THE COLLECTED WORKS OF JULIAN FANE
VOLUME ONE

BY THE SAME AUTHOR

Morning
A Letter
Memoir in the Middle of the Journey
Gabriel Young
Tug-of-War
Hounds of Spring
Happy Endings
Revolution Island
Gentleman's Gentleman
Memories of My Mother
Rules of Life
Cautionary Tales for Women
Hope Cottage
Best Friends
Small Change
Eleanor
The Duchess of Castile
His Christmas Box
Money Matters

Harlequin Edition

Three Stories of Boyhood
Secrets of the Confessional
A Reader's Choice

THE COLLECTED WORKS OF

JULIAN FANE

VOLUME ONE

MORNING

❖

TUG-OF-WAR

❖

GENTLEMAN'S GENTLEMAN

❖

CONSTABLE · LONDON

Morning
first published in Great Britain 1956
by John Murray Ltd
Reprinted 1956 (twice), 1957
Published in the USA, France and the Netherlands
Published by Hamish Hamilton Ltd and St George's Press 1986
Sceptre (paperback) edition 1988

Tug-Of-War
first published in Great Britain 1975
by Hamish Hamilton Ltd and St George's Press

Gentleman's Gentleman
first published in Great Britain 1981
by Hamish Hamilton Ltd and St George's Press

This edition first published in Great Britain 1997
by Constable and Company Ltd
3 The Lanchesters
162 Fulham Palace Road
London W6 9ER
ISBN 0 09 477080 8
Set in Monophoto Bembo by
Servis Filmsetting Ltd, Manchester
Printed in Great Britain by
St Edmundsbury Press Ltd
Bury St Edmunds, Suffolk

A CIP catalogue record for this book
is available from the British Library

CONTENTS

MORNING

FOR

J.C.F.

CONTENTS

1938

A DAY

A figure appears in the open schoolroom french windows at the corner of the house, raises her hand against the brightness and calls, 'Vere?'

The seven-year-old boy on the terrace, staggering under the weight of three half-rotten planks, answers, 'I'm coming!' Then, conscious of being concealed from view, he carries the planks to the wall that borders the grove of trees and carefully drops them over. One breaks. He turns away, considering the uses of the broken plank, picks up his tweed coat, feels in the pockets for the box of matches and the five cigarettes in their fragile paper holder, folds the coat across his arm and walks on down the terrace.

Suddenly he begins to run, leaping and skipping, revelling in the sunshine, in the summer, in his schemes and ambitions, in the reliability of his leather shorts and the springiness of the rubber soles of his sandals.

'I'm coming, Mal,' he calls. 'I'm coming.'

Mal is now standing on the smooth grass of the lawn, looking as if she had been planted there many years before like some proud and ancient tree. At the sight of the boy she exclaims in her singsong voice, savouring the Frenchness of her accent and the sweet airs of the day, 'Oh, darling, it's so lovely, isn't it? Do you see the blue sky? I love it so!' And she gestures comprehensively with her hand, flirting it somehow in a gay lighthearted fashion.

'Quelle vie,' says Vere, teasing.

'Quelle vie, quelle vie! I love it so!' Enjoying the joke she starts regretfully for the schoolroom door. Her walk is heavy, powerful. 'Now lessons, darling. Les leçons, les leçons,' she chants.

They sit together at the schoolroom table, enveloped in a cloud of the scent Mal always uses, half eau-de-Cologne, half disinfectant. Furniture looms into view as their eyes grow accustomed to the shade. Scamp the dog sleeps in the sunlight on the paving outside.

'And then, you see,' Vere is saying, trying to convey something of his excitement, 'my house is going to have two rooms. At least two rooms. And it'll be watertight, so that I can sleep in it. And have a fire . . .' He notices a flicker of amusement on the lips and in the brown eyes, and continues in a changed persuasive tone. 'Besides, it's going to be so useful. Probably I shall live there most of the time . . .' He breaks off, knowing that he has overstated his case.

Mal laughs, losing the high poise of her head. 'But chéri mignon,' she says, 'with what are you building your house?'

'Oh – odds and ends and bits and pieces.'

He is content to joke. He is prepared to wait for his moment of triumph. When the house is finished that will come. He imagines the admiring throng, the cries of wonder and congratulation, the stream of eager visitors. He laughs partly because he knows that one day his house will be no laughing matter.

The room is cool. He begins to put on his coat, cautiously, remembering its delicate precious cargo.

'And now,' Mal says, 'we must work. We will turn out your pockets, come along.'

Oh glory, thinks Vere. Pleasure, sunshine, dreams are swept away. The room is black and stifling. Why did he put on his coat? He does not even need it.

Mal points to his breast pocket. 'Et maintenant, qu'est-ce que c'est?'

'The handkerchief.'

'Le mouchoir.'

'Le mouchoir,' he repeats, thinking, Fool, fool. He has missed his chance, already it is too late to avoid the inquisition. He should have rebelled at once. Or does she know his secret? Did she search his pockets when his coat lay on the terrace wall?

'Allons vite, mon chéri, vite!'

The situation is beyond his control. He is hot, unhappy. He delves into the pockets of his leather shorts, pulls out string, chewing-gum, his knife. He repeats the names of the objects automatically as they are placed on the table before him. His hand rattles the box of matches: he raises his voice to drown the sound. He understands nothing, all is altered. Mal is unsparing: he is lost.

'Le couteau, la ficelle . . .'

He cannot bring himself to say, 'Why, Mal, that's everything.' He imagines too clearly the plunging hand, the withdrawal of the green paper holder, the merciless question: 'Et ces cigarettes, Vere?' Even if Mal does not know – and obviously she does, she is playing with him cruelly – but whether she does or not, disaster is still bound to overtake him: the cigarettes will fall from his pocket, the matches spontaneously ignite. He wonders if he should kill Mal, run away, make a last stand in his house. He is really a fugitive, a desperate man.

And his pockets are nearly empty. His fingers close over the box of matches, release them for the tenth time, pry into the deepest recesses, touch something and emerge.

'A feather, Mal!'

'Une plume.'

'Une plume.'

And now, now there is no turning back. He slaps the pockets of his coat, in the manner of his father, absent-mindedly almost. The matches rattle.

'Why, that's funny,' he says, opening his pocket wide with both hands and peering in. 'I seem to have a box of matches, don't I?' He looks Mal full in the face. A heady freedom possesses him. He begins to laugh. 'I wonder how they got there, don't you, Mal? A box of matches, dear, dear.'

He lays the matches on the table, a little away from the other trophies, and for a second both he and Mal regard them with surprise and interest.

'Les allumettes, Vere.'

'Les allumettes.'

'Les all-um-ettes. . .' There is a finality in her tone, a twinkle in the brown eyes. 'Et maintenant, la dictée.'

Vere begins to refill his pockets, the mirth still welling inside him. Mal, with a precise movement, stretches the waxed cover of the exercise book and writes in her strong script: 'Dictée. Le 2 Mai, 1938.' The matches remain on the table.

'I'd better leave those matches here, hadn't I, Mal?' he inquires. 'They might come in useful, for lighting fires or something.'

'Merci, Vere.'

Whereupon such a feeling of love seizes the boy, such a warmth of affection, such gratitude, such relief and such joy overflow in him that he is sure – he is certain – his heart must break. He catches hold of the large hand, kisses the cheek and lays his head on the soft shoulder, talking and laughing. He has never been so happy, never known the world could be so full and kind, so true and beautiful. He makes Mal gobble like a turkey and produce the potato she keeps in the top of her stocking against the rheumatism: he whistles through the gap in his teeth and blows through his fingers, imitating the hoot of an owl: he invites Mal to be the first to visit his house: and little by little the storm of emotion subsides. The dictation book is opened, the exercise book is arranged at the correct angle, the paper begins to wrinkle under the heat of the small hand, the voice to intone and the uncertain characters to spread across the page.

'Où est le chat de ma tante ...?'

Scamp the dog, drunk with the sun, struggles to her feet, waddles indoors and collapses with a sigh. The razor-edged shaft of light swings imperceptibly from right to left over the pale carpet. Sounds break from time to time, electric with distracting associations, into the somnolent peace of the schoolroom.

Bella the parlourmaid is starting to lay for luncheon. Her prim step clips across the oak floor of the dining-hall next door, stopping mysteriously when they reach the rug. Silver clinks at intervals as it is placed on the long refectory table, and the hand-bell tinkles, muted, discreet. Out of doors the iron rim of a wheelbarrow crunches lethargically over the grey gravel of the drive. Bruise and Harris, the under-gardeners, are weeding and smoothing the square turnabout in front of the house. From farther away comes the quick clatter of horse's hooves; somebody shouts. Vere imagines his father, thumbs hooked in the pockets of his coat, one foot turned outwards, lips pursed as he softly whistles, eyeing a nervous animal. Voices are heard; a car; the sweep of twig brushes; cries of fledgling birds; bees.

The clock on the mantelpiece whirrs and chimes.

'Mal, can I go now?'

'Yes, darling, yes. C'est fini!'

Vere runs through the french windows, sees his father advancing from the other end of the house, breaks into an imitative walk as he goes to meet him, bending his legs loosely at the knees and thrusting a hand in his trouser pocket, and calls out a greeting.

His father says, 'What have you been doing, you little monkey?' and pretends to squeeze the boy's nose between the fingers of his clenched fist. 'Have you been good?'

Vere laughs and says, 'You've been looking at a horse, haven't you?'

'How do you know that?'

'I heard you. I guessed.'

'What a clever boy you are.' The blue eyes crinkle at the corners in the way that Vere loves and the humorous quacking noise is made with the side of the mouth.

'Dad, are you staying here this afternoon?'

'No, old boy, I'm playing golf. I must change.'

'Will you drive an old golf ball into the wood?'

'I will tomorrow. You go and see what Nanny's doing.' A double quacking noise: the long legs mount the stairs two at a time, unevenly: the hard wood screeches beneath the clusters of nails in the shoes: a door slams.

Vere swings on the banisters. 'Bella,' he says, 'can you whistle through your teeth?'

'No, Master Vere,' she replies shortly, folding the napkins.

He wonders if she has something wrong with her teeth. But surely not, he decides; they look so incredibly white and even. 'My front tooth's loose,' he says. She does not answer. 'Bella, what's the time?'

'Ten to one, Master Vere.'

Ten minutes to luncheon: nothing to do: no time for anything. A delivery van is bumping along the back drive. He runs out of the house and over the paving and gazes through the gate in the garden wall. The van sways round the dovecote and pulls up in a perfect position, hidden by a circular yew-tree from the nursery windows. It is Mr. Trent the baker from Long Cretton.

Vere lifts the latch of the gate and saunters towards the van. 'Oh, good morning, Mr. Trent,' he says. 'How are you?'

'Why, Master Vere, good morning. I'm nicely, thanks, and how's yourself? Come to see what I've brought along, have you? Let's take a look.'

'I was on my way in actually,' Vere protests, following the baker to the rear of the van.

The doors are unlocked and opened. The sweet smell of fresh-baked bread assails his nostrils. Mr. Trent, talking all the while, searches under the crisp loaves for the white cardboard box. He finds it, shakes it, clasps his hands together. 'What have we here?' He laughs. The box is crammed with bars of chocolate.

'They do look delicious,' Vere enunciates with difficulty, his mouth watering, his fingers twisting the sixpence in his pocket.

'They are delicious too! Now what are we going to have today? These Mars bars are very nice, and so are the Crunchies, and here are some whipped-cream walnuts. Oh, just you look at them – but don't tell Nurse, Master Vere!'

'How much are the Milky Ways, Mr. Trent?' Vere asks hurriedly.

'The Milky Ways are very very good. They're tuppence.'

'Can I have a Milky Way then, please? No, perhaps I'll have two, please.'

'Two Milky Ways. Not three? That'll be fourpence, Master Vere, and mum's the word.'

Vere pays his sixpence and receives his change. But then he hesitates.

The baker says, 'What, Master Vere, I do declare, you haven't seen your favourites today,' and the fatal tray full of cream-buns is held out for inspection.

The buns are brown and soft and slit in the middle, and the scent of the cream with the indescribable flavour which rests in the slits is wafted upwards.

'I can't afford one,' Vere says faintly.

Mr. Trent seems not to hear him. In a voice as creamy and tantalising as his buns he continues, 'Isn't that a pretty sight? Shall I tell you what we'll do? You keep your tuppence. Now you choose a little favourite. How's that? – But eat it up quick, before Nurse catches you. Oh listen, there's the bell!'

Vere feels liquid with desire and apprehension. The luncheon bell is ringing from the nursery window, the forbidden bun is proffered temptingly, the pennies are already in his pocket, time is passing. If only Mr. Trent had come earlier. The lack of appetite at luncheon will be suspect for certain.

'Thank you very much, Mr. Trent. Good morning.'

Vere takes the bun. His hand is trembling though his voice is controlled. He walks with faltering steps towards the stable archway, sits on the stone mounting-block, bolts the bun in four mouthfuls, unable to indulge the ecstasy of the cream filling, runs into the yard and across it, and starts to climb the fire-escape to the nursery window.

Mr. Trent calls up to him, 'See you tomorrow, Master Vere!' and puts his finger to his lips.

Vere hiccups, squeezes through the window, drops onto the floor, then goes into the day-nursery. Flora the nursery-maid is trying to decide if she has laid correctly for luncheon. Her eyes when she looks at him are wide and abstracted.

'Flora, I've got you a present,' he says, giving her a Milky Way.

'Oh Vere, you shouldn't have.' Her voice is caressing, rather broken, sometimes throaty, sometimes clear. 'You haven't been with Mr. Trent?'

'Don't tell Nanny, Flora.'

She jerks her head in a manner denoting trouble in store, the eyebrows raised and the tongue clicking, and sends him to wash his hands.

When he returns luncheon is on the table. There is a dish with a domed silver cover: two vegetable dishes stand beside it. He hopes they contain something fresh and tasty: roast beef, for instance, dark sharp gravy, flowery boiled potatoes and those French beans, succulent and steaming, scraped to a tender green and with the strings removed. – That is what he could eat today, that is what he would prefer above everything. Nanny enters, the baby is strapped into the high chair, grace is said. Vere closes his eyes, praying fervently for French beans. The lids are lifted.

Under the silver dome is a fricassée of chicken, drops of melted butter gilding its rich surface. Mashed potato and stalky spring greens have been squashed flat by the covers of the other dishes.

'Not too much for me, please, Nanny,' Vere says, and to hide his despair turns to the baby. 'Hullo, Faith. Hullo, Faithie.'

The baby, gazing greedily at the food and kicking her chair, seizes his finger in a vice-like grip.

'Where's your appetite, Vere?' Nanny asks.

'Let go of my finger, Faith. I'm just not hungry, I'm afraid.'

'You'll never grow up to be big and strong if you don't eat.'

I will, he thinks with dull resentment. A plate is laid before him and he starts to pick half-heartedly at the white concoction. Everything tastes of Mr. Trent's bun.

Nanny says, 'Now Vere, eat up this minute.'

The rebuke injures him. He assumes a reproachful expression, but a chasm of sharp indigestion suddenly yawns beneath him. Faith's excited cries between each mouthful, the click of cutlery, the twittering flutter of the budgerigars – all are unpleasant, threatening. He cannot move – he must not even try: the weight of his fork disturbs his balance: the sunlight is too bright and too hot: he feels sick.

'Come along, sweetheart, eat a bit for me.'

'No, thank you, Flora.'

The care with which he speaks makes the words sound cold. He attempts to smile at Flora, but manages only a pained grimace.

'And it's no good making up to Flora,' Nanny says. 'Just get on with your lunch.'

He denies the accusation. But now his voice, instead of ringing tart and rebellious as intended, sounds sour and sulky, and he immediately wishes he had kept silent.

'And please don't answer back, Vere,' Nanny adds.

The baby, stimulated by the currents of discord in the atmosphere, grins round the table and turns a vacant windy stare on her brother.

'Oh Faith, go away,' he says.

The baby cries.

'That's wasn't kind, Vere, I'm surprised at you,' Nanny says as she comforts the child. 'Poor Faith. You ought to be more gentle with your little sister. There there now, there.'

What has happened, what has he done? He ate a cream-bun: it is his own affair. There is no need for anyone to be upset or cross. He tries to show by a gesture that he wishes Faith at any rate no harm, but her face grows purple as his hand approaches and her bellows drive the budgerigars half mad.

'Now Vere!' Nanny exclaims. 'You're being most aggravating. Leave the poor girl alone for any sake.'

Faith is unstrapped, swung soothingly in Nanny's arms until her bellows become sobs and then gurgles, replaced in her chair and coaxed into accepting another spoonful of food.

Vere meanwhile sits silent and hunched at the table, his hands in his lap, his eyes on a mustard-pot. He no longer feels sick, only miserable. He studies the mustard-pot. He is expected to cry, he knows it, but he will not, he will not – nothing will make him.

'Please, sweetheart, please, you must eat up, you know.'

He does not answer. He cannot. Flora's soft voice, the whole idea of Flora and her kindness and love, is insupportable, the blow for which he is not prepared. His eyes prick and he is unable to control the quivering of his lower lip. The outline of the mustard-pot blurs, the lump in his throat prevents him from swallowing. A tear trickles down his cheek, quick and damp, and falls onto his leather shorts.

'Do you want my handkerchief, sweetheart?'

'No.'

His heart is hardening. He glares at the mustard-pot. Indignation mingles with his brimming self-pity. He can never be the same: gone is the tender amenable boy who sat down at the table. As Nanny will learn, he in his turn can be harsh and cruel and unforgiving. Such, henceforth, is going to be his natural state, and no apologies or pleas will ever recall that other Vere.

Nanny asks Flora, 'Have you any idea why he can't eat?'

Flora pauses. 'He's never much appetite, has he?'

'But he must eat something. A growing boy.'

'Shall I make you a castle, Vere, and you can eat it up?'

'All right, Flora,' he agrees, forgetting his notions of revenge and suddenly feeling hungry.

'You've not been eating sweets, Vere?'

'No,' he replies in a shocked voice, taking an active interest in the layout of the castle, the moat of sauce, the walls of mashed potato and the wood of greens in the castle grounds. 'What about a drawbridge? Oughtn't it to have a drawbridge?' He makes the query general, but Nanny supplies no answer. She is not to be diverted. He feared as much. He might as well try to divert the sea. He looks at Flora hopelessly. 'It ought to have a drawbridge,' he says.

'Has Mr. Trent been up today?' Nanny asks.

'Mr. Trent? I think he has,' says Vere.

'I see.'

'Shall I eat some of the moat, Flora?'

'What did Mr. Trent give you, Vere?'

'Thank you, Flora – look, the moat is leaking now!'

'Those buns, I suppose, Vere?'

'Wait a minute, Nanny!'

'Has Vere been eating buns, Flora?'

'Oh, oh, the moat is running away – '

'Please answer me, Flora. Has Vere been eating Mr. Trent's buns?'

'Yes,' he interrupts, 'I have been eating buns.'

Everyone is surprised, even the baby. Nanny is the first to collect herself.

'Well, Vere, in that case you're a very naughty boy,' she says.

'I only ate one,' he replies. 'And I don't feel hungry. And that's all.' He looks boldly about him. He is really strong and daring enough for anything.

'That's most disobedient of you, Vere. And Mr. Trent ought to be ashamed of himself.'

'But I made Mr. Trent give me the bun.'

'What?'

'I made him, I forced him.'

The baby laughs. Vere joins in and pats her head. The baby goes on laughing, then begins to grind her five teeth.

'Don't do that, Faith. Vere, listen to me, please. Vere!' Nanny and

Flora exchange a bewildered glance. 'You are a bad boy. If you eat Mr. Trent's buns again I shall punish you. And this is my last warning. Now finish what you can of your lunch and hurry up about it.'

'Yes, Nanny,' he says, and a minute later adds with a penitent smile, 'I'm sorry.'

After luncheon Flora disappears with Faith. Vere fetches his book, takes it to Nanny and begs her to read aloud to him. She puts down her newspaper and, while he curls himself up at the other end of the sofa, looks for their place and then in a steady voice begins.

The story is about little Jack Rabbit and his mother, and their home under the Bramble Patch in Sunny Meadow. The characters are varied, kind Owl and wily Danny Fox, the scene golden and evocative. Vere listens rapt, translating the wonderful tale into terms of his own experience, placing the Bramble Patch and Shady Forest, until Nanny's head gradually sinks forward. He watches her jerk it upright, but only half-listens when she resumes her reading. The square glass clock ticks away on the mantelpiece, the heavy pendulum swings. Again the words slur and drag. Nanny jerks her head a second time.

'Vere, I'm sorry,' she says, 'but I can't read another word. We'll have some more tomorrow. Go to sleep for a minute. And I'll have forty winks, my eyes are just closing.'

She shuts the book and puts it to one side, folds her arms and allows her head to droop. Even in repose her compact figure is alert and energetic. Vere listens for her light reassuring breathing. Soon he is sleeping too.

When he awakes the nursery is empty. He jumps off the sofa, runs along the nursery passage and down the stairs, steals two ginger biscuits from the tin in the pantry, pockets a box of matches and goes out to his house. For a while he regards it critically, munching the biscuits and considering what he must do. Then he sets to work.

The shadows have deepened under the chestnut trees. Wood pigeons coo in the high branches and make leisurely flights, dipping, rising, clapping their wings behind their backs. A distant cuckoo calls and a horse whinnies and stamps its feet in the stable-yard. The earth seems to drowse in the afternoon sunlight, peaceful, replete.

For an hour and a half Vere works without pause. Then, his head aching slightly from his exertions and his hands shaking, he sits on the trunk of a fallen tree and produces the packet of cigarettes from his pocket. He selects a cigarette and puts it in the corner of his mouth.

Deliberately, as if his mind were on other things, he opens the new box of matches, strikes a match and shields the flame professionally against a non-existent breeze. He puffs, shakes out the match, flicks it away and looks at the cigarette to see that it is fairly lit.

This is the well-earned rest from his labours, the reward. He surveys his work, finding some cause for satisfaction. He has made progress, there is no doubt about it, but tomorrow he will redouble his efforts. He must have some long nails and the head of that hammer needs attention. What a lot there is to be done, more even than he thought.

Blue-grey smoke from his cigarette spirals and drifts languidly in the air. Its redolence suggests maturity and honest toil and skilled workmanship. He clenches and unclenches his hand, enjoying the thought that his palms are hardening and his muscles growing strong, and puffs again at his cigarette. Smoke gets into his eyes. The sudden sharp pain makes him rise to his feet, but a dizziness overcomes him, his head swims, and he quickly sits down again and blindly stubs out the cigarette. He doubles himself up and rests his head on his knees, keeping his eyes tightly closed. The dizziness passes and also the pain in his eyes, and the mood of quiet confidence and pride returns. Two or three days at this rate should make a big difference . . . He stands up, swings his coat over his shoulder and starts to plod towards the house, a real labourer, hungry, thirsty, heavy-footed, bent-kneed.

Flora, with the last of their luncheon, has made him a pie in a white dish. It is richly browned on the top and gives off a burnt and savoury aroma when she places it before him on the tea-table. But apart from this, apart from the delicious crispness of the potato crust and the smoothness of the creamed chicken within, the great charm of the pie lies in its being especially his own, and he eats it slowly, in small grateful mouthfuls. And when Nanny mentions that tonight is Flora's night off he begins to question her in a fondly authoritative fashion.

'What are you going to do, Flora?'

'I'm away to the whist-drive, Vere.'

'Where's the whist-drive?'

'At Long Cretton.'

'Are you going alone?'

'No.'

'Who are you going with?'

Flora looks at Nanny.

'But who are you going with, Flora? You must tell me.'

'Eat up your tea, Vere,' Nanny says.

'Will you win a prize, Flora?'

'I don't know.'

'But if you do win, will it be money?'

'Yes, I expect so.'

'Will it be as much money as Nanny will win if she gets the crossword right?'

'Good gracious, child,' says Nanny. Flora laughs.

'But honestly, will it?'

'No, sweetheart. If I did win I'd perhaps get thirty shillings.'

'Is that enough for us to keep ducks?'

Both Nanny and Flora laugh. To have made Nanny laugh is a feather in Vere's cap, and although he intended no joke, he begins to feel droll and amusing.

'If we kept ducks,' says he, 'we could fatten them up and sell them to Mummy and go away and live on the money. Couldn't we, Flora? We'd get married probably, and have lots of chickens and ducks, and sell them all to Mummy. We'd be quite rich, I expect. Wouldn't you like that, Flora?'

Laughter greets each sally. He does not understand why. His success amazes and delights him, he wants to go on being funny, but is not sure what new note to strike. He turns to traditional humour, raking up incidents which have been laughed at many times before: when Mrs. Lark the cook, for instance, was seen to scratch her back with the long-handled soup spoon. But try as he will he cannot prolong the joke. Flora, who always cries when she laughs, starts to dry her eyes and Nanny advises him to finish his tea.

He does not mind. He is so well-pleased with himself that he eats several slices of bread and butter spread with honey in the comb, and drinks three cupfuls of milk straight off. Every so often he bursts into laughter, remembering his witty remarks, and he hums while he chews until Nanny stops him, and then blows bubbles in his cup. As soon as tea is finished he jumps from his chair and starts running round the nursery table. Each time he passes Flora, who is clearing the crockery away, he says either 'Hullo, sweetheart,' or 'Christmas is coming, the ducks are getting fat.' These phrases reduce him to such a state of uncontrollable laughter that he can hardly keep his feet and wobbles about like a drunken zany. Nanny, sitting with Faith on a low chair in front of the fire, tells him not to be silly: but this is only a fresh cause for merriment. His older sisters, dressed in blue school tunics, enter the room. They are going to play cards with Mal downstairs and are full of the doings of their day at school. Vere will hardly let them speak. He dances in front of them, his head cocked to one side, flapping his arms as if they were wings. The two girls look at him oddly, ask Nanny to make him stop and finally leave the room, shaking their heads. He bows them out, skips back to the sofa and turns two clumsy somersaults. Nanny warns him that it will all end in tears. Tears? What are they? Faith, watching him over Nanny's shoulder, grins encouragement. He falls onto the floor, makes faces, performs mad antics for her benefit. She screams and dribbles with amusement. He crawls to the chair by the window, racked with laughter, gripped and dissolved by it, as weak as water, almost incapable of movement, and struggles and sways and slips, hysterical and helpless.

Suddenly he stops.

Something dreadful, terrible, frightful has happened. He cannot believe it. He cannot even bear to verify his suspicions. He gives a small choking laugh, almost a sob, a mocking echo, and sits with his mouth clamped open.

'Nanny!' he wails without closing or in any way disturbing the wide set of his mouth.

Nanny turns to look at him. 'Whatever is the matter, Vere?'

'Nanny, Nanny!'

'What is it, child, for any sake?'

'My tooth!'

Nanny picks up the baby and comes across to him. 'Have you given it a bang, or what?' she says.

'I've lost it.'

'I can't understand you.'

He yells at her, using neither his lips nor his tongue: 'I've lost it, look!'

'You've lost it? But it's still there. I can see it.'

He moves his tongue a fraction of an inch. He tastes blood – there is blood on his tongue! Feeling cold all over he yells louder and more furiously, 'But it's come out, I tell you!'

Nanny laughs. How can she? And yet it is funny. He can see the funny side himself. Oh glory! What is he to do?

'Don't laugh, Nanny, don't!' he cries.

'Well, pull it out, Vere.'

'No!'

'But it's hanging by a thread.'

'No!'

'Well, shall I tie it to the door with a string?'

'Nanny!!'

'Vere now, don't be silly.'

'I'm not!'

'Well then, be brave.'

'I am, I am!'

'Go on and pull it out then. Let me pull it out.'

'No, no, no, no!'

'Yes, Vere, come here.'

'No! No! Nanny! Nanny!!'

Nanny is laughing, reaching down! He makes an abrupt dodging movement. Something falls onto the floor. What is it on the brown linoleum? He squints, trying to see. It is his tooth, his front tooth.

'Now you're not hurt, Vere, it just dropped out. What did I say? I knew all that carrying-on would end in tears. Don't be stupid, child, it's all over.'

Yes, but his tooth is on the floor; there is an empty space in his mouth which he dare not touch; he is afraid to swallow because of the taste of blood.

Flora enters the room. Nanny, walking up and down and patting the baby, tells her the story. Flora laughs, then kneels beside Vere who is still sitting rigidly in the chair.

'Let's have a look, sweetheart.'

'Here.' He raises his hand and points. 'Is it bleeding, Flora?'

'Oh yes, I see. Where's the tooth, Vere? You haven't swallowed it?'

'No, no!' How can she think of such things? 'Please, Flora, is it bleeding?'

'No. I don't think so.'

He closes his mouth gradually. The gap feels strange against his lips. He moves his head. The muscles in his neck are stiff and aching. He gets up and walks – or tries to glide at least – over to the looking-glass. The sight of the empty socket makes him shudder.

'I thought he'd have to have it pulled by the dentist,' Flora is saying to Nanny. 'It's been loose I don't know how long.'

'Yes, it's a blessing, Vere. You ought to be grateful, instead of looking as if the end of the world had come.'

Impressed by this consideration Vere asks if he can see the tooth.

'Is it alive?' he questions Flora.

'No, sweetheart.'

'It's small, isn't it?'

'It's a milk-tooth, a baby-tooth.'

'Like Faith's?'

'Yes.'

'Shall I show it to Faith, Nanny?'

'What notions you do have, Vere. Yes, if you want, before I put her to bed.'

He takes the tooth gingerly between finger and thumb and exhibits it. To his surprise Faith is not interested.

'But look, Faith.'

'It's no good, she doesn't know what it is.'

'It's my tooth, Faith.'

'Kiss her goodnight, Vere, it's past her bedtime.'

'But it's my tooth. It's come out of my mouth. Faith, will you look!'

'Leave her alone, child, she doesn't understand.'

After Nanny and Faith have gone Vere sits with Flora on the sofa. The sun has moved round and the big low-ceilinged room is now in shadow. Looking at the tooth which reposes in the hollow of his hand, Vere is filled with morbid fascination, wonder and relief.

'It must have been pretty loose, mustn't it,' he remarks, 'because my lips aren't bruised at all.'

'You probably just caught it with your knee.'

'Why was it so loose do you think?'

'I expect you've another tooth coming.'

'In the same place? A baby-tooth?'

'No, a grown-up one.'

'To last forever?'

'Yes.'

'Until I die?'

'Now, Vere.'

'It was awful, Flora. I was laughing.'

Although he still shudders from time to time Vere's experience now seems to him both humorous and exciting; and the free, generous, confidential mood produced by it he would like never to end.

'Flora, have you eaten your Milky Way?'

'To tell you the truth I'd forgotten it.'

'I'd forgotten mine too. Shall we eat them now, together?'

'Yes, all right.'

He goes to the drawer in the dresser and fetches Flora's Milky Way. His own, he is afraid, having been in his pocket all day, will be broken and melted. But when he extracts it and his suspicions are confirmed, and Flora sees it and offers him hers, he refuses, saying that he likes his Milky Ways to be just so.

They sit side by side on the sofa, the girl's eyes dreamy and faraway, the boy eating slowly and with care, and converse quietly together. Vere asks questions to which he already knows the answers, wishing to perpetuate the perfect atmosphere, and Flora summons up her gentle voice in reply. The budgerigars twitter and flit about their cage, and the freshly-lit fire smoulders and smokes in the grate.

'Milky Ways are awfully milky, aren't they, Flora?'

'Does it hurt to eat, Vere?'

'Not really. I only use one side of my mouth, you see.'

A pause. 'Aren't you pleased I thought of the Milky Ways? I'll buy you another tomorrow.'

'You mustn't, sweetheart.'

'Why?'

They study his tooth through Nanny's magnifying glass, and Flora tells him he must keep it to show his parents when they come to say goodnight. She says they may give him sixpence for it. When it is time for Vere to have his bath therefore, he runs ahead of Flora into the bathroom and polishes the tooth with his toothbrush until it shines: then he wraps it in cotton wool and puts it in a pill-box which she has found for him. After his bath he places the box beneath his pillow, says his prayers, gets quickly into bed and waits.

What can be detaining his father and mother? He considers how best to describe his ordeal. How curious and concerned his parents are going to be. He dwells pleasantly in his imagination on their amazement and anxiety. His father may judge his pain and suffering worth a shilling, his heroism worth two. Sweet vistas begin to open before him. If only they would come!

But his father, he suddenly remembers, went to play golf. He might not be back for hours! And his mother, where is his mother? He learns that she is fetching his father from the golf-course. Have they returned? Not yet. When will they return?

'Soon, sweetheart, I expect. You needn't go to sleep for a bit.'

He will not see them: they will not come in time: that is obvious. It is sad when he has so much to tell and to show them, when he has made such preparations. He might as well go to sleep – are those voices on the stairs? Of course not. It is foolish of him to strain his ears. He knows that they will not come: he is sure of it.

He starts to sing to himself. He has not seen his mother since he knocked on her bedroom door, kissed her across the breakfast-tray and asked her how she was: except once, he recalls, during the afternoon. She was in the garden, tying back the purple clematis with raffia, a basket with secateurs on the ground beside her and a large pink floppy straw hat on her head. He paused and watched her, taking pleasure in the sight. Her presence seemed to complete the sunlit peacefulness of the scene, her intricate operations to complement his own furious toil. He wishes. . . But no; he will wish no more. He notices that his song has assumed a form. He tries to recapture and repeat it, but it eludes him. Will they never come?

When he first hears the soft rubber footfalls on the nursery passage he smothers them with song because he thinks they are a trick of his imagination. But his mother's following steps are undeniable. He listens, catches a snatch of tuneless whistle, sits up in bed and calls.

His father says, bending his head as he comes into the room, 'Well, you monkey, what have you been up to?'

'Darling,' his mother says, going to sit on the rail of the fireguard.

Vere hides his excitement so well that his greeting sounds detached and cool.

'Have you had a nice time, darling?' his mother asks, smoking elegantly, while his father regards his reflection in the looking-glass on the cupboard-door.

'Yes, thank you, Mummy,' Vere answers, suddenly uncertain about the best way in which to approach the great subject, in which to claim his parents' interest. 'I've got something to tell you,' he starts.

'What's that, old boy?' says his father, not turning.

'Well, my tooth's come out. Here, this one, it was loose.' His words are conveying nothing, he senses it. What has become of his thrilling account? 'I was laughing, and I knocked it with my knee, and it came out,' he says.

'Why, so it has.'

'Oh yes, darling.'

'Open your mouth.'

'Was it terribly painful?'

'A bit,' he admits, feeling better.

'Are you all right now?'

'Oh yes,' he says impatiently.

'But it's horrid when you lose a tooth,' his mother continues. 'Did it bleed much?'

'Yes, a little . . .' Is it dangerous if your mouth bleeds, he wonders.

'You won't be able to whistle through your teeth,' his father says with a smile.

'You will when your new tooth grows, darling.'

'But would you like to see the old one?' Vere insists.

'Good God, have you got it in bed with you?'

His mother gives his father a nudge and says, 'Yes, darling, let's see it.'

He shows his mother and calls to his father, who has turned back to the mirror. 'Don't you want to see it, Dad?'

His mother says, 'Do come and look, David,' without looking herself.

'Here, Mummy.'

'Isn't it clean?'

'I brushed it.'

'Cleaner than your other ones are sometimes, I'm afraid, darling.'

'Yes ...'

His father asks him what he is going to do with it.

'Well, I'm going to keep it.'

'What for?'

'Well, I don't know, I might sell it or something.'

'Sell it? Who to?'

'Oh, someone.'

'What a little rat you are.' A quacking noise. 'Is Faith asleep?'

'Faith? Yes, I think she is.'

'We ought to go down.'

'Oh don't go.'

His mother inquires if he would like his curtains drawn and his father wanders restlessly about the room. Vere regrets having asked them to stay. Nothing is happening as he expected, as he hoped, none of his lovely expectations are being fulfilled. 'What is the time, David?'

'Well, it's after seven.'

'Perhaps we should go.'

'Come on, you cuddle down,' says his father, 'as snug as a bug in a rug.'

But Vere makes a final effort. 'Dad, don't you really think I'll be able to sell my tooth?'

'I shouldn't worry about it, old boy.'

'But I am worried.'

'Daddy might buy it from you if you ask him nicely. Go on, David.'

'That's all very fine. All right, all right. How much do you want for it?'

'I didn't mean I wanted to sell it to you.'

His father jingles the money in his pocket and produces a handful of change. 'What's the price?'

'No, honestly.'

'There's two-and-six. That's more money than I ever had at your age.'

'No, thank you, Dad.'

'Stop talking and take it, there's a good boy.'

'No, Dad.'

'I'd take it, darling.'

'No.'

He cannot accept the money now. Surely they can see that? It is unkind of his mother to shake her head, of his father to shrug and turn away. He has never, never wanted money – money alone. But he cannot explain. He lies back in bed and pulls the covers up to his chin.

'Is something the matter, darling?'

'No, Mummy ...'

'Well then.'

'Going, going . . . gone! You are a silly boy. You'll never be rich. Come on, we're late.'

His mother leans over and kisses him and asks him if he will sleep. His father makes quacking noises and pinches his cheek.

'Goodnight, Mummy. Goodnight, Dad.'

'Goodnight, sleep tight, mind the fleas don't bite.'

Is the tooth so soon forgotten? Does his refusal of the halfcrown and all that it entailed count for so little?

'Are you sure there's nothing wrong, darling?'

'No.' He smiles wanly.

'Well, goodnight then.'

'Goodnight, Mummy.'

'Dream of bunnies in the night.'

'Goodnight, Dad.'

'Goodnight, old boy.'

They go into the day-nursery. He can hear them speaking to Nanny. Flora slips into his room, closes the door, comes and sits on his bed.

'What is it, Vere?' she asks.

'Have they been talking about me?'

'Your mother thinks you're looking sad.'

'I'm not.'

'What is it, sweetheart?'

'Nothing.'

'Let me put your pillow straight. Oh – did they give you a sixpence for your tooth?'

'No. But it isn't that, Flora. Daddy wanted to give me two-and-six, only I wouldn't take it.'

'Why though?'

'Well . . . I didn't want it.'

His parents' steps recede down the nursery passage and Nanny comes into his room.

'Vere, whatever have you been saying to your mother and father? They were quite worried.'

'It isn't my fault,' he answers. 'I haven't done anything.'

'I know what the trouble is with you. You're overtired. Look at the time. That's what it is, isn't it?'

'I am a bit tired,' he says, grateful for this simple explanation of the unhappy tightness at the pit of his stomach.

'Of course you are,' Nanny goes on, pulling down the blue blinds, and Vere believes her. 'You ought to be asleep. You're always like this when you're tired. I know you.'

And of course he is, it is perfectly true. He needs his sleep – he is a worker after all.

'Kiss Flora goodnight.'

'Goodnight, Flora.' He gives her such a hug that she nearly loses her balance.

'Vere!' She laughs. 'Goodnight, sweetheart.'

'Have a nice time.'

'I will.'

'And win the prize, Flora!'

'Are you thinking of our old ducks?'

Nanny says, 'Goodnight, Vere,' from the doorway.

'But Nanny,' he cries, 'aren't you going to kiss me goodnight?'

'Heavens, child, there's no end to it, is there? Goodnight, sleep tight.' She accentuates the words heavily, making a gesture with her hands as if to say: I suppose you think you won't be there for me to kiss tomorrow night, or the night after, or all the other nights.

'Tuck me in.'

'You are tucked in.'

'But my toes!'

'That's enough, Vere.'

'Goodnight, Nanny.'

She takes his head firmly in her hands and plants a kiss on his forehead.

'You will leave the door open?'

'Yes.'

'And you won't go away?'

'I may for a minute. I'm making no promises. Have you everything you want?'

'Yes, thank you, Nanny.'

'Well, go to sleep then, go to sleep.'

She half-closes the door, adjusts the stopper with her foot and turns on the day-nursery light. Flora patters down the passage. The budgerigars scold as they are covered up for the night. 'Goodnight, budgies,' Nanny says softly. 'Don't be afraid, you silly creatures, I'm not going to hurt you.' Even the birds seem subject to that effortless authority for they quieten immediately at the sound of her voice. Will she sit down and read by the fire? No; she is moving about, humming a hymn-tune, and now she is opening the other door, and now she is following Flora down the passage. Where is she going? Will she be long? Should he call? Anything can happen without her, Faith be ill or the house catch on fire. She ought not to desert him: she virtually promised . . . He will give her a minute before he calls.

He lies in bed and listens.

Out-of-doors the birds are singing. Would that be a blackbird beneath his window? Its song is still and clear. Rooks fly over the house. He can hear the weighty flapping of their wings as they head for their nests in the tall trees of the grove. The wheels of a farmcart grind along the drive, a whip cracks. Silence. The cooing of the white doves, sleepy and intimate, drifts from the crowded dovecotes. A late lark ascends from the buttercup field by the farm, and the swallows swoop shrilly on the insects of the hour. Soon the chill dimness will turn into night, full and blue. Bats will emerge squeaking from their secret haunts; owls will hoot; foxes bark; dew fall.

What is that?

Nanny is returning. Her steps weave down the passage, she enters the nursery, the springs of the sofa creak.

'Nanny?'

'Aren't you asleep yet, Vere?'

'Is everything all right?'

'Yes, yes, child. Close your eyes.'

'Goodnight, Nanny.'

'Goodnight, Vere.'

The boy turns over in his bed. He might have trusted Nanny: she would not let him down. She is next door, she will always be next door: her sure light will always shine: she will watch over him: he is safe forever.

The dusk blurs on blinds and curtains. Tomorrow . . . He hopes for fine weather. He has so much to do . . . Tomorrow . . .

THE BEE-STING

One morning Vere meets Mr. White the milkman in the backyard.

'Good morning, Mr. White,' he says.

'Morning, young fellow-my-lad,' Mr. White replies, as he kicks at the starter of his motorbicycle. 'You coming for a ride round to the garage?'

'Not today, thank you,' says Vere.

'Well, ta-ta for now.'

'Mr. White!' Vere restrains him. 'Mr. White, how does your motorbike work?'

'Can't stop now, young man. Jump on and see for yourself.'

'Round to the garage?'

'That's it.'

'I'll walk, Mr. White, and then you can show me.'

'Not afraid, are you?'

'Afraid?' Vere laughs. 'I just want to walk.'

'Right you are!'

With a great rattling of the piled milk-bottles in the sidecar the machine rolls down the incline and roars round the corner.

Vere watches it out of sight, hears the gears change and the engine abruptly putter to a stop, and wonders what he should do. For many months now Mr. White's morning visits have been a thorn in his flesh. He is possessed of a nagging and unfulfilled desire to take the milkman at his word. To ride on the motorbicycle, for however brief a spell, would be exciting, delightful, and also, he feels, a worthwhile experience. But Nanny, threatening the severest penalties, has expressly forbidden him to do so.

Mr. White of course does not know this. Receiving unchangingly polite refusals of his repeated and now challenging offers, he has not hesitated to draw his own conclusions and to state them. Thus Vere's pride has become involved in the matter, his courage has been called in question, and, absurd though they are, it rests with him sooner or later to prove Mr. White's suspicions false.

He sets off in the direction of the garage.

If he is to be perfectly truthful he has to admit that Nanny's attitude has raised a certain doubt in his mind. Is pillion-riding perhaps less simple than he imagines it to be? – That is the question. Is it in some unsuspected way difficult or dangerous? The mere idea of it perturbs Nanny: and although Mr. White does not share her view and clearly ought to know best, Nanny is seldom wrong. Not that Vere is afraid. He wants to ride on the motorbicycle, he is really keen about it, and one day he will, even if it means taking his life in his hands.

The machine is parked by the henhouses. The boy approaches it and touches the controls on the handlebars. How frightful, he thinks, if I touched the wrong switch and the engine started and the whole affair shot down the drive. He withdraws his hand and begins to whistle. He picks up a stone, throws it at a telegraph-pole, then flashes round suddenly and punches the pillion-seat with his fist. It is shaped and spongy, he knows it of old: he could sit there in comfort and in safety, he is positive. He would mount by placing his right foot on the adjustable foot-rest – here: he clicks it down. Right foot on the rest – so, and the left leg thrown over. It is as easy as falling off a log. Then a firm and upright position and a good grip with the knees, as on a horse, and what harm could possibly befall him?

'Well, well, well! Coming for a ride after all?'

Vere starts. 'Oh, Mr. White, I was trying the pillion,' he says. 'It's very springy, isn't it?'

'You wait till we get going.'

'What?' Vere starts to dismount. 'I was only trying it, Mr. White.'

'No need to move, I can manage, stay where you are.' And laying a heavy hand on Vere's shoulder to balance himself the milkman poises his foot for the strong downward kick.

Vere is absolutely trapped. He bitterly regrets his actions of the last few minutes. 'Wouldn't it be easier if I got off, Mr. White?' he asks.

'No no, that's all right,' Mr. White replies as he bears down on the kick-start and twists the hand-throttle. The engine puffs a couple of times. 'I can manage fine,' he says.

'Can you really?' says Vere, feeling helpless and ill.

The engine roars.

'O.K.?' Mr. White shouts, a broad grin on his frank fresh face.

'O.K.,' Vere answers, robbed by the rapid development of the situation of all power to protest.

Mr. White snaps on a pair of goggles, shakes the wire milk-bottle frames in the sidecar, climbs over the petrol tank, sits down and calls, 'Mind you hang on now!'

'How? Like this?' Vere beseeches, clinging to the milkman's coat-tail.

'Arms round my waist.'

'Like this, like this?'

'That's the way,' sings out the milkman above the noise of the engine. 'Hold tight, off we go!'

The clutch engages, the motorbicycle moves, lurches round in a tight circle and then starts to splutter down the drive. When Vere opens his eyes he discovers with relief that he is hidden from the nursery windows by the garden wall. As long as no-one has seen him! But he cannot worry. The air is rushing through his hair and tousling it, the milk bottles are clinking merrily in the sidecar, the pillion-seat is even more comfortable than he expected. He screws up his eyes and peeps over Mr. White's shoulder at the quickly-passing landmarks. There go the potting-sheds and the greenhouses. And here is Mr. Bruise with a surprised expression on his face – and there, already, he is left behind. They must be touching fifty miles an hour. How intoxicating it is to speed along like this – it is worth anything – how right he was to accept the ride! He is a bird, a swift; he is borne on the wings of the air; he is flying through it, free, unhampered; he is gulping it into his lungs; he is feeling it tingle on his skin. He relaxes his hold of Mr. White and cries, 'It's lovely.' He swings back in his seat and looks up at the sky. He grips with his bare knees and wishes he was going all the way to Long Cretton. He is light-headed with motion. 'It's lovely, Mr. White,' he cries.

As they near the bottom of the drive they slow down. Vere is just beginning to feel disappointed when he becomes aware of a pricking sensation in his knee. It is probably the air, he thinks, the pressure of the air. But the slower they go the more insistent it grows, and when they stop he realises with dismay that it is not a pricking sensation any longer: it is a pain, and a pretty sharp one at that.

'How did you like it?' calls Mr. White.

'Very much,' Vere answers, looking at his knee which has a round red spot on the inside.

'Well, hop off, young man, hop off. I must be getting along.'

'Mr. White,' Vere says, dismounting, 'there's something wrong with my knee.'

'What's that?'

'I've got a pain in it.'

'You kept your knees turned out, didn't you?'

'No, I gripped, like riding. Ow, it is painful.'

'Well, you've gone and burnt yourself. That's what you've done.'

Horrorstruck, Vere says, 'Oh, Mr. White, I haven't, have I?'

'That's what it is. A burn. And a nasty one too. You ought to have kept your legs well away from the exhaust pipes. They're bound to be hot, aren't they?'

'But I didn't know, Mr. White.'

'Oh, never touch the exhausts,' the milkman says in the same tone that somebody might say: never jump out of windows.

'But what shall I do?'

'You rub some butter on it. That's the thing. All right?'

'Are you going?'

'Got to be on my way. You're all right though, aren't you?'

'I suppose so.'

'Well, ta-ta, young fellow-my-lad, ta-ta.'

'Ta-ta, Mr. White.'

The milkman winks and grins, revs up his engine and disappears along the road.

Vere is most unhappy. He examines his burn and begins to hobble up the drive. His knee must have been sizzling against the exhaust pipe for ages, whilst he was pretending to be a bird et cetera. He might have known the ride would end in disaster. He was warned, and he never would have agreed to it except for Mr. White; who forced him against his will to stick on the blessed motorbicycle – when he tried to get off – and who is therefore responsible for the burn! Oh yes, he attempted to prove it was Vere's fault, suggesting virtually Vere burnt his leg on purpose. No doubt, Vere thinks, he has burnt in his time many boys' legs and excused himself in the same way: he probably makes a habit of it. And leaving without any offer of help, without so much as a kind word or a thought for the consequences . . . The consequences, Vere repeats to himself with a shiver: and forgetting Mr. White and his outrages he dwells with gloom and apprehension on the form that they are likely to take.

As he tops the rise by the greenhouses Mr. Bruise catches sight of him and stops sweeping, and as soon as Vere is within earshot clears his throat and calls, 'Morning, Master Vere,' in a knowing manner.

Vere conceals his limp as best he can and answers, 'Morning, Mr. Bruise.'

'I saw you, Master Vere.'

'Oh, did you?'

'I saw you on the motorbike. That's not allowed, is it?' And the old man winks a rheumy eye.

Vere is in no mood for winks and jokes and he says coldly, 'Yes, I saw you too.' He would like to ask Mr. Bruise to keep his knowledge to himself, but because he feels that one should only ask favours of friends – and Mr. Bruise's leering looks are not friendly at all – he maintains a haughty silence and passes on his way.

The gardener is not impressed. 'I saw you, Master Vere,' he crows with a grating laugh. 'You'll cop it. Wouldn't like to be in your shoes. Not half you're going to catch it – what a rumpus!'

Vere's heart sinks. His knee is really painful. The crimson circle has spread and the air burns and stings it horribly. He will have to go indoors. But then he will have to explain how he received the burn. And then he will catch it, as Mr. Bruise so happily understated.

He must find Flora. It is his only chance: find her, tell her the truth and enlist her aid. Flora will help him, Flora will think of something. Flora is sweet and good and sympathetic; if Nanny will not understand, then Flora will. Where are you, Flora? he thinks. Flora, Flora, he says under his breath as he limps along in the shadow of the garden wall. Flora, Flora, he reiterates a hundred times, until the name loses its meaning and becomes a mere jumble of pained and fearful syllables. Flora, Flora, come and help me.

He skirts the backyard and calls softly up to the night-nursery windows. Receiving no response he goes round and stands beneath the day-nursery windows and calls.

'Oh Flora, Flora!'

Once he imagines he sees her behind the glinting panes. He waits for the window to be thrown up, for her head to appear, but nothing happens. He dare not raise his voice in case Nanny should hear him.

'Oh Flora.'

His knee is becoming more and more painful. He cannot postpone things any longer. He enters the house by the back door, still calling for Flora, drags himself up the stairs and pauses at the top. If Flora is not alone in the day-nursery, if Nanny is there, then he is done for. He starts to tiptoe along the passage.

At the nursery door he stops and listens. All is quiet within. Perhaps Flora is darning. He opens the door a few inches.

'Who's that?'

Nanny's voice.

'It's me.'

'Oh, you gave me a fright, Vere. Well, come in or go out – make up your mind.'

'Nanny, I'm hurt.'

'For any sake.' She comes to his assistance. 'Where, child? What is it?'

Is she not angry, or even suspicious?

'It's painful,' he groans, playing for time and pointing to his knee. Somehow he expected her to know. If she does not, perhaps he might tell her a bit of the story, not everything at once? He could explain to Flora later, tell Flora the truth.

'Dear oh dear, it must be agony, child,' she says. 'How did you do it?'

'Don't touch it, Nanny!'

He racks his brains.

'I'm not touching anything. But how did you do it, Vere?'

'I was stung by a bee.'

'A bee?'

'Yes – ow, ow! By a bee, Nanny. It stung me – ow!'

'Come and sit down,' she says.

He has told not a half-truth but a black lie. It occurs to him and is out of his mouth before he can weigh it or restrain himself. If it is not accepted he is sunk.

'Tell me, Vere, now tell me. Have you taken the sting out?' She believes him.

'No.'

'Let me have a look. This is a funny sort of sting, Vere.'

'Why?'

'Well, it's all over red, and it's such an edge to it, and it's not much swollen.'

'I think it was a funny sort of bee,' he says.

'Whereabouts were you when you were stung?' she inquires, fetching her magnifying glass and peering through it to find the sting.

'Down the drive,' Vere answers.

'And what did the bee look like?'

'It was black and yellow, and furry, and big too.'

'Was it a wasp?'

'Oh no.'

'Well, I can't see any sting. Tell me what happened, exactly.'

'Well,' he pauses. 'I was walking down the drive. And suddenly the bee settled on my knee and I felt a terrific pain. I looked down and the bee was stinging me. It was as big as my thumb.'

'It must have been a queen bee.'

'I think it was.'

'Was there a swarm anywhere?'

'I don't know.'

'It's not like a bee to go and sting though. I can't understand it.'

'Well, this one did.'

'And what did you do, when you were stung?'

'I jumped. Nanny, it's painful. Won't you put something on it?'

'Vere, you're sure it was a bee and not anything else?'

'What else?'

'Well, a horse-fly or something.'

'It was a bee, Nanny, I promise you.'

Deeper and deeper he commits himself: he is up to his ears in falsehood and deceit. He is amazed by himself and by Nanny's credulity. He feels faintly embarrassed at being able to practise so successfully on her trust, but he resolves that as soon as the pain is relieved he will make a clean breast of the whole affair.

Nanny says, poking about in the medicine cupboard: 'Where's that blue-bag, let me think. I hid it somewhere for safety, and now I can't remember.'

'Nanny, do you put butter on stings?' he asks.

'Butter's for burns,' she answers.

'Oh, I see.'

'Well, here's some ammonia. I can't find the blue-bag, but ammonia's very good for stings, they say. Hold out your leg, Vere.'

'Will it hurt?'

'No, it'll be soothing. There. You poor boy, it is a bad place. There – is that better?'

She dabs his knee with a piece of cotton-wool soaked in the liquid from the cloudy bottle. The smell of it is acid and stifling.

'How does it feel, Vere?'

'Worse.'

'It can't.'

'Much worse.'

'There's not something else in the bottle, is there? No.' She sniffs. 'It's ammonia all right.'

'Nanny!' The pain is becoming intolerable.

'You must be exaggerating, Vere.'

'Oh, what can I do? It's smarting, Nanny, it's smarting so.'

'Now, Vere.'

He cannot sit still. He jumps up and hops round the room.

'Come here and let me look at it again.'

'But it's dreadful, Nanny. I can't bear it!'

'Well then, come here!'

He runs back to the sofa and hurls himself about on it, gritting his teeth and butting his head against the cushions.

After a glance at his leg, which she has seized, Nanny exclaims, 'Good heavens, child, it's all over blisters!'

She sounds so worried that Vere pauses and looks at the leg himself. At this moment Flora enters the room.

'Flora,' Vere moans, 'my leg's all blisters. Where have you been?'

There is a puzzled and doubtful expression on Flora's face. 'I've been collecting some watercress down the garden,' she says. 'I saw Mr. Bruise. Oh Vere, what have you been doing?'

'Flora, will you come and look at this sting on his knee,' says Nanny. 'I can't make it out.'

'Sting?' asks Flora.

'Yes, he was stung by a bee.'

'Were you, Vere?'

'Mmm,' he says, not liking actually to enunciate the lie a second time, for he knows that the game is up, he knows that Flora knows.

'Why are you smiling?' Nanny asks. 'It is a bee-sting, isn't it?'

'It is a sting,' he answers, 'in a way. It's a sort of sting. You see, I was stung by the exhaust pipe of Mr. White's motorbike.'

'What are you saying, Vere, what do you mean? This isn't a burn?'

'Yes, it is, sort of.'

'A burn? And I put ammonia on it? Oh child, child. Go down and fetch his mother, Flora.'

'No, Nanny,' Vere says.

'Quickly, Flora, and tell her it's urgent.'

Flora goes: Nanny rummages in the medicine cupboard: Vere sits fearfully on the edge of the sofa. Nanny's consternation and now her threatening silence, the unwonted summoning of his mother, the pain in his leg and the dire consequences he imagines will result from the application of the ammonia – all these things terrify him. He starts seriously to regret his lies. But when his mother arrives she is full of sympathy, and also, he notices, secretly amused by the story he has told. She asks him questions as she dresses his knee, her touch deliciously deft and gentle, and looks once or twice as if she is going to laugh out loud. This makes him think of the lie less as a crime and more as something excusable, jolly and sly. Of which he is the victim after all, he argues, when, a trifle resentfully, he meets Nanny's glum forbidding gaze.

He manages not to wince during his mother's operations and is congratulated on his courage, though his knee is now only numb. Flora shakes her head and clicks her tongue a certain amount, and his mother says, fastening the bandage with a safety-pin, 'Well, darling, let this be a lesson to you not to tell lies': but Vere, reflecting what seems to be the view of the majority, cannot feel unduly depressed. His ruse has fulfilled its intended function – and it was a ruse, he insists to himself as he meets Nanny's eye a second time.

His mother helps him to his feet and supports him when he tries to walk. He leans heavily on her arm, determined to make the most of her in this much-loved role, and suggests that they venture farther afield. Leaving Nanny to tidy the nursery they go along the passage and down the stairs, and find Vere's father in the hall. On being told what has taken place he smiles, his eyes crinkle and he calls Vere a monkey.

'Would you like to walk a little in the garden, darling?'

'Oh yes, Mummy, please.'

Together they stroll over the lawns, along the paved paths and between the yew-hedges.

'What did you say the bee was like, darling?'

'I said it was covered with fur, like a dog.'

'How big did you say it was?'

'Awfully big. And I said it had nine legs.'

'Good God.'

'And a sting like a knitting-needle.'

'Darling!'

'I did.'

'And Nanny believed you?' asks his father.

For some reason that he does not understand Vere pauses.

'She must be mad,' his father comments.

'Well, I made it all sound true.'

'You must have had a job.'

'Well, yes,' Vere laughs, and continues to give extravagant replies to the questions he is asked.

After several circuits of the lilypool his mother says that it is time for luncheon. With a light heart Vere bids his parents goodbye, hobbles to the gate in the garden wall, and then, screened from their sympathetic view, walks briskly into the house and up to the nursery.

He is unpleasantly surprised during the meal by Nanny's accusing looks and curt rejoinders; they slightly damp his carefree mood; but judging it only a matter of time before she sees the funny side of the events of the morning, he refuses to pay any great attention. When she declines to read to him after luncheon however, saying he does not deserve it, he considers she is carrying her disapproval too far and feels slighted, hurt, then angry. He tells himself she is humourless, obstinate, stuck-up, stupid and unfair. He does hope, all the same, that matters will have improved by teatime.

At teatime, if anything, they are worse. Although Vere makes one or two attempts at conversation most of the meal passes in silence. He leaves the nursery as soon as he is able, furiously resolving not to let Nanny's displeasure upset him, and seeks distraction out of doors. But he can find nothing to absorb or even occupy him: he wanders about the garden, idle and disconsolate, for an hour: and when the curfew is rung from the nursery window is still trying to persuade himself that her behaviour is unreasonable.

His mother arrives to rebandage his knee before he goes to bed. The burn, exacerbated by the ammonia, is raw and sensitive. On impulse, as a peace offering, in consideration of the blame that he knows Nanny assumes for its condition, he minimises his discomfort. But her steely glances show no sign of softening: and after healing anodynes have been applied, the pain has been eased and his mother has laughed again at his account of the morning's adventures, the spirit of rebelliousness once more flares within him.

This feeling persists – he clings to it at least – until Nanny comes into his room later in the evening, carefully closes the day-nursery door and subjects him to a long and searching scrutiny. He has been sitting up in bed, singing with revolutionary if uneasy vigour. His song weakens as she crosses and sits on the end of his bed, and, when she asks if he has anything to tell her, suddenly dies.

'Well, have you, Vere?' she repeats.

'No, I haven't,' he answers, marshalling his forces and giving her stare for stare.

'Are you sure, Vere?'

'Yes.'

She tries a flank attack. 'I want you to think what you did this morning.'

He goes to meet it. 'Nothing. I didn't do anything.'

'That's not the truth,' she says, bearing down on him. 'What did you do?'

'I rode on the motorbike.'

'I know, but I'm not speaking of that. What else?'

'Nothing else.'

'You told me a lie.'

'Oh Nanny!' He essays a laugh – for it is laughable, this mountain she is making out of a molehill. 'It was a fib.'

'It was a lie, and why did you tell it?'

'All right, I'm sorry,' he says abruptly and looks away, not beaten yet.

'That's not the way to say you're sorry and look at me, please,' she says. 'You told me a lie to get out of your punishment for riding on the motorbicycle, when you were forbidden – that's why you told it me.'

'But it was funny,' he exclaims.

'I think it was cowardly, Vere. I do.'

He repudiates the charge without conviction. Before he has time to collect himself she thrusts home her advantage.

'And I didn't expect it of you. I'm afraid you're not the boy I thought you were.'

'I am, Nanny,' he says, pressing back against his pillows and regarding her with round and nervous eyes.

'Another thing, Vere.' What now, he wonders, gathering his deflated forces together. 'I believed you, I believed your lie, and you set me up as a laughing-stock in front of your mother and father.'

'Oh Nanny, no.'

'Yes, Vere. Laughing like you did, because I believed you – it was inconsiderate and thoughtless and unkind.'

'Oh Nanny, please,' he whispers in surrender. His position collapses: it was always undermined. His strength ebbs away in his guilt, which he has felt but not till now comprehended. He is defeated.

'Well, Vere, goodnight,' Nanny says.

He has imagined his defeat was total: he has expected peace. Now he discovers his mistake. A truce is still war. Peace without reconciliation he cannot endure.

'You can't go!' he cries; and in his quick unhappiness he sees at last the real error of his ways, understands of a sudden how he has made her suffer, knows that he has been in truth unfeeling, heartless.

'I can do as I like,' she answers, rising to her feet.

In the light of his unhappiness he understands that too. She is free and independent, for he has severed – severed unthinkingly – the bonds of love, of respect and trust, which linked them. Clearly he perceives the tenderness of friendship – the risks and dangers of each careless word, each unweighed action. But if she will not leave him now – if only she will stay – how he will prove his love!

'Nanny, please don't go,' he says, and holds her square hands tightly in his own. 'I didn't mean to laugh. I won't again. I thought it was funny. I didn't know. I won't tell any more lies. I promise you. I do see now. I'm very sorry. Only don't go, Nanny, not like that.'

She sits on his bed. 'Now child, there there,' she says. 'I'll stay a minute. Don't cry, I know when you're sorry. We'll let bygones be bygones. Dry your eyes, here's my handkerchief.'

He takes her handkerchief and blows his nose. A pent-up flood of warm relief, of thankfulness, of love, courses and sweeps throughout his being. Kneeling beside his bed he says his prayers.

'Oh Nanny.'

He hugs and kisses her goodnight.

'There, child, it's forgiven and forgotten.'

'I'm going to be really good after this.'

'We must all try.'

'Always though.'

'It's not easy.'

'I don't mind.'

'Goodnight, my boy.'

'Goodnight, Nanny.'

HOUSES AND A BOOK

VERE'S first house was no more than a nest, hollowed out of the tall grass bordering the drive, into which he used to leap from a distance so as to leave no tell-tale trodden path, and from which he could spy secretly on the garden, the lawns and the front door. Crouching there by the hour, eaten alive by ants, midges and harvest-bugs, only his hair and forehead showing between the waving stalks, he would wait patiently for the reward of unsuspecting steps or the rare delight of an overheard conversation. His nest was not enduring. One morning he was lying in it on his back, gazing through the clean branches of the beech trees at the blue sky above, when he became aware of a recurrent and rhythmical scraping sound that set his teeth on edge. He rolled over and scanned the horizon. Old Harris, the gardener, not ten yards away, was sharpening the curving blade of his scythe with a whetstone. As soon as Vere heard the close and regular rush of the blade, laying the grass – the very walls of his house – in wide semicircular swathes, he jumped to his feet. Harris dropped the scythe, opened his mouth, told him to clear off. Convinced by the gardener's anxiety that he had had a narrow shave, Vere did as he was told. Revisiting the scene later in the day he was unable to discover the exact position of his nest. The grass was uniformly short and tufty, and landmarks like twigs and stones had been removed. He regretted his loss, then he forgot it. Such was the seed of later enterprise.

But that was long ago, the previous summer. Winter comes. Crude shelters begin to appear about the place, branches resting against the trunk of a tree or a piece of rusty corrugated-iron enclosing the angle of a wall – shelters constructed in an hour or two and hardly occupied as long. Christmas passes, and the holidays with their interruption of Vere's activities. Alone again he idly thinks of houses, awaiting some sign, some impetus. One winter's evening, when the wind howls round the corners of the house and the cowl on the nursery chimney moans and whistles, he receives it.

Nanny, after offering to read to him, searches in the bookshelf and takes down a thick-leafed volume entitled *Settlers in Canada*.

'Has it any pictures?' he asks.

'No, but it's a nice book just the same. Come and sit down.'

'Can I see it?'

'You ought to read to yourself. You read quite well, Mademoiselle was saying.'

'No, you read, Nanny. But this looks awful. Couldn't we have *Little Jack Rabbit*?'

'I've read *Little Jack Rabbit* till I'm sick of it,' she says. 'You must know it by heart. Besides, a big boy like you – you're too old for *Little Jack Rabbit*. We'll try this one. Pull up to the fire and listen.'

'Can I have a marshmallow first?'

'They're in the top drawer, Vere. And you might fetch me a peppermint while you're there.'

'I've brought you two peppermints, Nanny.'

'Oh, very well. Thank you, Vere. Now.'

Clearing her throat and sucking on the peppermint, Nanny reads: '*Settlers in Canada*. Chapter One.'

The first chapter is not long and concerns a noble English family which, somehow disinherited, decides to emigrate to the New World. At the end of it Nanny inquires if she shall continue. 'Please,' Vere answers, happily nibbling his damp marshmallow and feeling the heat of the fire on his face.

In the second chapter the settlers arrive in Canada, penetrate into the virgin country and search for a site on which to build their home.

And from this point onwards Vere ceases to nibble. He swallows the marshmallow, forgetting to chew it properly or to lick his fingers, and heedless of the interesting outdoor noises, starts to attend in earnest. For these people in the story, without professional experience and with only limited and natural resources, are about to build themselves a house, a fastness capable of resisting both the weather and attack, in a strange and trackless countryside from which they will have to wrest their livelihood. The significance of it all, like rain in a dry summer, transforms his landscape. It is this, precisely this, for which he has been waiting. It is the sign, the revelation. He too will sally into the wild country; he too will build himself a strong house; he too will live by the sweat of his brow. The example of the settlers fires him with unconquerable enthusiasm. He wants to begin at once, this evening. His teeth chatter with zeal and excitement.

'Oh Nanny, read that bit again!'

'Which bit?'

'The bit where they start building their house.'

'I've read it once.'

'Yes, but again.'

'Do you like it, Vere?'

'Yes, I do!'

The words are like fairy gold which he can harvest and glean at his leisure, leaving no speck behind, and treasure ever after. Or they are like some magical solution transmuting the dross of vague unformulated longings into the precious gold of a clear object, an aim. Either way they are gold – they shed a golden light on present and future – gold unalloyed, priceless, glittering.

Nanny reaches the end of the second chapter and the time comes for Vere to go to bed. He runs into the bathroom, taking the book with him, washes, cleans his teeth, puts on his pyjamas, dashes back to the night-nursery and is reading by his shaded bedside lamp – all within three minutes.

The settlers decide to build their house by the banks of a broad and tree-lined river. A great plain opens around them, fringed by a distant forest. Receiving help from the soldiers of a fortress situated some miles down river, they build first of all a stockade as a protection against the Indians and packs of fierce wolves that infest the countryside. Surrounded by threats and dangers, in an atmosphere of trust and reliance, they work without pause through the sweet summer days, felling the forest trees and setting up the saw bench, jointing the broad stakes for the stockade and laying the foundations of the house, constructing a yard and outbuildings for the animals.

Vere has just finished the third chapter when Nanny comes to say goodnight. He feels full, as if he has eaten a large meal and needs time to digest it, and is therefore not sorry.

'What a lot you've read, Vere!'

'Yes, I've read a whole chapter.'

'Goodness gracious.'

'It is a tremendous lot, isn't it?'

'You must like the book.'

'I do.'

'Goodnight, Vere.'

'Goodnight, Nanny.'

While the wind batters against his windows and the farmdog from its cold kennel faintly bays the fleeting moonlight, Vere lies in his warm bed, thinking disconnectedly. When he moves he notices that he aches slightly all over and his muscles are tense, as if from much exertion. The settlers slept under the stars, he thinks, the roar and eddy of the river filling their ears, the smoke from camp fires rising into the night. But not in winter, he recalls. He curls up and shuts his eyes. Still he sees the wide Canadian plain and the great trees. Like the settlers he is a breaker of new ground, a pioneer. He also belongs and does not belong; he also will build a house, a place of his own. And there he will live, lapped by Nature, resisting and loving it, forever contented, forever hardworking, self-reliant and admired. He falls into a dreamless sleep.

Waking in the morning refreshed he restrains himself with an effort from setting to work immediately. Instead, judging he can gain more from a quick but thorough study of the settlers' methods, he reads intently through the succeeding days.

The first snows of winter hold off until the homestead is ready. Then, with the gates of the stockade closed and the beasts in the byre, and with all sounds deadened by the softly descending flakes, the settlers resign themselves to the enforced inactivity and isolation of the cold season. They are not idle: furniture has to be made, animals have to be cared for. Nor are they dull: one night, in the middle of a frightful blizzard, starving wolves break into the stockade. But at length the ice on the frozen river is swept away, the water begins once more to flow and to gurgle and the tireless work is resumed.

The story develops. A friendly Indian is introduced, complete with wigwam and blanket. Then the youngest settler, a little girl, is abducted by a party of marauding braves. A chase ensues. The settlers, the Indian and the soldiers from the fort track down the culprits, and after desperate expedients – the climax of the book – rescue the child. Finally the settlers inherit their rightful English property and title, and prepare to leave Canada.

Over the tea-table on the afternoon that he finishes the book Vere discusses it with Nanny and Flora.

'Well, did the settlers save little Rosemary?' Nanny asks as she pours the tea, having heard at luncheon that the child was missing.

'Yes, they saved her all right,' he answers.

'I'm glad to hear it.'

'How did they manage?' Flora inquires. When he has explained she says, 'It must have been exciting.'

'Yes, it was,' he admits, meaning, Not nearly so exciting as the building of the house.

Nanny says, 'And what happens in the end, Vere?'

'The father becomes a lord – he is one really all the time – and he's awfully rich, so the settlers come back to England.'

'Well, that's very nice,' Nanny observes.

Vere munches thoughtfully, then asks, 'Why do you suppose they want to leave Canada?'

'They've inherited the money and the name, and they have their place to keep up – it's quite natural,' Nanny explains.

'But they're happy in Canada, aren't they?' he reasons. 'Why should they want to leave?'

'Perhaps they don't like it, sweetheart, not really.'

'Oh but they do! It's lovely there.'

'It's a hard life, Vere.'

'Yes, I know,' he says, uncomprehending. For it is exactly the hard life that he finds so attractive. The settlers have not been making the best of a bad job in Canada: they have been engaged in an enviable and inspiring work. Is it possible that they can wish to exchange their freedom for money, titles, places in England?

'Of course they'll not be happy, will they,' he says, 'when they get back, I mean?'

'Why not, Vere?'

'Well – they won't have anything to do, a house to build or anything.'

'I expect that's why they're returning. They don't want all that bother and nuisance a second time.'

'Bother, Nanny?'

'No.'

'Eat your cake, sweetheart.'

He begins to feel depressed. If Nanny is right, then all that he has loved in the story is meaningless.

'I'm sure they won't be happy,' he says. 'Not in the same way.'

'It's only a book, Vere, remember.'

'Well, they won't be happy. I know they won't.'

He denies the settlers happiness. If they regard the wonder of their life in Canada as no more than a nuisance, they will have to pay for their mistake with a sorrowful future. He commits them to misery and feels much better.

'How long did it take you to read the book?'

'Four days,' he answers, diverted by Flora's question.

'And you read it all yourself?'

'Yes.'

'Most of it, Vere.'

'Most of it I read by myself.'

Soon after this the rough March weather changes. The days are quiet and misty, and the trees drip although no rain falls. Vere gives up worrying about the complications of the settlers' story. He has his essential treasure, he cares for nothing else. With a knapsack containing biscuits and string over his shoulder he starts looking for a site on which to build his house. He combs the countryside, keen-eyed, heavily trudging, poking into unlikely parts of the garden and the grove of trees. Eventually, in the undergrowth behind the tennis court, he finds his ideal situation. On the first sunny day in April the work is set in motion.

He has chosen the angle formed by two walls for his purpose. The property is squared off by willows and evergreens on one side, which screen him from overlooking windows, and by the corroded iron wheels and splintered wood of a disused water-pump on the other. There are empty outbuildings nearby which he can plunder, and an untended path, winding away from the pump and through the grove of trees, leads up to the terrace. Since the floor-planks of the old summer house on the terrace are rotten and easily dislodged, this path is not without its uses. But he is careful on his journeys not to crush the nettles and sturdy weeds that surround his house, protecting it from chance discovery.

So begins for Vere a period of activity the like of which he has never known. His heart pulses with a steady and productive excitement. He is stronger and more resourceful than ever before. He glories in the size of his undertaking and the problems that confront him. His entire energy is concentrated on the project, every spare moment devoted to a form of toil connected with it. He can think of nothing else. Ideas come to him at meals or in his bath: he forgets to eat, to wash himself. Too absorbed to notice his happiness, too young to measure its depth, he works without respite.

Flora sometimes asks, 'When can we come and see your house?'

Pleased yet oddly not pleased by the question he usually parries it, saying either 'What?' or 'I'm deaf in that ear, Flora.'

'When are you going to let us come and see?'

'Oh, soon. Not long now.'

'Where is it, Vere?'

'Don't you know?'

'I don't.'

'Honestly?'

'I promise.'

Indulging himself he says, 'Where do you think, Flora?'

'I couldn't say.'

'Have a guess.'

'Round by the chickens?' He shakes his head. 'In the woodshed?'

'Indoors?' he exclaims. 'No, Flora, it's miles from there if you want to know, miles and miles. I'm afraid you couldn't guess.'

'I said I couldn't.'

'But I'll give you one more try if you like.'

'It's no use, Vere.'

'You probably think it's in the garden, or behind the tennis-court, don't you, Flora?'

'It must be in one of those places.'

'Do you think so?'

'Where else could it be?'

'Well, it's not behind the tennis-court. Fancy you thinking it's there! You'll have to wait and see, won't you?'

'I don't think I can much longer.'

At the time these conversations induce feelings of elation and superiority, but afterwards he regrets them. They leave a boastful and unpleasant taste in his mouth. Although he longs to broadcast the tale of his triumphs, the least word that he lets slip causes him a pang as of betrayal. He does not understand his contrary emotions until one afternoon, passing the front door with his star piece of material – the sheet of rusty corrugated-iron – balanced unsteadily on his head, he happens to meet his father.

'Hullo, Dad,' he says, lowering the iron with difficulty onto the paving and already, without knowing why, regretting the encounter.

'What the hell have you got there?' asks his father.

'It's a piece of corrugated-iron.'

'I can see that.' Vere's mother emerges from the front door and his father says, 'I thought I was seeing things. Vere was carrying that damn great piece of iron.'

'Darling! You'll cut your fingers to ribbons! Leave it there and the gardeners will fetch it.'

'My fingers are all right, Mummy.'

His father inquires, 'Where on earth did it come from?'

'Yes, darling, where did you find it?'

'Oh, I've had it for years,' claims Vere.

'But really, you mustn't just take things,' his mother says.

'I haven't taken it. It's mine. The gardeners gave it me ages ago.'

'Well anyway, you'll have to let somebody help you.' As an afterthought his mother asks, 'What do you want with it?'

'What?'

'What do you want it for?'

'I'm building something.'

'What are you building?'

He pauses and says, 'Well, it's a house. I've built lots of houses but this is a better one, much better. Will you come and see it when it's finished?'

'I don't think you'll need that bit of iron though, will you, darling?'

He raises his voice, wondering if she has heard him. 'It's for my house, it's for the house I'm building.'

'Well, go very carefully – promise?'

'Yes, Mummy,' he says. 'You will come and see my house?'

'I can't today, I'm afraid.'

'No, when it's finished?'

'Another day, darling, yes.'

'And you will, Dad?'

'Yes, but for God's sake mind out with that iron.'

Vere shoulders his burden, trying not to show how unbearably heavy he actually finds it, and stumbles away.

To begin with he is furious with himself for having risked the front of the house; then he is saddened by his parents' reaction; finally he realises that he must not speak of what is closest to his heart. No-one can share his excitement: no-one believes in it, in his house or in him. But one day they will. Until his house is finished – only till then – he is on his own.

Day by day meanwhile, notwithstanding setbacks, the work advances. The stones on the top of the walls are rearranged, levelled and packed with earth. The planks from the summer house are laid across to make a triangular shelter. This is so low that he excavates the soil, to the depth of about a foot, beneath it. The planks do not fit, their crumbling edges admit the light, and he begins to throw the excavated soil onto the roof. It falls through the gaps quicker than he can throw it. He fetches newspaper and spreads it over the planks. The soil after that remains pleasingly in position: he throws it up by the trowelful: it becomes a mountain. He would like to climb onto the roof to smooth it, but the planks sag alarmingly and he does not dare. At least no chinks of light remain: and when trees and bushes grow on the mountain, how secret his house will be – a sort of natural cavern!

The corrugated-iron – the largest part of the outside wall – he fixes against the roof, filling in at the sides with more planks. Over everything he then drapes sacks, wedging branches against them and driving in stakes for greater strength and solidity. He also hangs a sack above the narrow entrance to serve as a door.

The house inside is damp, pitch-dark and musty. By the light of a candle which he has borrowed from the cupboard in the pantry, he pats down the earth in the well of the floor and fashions a doorstep. He drives wooden pegs into crevices in the stone walls, for his coat and for tools, and makes an insecure shelf on which to keep stores such as candles and matches and biscuits.

Discovering that he can only stand upright in the very corner of the angle formed by the two walls – elsewhere the sag of the ceiling prevents it – he arranges a seat with a plank and some stones. Leaning right forward, in order not to collapse the outside wall, it is possible to sit there – it is really quite comfortable.

Three days after his eighth birthday he surveys his work. The earth on the roof has settled down and already one or two weeds are sprouting. The thick wall of iron, planks, branches and sacks scarcely moves when he touches it. The floor of his house is level and hard, his knapsack and tools hang from the pegs. He climbs onto the water-pump. Beyond his house stretch fields and distant woods. The sun is shining on the wide landscape, but the corner of it that he has conquered and made his own is in shadow. He turns and edges through the nettles.

'Where have you been, Vere?' Nanny asks when he comes in late for tea. 'Didn't you hear the bell?'

'My house is finished,' he answers.

Flora enters the room and is told the news.

'Can we see it this evening, Vere?'

'Not till tomorrow,' he says. 'I've still one or two things to do.'

'Are you pleased with it?'

'Quite.'

'House,' says Faith.

'You can come too if you like, Faith.'

'House,' she repeats.

The rest of the evening is spent in a ferment of excitement. Vere is restless and talkative. Every conversation seems to wind up with a reference to his house. He tries without success to speak and to think of it calmly: he changes the subject a dozen times: the result is always the same.

Before going to bed he slips between the night-nursery curtains, and resting his forehead against the cool windowpane, looks out at the night. So much depends on the weather. Another clear day, he prays. If without sun, let it at least be dry and balmy. No rain, he pleads, no rain.

He sleeps fitfully. Waking with the first light he gets up and goes again to the window. The sky is overcast, there is a gusty wind. It may change, he thinks, it is still early. But by breakfast a light drizzle is falling. Nanny says it cannot last. He wants to believe her: yet how grey the sky is – no blue anywhere! As long as there is not a downpour. If necessary a drizzle, but please, he implores, please, please, no downpour.

The downpour comes at eleven o'clock. Vere is with Mal: this is the time, during his break, when she was to pay her promised visit.

'But after luncheon, chéri, we will go.'

'It'll be raining.'

'Then tomorrow.'

'It was all arranged for today, Mal. Everything was ready.'

'I know.'

The rain streams down. One hour, two hours pass. The sky is shrouded. Millions of drops of rain like sharp spears pierce and mutilate Vere's tender hopes. Wistfully he looks through the windows, mourning and grieving: and when Nanny at luncheon says that she thinks it is brightening, he smiles sarcastically and does not even bother to turn in his chair.

But Nanny is right. By two o'clock the clouds have lifted and beams of watery sunlight catch the silver spatters of late raindrops.

'Put on your wellingtons, Vere,' she says. 'You can fetch Mademoiselle on your way down.'

'Do you think it's worth trying to go?' he asks, anxious not to suffer fresh disappointment.

'Of course it is.'

'But the whole place'll be sopping wet.'

'Well, if it is, it is.'

'But you do understand, Nanny?'

'No, I don't understand,' she says. 'Stop worrying and put on your coat. We'll be out in a jiffy.'

'You don't know where to go, do you?'

'Yes, we do.'

'You do? Who told you?'

'A little bird. Run along.'

She hustles him out of the nursery. What little bird, he wonders as he walks along the passage. How can she know or think that she knows? He descends the staircase slowly, unable to ponder properly because of the revival of his vivid hopes, and finds Mal in the schoolroom wearing her soft raincoat and green hat with the jay's feathers.

'But you're all dressed,' he exclaims.

'I am dressed for the visit to your house,' she says. 'Can Scamp come with us?'

'She might as well.'

He leads the way through the side door, feeling with every step more nervous and unwilling. He has made so much of his house: now he remembers a hundred faults in its construction, recalls that the job is not complete. It occurs to him that the rain may have injured some part of it, may even have destroyed the whole. And he does not know: what then is he doing? He warns Mal not to expect too much, blaming the weather for whatever deficiencies they may find. Mal says only, 'We will see.' He dislikes this answer, begins to feel that the expedition is being forced upon him, wishes he had never mentioned his house to anyone, hopes for more rain.

They reach the willows.

'Through here, Mal,' he says breathlessly.

She stumps forward, poking with her stick, and says, 'I can't go through there. It is too thick, Vere.'

'Yes, you can.'

'No, chéri.'

'Well, come round to this side.'

Trembling with controlled impatience, with excitement and uncertainty, he brushes through the undergrowth and climbs onto the water-pump. His house is still standing. It looks so natural and hoary with its branches and damp sacks and mountain of earth on top, as if it had stood there, in its concealed neglected corner, for all of time, that a sudden wave of relief and affection surges over Vere at the sight of it.

'Mal, here!' he cries, jumping down from the pump. 'You can get through easily!'

'But it is thrilling!' she says.

'Can you manage?'

'Mais oui.'

'There's my house, Mal.'

'Where?'

'There.'

The large woman and the boy, surrounded by the dripping trees, halt together at the edge of the open space. The warmth of the sun makes the earth steam around them. For a few seconds they gaze at the house in silence, then Vere says shakily, 'Mal, you see, it's only rough. I've hardly started on it yet. I just thought you might like to visit it sort of halfway – it's about half-finished.'

'It's lovely,' she says.

'It may be one day.'

'But now.'

'Do you think it is?' He cannot help smiling.

'Mais oui, mais oui! Lovely!'

She is speaking in her businesslike voice, she means what she says.

'How did you do it, Vere?'

It is this – the astonished question, the admiring glance, the unfeigned earnest interest – it is this for which he has slaved. By means of this house which he has created from nothing with his lonely labour, by means of this lasting expression of his deepest, strongest and best-loved mood, he has made his mark, he has gained his prize. Troubled no longer by fear or anxiety, his personality enlarged by his sweet success, he feels new powers stirring within him, unbreakable resolves, noble intentions.

'Tell me, how did you do it?'

'It took me a long time.'

'How long?'

'Weeks. Three weeks.'

'That is not long.'

'I worked awfully hard.'

'Amazing. Explain it to me. What are these sticks?'

'Sticks? That's the stockade.'

'I see.'

'I'm going to grow food here.'

'What sort of food?'

'Radishes and carrots.'

'And the house?'

'I'll show you. This is the door, this sack. Now you see these nails in the wall? I can fasten the door to whichever I want. For cold weather, or warm, or hot.'

'What made you think of such things?'

'That's nothing. Come in, Mal.'

Vere is so proud and happy. There are some beads of moisture on the ceiling planks, but the floor is almost dry. The house must be remarkably well-built to have withstood such an onslaught of wind and rain. And the faults? Why, he will put them right another day.

'Come in,' he calls.

'I can look from here, chéri.'

'But Mal, I've made you a seat. You must come right in.'

'I think I am too big for the door.'

'No, you're not,' he says, although she does seem enormous – her head alone completely blocks the doorway. 'Wait a second and I'll light the candle. There, that's better. Come on, Mal, you'll get in easily.'

'But chéri, I don't want to knock anything down.'

'You couldn't. It's tremendously strong. You see the step, don't you? Entrez.'

'Merci, Monsieur.'

She places one foot on the step and heaves her shoulders through the aperture.

'That's fine,' Vere encourages her. But Mal begins to laugh. 'What are you laughing at?'

'Eh bien, chéri – I am stuck.'

'No, Mal, you're not.'

'I am!'

'Where?'

'My hips.'

'Put your other leg in.'

'That is the leg with the rheumatism. I cannot move it an inch.'

'Try, Mal.'

'Quelle horreur!'

Whenever she laughs the drops of water on the ceiling shiver. Vere wishes she would not; there is nothing humorous in the situation; for both of them it is plainly becoming serious.

'No, Mal, please,' he says, 'try and move. You must now. Please, Mal. Are you ready? There!'

She enters the house. The entire structure rocks as she does so and little remains of the doorstep, but at least she is in. Bent double, refusing to sample the seat, saying that if she did she would never get up again, her face in the candlelight looking red and hot, she is nonetheless appreciative. Although he can scarcely move, Vere points out the various pegs in the walls and describes their uses, and recovering gradually from the shock he received when Mal stuck in the doorway, begins once more to glow and exult.

'It is all right, Mal, isn't it?'

'Really, I congratulate you.'

'Do you really?'

'Really.'

They are just preparing to leave – Mal is swinging round and he is pushing her – when suddenly and without warning the roof creaks dully and the candle goes out.

'What has happened?'

'What?' he says. 'Nothing. Go on, Mal.'

'But I heard something.'

'I don't think you did. Please go on.'

'Is it safe?'

'Of course.'

A plank breaks. One end of it catches Vere a wicked blow on the head, the saturated earth of the mountain pours onto Mal's bent back, the sunlight streams through the rent in the roof, illuminating the wreckage.

Vere is suffering and in pain. He rubs his head with his hand and his eyes water. Mal, who cannot see the full extent of the catastrophe, calls to him.

Confused, frightened, not understanding what has happened yet determined to be equal to it, he answers calmly, 'There's nothing wrong, Mal. One of the planks, that's all. Can you get out?'

'But are you hurt?'

'No.'

She accepts his statement. He longs to tell her that he is hurt, badly hurt, that the bump on his head is the size of a pigeon's egg; but he only asks her how she is managing. He wishes he were alone. He cannot face explanations, the thought of them makes his blood run cold. And there is Flora now: she is calling out: and Scamp is barking: and Nanny and Faith will be up by the willows.

He hears Flora say as Mal emerges from the house, 'Isn't it grand, Mademoiselle?' And then, 'Why Mademoiselle, you've mud all over your back!'

He hears Mal's worried answer, braces himself, then climbs over the broken doorstep into the sunlight.

Nanny appears beyond the water-pump with Faith in her arms.

'Where is it, Vere?' she calls.

'Hullo, Nanny.'

'Heavens, Mademoiselle, have you had a fall?'

Mal answers, 'Oh Nanny. No, we went into the house and part of it came down – it was an accident.'

'Oh dear,' Nanny says. 'Well, I'm sure the coat'll clean. So there's the house, Vere. It's fine! Mademoiselle, you let me have your coat afterwards, will you?'

And they converse together.

Flora, who has been looking at Vere and chewing her lower lip, asks where the house is damaged.

'All over,' he replies in an undertone.

'But no, you will mend it, Vere, it is not bad!' says Mal.

'Whatever's wrong with it you wouldn't know,' Nanny agrees. 'Well done, Vere.'

'And inside, Nanny,' Mal comforts him, 'it is wonderful! I love it!'

But the house is broken, he thinks. 'Let's go,' he says. 'Let's leave it.'

'You are not worried, are you, chéri?'

'No,' he replies.

'It is my fault?'

'No, Mal.'

'And you will put it right?'

'I don't know.'

Flora asks him if she can have a look. He says he does not care.

'Now Vere,' Nanny reproves from beyond the pump. 'What a way to speak to Flora. She's only trying to help. Show her what's the matter.'

He kicks at a stone while Flora and Mal stand by his house, discussing the damage. He notices that the roof is no higher than their waists. His enduring monument is a doll's house, clumsy, ramshackle, broken!

'Sweetheart,' Flora asks, 'it's just this plank, isn't it?'

'Could we not replace it now, Vere?'

'No,' he says. 'I'm afraid not, Mal. I'm afraid it's absolutely ruined actually.'

'But no!'

'Yes!' He laughs shortly.

'Oh Vere, I'll help you do it.'

'Will you, Flora? What about all these other things? This plank's pretty well bust too.' And he tugs viciously at the outside plank, the one with the heaviest sag. It does not move.

Nanny calls, 'What are you doing, Vere? You will bust it if you're not careful.'

'It is already,' he calls back angrily. That this weak plank should not even break at the correct moment enrages him.

'Don't, Vere,' says Mal.

'Look!' he cries. 'You see?'

The plank has cracked. Earth from the mountain cascades into the house.

'And this too!' he says, yanking at the corrugated iron.

'Stop him, Flora,' Nanny calls.

'Sweetheart, Vere!'

The iron flops onto the ground, exposing the debris within.

'There!' he shouts. 'Do you see now? It's a rotten mess, that's all! I'm only showing you!'

He has never been so violent in his life. He scarcely knows what he is doing. A hard core of destructive furious misery sticks in his throat and chest.

Mal says, aghast, 'How could you, Vere?'

'Why not? Why shouldn't I? It's damn rotten anyway. All of it. Goodbye. I'm going.'

He flings away, but the excess of emotion makes his head throb and stars dance in front of his eyes. He stumbles over a wet sack.

'Vere!' Flora picks him up. 'What's the matter, Vere?'

'Nothing,' he sobs. 'I've hit my head. Goodbye!'

But he is not allowed to go. Flora feels the bump on his head and calls to Nanny. Mal feels the bump. Nanny takes him into the house. In the bathroom she applies lotions and reproaches him with having kept silent. This affords him some relief from his choking anger and despair. At least he has shown courage in the face of adversity. But he is ashamed of this sympathy won for the wrong reasons: he despises himself for welcoming it: and tearing himself from Nanny before she has completed her task he runs away down the nursery passage.

At the top of the stairs he meets Flora and Faith. Flora asks him where he is going. The gentleness of her question increases his anger. He answers bitingly, 'Out!' and deaf to her dismayed entreaties rushes down the stairs. On the bottom step he trips and turns his ankle.

Sobbing with fury he hurls the side door savagely open and hobbles onto the lawn.

'Vere!'

It is his mother. She is standing with his father outside the school-room french windows.

'You're not to open the door like that, Vere, you'll break the glass,' she says. 'Go back and shut it properly.'

He does as he is told and starts to cross the lawn.

'Vere! Say you're sorry to your mother,' his father calls.

'I'm sorry,' Vere shouts without pausing.

'Vere! Come here!' The boy stops. 'Come here.' But he does not move. He would rather die. 'Say you're sorry again.'

'I'm sorry, Mummy.'

'You mustn't bang doors like that, darling.'

Darling, he thinks – that empty word.

'You won't bang them any more, will you?'

He says nothing.

Uncomfortable, his mother calls across the lawn: 'Did you take Mal to see your house?'

He still says nothing.

His father mutters, 'Leave him alone.'

Yes, Vere thinks, leave me: I ask for nothing better.

'Would you like us to come and see your house, darling? We could now.'

'No,' he replies. 'It isn't ready. Thank you, Mummy.'

His father says, 'Come on,' and strolls off, whistling.

'Well – goodbye, darling,' his mother adds, smiling and waving her hand.

He turns away. At the mention of his house his heart has contracted. Even his parents' knowledge of it shocks him. But now his heart contracts at their lack of interest. He cannot comprehend his feelings.

He clambers onto the terrace wall and drops into the field of uncut hay. The fall jars him and hurts his ankle. He does not care. Water trickles down his legs inside his wellingtons as he limps through the wet hay. Clouds scurry and the sun warms – he does not notice: birds rise from beneath his feet – he does not start. On and on he walks without any sense of direction, conscious only of the turmoil within and the weight of his sorrow.

In a patch of purple clover he catches his foot and measures his length on the ground. He does not rise, he can bear no more. An endless aching sob is wrenched out of him, and another, and another. He has not the strength or the will to fight his sobs: they engulf him entirely. The tears course down his cheeks and mingle with the raindrops in the rich clover. He lies face downwards, clutching at grasses with his hands and resting his hot forehead on the soaked and soothing earth, and cries bitterly.

After a time his sobs lessen. There is an occasional catch in his throat and sometimes he shudders, but he feels drained, the causes of his misery recede, and he has to admit to himself that he is more hungry than anything else. He raises himself on an elbow and looks round.

He is not alone.

A startled hare is crouching only a few feet away, regarding him with flat and frightened eyes. He stares at the hare and the hare stares back. But this tawny animal, he thinks as he recovers from his surprise, is a fellow-creature, a friend; and he begins to rub his thumb and first finger together and to murmur softly, 'Come on. Come closer. Don't be afraid. Come on then, come on.'

The hare seems to hesitate. It lowers one ear a fraction of an inch and twitches its nose. Vere slides his hand along the ground, murmuring the while, but suddenly the hare is gone, bobbing unevenly, all legs and tucked-in tail, away into the hay.

Vere scrambles to his feet. The hare is nowhere to be seen, but under a tuft of grass beside the clover patch he finds a small smooth nest. Perhaps this is where he caught his foot: it is the hare's house and he has trodden on it. He kneels down, greatly distressed, places his hand in the oblong hollow and examines it from above and below. It is a perfect house, so snug and well-hidden, so natural. The hare must have been returning to it, full of pride and anticipation, only to find it crushed and overlaid by a fearsome stranger. What cruel fates, he thinks, await builders of houses. He tries to reshape the nest, but without success for the grasses are bruised and broken beyond repair.

He takes stock of his position. The tops of the grove trees are barely visible: he is miles from anywhere. After a last long look for the hare he sets out for home.

Whatever brought him so far into the field? Nanny and Flora must never know of his flight. No-one must know that he wept in the patch of clover, and no-one will know, except the hare. He and the hare are fellow-sufferers, he thinks. He wonders if the small animal is lying somewhere in the field, its eyes filled with tears, its brown body shaken with sobs, for like Vere the hare has lost its house. Their situation is the same. But no, he decides: the hare would accept its lot more philosophically. A hare's life probably consists of building houses and finding them destroyed. But then, he remembers sadly, so does my life . . .

The truth is, he thinks as he tramps through the hay, that one builds not for other people but for oneself: not really for praise or approval, but because one cannot do otherwise. Houses collapse, he thinks, are trodden on, are deserted when complete: but more houses are built, they always will be, he cannot imagine life without them.

His house is a failure. When he was building it – until a few hours back – he thought it beautiful. How can he have been so slapdash, so easily satisfied? He was going to have two rooms, a fire: he was going to sleep in it. What became of all his visions – that splendour, that magnificence? His broken house is a thing of the past. He will not visit it again. He is older now and not so hopeful, and the sweet and sanguine path that he has recently pursued is barred to him forever. One day, some day, he may build another house; but then he will build for the sake of building, modestly and in private. One day, perhaps . . . He cannot tell.

His resolution fortifies him, his spirits revive. The sun is shining blindingly after the rain. As a sign of fair weather the swallows mount and circle in the sky. Curiously, like some returning traveller, Vere observes afresh the gravel drying on the drive, the bare trunks of the beech trees, the grey extended house with white sash windows, the lawns, brick walls and climbing roses: and at sight of the dear unchanging scene, love that is remembered and new love unite in his heart, producing a tentative happiness, fragile yet pure and true.

It is five o'clock when he enters the nursery and tea is on the table. Flora greets him and helps him off with his wellingtons, but does not refer to the events of the afternoon. This raises a barrier between them, which Vere is considering how to broach when Nanny comes in with Faith and bluntly asks him where he has been.

'Out for a walk,' he says. 'I saw a hare.' Then he adds quickly, 'I'm sorry about earlier.'

Nanny accepts his apology as she straps Faith into her chair, asks after the bump on his head which he has forgotten, and says, sitting down, 'It was a shame about your house, Vere.'

'I know,' he says.

Flora sympathises and inquires if he will repair the damage.

'No,' he replies. 'I don't think I will, Flora.'

'You'll just have to build another house, Vere. That's what you'll have to do,' says Nanny.

'Yes,' he answers. And all of a sudden, to his utter amazement, he realises that he is once again in the grip of familiar excitement. The future, the radiant future with its smiling countenance, is holding out its hand, is claiming him again. He is already thinking where to build his house, his new house, a final and a faultless house, a house to end all houses.

He cannot escape: he does not wish to. The frenzied yearnings of his soul, the singular joy, the labour and the pain – he embraces them like long-lost comrades. They are his destiny.

'Yes,' he says quietly to Nanny, 'I am going to.'

LEO'S BIRTHDAY

NANNY, how long before Leo comes back from school?'
'A week . . . Five days, three days, two days . . . Tomorrow, Vere.'

'Leo comes back tomorrow! And it's his birthday the day after, isn't it? Oh Nanny, what shall I give him?'

'Some little thing, Vere. Leo will have lots of presents.'

On the morning of the day of Leo's return Vere goes shopping in Long Cretton. Because of what Nanny has told him, wishing his present to be noticeably nice, he buys a flat chromium-plated knife for his brother, price five shillings and sixpence, which is more than he can afford. During the afternoon he uses it to carve his initials on the linoleum of the nursery passage, then he wraps it in tissue paper and puts it in his pocket, and with time to spare before leaving for the station, wanders into his brother's bedroom.

The figured bedspread is crisply white and unruffled, the windows are open, the tables bare, the drawers empty. Leo will live in this clean room, he thinks: Leo's things will litter the tables and overflow the drawers: this will be Leo's room. All will change here. All will alter in other ways. Private enterprises will be shelved: successes, failures, ideas, amusements will be divided, halved: the life with Leo, the happy active life, is again about to begin.

'Vere! Albert's waiting in the car.'

He runs downstairs. The house is neat and quiet, ready for his parents, ready for Leo. He will laugh with Leo, tell and listen to stories; they will quarrel and fight. In a quarter of an hour Leo will be home. Vere is really looking forward to his arrival, to the excitement and disturbance.

'Are we late?' he asks anxiously, climbing into the car.

'Not unless the train's early,' answers Albert as he slides into his seat, closes the door, switches on the ignition, presses the self-starter, slips the car into gear and disengages the brake.

They move smoothly away.

'How do you do all those things so quickly?' Vere inquires.

'You ask your brother. He'll make a driver one of these days.'

'I'm going to learn to drive too,' says Vere.

After a pause Albert remarks, 'Well, you'll be getting up to some games now, I expect.'

'Why?'

'With that big brother of yours.'

'Oh, yes.'

'Give you someone to play with, won't it?'

'Yes, it will,' Vere agrees, starting to whistle.

'But you like playing on your ownsome, don't you?'

'Yes,' Vere replies.

On the station platform Mr. Pick the station-master, red and green flags under his arm, greets Vere.

'Come to meet your brother, I expect?'

'That's right, Mr. Pick.'

'He's the gentleman nowadays, isn't he, just like his father.'

'Yes.'

'Keep back from the line, sir, if you please.'

Although he buys a bar of slot-machine chocolate and weighs himself, Vere begins to wonder why he came to meet the train. Instead of wasting his time and money he thinks of a hundred interesting things he might be doing: and as for gaining a few extra moments of Leo's company – Leo will be home for weeks and months.

A bell clangs. Mr. Pick unfurls his flags with a flourish and cries, 'London train, London train!' A hefty porter jumps onto the tracks, saunters across and heaves himself onto the platform.

'Where's the train?' asks Vere.

'Search me,' says the porter, winking at Albert.

A second bell clangs and a distant rumble is heard. Vere turns to the right, and here comes the train, streaming through the tunnel like a centipede, screaming and whistling, blasting out steam and smoke, tearing along!

'Back from the line, please!'

Now the train is close, slowing up, but it cannot stop – it will never stop in time! Mr. Pick blows his whistle, waves his flags and his arms, knocks his gold-braided hat askew. The engine-driver, big and grimy, grins at Vere as he passes, taking no notice of Mr. Pick's obscure signals. The brakes wheeze, the carriages jar. 'That'll do it, George,' calls the hefty porter. The train halts.

'Where are they, Albert, can you see them?'

A window is lowered and a round face pops out.

'Leo!' Vere rushes along the platform. 'Here they are, Albert! Leo, Leo!' He tugs at the heavy door. 'Hullo, Leo!'

'All right, don't shout,' says Leo, blushing. 'Hullo, Albert.'

'Good afternoon, Master Leo.'

'My trunk's in the van, Albert.'

'Right you are, Master Leo.'

Vere's mother steps down from the train. His father, inside the compartment, calls, 'Don't stand there, Vere, come and take my bag.'

'Help your father, darling,' his mother says.

'Go on, sloppy,' adds Leo, and the passengers in the compartment laugh.

Whistles blow: luggage is piled onto the platform: doors slam. The porter approaches.

'How many pieces, sir?'

'What?'

'Seven pieces, Dad, I counted them,' says Leo.

'Good boy. All right, come on. Don't lose my case, Vere.'

With a long-drawn sigh, a whistle and a puff, the train pulls out of the station.

Vere carries his father's attaché-case to the car. Leo is shaking hands with Mr. Pick, who beams and touches his cap deferentially. Luggage is strapped onto the roof of the car and stowed in the boot. Albert mops his brow and orders Vere out of the way. Leo comes through the station gate.

'You sit in the front with Vere,' says his mother.

'Do I have to?'

'Oh Leo, don't be unkind. Vere's been longing to see you.'

'I don't mind,' Vere shrugs.

As they leave the station Mr. Pick blows his whistle for the amusement of Leo, who laughs and waves, then the car swings away onto the main road.

How low Vere feels! If the holidays begin like this, how will they end? They last for years too. He wishes he had not spent so much money on the chromium-plated knife. He will have to keep it for himself, and give Leo as a birthday present the bar of railway chocolate. Why did he come to meet the train, what did he expect of his brother? He has never even cared for Leo. And Leo clearly does not care for him.

'Got me an expensive present for my birthday?'

'Yes,' Vere replies, taken by surprise.

'What is it?'

'I'm not going to tell you.'

'You are.'

'I'm not.'

'You lovely boy.'

'A jolly sight too expensive,' says Vere.

Leo pokes him in the ribs with his elbow and turns to talk to Albert.

Vere, winded by the blow, looks out of the window. He will certainly not give Leo the knife. He hates Leo. Never again will he be deceived by smiles and sudden questions. His brother is vile, horrible, whatever anyone else may think, rough, cruel and heartless: henceforth he will ignore him completely.

In spite of his firm resolve, at tea and during the triumphal tour of gardens, garages, stables and house, Vere continues to be tricked by flashing smiles and unexpected jokes into thinking he may be wrong in his estimate of his brother. Once or twice he even tries a joke and a smile himself. But his incautious hopes revive only to be crushed, and he grows sullen and wary, despises himself for being so lightly won, detests Leo, particularly for his assurance and fatal charm; while the pleasure that everyone appears to take in his brother's presence and jolly ways he does his utmost to discount.

Such is Vere's frame of mind at suppertime. He vows it will never change. However, when in the nursery Leo proposes that they should sleep in the same room, that they should straightaway move Vere's mattress and eat their soup and toast in bed, he finds himself not only listening with interest but actually agreeing; and a few moments later, as they struggle with the heap of bedding, he catches himself joining in Leo's infectious laughter; and when Leo says to him, 'Let's wash quickly, then we can play the wireless and have a chat,' he really wonders if he has not misjudged his brother.

Later still, snugly in bed, sipping cups of strong clear soup and munching dry toast, Leo observes, 'We might be in a theatre or a club, mightn't we, Jackson?'

'Yes,' Vere answers, once more taken unawares. This Jackson with whom the brothers sometimes identify themselves, the embodiment of all they consider grand and worldly, is a creation of their rare accord. For Leo to summon Jackson after the dissension of the afternoon is therefore curious. But pleased by what he accepts as a gesture of peace, Vere suggests, 'Have a cigar, Jackson,' and pulls a propelling pencil out of the pocket of his pyjamas.

'Light, please.'

'Coming up.'

He pretends to strike a match, Leo to puff and wave away smoke. They speak in deep voices, address each other as old boy, old man, old thing, and offer each other loans of a thousand pounds.

'What are these cigars, Jackson?' asks Leo.

Vere gazes at him blankly, but remembering a phrase from *Settlers in Canada,* replies, 'They're some weeds I bought in Montreal.'

Leo giggles. 'Not bad at all,' he says. 'Waiter, more oysters for Mr. Jackson. And I'll have another dozen or two. Thank you, waiter, keep the change.'

They dip their pieces of toast in their soup and with difficulty swallow mouthfuls whole. 'Good place, this,' they say. 'Nice to see you again.' Safely out of character they express their thoughts more freely.

'I say, Jackson, did you give the waiter a quid?' Vere inquires.

'I gave him a fiver, if you must know.'

They giggle. It seems so odd to say 'if you must know'. Leo calls for music and switches on the wireless. Vere conducts with serpentine movements of his long arms, tangling and disentangling them. Leo laughs and sips his soup, and, when Vere pretends that he cannot unwind his arms, cries with laughter and eventually dribbles.

Nanny comes and says goodnight. The light is turned off. Vere, lying on his mattress on the floor by Leo's bed, can just distinguish his brother's face above him, faintly picked out of the darkness by the glow of the wireless dial.

'Leo,' he says.

'Yes?'

'Happy birthday tomorrow.'

'Thanks. What's your present, Vere?'

'It's a chromium-plated knife, one of those really strong ones, Sheffield steel blades, you know.'

'Gosh, I've always wanted one like that.'

'Honestly, Leo?'

'Do you know what Mummy and Daddy are going to give me?'

'No,' says Vere.

'I asked for a bicycle or a gun.'

'Did you?'

'Yes.'

'Golly,' Vere bursts out, 'if they've given you a gun, Leo! I'd rather have a gun than anything in the world.'

'You can use mine.'

'Thanks awfully!'

Leo says, 'I'd rather have a bicycle. Do you swear you don't know?'

'Yes, I swear.'

'What shall we do tomorrow?'

'Let's go shooting.'

'Has Mrs. Lark made me a cake?'

'I think so. I know, let's cook our lunch out of doors.'

'They'd never let us.'

'Yes, they would. It is your birthday.'

'Gosh, I'm sleepy.'

'Don't go to sleep yet, Leo.' A pause. 'Leo, let's make tomorrow specially nice.'

'All right.'

'Do you think it will be a gun?'

'I hope it's a bicycle.'

'Leo . . . Thanks for saying I can shoot with it.'

'That's all right.'

'Well . . . Goodnight, Leo.'

'Goodnight, Vere.'

The wireless is switched off and the room is in total darkness. Leo tosses once in his bed, then begins to breathe regularly. A suggestion of light, blue-green like the depths of the sea, tinges the still curtains. Vere lies awake on his hard mattress.

Leo is his best friend, there is no escaping the fact. Leo is the most decent, the kindest, funniest – the closest friend he has. He could not have been more generous about the gun: perhaps he will give Vere a share of it: and how he enjoys a joke, how he laughs! He can be nice when he tries, that is the truth about Leo: and when he does not try, then he is nasty. He ought not to have called Vere 'sloppy' on the station platform. For that matter he ought not to have behaved in such a careless and high-handed way. But, Vere wonders, is he in any position to complain? Of his own free will he is lying on the floor while Leo comfortably reclines in bed; without persuasion he spoke of the knife; and he said goodnight, although he wanted to go on talking, because Leo decided he was sleepy. It is strange, Vere thinks, that he should permit Leo to twist him round his little finger, strange and discreditable. For Leo has behaved badly – that blow in the car was outrageous. No; his brother's conduct does not stand examination, and it is weak to be taken in, deceived by random smiles and sweet words, when Leo has proved himself times without number brutal and unloving.

He turns over in bed and closes his eyes. In future he will be more careful. He will not commit himself so readily or to the same extent. He will question and weigh, and with steady judgment control their relations. Feeling that he has freed himself from Leo's subtle spell, feeling once again thoroughly Vere, with a final happy twinge of anticipation at the prospect of the following day, he goes peacefully to sleep.

The next morning the brothers wake at seven-thirty. Vere wishes Leo a happy birthday and gives him the knife. Leo thanks him warmly and lays it on his bedside table. For an hour they fight, struggle, laugh and tumble about on the beds. At eight-thirty their father, in pyjamas and down-at-heel slippers, a shaving-brush in his hand, a heavy lather on his chin, comes to bid them good morning. But neither he nor the boys can think of anything to say to each other, and after he has left Leo and Vere dress and go to breakfast in the nursery. Nanny, Flora, Faith, and Mary and Karen, the older girls, enter and give Leo their presents. From Nanny he receives four marked handkerchiefs, from Flora a box of peppermint creams, from Mary a book about a boys' school, from Karen another box of peppermint creams, and from Faith a jersey which Nanny has been knitting for the last two weeks. He accepts the gifts gracefully, with exclamations and kisses, leaves them on the floor and takes his place at the table.

As soon as grace has been said Vere puts forward his plan for the picnic. Mary and Karen are full of enthusiasm, which Leo now reflects. They plead with Nanny: provided they can obtain their mother's consent she at length agrees to help them. Cries of glee break out on all sides. Where will they have the picnic? Faith batters her plate with her spoon. Who will they ask? What will they eat and how will they cook it? Who will cook it? Will it be fine, will they obtain permission?

Breakfast is finished and the children, flushed, bright-eyed, eagerly chattering, approach the solemn door at the top of the front stairs. They try to decide who shall knock on the door, giggle, hush one another, giggle louder and push Leo forward. He scratches at the panel with his fingernails.

'Come in.'

The children enter their mother's room. She is lying in bed, pale and composed, eating her breakfast of a boiled egg and white bread-and-butter with the crusts removed.

'Good morning, darlings,' she says.

'Good morning, Mummy,' they answer, as in turn they lean across and kiss her.

'Happy birthday, Leo darling.'

'Thank you, Mummy.'

'Your present is downstairs. Will you wait to see it till I get up, or would you like to go now?'

Leo, who in the general excitement has forgotten about his birthday, tactfully agrees to wait.

'It's from Daddy and me,' his mother says. 'I hope you'll like it.'

Leo replies, 'I bet I will,' and glances at the others. 'Mummy,' he starts, pauses, then inquires, 'Don't you like toast with your egg, Mummy?'

But Mary interrupts in a commanding voice, 'Leo!'

'What's the matter, darling?'

'Go on, Leo,' orders Mary.

'What is it, Leo?' asks his mother.

'Well, we were wondering, Mummy, actually, if you'd let us have a picnic, as a sort of birthday treat? Nanny says she doesn't mind and we would love it. Could we?'

'But tea is all arranged indoors.'

'No no – for lunch!' chime in the others. 'We want to cook our lunch. Oh Mummy, please!'

'As a special treat,' repeats Leo appealingly.

'Yes, I think you could, if you really want to.'

The children, who have been standing in tense postures round the room, look at each other, draw deep breaths and thank their mother. Smiles spread across their faces and they troop modestly through the door which Leo, after making an arrangement to meet his mother in half an hour, discreetly closes. The door-handle clicks: they tear along the passage and hustle helter-skelter into the nursery. They shout the glad news at the tops of their voices, leap about, congratulate Leo and pat him on the back as hard as they can. Laughing and arguing they mill round Nanny and Flora, planning the picnic. They will roast a chicken on a spit: no, they will fry eggs, bacon and sausages: no, they will bake potatoes in the bonfire: no, they will – shall – must have mashed potato. And what pudding, heavens above, what pudding? Banana fritters, treacle tart? And where will they have their picnic, where, where?

'Mary and Karen,' Nanny says at last, 'you go to Mrs. Lark and ask her nicely, nicely mind, what she'll let you have. Flora, run after the girls and see they don't get into trouble. And Leo, you go with Vere and say good morning to Mademoiselle and ask her if she'd care to join us. And we'll meet back here. Off you go now.'

The boys caper down the passage, find Mal and invite her to the picnic. She accepts with pleasure and gives Leo his present, a tie with a design of Sealyhams' heads. Leaving her they go to the smoking-room, where they meet their father.

'Is Mummy down?' asks Leo.

Vere tells his father about the picnic.

'Are they going to roast you and eat you for dinner?'

'Oh Dad!'

Leo has run out of the room and now returns arm-in-arm with his mother. She loves these little attentions and is smiling happily.

'Shall we let him have his present?' she asks, laying her hand on Leo's head.

They form into a procession, pass through the study, go out by the back door, cross the yard and enter the hot and musty brushing-room. On the deal table, stained and shiny with boot-polish, is a long canvas gun-case.

'It's a gun,' says Vere from the doorway. The sight of the case, bulging and reinforced with strongly sewn leather, so new, clean and manly, makes him shiver with delight.

'A gun! Oh Mummy, Dad, that's marvellous,' says Leo, kissing his parents. 'I wanted one more than anything. Thank you so much!'

His father, with red and slightly shaking fingers, begins to unbuckle the end. 'You go very carefully with this now, Leo. Stand clear,' he says, sliding the gun out of the cover.

Vere says, 'It can't be loaded.'

'You be quiet and do as I tell you.'

'Yes, you be quiet,' adds Leo.

But Vere is too intent on the wonderful object which his father gingerly handles even to laugh. He has eyes for nothing but the gun, a small shotgun, exquisitely made, reminiscent of a hundred beloved passages from *Settlers in Canada*. His father opens and closes the breech, looks down the barrel, raises the gun to his shoulder once or twice, then holds it out to Leo. Vere leans over his brother's shoulder. The gun's stock is of walnut, intricately whorled; the breech and trigger-guard are chased and figured; the blued steel of the barrel is dark and thinly oiled; the foresight is brassy and bright.

'Do you like it, darling?'

Leo, copying his father's actions, answers, 'I certainly do!'

'Can I hold it?' asks Vere.

'Don't go and drop it.'

'Of course I won't.'

He takes the gun and opens the breech. Its mechanism is as fine and precise as a watch. Pointing the barrel towards the light he stares through it. The silver barrelling is perfect. The winding rings, which give direction to the shot, glint and gleam with trapped brightness. He closes the gun gently and traces with his finger the circular markings on the smooth stock.

The others are talking. 'Can we let it off?' he interrupts.

'What, in here?' jokes Leo.

'You must take the boys out shooting, David.'

'Oh yes, this evening – after tea, Dad!'

'Perhaps you could shoot a pigeon, just to show them, David.'

'It's the wrong time of year.'

'Oh please, Dad!'

Leo begs his father, Vere beseeches him. Eventually he consents. The boys must behave, do as they are bid, sit very still and quiet. They agree to everything. In that case, as long as it does not rain, he will take them shooting.

The gun is replaced in its cover and stood in the gun-rack. Leo once again thanks his parents and the brothers return to the nursery.

Preparations for the picnic are proceeding apace. Chops, tomatoes, carrots and potatoes have been wheedled out of Mrs. Lark, also a frying-pan and a kettle. Packages in greaseproof paper, baskets, rugs, newspaper and sticks are scattered over the nursery table.

'What about our pudding?' question the boys.

'Oh, didn't we tell you? Ice-cream,' answer the girls with sly smiles.

Nanny enters the nursery and issues orders like a general. 'Now, have you salt and pepper?'

'Salt and pepper, Vere,' says Flora, pointing to the dresser.

'And milk?'

'Mary, ask Mrs. Lark for milk, we forgot that,' says Flora.

'And now, where shall we have our picnic?'

Mary suggests the farm, Karen the wood, Leo a field or down the drive.

Nanny says, 'Flora, you take these things when you're ready, and you and the children choose the place. Not too far away, and let's have some water close, and sticks for the fire. And I'll come soon with Faith and find you.'

Everyone hurries to obey Nanny's commands. The table is piled higher and higher with stores and equipment. Flora stands beside it, saying to herself, 'Oh dash, the orangeade . . . Oh dash, the ice-cream wafers!' As each omission occurs to her she clicks her tongue and tosses her head, and once, when Vere points out that they have forgotten a box of matches, she laughs through her teeth and buries her face in her hands. But finally all is complete. The children, reassembled in the nursery, load one another like pack animals and shout instructions over their shoulders. Karen leads the caravan down the passage and out of the house; Mary and Leo follow; Flora, with Vere trotting beside her, brings up the rear.

It is a day of sun, cloud and wind. The shadows of the trees seem to be blown across the gravel and short grass of the drive. Jackdaws wheel and plummet round the hollow elm, cavort in the swift currents of the air, uttering cracked and piercing notes, settle on swaying twigs and soar again into the sky.

The spot that Flora chooses for the picnic is a mossy bank under the nut-hedge at the end of the garden. The children gratefully deposit their loads, and Leo and Vere are despatched to gather wood for the bonfire. It is lit by the time they return and Karen is blowing it up, her nose an inch from the undecided flame. The wind changes. She emerges from smoke and fire with singed eyebrows and a cry of despair that turns into laughter. What does it matter? Nothing matters today. Everything is funny, everything amuses. The children settle to their tasks. Flora lifts the lid of the ice-cream machine and allows them a taste. They reach into the freezing container, packed round with chips of broken ice, and scrape the dripping whisk with their fingers.

Nanny arrives. Fat begins to bubble and spit in the frying-pan, blue smoke to rise. Flora and Mary prod at the white potato slices with palette-knives; Leo lies on his stomach, tending a pile of ashes that he calls the oven; Vere fetches and carries, filling the kettle, supplying Karen with fuel. Returning from one of his errands he finds his father, leaning with crossed arms on a tall thumb-stick, watching the others.

'Hullo, you little rat.'

'Hullo, Dad.'

'Doesn't it smell good?' His father sniffs.

'Stay and have lunch,' says Vere.

'No, old boy.'

'Please do.'

'There won't be much left by the time you've finished, will there?' His eyes crinkle. 'I've got my lunch indoors.' And scarcely noticed by the picnickers he strolls away.

Sensing of a sudden his father's exclusion, his loneliness, and recalling his early morning visit – the way he smiled through his shaving-soap, not knowing what to say – Vere feels unexpectedly sad, sorry that he cannot share with his father the wonder of this day, glad that at least he asked him to stay. Later, he thinks as he watches the broad retreating figure, we will go shooting together.

The brisk wind hustles the clouds across the sky, and this cloud, which for a second masks Vere's sun, passes like those above. Warmth and light are everywhere again, movement is general. 'Vere, more sticks. Wash this pan, Vere.' He steps with perilous agility between the crouched and concentrated figures, smoke in his eyes, smuts in his hair, laughter never far from his lips. The tempo of activity increases. He receives a blow on the leg from Leo – 'Get your great foot out of the chips' – upsets water over Mary, but he only laughs, amused even by his repeated apologies. 'Sorry, look out, sorry, sorry . . .' He hugs Flora – she is working so hard – lifts her linen hat and kisses the top of her head. 'Sweetheart,' she cries. 'Sorry, Flora.' When he replaces her hat the shadow of the soft white brim unevenly divides her smiling face. 'Oh Flora, sorry,' he says.

His mother and Mal approach. 'How are you getting on?' 'You don't know what fun we're having, Mummy!' 'Come and look in my oven,' calls Leo. 'My eyebrows are burnt off,' Karen says. Vere has never seen his mother so lively. He leads her round by the hand, pointing out this and that, offering her a chip, a carrot, while Mal crows her appreciation in broken English. 'Stay, Mummy, you and Daddy stay.' 'No, darling, we'll be out afterwards. Have a lovely lunch.' 'We will!' 'Goodbye, darlings.' 'Goodbye, Mummy.' A rug is spread on the bank and Mal lowers herself onto it with groans and laughter. Flora says, 'I think we're ready.'

The children circle the fire with burning faces, eyes fixed on Nanny and Flora, mouths watering. Crumbling fried potatoes are ladled onto the plates they hold out, burnt carrots and tomatoes, sizzling chops. They mutter in indistinct voices at the least injustice, wishing their helpings could be weighed on a pair of scales. Hunks of crisp bread are cut, knives and forks distributed. Grace is said. They sit, and in hushed and reverent silence gulp down the first unforgettable mouthfuls.

But every mouthful of that luncheon under the nut-hedge is unforgettable. As it begins so it continues. The chops are different from any Vere has tasted: everything is different: ice-cream was never, never like this.

Satisfied, replete, partly sheltered from the wind which rustles and shakes the branches of the hazel-trees and causes the embers of the fire to glow intermittently, the children loll on the bank in easy attitudes. The filtered sunlight flecks the rich mosses: they lie on their backs and touch them with their outstretched hands. Wouldn't it be nice, they ask each other lazily, to have a carpet of moss? It would be soft, springy, and the merging shades of green, the specks of gold and purest white – why, they would provide variety and contrast. Wouldn't it be nice, they murmur, to live always in this pleasant mottling sunlight, under the busy but reflective sky? To eat as they have eaten, to work as they have worked, to relax as they are relaxing – what a life that would be! Their thoughts, indolently voiced, play upon their separate imaginations, summon for each an individual heaven. Freely their fancies roam, distinct, personal – perhaps never to be shared. Yet as they dream, stroking the mosses, sinking their fingers to feel the deep hoarded moisture of the earth, the magic of this moment under the nut-hedge – the sunlight, the rapt peacefulness of the hour, the quiet conversation of the grown-ups, the fall of the fire – permeates their private worlds and unites in a way and for a brief instant the inexpressible longings of their ardent and tender hearts.

Somebody stirs. The moment is gone. But the children, after they have cleared the picnic and taken it indoors, return to the garden and lie on the mown grass. They stare at the sky, fling out their arms, as if they believe that by imitating their previous postures they will succeed in recapturing their previous mood. They discover that the moment is truly gone, truly lost. They wish to speak of it but do not know what words to use, how to express themselves. They enthuse over the picnic and pause; their lips part in secret smiles; their eyes are eloquent, lingering; they are silent. They feel that under the nut-hedge they experienced a closeness to each other and to all things that was unique and wonderful: but as their talk is forced into other channels their minds jib, doubt, shy away from the strangeness of their fleeting illumination. They speak of what is safe, understood. A desire to re-establish themselves in the characters by which they are recognised, and out of which they seem to have slipped, possesses them. They fear they have given themselves away, allowed strangers to trespass on the intimate preserves that they will one day, one day throw open, but not yet, not now, not like this: and a sense of discovery, of being found out, causes them embarrassment. So they turn from the memory of the moment on the mossy bank, the joy of that unspoken union, and grapple once more with the world they know, the world of other people, sure and familiar, normal, certain, right.

The wind dies down. The children roll into the shade of an apple-tree.

'Isn't it hot?' they say.

'It must be the hottest day of the year.'

They take off their shoes and socks and race each other to the lily pool. Dangling their legs in the cool water, dancing about on the hot paving-stones, applying their thumbs to the nozzle of the fountain, they pass the afternoon. When Nanny leans out of the nursery window to ring the bell for tea she sees four figures, two wearing only trousers turned up to the knees and two in clinging vests and blue knickers, darting with damp abandon round the pool. She rings the bell imperiously.

Astonished by the state in which they find themselves, the children collect their discarded clothes and straggle indoors. After washing and changing they go down to the dining-room and eat a large tea. As soon as the meal is finished Vere reminds his father of his promise.

'What promise?'

'To take us shooting, Dad.'

His father, who has been sitting silently at the head of the table, puts out his arm and catches the boy round the waist. 'You want to go, don't you?' he says, smiling indulgently and squeezing Vere's chin with the finger and thumb of his free hand. 'Don't you, little monkey?'

'Yes, Dad. Please, you will take us?'

'All right then, later,' he agrees.

It is past the brothers' usual bed-time when they meet their father in the brushing-room. He has put on a rough tweed coat and a cap, and carries a shooting-stick and a box of cartridges. They take the gun out of the rack and Leo is shown how to hold it in the crook of his arm: Vere is entrusted with the cartridges and they sally forth.

The wind has dropped completely. High gauzy cloud is drawn across the sky and the spreading scene is rosily sunlit. Midges swarm under the trees, early moths flutter from tufts of grass.

'Dad,' says Vere, running to keep up, 'one evening with Mr. Ball' – Mr. Ball is the farmer – 'I went shooting, and we walked for miles. And on the other side of the wood a really high pigeon came over and he shot it dead. It fell round and round, with its wings out, round and round – it took ages to come down. Do pigeons always fall like that?'

'Not always, no.'

'Another time Mr. Ball shot a pigeon, but that was with a rifle, sitting. It was frightfully difficult though, up in a big tree, and he got it through the heart. That one fell with a thump.'

Leo says, 'Shut up, Vere, you'll scare everything off.'

'Have you shot many pigeons, Dad?' Vere asks in a loud whisper.

'In my time I have.'

'Will we get one this evening?'

'We might.'

'Are you going to shoot flying?'

'That's the idea.'

They enter the wood. The boys follow their father down a rutted overgrown track. Amongst some dark fir-trees they stop.

'This ought to do it.'

'Here, Dad?'

'Yes. Now, I'll shoot through that opening.' He points up. 'Give me the gun, Leo. Vere, empty those cartridges into my pocket.'

'All of them, Dad?'

'Yes. Go and sit over there now, and listen, don't talk or move. Do you understand?'

'Yes, Dad.'

The brothers choose trees about ten yards from their father, sit with their backs against the trunks and clasp their drawn-up knees with their arms. The drooping branches cast a deep shade on the earth which is yellow-brown and strewn with pine-needles. Here and there shafts of light arrow down and fasten brilliantly on a skeleton branch or a fir-cone gnawed by squirrels. Motes whirl profusely in the sunbeams, the air is musky and resinous, a humming silence prevails in which the least sound echoes and multiplies.

A metallic click. Vere starts. His father, sitting on his shooting-stick beneath the patch of sky – blue between the fir-trees – has opened the gun. He slips a cartridge into the breech. Another click as he closes it and again Vere starts. His father reaches for a cigarette and strikes a match. It rasps harshly against the side of the box, flares for a second and is flicked aside. Tobacco smoke drifts in the clearing, heavy, blue, aromatic. His father begins to whistle softly, looking at his shoes, his back rounded.

Leo leans across and plucks Vere's sleeve. 'Which way will the pigeons come?' he whispers.

'I don't know.'

'It's exciting, isn't it?'

Vere nods. His father swivels on his stick, smiling. A jay scolds in a nearby tree. Suddenly there is a rushing flutter of wings as the first pigeon glides overhead and then veers widely away.

Leo calls out. His father stands up, throws his cigarette onto the pine-needles, grips the gun with both hands. Smoke from the cigarette clings to the ground. A second pigeon sweeps in, a third, a fourth. 'Why doesn't he shoot?' asks Leo, and Vere answers, 'They're all too far.' The boys gaze upwards, straining their eyes, the bark of the trees rough against their shoulders. A fly buzzes discordantly and settles on Vere's forehead.

'Dad,' warns Leo.

A fifth pigeon is sweeping in. Vere sees it and looks at his father. He is tense now, feet apart, gun slightly raised. The pigeon sails over the treetops. There is a loud bang and it swerves out of sight.

'Did you get it, Dad?' cries Leo.

'No.'

'Are you sure, Dad?'

His father reloads the gun without answering. More pigeons fly over the clearing. Vere picks up an empty brass-tipped cartridge and sniffs it. Thicker and thicker fly the pigeons, again and again the gun bangs. In the dimming light Vere can discern the taut expression on his father's face, and, as more of the looming birds are missed, can hear him cursing under his breath. He wishes he could tell his father how happy he is, or could be, sniffing the acrid cartridge, sitting in the shady wood: he wishes his father would not repeat, 'I can't shoot with this damn gun,' would smile or whistle or make a quacking noise. But Vere understands that his father cannot do any of these things because he is too fine, too splendid: that if he could laugh when he missed a pigeon, if he could eat ice-cream under the nut-hedge, then he would be different – a friend: and recalling his affectionate gesture at the tea-table, his wistful question 'Don't you, little monkey?' and his sad flattered smile, the boy senses for the second time that loneliness which touched him before the picnic and which he longs to be able to disperse.

It is evening now. A scarlet flash is visible when the gun is fired. The patch of sky takes on a sunset colour and under the fir-trees all is dusky, indistinct.

'Leo.'

'Dad?'

'Give me some more cartridges.'

'Have you got any more?' Leo asks Vere.

'No.'

'We haven't any more, Dad.'

There is a pause. Vere says carefully, 'Can you see to shoot, Dad?'

'I can see all right. There's something wrong with the gun, I don't know!'

'But it's fun, Dad, being here.'

His father remarks irritably, 'I've never known anything like these midges!'

Vere can think of no answer. In the unsettled silence he hears Leo sharply scratch his ankle, his father's foot scrape against the shooting-stick. The day is not what it was, none of it is the same. He begins to feel tired. He would like to go home.

Suddenly the gun explodes. There is a whirling overhead, then a curious thud. Leo is on his feet and his father is saying, 'I think I got that one – did I get it, Leo? Go and look to the left – I think I got it!' And his voice is changed.

Vere jumps up. Somewhere a branch cracks, another shivers. Something is falling to the ground – wings flap loudly once. 'Where is it?' calls Leo. They hunt under the fir-trees. 'Here, Leo, Vere, here we are!' The boys run – bent double – beneath the spiky branches. Their father is standing by the dead pigeon which lies with its head unnaturally twisted to one side. 'Well done, Dad,' they say. 'Good shot, well done! Oh Dad, well done!' Some feathers, pale, luminous, sway softly downwards and light on the dark earth.

'That was the last cartridge,' their father is saying in his excited voice. 'I was just going to give up. I couldn't see a damn thing. Then this chap comes over! Here you are, old boy, here's your gun. There's not much wrong with it if you shoot straight.' He laughs, feeling for a cigarette, and the boys laugh too. 'You take the pigeon, Vere. God knows what time it is. Come on.'

He goes to fetch his shooting-stick. Vere picks up the warm pigeon and follows Leo onto the track.

'It must be frightfully late.'

'Yes,' Vere murmurs.

'Gosh, I enjoyed that.'

'So did I.'

'Is the pigeon heavy?'

'Yes, Leo, quite.'

A cigarette glows and their father approaches out of the gloom.

'Come on, rabbits, time to go home.'

They file along the path, Vere stroking the pigeon and smoothing its ruffled downy feathers, and climb the gate into the field. A corn-coloured moon, round and low, rises already over the nestling farm. The grass beneath their feet is dim and dewy. Leo puts his arm through Vere's.

'Gosh, it's nice to be back.'

'Oh Leo, I wish it was always like this, always your birthday.'

'It's only the first day of the holidays.'

'It has been specially nice, hasn't it?'

'Yes.'

'Leo, I'm glad you're back.'

Their father waits for them. They run to catch up and walk on either side of him with stretching legs.

'Is the pigeon safe?'

'Yes, Dad.'

'Don't let it fly away.'

'I'm holding it in my arms.'

A snatch of tuneless whistle.

'Well, we got one after all.'

'Yes.'

'Did you think we wouldn't?'

'Well . . . For a bit.'

The boys look up at their father, smiling. He tosses his cigarette aside and rests his hands on their shoulders.

'Are you happy now?'

'Yes, Dad.'

'Are you, Dad?'

'You monkey . . . Yes, I am.'

They stumble over the uneven turf and bump against each other, as with full hearts they fix their eyes on the bright windows of the house.

1939

WINTER

LEO'S holidays pass. The sixty-five days succeed one another, some sweet, some sad, some light, some dark – none like Leo's birthday

Walking home from the wood that evening Vere's happiness seemed complete. He did not think – he was too happy – but he savoured his feelings of joy and fellowship, and as he bumped against his father in the twilit field, fully and without reserve he welcomed his emotions, believing he had won them for himself and they were his forever.

Vere's happiness does not last. The morning after Leo's birthday his father says to him, 'Don't you try to get me to take you shooting again, you monkey. Your mother says you're looking tired.'

These words confuse the boy. He does not know what to do or to say. The gap between him and his father, over which their hands had touched so warmly, so hopefully, widens and becomes impassable. 'Does she, Dad?' he replies eventually, raising his voice as if to make himself heard across the empty spaces.

The children never again approach the moment of union they knew under the nut-hedge. Rifts open between them as the holidays progress, squabbles break out. Leo becomes friendly with an older boy from his school. Once he has to be persuaded to allow Vere to join in their swaggering enterprises. After that the brothers go their separate ways, Leo laughingly with his friend, Vere distractedly, alone, unsettled. But the holidays end and Leo returns to school. Two days after his departure Vere finds the chromium-plated knife in the drawer of the bedside table. It is still wrapped in tissue-paper and there is a spot of rust on one of the Sheffield steel blades. He turns the knife over in his hand, tries its sharpness on the ball of his thumb, pockets it and does not go again into Leo's room.

Autumn comes and leaves are blown at night against the shuttered windows. Extra blankets are put on the beds and Albert comes in one morning to see to the radiators. Bonfires smoulder down the drive, flaring and dying out, and the gardeners pause in their work to blow on their red, chapped hands.

'When is autumn winter, Nanny?'

'It's winter now, child, winter now.'

Long cosy evenings are spent round the nursery fire. Loving without fear and certain of love, Vere regains his poise and concentration. Books are read, *The Last of the Mohicans*, *Children of the New Forest*. He gazes into the embers, bemused, contented, while Flora reads in her soft voice, looking up as she turns a page, and Nanny's knitting-needles click. His parents are seldom at home. They come and go, in dark London clothes, in tailored tweeds, in hunting clothes, changed for dinner: gentle, undemanding, they move like shadows through these quiet weeks. October passes, November ... The dashing exploits of the summer months seem far away. He is in tune with winter now, its stoic calm, its peace, its peculiar clinging sadness.

December . . . The windows of the shops in Long Cretton are tricked out with tinsel. 'Christmas is coming, the geese are getting fat ...' 'Go on, sweetheart.' 'Please put a penny ...' 'Go on.' 'In the young boy's hat!' How lovely to make Flora laugh. 'Flora, we never kept our ducks, did we?' 'We'll buy some after Christmas, sweetheart, and fatten them up and make a nice bit of money.' 'Really, Flora?' 'Honestly.' But Christmas is coming and Vere needs the money now.

Mrs. Lark calls him into the kitchen one evening to stir the Christmas pudding. 'Put the money in, my dear, and stir him up,' she says, pointing to a pile of sixpences and threepenny bits that stand by the big brown bowl. While Vere drops the coins one by one into the heavy mixture and wields the wooden spoon with both hands, Mrs. Lark leans on the kitchen table – her arm bent sharply outwards at the elbow – and regards him with her brooding black eyes. Suddenly she says, 'We're off to a dance on Christmas night.'

'Can you dance, Mrs. Lark?' asks Vere.

'Dance?' Her eyes flash. 'I was born dancing! Ethel,' she shouts to the scullery-maid, a stolid country girl supposed to be wrong in the head. 'Ethel, can I dance?'

'You can, Mrs. Lark,' says Ethel.

'Mister Vere and me's going dancing Christmas night.'

'Oh fancy,' Ethel giggles.

'Now then, none of that,' snaps Mrs. Lark, still without a smile, and turns to Vere. 'Made your wish, my dear?'

He closes his eyes, and unable to think of anything better, wishes for a happy Christmas.

'Right-ho,' says Mrs. Lark. 'Here's hoping your wish comes true and thanks for the kind assistance. And remember, Christmas night!'

This conversation with Mrs. Lark excites Vere unexpectedly. He begins to take a more active interest in the preparations that are stealthily going forward around him: he helps to deck the nursery with streamers and silver stars and, the day before Leo returns, with dark green holly: he wakes early with twinges of anticipation and counts the busy cheerful days. But he cannot throw off that peculiar sadness – that sadness of the season – a regret for what is past, a reaching out for what he does not know, a wistful hope, an unexplained despair, which makes him pause in the act of balancing a sprig of holly on a picture and gaze into Flora's eyes, or at Nanny drying Faith's clothes in front of the fire, as if for the last time.

On the afternoon of the day before Christmas the children wrap their presents. Vere's are already wrapped and put away, and he sits on the nursery sofa, watching, smiling, strangely untouched by the merry bustle and noise. From time to time he wanders between the intent figures, tries to tease Leo who tells him to go away, strokes Karen's hair and receives a cold look, and imagines that if only somebody would laugh at his jokes his depression would instantly vanish. After tea on the same day the children go carol-singing. Muffled in their warmest clothes they arrive at Albert's cottage, open their hymn-books with clumsy gloved hands, fumble with torches and raise their treble voices in uncertain unison. 'Silent night, holy night . . .' Leo leads them, and his clear notes, the simple carol, the crisp mysterious night which obliterates familiar landmarks, produce little by little a sense of wonder and release in Vere's heart. It is Christmas Eve, he tells himself, the bright stars are shining; nothing is the matter, nothing is wrong.

But that evening as he lies in his narrow bed Vere's sadness returns. And the next day – Christmas day – it is no better. As soon as tea is finished he slips out of the dining-room, where Faith is crying for the fourth time and Leo is performing card-tricks on the floor, and rests his head against the wall of the dark passage. Bella, emerging from the pantry, sees him and asks why he is not with the others. He replies that he does not know.

The character of his sadness has definitely changed. It is no longer peculiar, but actual – even dangerous. Bella invites him into the servants' hall. He follows her and begins to eat sweet chestnuts which Ethel is roasting in the fire. The room is hot and bright, and Ethel laughs at everything he says. Mrs. Lark comes in, dressed for the dance. Her black locks are oiled and curled, her black eyes glint and dart, she seems to be covered in black beads, and her powdered flesh looks luminous. He tries to excuse himself, but she seizes him by the hand and leads him into the kitchen. He is dancing with Mrs. Lark round the kitchen table, round and round, pretending to join in resounding laughter. Light is reflected from copper pots, staring faces fill the doorway. He bumps into the cook – she is like a cushion, feels her soft arms about him, hears her fruity voice, is stifled by her scent. His head is whirling. Flora calls. He goes upstairs.

That night, when all is quiet, Vere wakes and is sick. His illness has begun. He surrenders to it with relief as he could not surrender to his incomprehensible sadness. He is sick throughout the remainder of the night and in the morning feels pale and wasted. His mother appears – he is sick: his father, Dr. Gail – he is sick. The day passes, the night – the night again, the day. He loses count of time.

'I'm ill, Flora.'

'Yes, sweetheart.'

'I've been ill for ages.'

'Don't talk. Try and sleep.'

'When was Christmas?'

'Three days ago.'

'Oh Flora.'

'Yes, sweetheart, I'm here, I'm here.'

He is often frightened. His coughing and his sickness frighten him. Only Nanny's hand, or Flora's – only their ready hands, for which he reaches at all hours of the day and night, still his fear. He sleeps, waking to the smell of enamel bowls and clean linen, sleeps again and dreams. One dream terrifies him. He is being forced to swallow huge moving furry shapes: they balloon out as they approach him, dark and living: he swallows and swallows, but cannot swallow quick enough: they slide over his head like sticky sacks: he becomes a shape himself and is carried away. He has other dreams. Sometimes he is kissing his father, hugging and kissing him, speaking of his love and admiration, and his father is smiling fondly and laying his shaky hand on Vere's refreshed forehead. Or he is in the garden, pushing his way through one of the yew hedges: he sees his mother in the distance, gathering flowers, beside blossomy trees full of singing birds, under a blue sky: he wrestles through the hedge into the sunlit garden, and suddenly he is unbelievably happy, so happy that he wants to cry.

'What's the matter with me, Flora?'

'You've got whooping-cough, Vere.'

Detached incidents, like phrases of music, stick in his mind: shooting the pigeon on Leo's birthday, the chromium-plated knife, the hare's nest in the field of clover, the ride on Mr. White's motorbicycle. But the grinding rotation of his thoughts mill these recollections into a dust.

He is very ill. He knows this for certain when a nurse arrives. Stretching out his hand to Nanny or Flora and touching instead the nurse's starched apron, he cries. One evening he sits up in bed and says he is hungry. The nurse recommends calves-foot jelly, but Vere, with tears in his eyes, begs Nanny for oranges.

'Yes, Vere, in a minute, I'll prepare them.'

Nanny brings him the oranges. She has peeled and sliced them beautifully, removed all pips and skin, and sprinkled them with sugar. He eats voraciously, his mouth watering.

'Oh Nanny, how good they are!'

'I'm glad to see you eat something, Vere.'

'How many oranges?'

'Just the one.'

'I think I could eat another.'

'Finish this one first.'

But Vere is sick before he finishes.

'No more oranges for you, my lad,' comments the nurse. A day or two later she leaves. Vere immediately shows a slight improvement. One evening his father comes into his room and says he is going away.

'When, Dad?'

'Tomorrow.'

'Tomorrow! Where?'

'Abroad, America.'

'For a long time?'

'Yes, quite a time. When I get back you'll be as fit as a fiddle.'

The idea of this departure, although he has scarcely seen his father since his illness began, horrifies Vere. He wants nothing to change: he cannot bear that it should. He feels that an opportunity which he has privately treasured but never properly attempted to realise is slipping through his fingers: he feels because of his weakness that he can no longer observe the niceties which in the past have smothered his relations with his father: unprepared as he is, he still feels forced to take his chance.

'Dad,' he says, 'do you remember when you shot the pigeon?'

'What made you think of that?'

'I think of it often.'

'Do you?'

'Yes. Do you remember when we walked home, Dad?'

'Why?'

'It was dark, wasn't it? I loved that evening.'

The tears come into his eyes. He cannot master them any more: he seems to be made of tears. Sentimental and unsatisfying, they spoil his good intentions.

'Take us shooting when you come home, Dad.'

'Yes, Vere, yes, I will.'

'I wish you weren't going.'

'So do I.'

'You couldn't shoot the pigeon, could you, Dad – to begin with?'

'No,' his father smiles.

'But then you did, I knew you would. And we walked home together . . .' He is ruining everything with his senseless repetition. 'Leo and I ate the pigeon.' The tears run down his cheeks. He loved that pigeon – why did he eat it? How sad, how sad! 'Oh, Dad, I wish you weren't going away . . .' Although untrue, the expression of this wish again makes the tears start. Everything is too difficult; he is too tired. However hard he may grip his father's thumb with his moist hand he still cannot touch him. And he cannot explain. It is easier to dwell on the mere fact of his father's departure and to let the misunderstood tears flow. 'I wish you weren't going, Dad . . .'

'It won't be for long, monkey. We'll have a celebration when I get back. And you're better anyway. Don't cry – come on, old boy, come on now.'

A big silk handkerchief is produced which smells of tobacco. Vere wipes his eyes, sees his father's concerned face, tries to apologise for the tears he feels he has inflicted upon him, cries again. At length he controls himself.

'I'll send you some postcards.'

'Thank you, Dad.'

'Mummy's going to get the vet in if you're not well soon.'

'Is she, Dad?'

'Well . . . Goodbye, monkey.'

'Have a nice time, Dad.'

Lips a little pursed and head bent forward his father leaves the room. Vere lies drained and exhausted after he has gone, studying the firelight on the smooth ceiling.

Healing dreamless sleep claims him that night and the following nights. He wakes calmly from his slumbers, soon grows drowsy again, slips into cool sleep, once more wakes. His illness is over. It is as if the tears he shed with his bewildered father contained all the poison and pain in his system. He begins to anticipate his meals, to demand amusement. He leaves his bed for the first time, protesting, and gloomily sits beside it for an hour. The next day he sits gloomily for two hours, but when he climbs back into bed is hot and restless. The third day he eats his tea in the nursery and has to be persuaded to return to his bedroom. He is wheeled out-of-doors in the old wicker-work Bath chair. He plans complex routes and timetables which he follows closely, shouting directions to Flora while he grips the long steering-arm and consults his father's stop-watch. He lives from hour to hour, from day to day, happy with the happiness that is in the song of the cold robin, wistful, fleeting, borne hither and thither on the blustery wind, rising, falling, heard and unheard.

He is to go to the seaside with Nanny. On the morning of the day before he is due to leave he receives a letter from Leo. 'I am glad you are better,' his brother writes. 'We will share a room when you come to school next autumn. It will be great fun . . .'

After breakfast on the same day Karen tells him privately that Flora is going to be married. Although he can foresee no way in which this will affect him, for some reason Vere neither questions Karen on the subject nor mentions it to Flora.

That afternoon, for the last time, Flora wheels him out in the Bath chair. Halfway down the front drive they come across old Harris the gardener, sitting on the handle of his wheelbarrow in the lee of the garden wall. Vere steers the Bath chair alongside and greets him, then, noticing a short black pipe held in his knobbly hand, happens to ask after Mr. Bruise who possesses a corncob pipe that is nine years old.

'Mr. Bruise?' Harris lifts his worn tweed hat and drops it back on his head. 'He's bad, they tell me, Master Vere. Nice afternoon, isn't it?'

'What do you mean he's bad, Mr. Harris?'

'Ill, I mean, after his operation.'

Vere looks at Flora. 'Has Mr. Bruise been ill? I didn't know.'

'Yes, sweetheart. Come along.'

'It's all right, Flora, I've allowed us lots of time. When did he have his operation?' Vere asks idly.

'That was just after Christmas. He was poorly a good bit.'

'Is he better now?'

'They say he's bad, I've not been up there.'

Vere glances at the stop-watch in his lap. Now they are behind their schedule.

'Is he able to eat?' Flora is asking.

'He's this here pipe in his throat. Poor old man, he won't last winter. He can't take no nourishment.'

'What sort of pipe?' Vere inquires curiously, imagining for a moment that the words must refer in some way to Mr. Bruise's corncob.

But Flora interrupts. 'Give him my kind regards, Mr. Harris, if you see him. Good afternoon. Which way, Vere?'

'Down the drive, turn left,' he answers. After they have creaked along for a bit he asks, 'What does it mean, Flora?'

'Nothing, sweetheart. How are we getting on?'

'We're late.' He raises his voice: 'But you must tell me, Flora. I understood.'

'Mr. Bruise went into hospital, sweetheart, and they found out there was something wrong with his throat, that's all.'

'And they put a pipe in it – in his throat?' He emphasises the words strongly.

'Yes.'

'Why?'

'Well, so he could swallow.'

The wheelchair bumps and trundles over the ruts. In an angry tone Vere continues. 'Do they feed him through this pipe?'

'Yes, but don't ask me any more about it.'

'Where is the pipe?' he returns in his angry tone.

'I've told you, Vere.'

'But how do they feed him? And what with?'

'Now, Vere.'

'Tell me, Flora.' She does not answer. 'Flora!' His heart thumps. 'I can find out easily, don't worry.' Flora says nothing.

They turn left at the bottom of the dipping drive, left again up the back drive.

Flora says, 'I don't know more than I've told you, Vere.'

'Is Mr. Bruise going to die?' Vere asks sadly.

'He's very ill, that's all we know, sweetheart.'

By the greenhouses they again meet Harris. He lifts his crumpled hat a second time and exposes a bald white head. Vere calls to Flora to stop.

'Mr. Harris,' he says. 'If you see Mr. Bruise...' He shudders and looks away. 'Will you tell him I've been ill?'

'Yes, Master Vere. He likes news of the family, always did.'

'Mr. Harris, can he smoke?'

'I don't expect he can.'

'I wonder what's happened to his corncob.'

'He'll be missing that.'

'Goodbye, Mr. Harris. I'm going away tomorrow.'

'You get well then, Master Vere. Goodbye.'

Flora pushes the Bath chair along the cinder path and asks which way to go.

'Just home, Flora,' he replies.

Vere does not think again of Mr. Bruise, of school or Flora's marriage. A merciful gauze descends and surrounds him, softening the hard edges of unpleasant facts, blunting their sharp implications. He leaves for his holiday without noticing Flora's strained looks when she bids him goodbye and the unwonted warmth of her final hug.

Nanny and Vere spend ten days by the seaside. Gradually the colour floods back into the boy's cheeks. He eats enormously and after the first two days refuses to be wheeled in the battered bath-chair. Morning and afternoon he goes for lengthening walks along the front with Nanny. He breathes the keen salty air, watches the rough green sea, wishes he lived by the seaside. In the evenings, in their bedroom which smells of sand and rubber shoes, Nanny and he sit by the fire over a jigsaw puzzle or a game of Old Maid. The days pass in a happy blur: they are unpacking, they are packing: Albert arrives to fetch them home.

During the drive, at first regretful, then excited, Nanny says, 'Vere, I want to warn you that Flora's leaving us.'

'For her holiday?' he asks.

'No. She's to be married.'

'Oh yes.' He nods. Then he says incredulously, 'She's not going away?'

'I'm afraid she is.'

'When?'

'She'll be leaving tomorrow. She's being married the day after and she'll spend the night at Long Cretton.'

'I see,' he says.

Later he says, 'I never thought she'd have to go away.'

'She's going to live at Long Cretton. You'll be able to visit her quite often.'

'Does she want to leave us?' he inquires.

'Well, she wants to get married.'

'What's her husband's name?'

'Rodney Marston.'

'I see,' he says again.

At home everybody is delighted with the changes in Vere's appearance. He is full of his holiday, spends the remainder of the day describing it, and only remembers Flora's impending departure after he has gone to bed. The next morning, before leaving for school, Mary and Karen come to say goodbye to Flora who is wearing a new dress. When they have left Nanny takes Faith into the night-nursery.

'Sweetheart,' Flora says as Vere makes for the door into the passage, 'I think I'd better be saying goodbye.'

Vere, who has assumed that Flora would be staying until lunchtime anyway, stops and asks in a shocked voice, 'Now?'

'I've lots of things to do in Cretton,' Flora explains.

'Oh, all right,' he says grudgingly, then, gaining time in which to steel himself for this vaguely threatening scene, he inquires, 'Flora, whereabouts in Cretton are you going to live?'

'We've a bungalow. It's just off the High Street. Will you come and see us, Vere?'

'Yes, I will.'

Flora's dress is dark blue with a white collar and white cuffs. Her face is white too, he notices. And her eyes are huge, pale, abstracted but searching.

'What's your house called?' he asks quickly.

'Well,' she smiles, 'it's a funny name. Little Lodge.'

'Little Lodge. Yes,' he smiles in reply, thinking, What is the matter with Flora? She is making everything so strange and difficult – she is even speaking strangely. He wishes she would say goodbye. He feels that the veil which has protected him since he learnt of Mr. Bruise's illness is in danger of being parted, being rent. And he clings to his veil. Afraid of emotions which have betrayed and pained him in the recent past, he does not want to feel strongly – he does not want to feel more than wistful and melancholy. Goodbye, Flora, he says to himself: I love you, Flora: later, later I will feel sad: but now, goodbye.

Aloud he says, 'I'll come often and see you, Flora, it's not really like saying goodbye,' hoping thus to belittle their parting, to make of it a light and trifling affair.

'No, it's not like saying goodbye,' Flora repeats after him, and there is a pause.

He stands by the combined cupboard and chest of drawers, Flora by the dresser in between the windows. The budgerigars scratch on the sanded floor of their house-like cage at the end of the low room. It is a grey day. He steals a glance at Flora, but hastily looks away. Surely her eyes were shining unnaturally? Although uncertain he dare not look again. She cannot – must not cry. He starts to panic. He does not know what to say, he cannot abide this heavy silence. The door of the scrubbed-oak cupboard suddenly swings open. He laughs.

'Look,' he says with relief, banging the door. But again it swings open.

'Where's the piece of paper that wedges it?'

'I don't know.'

Flora crosses the room. He wishes he could see that piece of paper, find and replace it. Flora's nearness adds to his panic. If only she were still by the dresser, still at a distance! He kneels, making as much as he can of the movement, and lowers his head until his eye is level with the floor.

'I've got it,' Flora says above him, 'it was in the cupboard,' and she wedges the door.

Vere straightens up. But his exertions have released some essential spring of his control. His legs shake, he feels brittle, as if at the least jar he will break, and also exposed, undefended. And the tension steadily mounts. He holds his breath. All depends on Flora, he is at her mercy. Not that same sadness, not that pain – not again, Flora, he prays.

'Sweetheart,' she speaks in an ordinary voice and pauses. Her back is turned to him – neat dark head, white collar – and her hand rests on a ledge of the cupboard door – supporting her, it seems, holding her up. 'What am I going to do without you, Vere?'

She turns. Her blue eyes swim with tears and her lower lip trembles.

'How will I get on, Vere? I don't know. I don't know how I'll manage at all.'

He seizes her hands, her firm arms, her neck above the white collar. She bends down and embraces him.

'I've made you cry. And I didn't mean to. There, sweetheart, don't, don't.' But she is crying so much that she speaks indistinctly. 'I'm going.'

'No, Flora.'

'I must.'

'Nanny and Faith . . .'

'Not now.'

'Please, Flora . . .'

'Goodbye, sweetheart, goodbye, Vere.' She opens the passage door. 'Come and see me soon,' she says, stumbles down the two steps and passes out of sight.

Vere remains by the scrubbed-oak cupboard for some time, then goes and sits on the window-seat. He wipes his eyes with a handkerchief that still smells of the seaside, and remembers his father's handkerchief that smelt of tobacco when last he wiped his eyes. Recalling those paltry tears he smiles: never before has he felt so sad. And thinking of Flora he continues to cry and to stare through the window.

But now it is an entirely new sadness, not peculiar or clinging, neither senseless nor exhausting, that causes Vere's heart to ache. Although he feels sad all over, even in his feet and the tips of his fingers, he is free, and his spirit is clear as it has not been for many months. His fears scatter. He opens his heart to life, and his true sadness, faithful, looking forward, liberating, swells within him.

He is well.

SPRING AND SUMMER

WINTER passes and spring comes. Under the influence of the spring sun and air Vere's health improves; and like the light which changes perceptibly, becoming ever finer in quality, more colourful and of a softer, sweeter texture, he too feels himself changing. Once more his mood matches the mood of the season. The snowdrops in the drive, the daffodils, the first green of the trees, the clear evenings which lengthen: these transformations of atmosphere and landscape reflect the processes taking place inside himself. The spring is his own: he unfolds with it: yet as the spring anticipates the summer, so he, with hope and fear, anticipates time that is still to come.

For now Vere's life is overshadowed by the endless and insuperable cliff of school. All his fancies are limited by that dread finality, all his activities curtailed by it. He is conscious of the months that remain to him: he is no longer carefree: the simple present does not satisfy: the future is not forever. Filled with longings, sweet and languorous, for some mysterious happening – some vague but beautiful happening – which will disperse this black shadow, which like sunlight will dazzle and blind, he waits, he hopes, and his expectant hours become days, his days weeks, his weeks fortnights and precious months.

In search of his beautiful happening he recalls the old days. But Flora is gone – and Edith the housemaid who does her work cannot replace her – his father is abroad: nothing can ever be the same. Yet what times they had, how happy they were! He thinks of Leo's birthday, of the moment under the nut-hedge. The holidays are approaching and he thinks of Leo often. He is convinced that his brother will be struck by his many new qualities – his increased understanding and affection, for instance: and he feels that if only he can confide in Leo as he never has before – really reveal and explain himself – their friendship is bound to become tender and true. And since he reaches out towards truth, towards tenderness, towards love and trust, and the absorbing joy that they will bring, he awaits his brother's return with impatience and devouring hope.

Leo arrives. Vere moves his mattress into his brother's bedroom and sleeps on the floor for five nights. There are jokes and happy laughter, enjoyable tussles and fights, even the occasional conversation, but he does not confide in Leo. Something always seems to prevent him from doing so, some joke or inattention on his brother's part. In the end their constant laughter, unravelling and then disintegrating, makes Vere feel weak when he remembers the onus of his intricate explanation. Overcome by a sense of futility and failure, of disappointment and dissatisfaction, he is not sorry to return to his comfortable bed.

The brothers have decided to build a house. Vere believes that the work will unite them, that as they near the supreme moment of completion the confidential climate must improve, and that once he has spoken frankly to Leo their relationship will enter into its desired phase. With liberal use of the word Jackson the house is planned. Leo's conception of it is grand, radical: Vere's, by comparison, modest and rather dull. Vere quotes from his experience, but Leo sweeps aside difficulties as if they did not exist. He insists on some means of heating their house. Vere says he has considered this before but found it impracticable – 'What sort of a fire, Leo, and where do you think you're going to get it?' he asks. By way of answer Leo requisitions the stove in the old potting-shed, blithely informing his mother of the fact some days afterwards. To start with Vere is delighted by Leo's ruthless methods, his knack of obtaining what he wants almost before he has decided if he wants it. But when he orders planks from the local timber-merchant, Vere, discovering that he is expected to pay half their cost, cannot help feeling that the whole principle of building houses is being betrayed. There is nothing secret about Leo's house, nothing personal or magic – it is a house: he makes no attempt to adapt materials to his uses, does not employ ingenuity, does not contrive – he buys or borrows what he needs, requests aid and suggestions from everybody, is always ready to discuss the project. And this approach of Leo's palls on Vere. He ceases to contribute his usually despised ideas and waits for the actual physical labour which he finds so pleasant to begin.

But here again there is trouble. Leo starts with a flourish, working throughout the day, and only Vere's pride prevents him from begging for a respite. The next day Leo works intermittently, pausing often to admire Vere's concentration and craftsmanship. The third day he wants to bicycle into Long Cretton. Vere dissuades him and they return to the house, but Leo picks holes in everything they have so far achieved and expresses doubts as to whether they should in any case continue. Vere is shocked, the brothers quarrel, and for some days Vere works alone: then Leo apologises and proceeds to take an enormous amount of trouble over the positioning and lighting of the rusty stove. Eventually the house is finished. But although it is more solid than any of Vere's other houses, although it has a bright crackling fire, and is watertight and windtight, and a real object of admiration, it affords him scant pleasure. Leo's attitude – his lack of interest, unequal bouts of labour, inconsistency and public ways – seems to have rendered the whole undertaking hollow and meaningless.

The brothers are sitting in the house one morning when Leo says, 'Pretty good bit of work we've done here, Jackson.'

'Yes,' Vere replies, picking a dry twig from the heap beside the stove and cracking it in his fingers.

'Lovely and warm and snug, isn't it?'

'Yes,' Vere agrees, poking the twig into the red roaring fire.

'What can we do now?'

Leo is always wondering what he can do.

'Well, we can sit and talk. And we might build a sort of outhouse.'

'Oh don't let's build any more.'

'Well, we could . . .' But Vere suddenly feels tired of devising amusements for Leo. He recalls his dream of friendship with his brother. Because he has strayed so far from it – down the old hopeless path, he realises: permitting Leo to dictate, resenting his dictation – he answers angrily, 'I don't know what we can do.'

Leo appears not to notice. He clicks his tongue and says, 'There's never anything to do here. Let's ring up Tim.' Tim is his school friend.

'Go ahead,' says Vere.

'Well, what are we going to do?'

Vere gazes at the rough stakes in the wall of the house, and craning his neck unnaturally, at the dark planks of the roof. 'You don't want to stay here, Leo, do you?' he says bitterly. 'Just stay here, I mean, quietly, and do things here?' He glances at his brother, whose blue-green eyes are cool and critical.

'What are you talking about?'

'Nothing, Leo.'

'We built the house together, didn't we?'

'A fat lot of building you did.' He thrusts his finger into a knot-hole in one of the planks. He is not sure if he is confiding in Leo or denouncing him. He is only sure that he is making a fool of himself.

'Go away, baby,' says Leo.

'All right, I will.' Vere rises to his feet.

'Sit down and stop being so silly.'

But Vere walks out of the house.

Leo announces at luncheon that Tim is coming to tea. Turning to Vere he says, 'Is my baby brother feeling better?' Vere does not answer. He scarcely speaks for two days. He cannot surmount his sense of grievance. Tim comes to tea with Leo, Leo goes to tea with Tim. The brothers' house is dismantled by the gardeners.

For some time after this episode Vere is very cautious and reserved in his dealings with Leo. But towards the end of the holidays, securely armoured as he feels himself to be, he relaxes his tight defences. One morning – always a tricky period where Leo is concerned – he is reading an interesting book in the nursery when his brother again asks what they can do.

Vere ignores the question. Leo repeats it. Vere replies that he is reading. Leo proposes they should take a walk. Vere remains silent. Leo begins to taunt him. Vere pretends not to hear.

'Afraid to get your feet wet? Frightened of the fresh air? It'll make you look a bit more healthy. You don't understand that book so I don't know why you're reading. Jump into the pram and I'll wheel you into the garden.'

'Leo,' Vere says reasonably, 'why don't you go out alone?'

'Oh, I wouldn't dare without you to protect me. Come on, baby.'

'Don't call me baby, Leo, and please leave me alone.'

Leo crawls across the floor and starts to tickle Vere's legs. Vere changes his position: Leo follows him: he goes into the night-nursery, his finger marking the place in his book.

Leo inquires, 'Ready for bed? I'll fetch your pyjamas.'

Vere proceeds into the next room, bangs the door and leans against it. Leo pushes. Vere jumps away and his brother falls forward: he laughs and sits down on a chair.

'Trying to be funny, are you?' says Leo, 'I'll tell you a good joke,' and he snatches away the book.

Roused at last Vere demands its immediate return. Leo laughs successfully and runs away. Vere chases him all over the house, catches him, hits him twice on the shoulder as hard as he can, then picks up the book which has been thrown aside, dodges into his mother's bathroom and locks the door. Leo, pained by the blows, loses his temper. He hammers on the door, looks through the keyhole, shouts insults through it, swears that he will not budge until Vere comes out. But his temper never lasts and soon he is laughing and enjoying himself.

Too angry to wait for Leo to tire of this sport Vere silently raises the bottom sash of the bathroom window and looks out. There is a drop of twenty feet onto the paving-stones of the backyard, but a few feet to the right of the window-sill is the sloping slated roof of the nursery-passage. If he were able to reach that roof he could climb along it and get into the house by one of the passage windows. And whilst Leo continued to thump on the door of the empty bathroom, he would be free to read undisturbed in the nursery. In spite of his rage he is sourly amused by his crafty and audacious plan. He stuffs the book into his pocket and swings himself out of the window.

He is less amused when he tries to straighten his knees: less still when he realises he cannot reach the roof with his outstretched leg. He will have to jump. But now the paving stones look grim: and he notices that some of the slates on the roof are perilously loose. 'Having a bath, baby?' he hears Leo call. 'Come out and I'll give you a present – something you'll remember. Come out, little man. Come out, you sulky boy.' He shifts his balance to the outstretched leg and shoves himself sideways and backwards with the aid of a drainpipe. He seems to waver in mid-air for a second – his heart shrinks to the size of a pea and his scalp pricks – then his foot touches the roof. On all fours he slithers over the slates as quick as he can, squeezes through a window, tiptoes into the nursery, resumes his initial seat, produces his book and once more finds his place.

He is much too angry to read. The book shakes in his hands and the words swim. Now his heart is swollen – distended with anger. He has been stripped of his armour, goaded into this destroying frenzy, into risking danger, into suffering fear – at Leo's will, for Leo's pleasure. He smarts from ancient hurts, revives injustices. With shame he recalls his mistaken hopes of friendship with his brother. Schemes of revenge swarm in his throbbing head. He forgets that he has won the day – but it is not today for which he wishes to revenge himself – rises to his feet and stalks stiffly down the nursery passage, intent on dealing Leo a final, absolute and crushing defeat.

Leo is still shouting and banging on the bathroom door. Vere watches him for a moment, then says, 'Do you want anyone, Leo?' But he is so terribly angry that he sounds as if he is sobbing.

Leo turns. Instead of the unguarded surprise Vere hoped to see in his flushed face there is only cold hostility. 'Hullo, baby,' he says. Suddenly he laughs. 'I knew you'd get out, baby.'

Vere answers cuttingly, 'It's not hard to get away from you.' But again the sentence sounds like a sob.

'Anyone can get through that window.'

'It made you look a pretty good fool.'

'Why are you crying?'

'I'm not.'

'You'll have to go back and unlock the door.'

'I won't.'

'I don't mind. Anyway, it's lunchtime.' Leo laughs again, unexpectedly ruffles Vere's hair as he passes him, and runs along to the nursery.

Vere remains where he is – his hair disordered, tears of powerless anger in his eyes – outside the bathroom door. He longs to follow Leo, to catch, to beat, to pummel him. He is prevented by his anger, which calls for deeper satisfaction. Yet in no serious way – only by force – can he touch, let alone crush, his laughing brother. Bitterly he accuses Leo of his many crimes; but more bitterly he reproaches himself for his inability to convict or to punish him.

None of the wrathful arrows Vere continues to aim at Leo finds its mark: in fact they rebound off Leo's tough hide and wound Vere. He retires into miserable silence. Albert has to fetch a ladder in order to open the bathroom door. Since Vere refuses to explain what has happened he is blamed for causing Albert trouble. For several days he does not speak to Leo. He is repeatedly told to forgive and forget, but he cannot, and is blamed for this also. He relents only on the morning that Leo goes to school. It is the last time he will say goodbye to his brother: at the end of the next holidays he will accompany him. Alone once more, he is nervous and depressed, his numbered days overshadowed, his hopes proscribed. But the lovely weather soothes and consoles him, and gradually he begins to sort out, to piece together and to weigh, the hurried experience of the past four weeks.

And he cannot understand anything. He cannot understand why Leo is not the friend he desires; why his ready love for Leo was refused; why he hates Leo. He cannot remember how he came to entertain such thoughts about his brother. He cannot understand Leo's wounding strength, his own apparent weakness. He cannot understand his error. He dreamed of magic happenings, of joy, of friendship – then of Leo. He dreamed of Leo: that was his mistake. For Leo is as he has always been: he does not change. It was the change in Vere – his vain and vulnerable dream – which brought about his present injuries. But this he does not understand.

And because he does not understand he goes on dreaming. He is not sad. He spends much of his time with Nanny. Since Flora's departure she has become the pivot of his life. With her he can be true to himself as she is true. His confidence is always respected. But he does not try to speak to her of what concerns him most closely: he could not speak of it: and his silence, his recognition of the fact that explanation is unnecessary between them, is a measure of his love and trust, for with other people he often feels a pressing and fatal need to explain himself. Nanny is his friend in the same way that his right hand is his friend. Mal is his friend and Flora at Long Cretton is his dear friend. And after all he is happy with his friends. He is happy that he can run in the sunlit garden, can sit by Nanny's wicker-work chair under the apple trees, can play with Faith, can shout and laugh and look for birds'-nests in the thick hedges. But where nonetheless he wonders, where, where – is that peculiar friend his heart craves? Where is that happiness he can hold shining, like a nugget of gold, between his hands? Why, in spite of his friends, does he feel solitary? And in spite of his happiness sad? Ah, one day, one day. . . He will come on this extraordinary happiness of which he dreams. He will dig it up like buried treasure. He will shower it richly on his perfect friend, on all his friends, on all the people he has ever met, on all the people in all the world. Everyone will be happy and he will be happiest of all. The days will be composed of moments like the one under the nut-hedge on Leo's last birthday – a series of similar moments, strung everlastingly together: the nights will be starry and blue. And soon he will find this happiness, soon he will find his friend.

Vere dreams and the days pass. His few months of future are being whittled away. In order not to look forward to what is terrible, he hopes for his mysterious happening – how he hopes! – through May, through June. He does not know the form that it will take, he does not know from what quarter to expect it – there is still no sign: he believes in it more firmly. He cannot bear to do otherwise. But time is always passing. He grows impatient, fretful. Summer comes. His mother leaves for America. One day Vere receives a letter from his father.

'Dear old boy,' his father writes. 'Mummy has arrived safely with all the news from home and has made me feel very homesick. It must be glorious now, isn't it? Warm sunny days, I expect, so different from here. I wish I was with you. Do you remember when we shot the pigeon? It was fun, wasn't it? We'll go shooting again when I get back. It looks as if I may have to leave earlier than planned. So looking forward to seeing you, dear old man – Daddy.'

Vere reads and rereads this letter, keeps it in his breast pocket, sleeps with it under his pillow.

His father will be the friend for whom he has waited.

A HUNT AND KILL

VERE is in his father's bedroom – out-of-bounds to the children – when his parents arrive home.

It is an evening in late August. More than half the holidays have gone. The cliff of school menaces now, and Vere's dreams have become confused. Sometimes it seems as if he is climbing up a steep path known only to himself – climbing and climbing up this secret path, by means of which he is avoiding all the fears and frightful dangers of the cliff, and that soon he will emerge into brightest sunlight. But he cannot climb any higher without help from his father, without love and kind understanding. And now he is about to receive this help. He still does not know the exact form that it will take. He believes simply that it will be different from anything he has ever known; that his father will be different; that his mother, everyone will be different; that his life will change; that dread will be quite removed; that certain joy will replace it. Sometimes it seems as if only a few yards of dark path separate him from this sunny upland: more often though his dreams are clouded by anxiety.

He sits in the single chair in his father's bedroom and strains his ears. He is sure he will hear the car. A myriad indefinable outdoor noises float through the open windows. Pleasant thrills begin to run up his spine. His father will soon be home. He leans back in the chair and opens the cupboard door. The owner of so many clothes, hanging suits and pairs of tilted shoes, must needs be a different and extraordinary person. Rising to his feet he goes over to the mirror and tries to smile gently, crinkling his eyes. It occurs to him that his imagination never carries him beyond his father's gentle smile. He makes a face like a monkey, then like a Chinaman. He starts to laugh silently, in a loose excited way, when suddenly, to his astonishment, he hears voices in the hall and steps on the front stairs.

He stops laughing and his heart beats very fast. All his serious hopes soar to a climax. Without thinking he runs out of the bedroom.

'Darling!' his mother says, reaching the landing and giving him a kiss.

His father, who also gives him a kiss, says with a frown, 'What were you doing in my room, you little rat?'

For a moment Vere is unable to speak. Nothing – nothing has changed. His parents look the same, wear the same clothes, say the same things in the same voices, kiss as they have always kissed. They might never have been away. Rather than being as he imagined and hoped, everything is as he has tried not to remember it. And his father's smile, of which he has thought so often, is like a barrier between them – just as it used to be: as it has always been, he now remembers. He manages to say, 'I didn't know you were here.'

'We've been in the garden with the others. You have grown, darling! Are you well?'

'Yes, Mummy, thank you.'

'But why were you in my room?' His father smiles but is obviously not pleased. 'You mustn't go in there.'

Vere smiles too, but cannot meet his father's eye.

'Were you in Daddy's room?' his mother asks, puffing at a cigarette. 'Well, shall we go along and see Faith?'

'All right, Mummy. She was waiting for you.'

'Oh, there's the new carpet,' says his father, pointing along the passage.

Vere follows his parents to the nursery. He blames the bedroom for everything. No more is said about it. He draws his mother's attention to this, his father's to that, hoping to make them forget the incident, but as a result he feels deceitful, and suffers from his old painful sense of nothing being either complete or clear.

He is relieved when they go downstairs. In the smoking-room his parents open their letters, tearing the envelopes and throwing them onto the floor, while the children loll on the sofa, talking in whispers. From time to time a remark is addressed to them – 'What are you up to?' 'We won't be long, darlings' – then more envelopes are torn and tossed aside. But the charming room with its shelves of unread books, beautifully bound, its shiny cushions, tall lamps and dulled discreet looking-glass – this harmonious room has never seemed to Vere more enclosed, and he believes that if he could only get out of it, passing through the wide french windows into the airy garden, he would feel a hundred times better and all things would again become possible.

In a way he is right. At length the family moves through the windows. The children chatter and hang on the arms of their parents, who listen abstractedly, smoking and smiling. Vere feels suddenly full of energy – like a piece of twisted elastic – and runs and leaps to everyone's amusement. But he is still dissatisfied. Whenever he pauses he looks questioningly at his father, and the winks and quacking noises he receives in answer are like added twists to the elastic inside him, which only a fresh series of wild leaps, hops and bursts of laughter on the part of the beholders, can unwind. Now he blames the clothes his father is wearing for his dissatisfaction – that diamond pin in his black tie, those pointed black shoes, the stiff collar and the blue suit. Now he blames the desired stroll through the garden, now the fact that he is not alone with his father. All the same he begins to feel better. And later in the evening, when he goes to bed, it seems to him that he is nearing the summit of his hard path.

Several days pass. One afternoon Vere comes across his father in the garden. He looks up from the seat on which he is sitting and says lazily, 'Well, monkey – what are you so busy about? Come and sit down.'

Vere starts to excuse himself. 'I was just going to the potting-shed,' he says, gesturing as if to emphasise the importance of his mission. But then, recollecting his dreams, he changes his mind. 'Oh – perhaps I will sit down,' he says, feeling clumsy and self-conscious.

'Isn't it lovely?' says his father.

'Yes,' Vere replies, and there is a long pause. He keeps on thinking of things to say, but none of them seems suitable and he remains silent. He knows that this is his opportunity, yet all he can do is stretch his toes with embarrassment and wait. The hot sunlight stupefies him. He gazes at a baked flowerbed and grows unreasonably angry.

'Why were you going to the potting-shed?' his father asks at length, lowering his head and leaning forward with his elbows on his knees.

'To get a saw,' Vere answers briefly, feeling that his father is not interested, that the question is beside the point.

'What do you want with a saw?'

'We're building a sort of cart, Leo and me.'

There is another pause. Covertly Vere regards the back of his father's head, the smooth hair curling crisply at the ends and the red neck with its pale furrows. Now that he cannot see his father's face he is free to imagine its expression: a kind expression, he is sure, and gentle, frank – the sort of expression he has often imagined in the past. His anger leaves him and he waits patiently, his mind revolving round his hopes and fancies, while the sunlight eases his constraint. All will be well: he cannot worry: he wishes his hair curled like his father's: he wishes he was like his father – had the same strong neck and big hands: he loves his father, they will be friends: it is too hot to worry anyway.

Without looking up his father says, 'What about school, old boy?'

The question seems to match Vere's mood so closely, seems to him so wonderfully intimate, that his heart, instead of sinking as it usually does at the mention of the word 'school', bounds upward. He replies 'I know,' but the two senseless words express for the first time a little of all he is feeling and longs to convey.

'When is it, the sixteenth of September?'

'Yes.'

'I'll have to come and see you.'

'Will you really?'

'We'll go out fishing in the sea, would you like that?'

'Yes, Dad, I would.'

'I took Leo last year.'

'Did you?'

Vere digests the information about Leo, determined not to let it mar his tentative happiness, then says, 'How old were you when you went to school, Dad?'

His father turns his head and glances out of the corner of his eye. 'About the same age as you. Why?'

'Well . . .' Vere pauses. The expression on his father's face is not at all as he imagined it. He studies the flowerbed, trying to forget that cold suspicious glance. Then he dismisses his fears. He tells himself that he is nearing the summit of his path, that his exertions are about to be rewarded; and so he ignores the warning signs, braces himself as if for a last effort, and speaks out.

'Dad, did you mind going to school?' he inquires.

'What?' His father sounds surprised. He stirs restlessly and continues with a half-laugh. 'Yes, I suppose I did a bit.' He lifts his head and leans against the back of the creaking lichened seat. 'But you don't mind, do you?' he asks.

Vere looks at his father, says 'No,' and rises quickly to his feet.

'Where are you off to?'

'I'd better get the saw.'

'Be careful with it, won't you?'

'Yes.'

As Vere walks away he hears the click of his father's cigarette-case and the rasp of a match, and he thinks, angrily again, How can he smoke? That his father should calmly smoke after what has happened seems dreadful to him. He feels suddenly hopeless and unhappy.

More even than Vere suspected hung on his question about school. He does not understand why he answered his father in the negative, but he knows he could not have answered otherwise. If only his father had said, 'Yes, I minded. Do you mind?' – if only he had said that, Vere could have spoken of what acutely concerns him and everything would have been transformed. Truth would have removed fear, love fulfilled hollow dreams. But his father did not ask or want to know whether Vere minded: he merely wanted Vere to say that he did not mind. His words, the tone of his voice, his expression, the movement of his hands – all made it plain that he required a certain unencumbering reply.

'You don't mind, do you?'

'No.'

To Vere, perched on his craggy and perilous path, that enforced concealment of the truth is like a blow on the head. He cried out to his father, released his precarious hold, reached upwards – he was so near the summit, so very close. He received no help. Therefore he falls, falls and is bruised, and an avalanche of hopes, of dreams, tumbles down on top of him.

His grand feelings for his father begin to resemble his old feelings for Leo. The cherished thoughts of many weeks cannot be wiped away at will. Although they shame him, an affectionate smile from his father or a kind word – the least demonstration is enough to prove, by the involuntary surge of longing and joy it produces, that he is not free of them. He pretends that he does not care; avoids his father; is cautious and reserved; forgets his fantasy about the path. But his hopeless and unhappy feeling steadily increases.

And the days flit by. Happening to pass the stable archway one afternoon Vere notices a commotion in the cobbled yard and goes to investigate. A little mare called Contact has arrived on trial for his father. She is a nervous animal, black, with a muscular neck and small head, and delicate tapering legs. After she has been stabled and the grooms have dispersed, Vere, possessed by one of those whims to which he is liable nowadays, begs a couple of apples from the head-groom and approaches the door of the loose-box. The mare swings round when he calls, and with nodding head moves towards him. He balances one of the apples in the palm of his hand and holds it out.

'Here, Contact, come on, Contact. Now don't bite me,' he murmurs.

The mare extends her head, eyes slanting curiously, breathes warm air onto Vere's hand through dilating nostrils, then nibbles the apple into her mouth with her soft mobile lips. Her yellow teeth show for an instant; she munches once, tosses her head, and stares at something on the other side of the yard. Delighted by her gentle ways and knowing expression, Vere offers Contact the second apple.

This is the start of a strange friendship which develops during the next few days between the boy and the little mare. Had he stopped to think Vere would have been surprised by his constant visits to the stables, of which he usually steers clear, and his complete absence of fear in all his dealings with Contact, when he has never before been anything but frightened of horses. But he does not stop to think, and his undemanding tenderness affords him relief from the intricate consideration of his feelings for his father. Perhaps the very oddness of the object on which he chooses to lavish his love and countless attentions stimulates him; perhaps he feels that the mare's unsettled future and his own are intertwined; perhaps he senses some sad dumb fellowship between them. Whatever the reason may be, the moments he spends clinging to the top of the loose-box door, talking to Contact, stroking and feeding her, become for him the most real and precious moments of this period.

On two occasions his father gallops the mare in the field by the back-drive. Sitting on the stone stile in the wall Vere watches proudly as she trots over the close grass, canters with a free but restrained grace, and finally gallops, hinting at her speed and well-knit strength.

On the way back to the stables after the second gallop Vere asks his father, whom he seems able to meet on this neutral ground, if he is going to keep the mare.

'I want to try her out with hounds first,' his father answers. 'I thought I might take her cubbing tomorrow.'

'Can I come, Dad?'

'Well, the meet's pretty early.'

'I don't mind.'

'Do you want to come, you monkey?'

'Yes, very much.'

'Well, we'll see.'

'And then you'll buy her, won't you, Dad?'

'I may. Do you like her?'

'Yes.'

Later in the day the subject of the cub-hunting is again broached by Vere. The other children join him in begging to be allowed to go. Permission is granted and Mal agrees to accompany them.

That evening Vere takes some lumps of sugar out to Contact. He steals across the deserted yard, peeps over the high door of the loose-box and whispers her name. The mare pricks her ears, turns, rustling the thick straw that covers her hooves, and comes towards him.

'What do you want?' he teases her, stepping back and showing his empty hands. 'I haven't anything for you. What is it then?'

The mare presses her nose against his chest, breathing gently. 'No, I haven't anything. Honestly I haven't,' he says, putting his hands in his pockets.

Contact raises her head and appears to lose interest.

'Contact!' he commands. She pays no attention. 'Why Contact,' he says in a sly voice, 'guess what I've found. Look at that, well I never.'

She dips her head and nuzzles his closed fist. He opens it gradually and, as she takes the sugar, slips into his favourite position, his back against the door of the loose-box, the mare's neck over his right shoulder.

'You just want the sugar, don't you? That's all you want,' he says, caressing the bridge of her nose with one hand and pulling down her head, while with the other he feeds her. 'You're awfully greedy. How much sugar could you eat? I don't know why I like you so much!' His eyes begin to water. 'Well, you've got an early start tomorrow. Now mind you behave.' He notices that he is speaking to Contact very much as Nanny speaks to him. This makes him smile. 'Otherwise you'll have to go away and I'll never see you any more. And that's the last lump, you greedy animal,' he says, feeling weak and sentimental. 'Goodnight then,' he says sternly, moving into the sunlit yard.

Contact blows through her nose, and Vere, pleased with that gentle parting whinny, leaves her and goes indoors to the early bed which has been decreed.

He sleeps lightly and is awake before five o'clock when Mal knocks on his door. His room is full of the dawn. Before switching on his bedside lamp he bends beneath his curtains and looks out of the window. A pale illumination shows the stable archway. The elm tree is a black shape against the sky which is still sprinkled with stars. The air is cold, and a ghostly patch of mist spreads over the field where Contact galloped.

He shivers, draws his curtains, and turning on the light quickly dresses himself in the thick clothes that have been laid out overnight. Then he tiptoes downstairs in his stockinged feet, puts on his wellingtons and short leather coat, and enters the bright front-hall where the others are slowly congregating.

After a pause the door at the top of the stairs opens and Vere's father appears. He wears breeches and gaiters, neat boots, a black coat of some thick material, and a white stock tied tightly round his neck and fastened with a large gold pin.

'Are you all ready?' he whispers.

His face shines as it always does after shaving, his eyes sparkle, and his presence has an invigorating effect on the children, who stop yawning and rubbing their sleepy faces, and begin to whisper and laugh amongst themselves. Mal comes in with a jug of hot chocolate and some biscuits. Mary opens the front-door. It is grey and cold outside, but much lighter than before. Standing in the porch they drink the frothing chocolate out of steamed glasses, the heat of which warms their hands. Cocks are crowing at the farm, birds are beginning to twitter, the black car is coated with dew.

Leo asks, 'Do you think you'll catch a fox, Dad?'

'We might. It's just the right morning.'

'How can the hounds see? It's so dark.'

'Oh Karen!' scoff the children, still whispering for some reason. 'It's only early yet. It'll be daylight soon. Besides, they use their noses.'

'There ought to be a good scent today,' their father says, whistling under his breath and seeming to sniff the sharp air.

'What's the time?'

'Shouldn't we go?'

Vere fetches his father's bowler hat, string gloves and riding-crop.

'Your hands are freezing,' his father says as he takes them.

'Are they?'

'What, didn't you know?' He smiles.

'No.' Vere shakes his head.

'Are you excited?'

'Yes.'

'Come on then.'

His father drives the car, lighting a cigarette with difficulty as he does so. Vere, who sits at his side, cannot look at him this morning without feeling tensely hopeful, and it is mainly on account of this that he trembles with excitement and clenches his cold hands. But now his father, Mal – everyone is excited. The meet is to be held in the park of a neighbouring landowner, and soon they pass beneath a stately archway, follow a bumpy road between two lines of chestnut trees, come up with some other cars – horses, bystanders – stop and get out. The sun has risen by this time. Huge sunbeams point into the violet and green sky, and the grass that can be seen through the flat mist gleams like a stretch of water. Sounds hang in the moist atmosphere and are magnified by it – the smart click of horses' hooves on the road, the jingling of bridles, voices, the whimpering of two terriers.

'Where are the hounds, Mal?'

'They will come soon, chéri!'

Several horses are being walked under the trees, and amongst these Vere recognises Contact. He wades towards her through the wet grass.

'Good morning, Kenneth,' he calls to the groom.

'Morning, Master Vere.'

'Hullo, Contact.' The mare blows through her nose as she did the evening before. 'Hullo there, Contact,' he says, stroking her neck and shoulder, and hurrying to keep up with her swishing steps.

'You come to see the sport?' questions Kenneth in his harsh voice.

'Yes. When will the hounds be here?'

'They'll not be long. Steady, old girl,' he cries as Contact tosses her head.

'Steady, Contact,' Vere repeats.

His father approaches.

'How is she, Kenneth?' he asks, taking a last puff at the stub of his cigarette and spitting out the smoke.

'She's fresh, sir.'

'Doesn't look it.' His father buttons up his coat.

'She's not seen hounds yet.'

'Bring her onto the road.'

'This way – this way, old girl,' says Kenneth, pushing the mare with his shoulder.

'Do you want your gloves, Dad?'

'I've got them. Kenneth, here!'

A little car noses its way along the yellow road and suddenly toots its horn. At the sound Contact tosses her head again and breaks into a springy trot.

'Steady!' says Kenneth roughly, dragging at the mare's bridle.

Contact grows calm, but Vere, who stands at her head while his father mounts, can tell by her breathing and her eyes which show more white than usual that she is in a strained uncertain mood.

'Now you behave, you behave,' he mutters, but because of his own excitement the words seem to carry no weight.

Suddenly he remembers the piece of digestive biscuit he has saved for the mare. He reaches into his pocket – crumbs get under his fingernails – glances at his father who is speaking to Kenneth, and holds out the morsel.

'Contact!' he says in a soft commanding voice.

She lowers her head and begins to nibble the biscuit with her lips.

'There,' he says, 'do you like that? That's your breakfast. Eat it up.'

'What are you doing, Vere?'

He raises his eyes guiltily.

'I was just giving Contact a biscuit.'

His father pulls at the reins, jerking up Contact's head. The biscuit falls from her lips into the grass. She starts sidestepping. 'Don't feed her!' His father frowns as he says this. Then he twists round and calls over his shoulder, 'Why don't you stay with Mal?'

Vere blushes and looks away. Why did his father have to say that, he thinks rebelliously, in such a voice and so loud? What wrong was I doing? All the same he feels he has committed an awful sin. Unpleasant twinges of dread riddle his fresh excitement, weaken and spoil it, and he walks towards Mal apprehensively.

The sun is now shining with cold brilliance. Everything is touched by it – the clearing mist, the trunks of trees, horses, cars. A whip cracks along the road, there is an odd throaty cry, a few deep barks and a whine, and the hounds come into sight. They approach in a compact mass – a single body with many legs and waving tails – the master riding in their midst, whippers-in on either side of them. Admiring cries break from the bystanders. The master, who looks like a hound himself with his wooden face and set expression, begins to greet people in rasping tones and to touch his velvet cap with his riding-crop. The two hunt-servants call the hounds by name and flick at them with their whips. Horsemen answer the master respectfully; everyone seems to be impressed and delighted by his safe arrival; anticipation mounts.

'Nice bit of trouble over there,' Vere overhears somebody say.

He guesses it is his father who is referred to. 'Oh Contact, be good, please be good,' he breathes quickly, half closing his eyes. Then he looks round. Between the trees, some distance off, he can see the little mare prancing on her slender legs and shaking her head. The master blows a short piercing blast on his hunting-horn. The mare begins to rear up and buck. 'Oh don't, Contact,' Vere implores silently. His father's face is very red and his bowler hat has fallen forward onto his nose. 'Don't make him angry, Contact,' Vere pleads; but he senses that his plea has come too late and of a sudden is filled with despair. Mal touches his arm and he turns away.

The hounds are moving forward. The dozen or so riders jostle after them, then come two cars and the people on foot. Mary, Karen and Leo pass with shouts of glee, their gumboots clumping as they run and their coats flapping open. Kenneth passes with bow-legged steps. The hunt disappears through a gate into a wood and Vere follows slowly with Mal. His father and Contact are nowhere to be seen.

'La chasse, la chasse!' Mal exclaims. 'Don't you love it?'

Vere answers disagreeably, 'There are an awful lot of hounds to catch a fox, aren't there?' Nonplussed, Mal smiles, tightening the corners of her mouth. 'What harm do foxes do?' he continues.

'They kill the chickens!' She looks at him as if she has explained everything. 'I have seen it, when I was young. They do not kill only one chicken. They kill all – in the neck they bite them' – she makes a blood-thirsty sound – 'ten, fifteen chickens!'

'How did you see it?' he asks.

'Well, the fox got into the chicken place and afterwards I went to see.'

'And were they all dead?'

'Mais oui!'

'Was there blood everywhere?'

'Yes – horrible!'

'Is that why foxes are hunted?'

'It is necessary. If not there would be no chickens or eggs.'

'I love chicken and eggs,' says Vere, feeling hungry.

'Moi aussi.'

'I'd love two fried eggs with fried bread and crisp bacon, wouldn't you, Mal – just cooked and hot?'

'Oh don't!' She laughs.

'But I still can't see why they have to have so many hounds,' he says.

They walk for a time without speaking. Then Mal halts and lifts her stick with the rubber thing on the end.

'What is that?'

They listen. They are in the wood, at the juncture of several grassy rides. The sun, more golden now, lights up the damp bracken in places and the tangled scrub. A startled jay swoops over their heads, turns silently – its white rump flashing – and vanishes amongst the ornamental trees. A moment later its note of warning is heard, raucous and scolding. A blackbird flies low down one of the rides, sees them, swerves frantically and also begins to scold. An alarmed hush falls over the wood.

'What did you hear?' Vere whispers.

'But there – there!'

A distant bell-like crying, interspersed with some deeper baying and a curious broken yell, comes to their ears.

'Are they killing a fox?'

'Je ne sais pas.'

'But what are they doing?'

'Hunting! Come on! It's thrilling!'

He begins to feel excited again and says to Mal, who is starting to plod down a ride: 'Are you sure that's the right way?'

She stops. 'Why not?'

'We don't know where they went.'

'Then we will find out.'

'Can you hear anything?'

'No.'

'Wait, Mal.'

'No no – come along!' She resumes her heavy walk.

He picks up a stick as he follows her and slashes at tufts of grass, scattering the dewdrops. He thinks of Contact and tries to feel depressed. 'Why is it called cub-hunting?' he asks, although he knows quite well.

'Because it is the cubs they are hunting.'

He wants to say, 'How cruel.' Instead he inquires, 'How will we know when they kill one?'

'We will hear the horn.' She imitates it, puffing out of the side of her mouth.

He smiles crookedly, drops behind, beats the grass with his stick. But all the time he is listening intently and feeling more excited than ever.

Soon after this they emerge from the wood. A bank on which huge pine trees grow stretches before them, sloping easily down to a lake. Beyond the lake, in a fine position, rises the bare wall of a great shuttered house. A stray hound lollops between the pine-trees and Vere calls eagerly to Mal, running to catch up with her.

'Do you see it? Look – did you see it, Mal?'

'What?'

'The hound! It's gone now.'

'Ssh, we will see the fox.'

'Where?'

'I don't know.' He laughs. 'In a minute.'

Two ducks quack and fly from the lake, splashing loudly.

'Look!' cries Vere. 'There's Contact! Contact and Daddy – look, Mal, look!'

Sunlight flashes on a horse and rider away amongst the pine-trees.

'I can see nothing.'

'They were there!'

'Are you sure?'

'I know it!'

And Contact was cantering! So all may still be well! He squeezes Mal's arm.

'Oh, we'll miss everything – please hurry, Mal!'

He runs ahead over the ground that is covered with pine-needles, hears a noise behind him, slithers to a stop and turns. Mal is lunging forward with her stick. He stares in amazement. Suddenly she tears off her green beret and hurls it towards a pine-tree.

'The fox!' he thinks, opening his eyes extremely wide and gazing up the slope.

Fifty yards away, in deep shadow, a small brown object is moving rapidly between the tree-trunks. As soon as he sees it, without knowing why, Vere shouts. The object increases its pace. He shouts again and dashes back to Mal.

'Tally-ho!' she is crying.

'Was it the fox?'

'Tally-ho, tally-ho!' she warbles in her singing voice, nodding her head.

He begins to shout with all the power of his lungs. The fox has gone – he does not look or care for the fox: but he shouts until he is hoarse.

'Mal, Mal!' He can hardly speak. 'They're all at the end here – the hunt and Contact – everything – come quick, Mal, quick!'

'You go!' she insists furiously.

He runs under the pine trees, attempting to take off his coat as he does so, but he slides and slips on the pine-needles, nearly falls, and allows it to billow and flap. He is unbearably hot and half-crying with the wild excitement that has now taken possession of him. He has seen the fox, he can hear the hounds giving tongue: he has seen Contact and she seemed to be calmly cantering. But not for these reasons alone does he feel so feverishly excited. The real climax is approaching – that is what he feels. Everything, one way or the other, is about to be resolved. This path is the path he has imagined: somewhere along it he will find what he is seeking. And therefore he plunges headlong, so breathless that he seems to have a prickly burr stuck in his throat, under the dark green trees.

He reaches an open space and stops. The bright sun is blinding. He screws up his eyes and looks round. Some riders are crossing a balustraded bridge on his right and galloping up the grassy slope. The horses' hooves throw divots of turf into the air as they pass him. On the other side of the glade in which he is standing an unfenced wood, with neatly-divided areas of bracken and sparse undergrowth, covers the hillside. The hounds are in this wood. He catches a glimpse of them and shouts. Then he starts to run across the glade. Two more horsemen thunder over the bridge. One of them waves at Vere and bellows something. He gazes at the charging horses blankly and scrambles in the nick of time out of their way. He begins to run towards the bridge, realises he is going in the wrong direction, turns about and races back to the last of the pine trees. A solitary horseman canters over the bridge. It is his father.

'Hullo, Dad!' He waves his arms.

As before, he thinks, if Contact is only cantering, not galloping or bucking, all must be well. And he runs forward a few yards, beside himself with hope and mad joy.

'Dad, Dad!' he screams.

But then he sees that Contact is not exactly cantering. Her head is drawn up and back. She is pawing yet only just touching the ground with her forelegs – which look abnormally long – while her hindlegs are awkwardly gathered underneath her. She seems to falter all the time, as if she wanted but was unable to bound forward. And her neck and flanks are white with hot lather.

'Contact,' he gasps, not understanding.

His father is standing in the stirrups now, dragging with his full weight on the reins. And Contact's head goes up, her neck bulges out, her forelegs leave the ground altogether.

His father's face – he can see it – is purple, contorted. There is a scratch on his jutting chin.

'What's the matter, what's the matter?'

Vere repeats the question several times, not knowing what he is saying.

'Where the hell is Kenneth?' shouts his father.

'Kenneth?'

'Where's Kenneth?'

'I don't know.'

'Go and find him!'

'What?'

'For God's sake go and find him!'

'What's the matter, Dad, what's the matter?'

But he can see what is the matter. He forces himself to move towards Contact, though he feels suddenly sick and paralysed.

'Her mouth is bleeding,' he sobs as if he were still excited.

'Get away from this something horse!'

Vere takes no notice. His father relaxes his hold on the reins for a second in order to obtain a better grip, and Contact lowers her head and stands still. Her mouth is injured and bleeding, her sensitive lips are covered with blood and foam. The steel bit pulls her mouth open. He can see it is full of blood.

'Oh Contact,' he moans.

The mare blows through her nose, which is cut and also bleeding – blows very gently, as if in response.

'Her mouth is bleeding!' he shouts angrily at his father.

'I don't mind if she's bleeding all over!' The reins jerk and Contact rises on her hindlegs.

'Leave her alone!' Vere cries.

'Get out of the way!' shouts his father at the same moment.

'Don't do it – how can you? Leave her alone!' cries Vere in a paroxysm of rage and grief.

'How dare you talk to me like that?' answers his father. 'Go and get Kenneth!' And swearing and muttering he gathers the reins in one hand, raises his ivory-handled riding-crop and whacks it down on Contact's quivering flank.

The mare whinnies. The veins swell in her neck and she careers up the slope, her head tugged savagely to one side.

'How can you?' Vere sobs. 'How can you, how can you?' he repeats over and over again.

He stumbles to his pine tree and flops onto the ground at its base. 'How can you?' he continues to mumble, sobbing and staring blindly at the bracken opposite. The glade is empty now, the hounds are momentarily quiet. But there, in the bracken, something is moving. He takes a deep jerky breath and focuses his eyes.

A fox is bobbing through the undergrowth. It is not twenty yards away: he can see it distinctly. Now it stops and listens. He can see it has one pad raised. He is reminded of Danny Fox in his favourite *Little Jack Rabbit*. This fox has the same pointed face he has imagined, and sly expression, big ears, sleek red coat. In spite of himself he feels excited again and stealthily stands up. The fox – but it must be a cub – emerges from the undergrowth and begins to step and jump delicately over the bracken. It reaches the grass ride and pauses, snapping unexpectedly at a fly. Then it leaps over the last clump of bracken, lands without a sound and trots away down the ride.

Ten feet ahead of it a hound appears. Both the fox and the hound stop. For some seconds nothing happens. The hound and the fox face each other without moving on the green sunlit turf beside the bracken. Then the pack of hounds, strangely silent in its approach, bounds into view. The fox turns. Vere tries to shout and runs across the glade. The hounds, with terrible cries and without checking, descend on the fox. One endless high-pitched scream rises above the baying. The fox is caught, torn apart – red limb from limb – tossed in the air, caught again, and worried on the ground by the circle of snarling hounds.

The master rides up, followed by the hunt. He blows a long call on his hunting-horn, then, smiling with pleasure, cheers on and encourages the hounds. The other riders join in and shout congratulations to the master, watching the murderous hounds with evident satisfaction. Beyond the group Vere sees his father, still having trouble with Contact, but laughing now and straightening his stock. He retraces his steps across the glade and finds Mal.

'It is the kill!' she says. 'Why are you so white? What is it, chéri?'

'Nothing, Mal,' he replies.

'Do you want to go back to the car?'

'Yes, please.'

But a man blocks their way. He has a strong nose and thin lips.

'Come with me, nipper,' he says. 'I'll have you blooded.'

Mal answers for Vere.

'Not want it?' the man exclaims. 'Aren't you a sport like your father?'

Vere raises his eyes. 'No!' he answers with cold conviction.

WAR

It is the first Sunday in September.

Vere wakes with a horrible start and immediately feels angry.

Leo is standing at the end of his bed, the jacket of his pyjamas open, the white skin of his chest exposed, and his pink shiny face lit by the sun that streams narrowly through the gap in the curtains. 'Wake up, wake up,' he is saying as he swings on the wooden bed-end.

'Go away,' answers Vere, jolted by the creaking motion.

'You go away,' Leo teases.

'Go away, Leo!'

But Leo jumps onto the bed and begins to bounce up and down on the springs. 'It's . . . time . . . for . . . small boys . . . to get up!' he sings out between bounces.

Soon the brothers are fighting. Leo gets the worst of it for Vere fights with fury, taking a certain perverse delight in this violent expression of his careless despair. But his victories are hot and bitter – Leo only laughs and giggles, undismayed by defeat, tirelessly provocative – and the sense of disaster to which he awoke, the anger and the dread, are not assuaged.

'Come on, Leo, it's time to get up. Now stop it.'

But Leo never knows when to stop. He laughs and pushes Vere, who falls backwards onto the bed and hurts his wrist.

'You fool, Leo, you've hurt me, look what you've done!' says Vere, swaying about on the edge of the bed and hugging his wrist. Perhaps it is broken and I will not have to go to school, he thinks. 'Fetch Nanny,' he groans. 'It's really bad. Go and get her, Leo,' he repeats angrily.

Nanny comes and examines the wrist which looks rather normal. 'It's usually Leo who gets hurt about this time,' she says, a reference to the maladies Leo is apt to develop towards the end of the holidays.

Vere pretends not to understand. 'It may look all right. I just can't move it,' he says. Nanny smiles. Angry with Nanny for smiling, and also for comparing him to Leo, he says with a sour laugh, 'Oh, don't worry, I expect it'll get better!' And he walks rudely past Nanny and Leo, enters the bathroom and bangs the door.

He wishes his wrist would suddenly swell and fill with poison. He wants something dramatic and terrible to happen. His mind revolves round catastrophe. He desires the discomfiture of all his foes, and in order to achieve it is more than ready to sicken and nearly die – or in fact die, and so be spared school.

The sunlight is brilliant on the bathroom floor – it warms his bare feet: and outside, on the roof of the stables, the dew is drying, the doves are stretching their wings and cooing, the weathercock is steady. All is sweet and familiar. And he finds it vile, hateful. He leans on the stone bathroom window-sill and imagines with relish some sudden shock – a tremor of the earth, some ruinous explosion – which would disturb the perennial lethargy of the scene he surveys. Only a great exterior tension, he believes, will snap the cords of misery that bind him, only a shattering upheaval free him from the prison of his inescapable rage.

He returns to his room and begins to dress. His fingers tingle under the stress of his emotion, his hair hurts when he combs it, and his skin aches from contact with his clothes. His shirt seems to be made of sandpaper: he feels raw, he positively smarts: and he has a dull pain in his teeth which he discovers he is grinding.

He wonders what is wrong with him. Remembering past pain, he throbs with present anger, future dread. But he shakes himself like a dog and determines to control his ill humour.

At breakfast there is talk of war. The children are full of it and Nanny's anxious expression adds to their excitement. Vere, obsessed by his efforts to keep his temper, says little, but he blushes every time he speaks or is spoken to, and his irritation increases. Towards the end of the meal Nanny asks after his wrist.

Colouring, he repeats stupidly, 'My wrist?'

'Have you forgotten it? It must be better,' Nanny says.

'I thought you couldn't move it,' says Leo, and proceeds to give an amusing account of the incident in the bedroom. 'I should jump out of the window,' he finally suggests. 'Then you'll probably always stay at home.'

'Yes, in a coffin,' adds Karen.

Vere is too angry and miserable to answer. He no longer feels ashamed of his rage; he discards his good intentions. Hatred flares in his heart: hatred for Leo, Karen and even Nanny, self-hatred for having laid himself open to attack. Incapable of giving vent to his fury, speechless as always in face of opposition, he glares round the table. But he cannot meet the intrigued stares that are turned upon him and his hatred melts into self-pity. Excusing himself in a thick voice he leaves the nursery and goes along to say good morning to his mother.

After he has kissed her, for want of something better to say, he mentions the war, but in a cool tone so that it should not appear that he shared the others' excitement. His mother says it is dreadful, and she does not know what they are going to do. Then she says, 'Darling, I found your School List last night. I think you ought to go through it with Nanny.'

Something in his mother's voice makes Vere answer sharply, 'What's a School List?'

'It's no good speaking like that, Vere,' she says, lowering her chin and giving him a reproachful look.

'How was I speaking?'

'In that cross way.'

'I wasn't.' He is startled by his abrupt and disrespectful tone, yet oddly gratified by it. After a pause, looking out of the window, he repeats his question. 'I asked you what a School List is.'

'It's your clothes,' his mother answers shortly. Then she asks, 'Are you very sad about school?'

Taken by surprise he glances at his mother. Her face wears an expression of fearful probing inquiry. Again something in her voice, and in her eyes which she quickly averts – a sort of nervous anticipation – seems to demand brutality; and when she reiterates, 'Are you, darling?' he answers, 'Of course not!' with cruel emphasis.

'And I can't go through the list today,' he adds.

His mother shuffles the newspapers that lie on her white satin eiderdown. 'Now Vere, go and get it finished,' she says. 'I'm only thinking of you, darling.'

He snatches the paper and leaves the room in silence.

A dull precise voice booms along the nursery passage. Nanny and Edith are listening to the wireless.

'We've got to go through this,' Vere says loudly, ignoring Nanny's solemn expression and waving the School List in front of her.

'In a minute, Vere, be quiet now.'

'Mummy says we must.'

'Put it down and be quiet, Vere, there's a good boy.'

He throws the paper towards the uncleared breakfast table, but it folds and flutters to the ground. He kicks it, then bends laboriously to pick it up. The blood rushes to his head, there is a singing in his ears, and the voice that issues from the leather-covered wireless seems unbearably loud.

'Nanny, we've got to go through this list,' he shouts.

Nanny rises and turns off the wireless. 'Well, Vere, what is it?' she asks mildly.

'How do I know?' He hands her the crumpled list, regretting the rough way he has spoken.

'Are you well, Vere?'

'Why?'

'You look rather pale.'

He begins to feel sorry for himself. 'I don't know,' he says.

'What is it, Vere?' Nanny asks as she follows him into the passage.

'Nothing, nothing,' he answers. 'Let's go through the beastly list!'

He stalks ahead of Nanny down the passage and enters the darkened spare room at the top of the kitchen stairs. Stumbling over shoes and piles of clothing he reaches the window and pulls the blind. It rattles upwards. The sight that meets his eyes makes him feel weak and he sits abruptly on the lid of his new brown trunk.

'You read out what's written here,' Nanny says, 'and I'll do the checking.'

Vere takes the list and reads. 'One Eton jacket and trousers. Two blue blazers. Three pairs of grey flannel trousers. Two pairs of short trousers, blue ...'

Nanny kneels on the floor and answers him at intervals. 'Am I allowed to take my tweed coat?' he asks.

'No, just the things on the list.'

'Am I allowed to take my sheath-knife?'

'You know you're not, Vere.'

'Or my yellow tie?'

'What comes next, Vere?'

He reads with heavy sarcasm. 'Five vests and pants ...'

The angry wasted minutes pass. I will regret this lost time, he thinks; but still the furious thoughts boil within him. Will I always feel the same, he wonders. And because his shocked reactions seem perfectly true, reasonable, and therefore lasting, he sees suddenly a lifetime of anger and hatred stretching before him, and this thought fills him with fresh misery. In order to interrupt the obsessive circle of his feelings he asks Nanny why she was listening to the wireless. She tells him of the threat of war, but he cannot concentrate on what she is saying. He finds himself studying her face with cold detachment, noticing the high hairline, the strong bristling eyebrows, the slightly crooked mouth and the small definite chin. He observes her face as if it belonged to a stranger. But the very barrenness of his response eventually evokes a blunt unhappy ache in his heart.

They continue to sort the clothes. 'Nanny, did you go to school?' he asks.

'Indeed I did.'

'But you lived at home, didn't you?' he challenges her.

'Yes, but it was two miles to school and we had to go in all weathers.'

'How? How did you go?'

'On Shanks's pony. Four miles a day, and often it was cold and wet.'

'I wouldn't mind walking four miles a day.'

'Read out the list, child.'

'One pair of black football boots. Did you like school, Nanny?'

'Well, I wanted to learn and get on.'

'Why?'

She laughs. 'It's natural, and that's how you must think about it, Vere.'

He would like to say, 'But while you were learning and getting on, you lived at home.' Instead, he reads out the last item on the list. He does feel calmer for the conversation, however; and his attempts to picture Nanny as a little girl, trudging to school through snow and sleet, with rosy cheeks and books under her arm, and perhaps an apple in her pocket, divert him. He examines her closely. Did she have those hairs on her chin when she went to school? He cannot imagine her without them. For the first time in the day he smiles.

'There, that's the lot. Oh my poor knees,' she says, rising to her feet with difficulty. Vere wonders if she rose from her school desk in the same way, begging the teacher's pardon for her rheumaticky joints; and once again he smiles. 'All over,' she says as she closes the spare-room door. He remembers that she says 'All over' when she fetches him from the dentist's house in Long Cretton, and is grateful for the tacit admission of his suffering and pain.

'Are you going to church today?' she asks. 'You will be, I expect.'

Wishing to convey his gratitude he thanks her for checking the School List; but the mention of the word 'school' churns up a new storm of dread and despair, and he leaves her in the middle of a sentence and hurries down the front stairs.

His father is sitting at the end of the long hall table. He lowers his paper as Vere approaches and inclines his head to be kissed. Then he says, 'Your hair needs brushing.'

'I know,' Vere answers quickly. 'Are we going to church?' Nowadays he does not address his father by name.

'Do you want to?'

'I don't mind. Are we?' He feels he can only make arrangements with his father.

'I think we'd better. What's the time?'

'Twenty-three minutes and twenty seconds to eleven.' Vere thanks heaven for his watch which he can safely regard and wind. 'What time will we leave?' he asks.

'Ten to eleven. You go and get changed.'

Vere returns to the nursery, enters his bedroom, and begins to bang the cupboard doors, tug at the drawers of the chest and hurl his Sunday outfit onto the bed.

'Now then, now then,' Edith warns him as she passes through the room.

'What are you saying?' he inquires insultingly.

'Don't take that tone with me, Master Vere,' she retorts, accentuating the 'Master Vere'. 'Perhaps school will teach you manners.'

'I didn't hear that, Edith!' Vere shouts. But Edith has closed his door.

He breathes hard as he climbs into his grey flannel suit and half-throttles himself with the yellow tie that he cannot take to school. Out of his window he can see the stable archway, through which Contact will never again walk with nodding head. Out of his other window he can see the roof over which he scrambled to escape from Leo. He busies himself with his clothes. He feels he must rush and hurry, and he fumbles with buttons and breaks a shoelace. He has a dreadful sensation of precious time going to waste – time that he does not know how he would use, except for further hurry, further rush: time that is nonetheless invaluable. He knocks over a photograph of his father on horseback and does not pick it up. His room is in disorder. He marches out of it, slamming the door, and enters the nursery.

Nanny straightens his tie and tells him to pray for peace. On the way downstairs he can hear his mother sending Mary to wash her hands, Leo and Karen arguing about what they will do if war is declared, his father saying angrily to Bella, 'But I left the blessed thing here!'

Out-of-doors the car drawn up in the shimmering sunlight seems to share and augment his restless impatience.

The children pile into it and chatter excitedly.

'If there's war, will you have to fight, Daddy?'

'When will we know for certain?'

'I'm going to buy some more cartridges for my gun.'

'Move over, Vere, or I'll fight you.'

'Yes, Vere, move over.'

'But when will we know, Mummy?'

And Vere wonders what he is doing with these people for whom he feels only hatred and distaste.

They arrive at the church and hurry up the gravel path between the gravestones. The bell stops tolling as they tiptoe through the porch and take their places on a bench behind the font. Vere leans forward in an attitude of prayer, but suddenly noticing that Leo is wearing a pair of his socks, he begins to tremble with rage.

The number of a hymn is given out in a reverberating voice, the organ intones the introduction and the congregation rise and sing. Vere compresses his lips until they pulse, tautens every muscle in his body, clenches his fists and holds his breath. Nanny knitted him those green socks. He would like to spring upon Leo and tear them from his feet. He would like to wound and mutilate Leo. He remembers the agile fox, snapping at a fly, neatly leaping over the bracken, and recalls its fate with a shudder. Let Leo be punished in the same way, let everyone be punished – everyone! His vision blurs; he shivers and sweats all over; his anger and his hatred reach a higher pitch of intensity than ever before.

The double doors at the back of the church are noisily opened. People turn. Mr. Pole the churchwarden limps up the aisle and exchanges a word with the parson, then limps to his position in the front pew and pretends to sing. The doors remain open. The parson signals to the organist: the music and the voices tail away. A gradual hush descends.

And although he feels sick and ill, and wonders if he is going to faint, Vere's spasm of rage passes.

For a few seconds the hush continues. Shafts of sunlight bar the church, coloured in places by the stained glass of the windows, and a rook caws lazily somewhere outside.

The parson announces that war has been declared and once more silence falls.

The congregation is larger than usual, Vere notices. Again the rook caws. And everyone is surprisingly still. His mother is looking down at her hymn-book, one edge of which she smooths repeatedly with her pointed thumb. His father's face is grave and pensive, and his jaw juts forward as he clamps his front teeth together. The curious silence is prolonged: it grows tense. Leo shifts his weight furtively from one foot to the other: Vere's back begins to ache.

'Let us pray.'

He sits down, feels slightly better, tries to think of the war, but a final wave of choking despair swamps him and bears him helplessly away.

The voice issues from the sunlight – like the voice of God, Vere fancies – 'Let us draw near to Our Lord in this time of our trouble . . .'

How true, how true, Vere suddenly thinks – this time of our trouble – and he grasps at the words as if to save himself.

'Grant us deliverance from the trials and dangers that await us . . .'

Oh Lord, grant that, Vere prays.

'Prepare us for adversity . . .'

Prepare me, Lord, Vere echoes.

'Forgive us our sins . . .'

He is reminded irresistibly of a picture which has floated lately in his mind: of a lagoon, reflecting a clear northern sky, dotted about with boats and ringed by mountains, cut-off, serene and infinitely peaceful. He sees the settlement at the mouth of the lagoon and the arrested drift of evening smoke above it, and he hears the voices that are carried across the water. He loves that picture: he can see it now so plainly. Why now, he wonders. But he dare not question. He closes his eyes and thinks of the rook, Mr. Pole, the war – of things that do not concern him. And all the time, like a freed bird, he is cautiously fluttering, a yard from his cage, another yard, afraid to spread his unaccustomed wings, still doubtful of release.

But the war may prevent me going to school, he thinks. Leo nudges him and he stands up. School will come sometime, now or later, he decides. And he smiles at Leo. The hot lump of dread and hatred dissolves in his chest. He opens his hymn-book and inhales the musty air of the church without hindrance. For a second he thinks of the meaningless war and the prayers that fitted his mood so strangely, then he joins in the singing.

NANNY AND FLORA

SEVEN days remain to Vere.

He remembers his seven days as he wakes from a long heavy sleep. Then he turns over quickly, curling up, and draws the bed-clothes round him. There is a draught beneath his left shoulder. He pulls down the pillow and settles his head into it deeply. He can feel the breeze on his forehead, cool and intermittent, and by opening his right eye a fraction he can see the sunlight and the faint undulation of the curtains. How warm he is, and comfortable. Seven days . . . He dozes and wakes. Seven days . . .

Is a week a long or a short time? He does not know. There are lots of hours in each day and he has only been awake for minutes, yet every second of those minutes has contained a thought, and even a spice of enjoyment. If he can fill his seconds in this way, every second of every minute, every minute of every hour, then a week is an age, a lifetime. He resolves to treasure his seconds, to extract satisfaction intensely from each. That is the secret, he decides . . . And once again he dozes.

But seven days make a week, he thinks, suddenly opening his eyes, and four weeks make a month, and I had a month left just the other day – a month is nothing, nothing! He shivers and turns over in bed, and a moan of regret for the briefness of his seven days escapes him. What can he do in a week, what is worth doing?

His access of despair sharpens his senses. He hears the muted ticking of the postman's pedal-cycle, the sharp rasp of his nailed boots as he dismounts, the sweet ring of his bicycle-bell as it touches the iron of the fire-escape beneath the nursery window. The postman is sorting the letters: Vere imagines he can hear the rustle of paper. And now he is entering the backyard. Bella will receive him in the pantry, Mrs. Lark will give him a cup of tea; he will collect the mail, stow it in his canvas satchel, comment on the coming heat of the day; then he will leave the slowly stirring house and bicycle unhurriedly, through the sunlight, back to Long Cretton.

If only I were a postman, Vere thinks with a sigh, as for the third time he turns over in his bed which now seems to him hot and confined. He recalls his anguished and impressive moan and tries to repeat it, but it sounds like the moo of a cow and he is forced to smile.

Still smiling he throws back the covers and extends his bare feet into the sunlight at the bottom of his bed. He wriggles his toes and hopes they will get sunburnt. Perhaps he will not have to go to school. The floor of his room is squared with brightness and the soft breeze billows across his legs. Perhaps on the morning of the day he is to leave Nanny will come and tell him that since he has been so brave he need never go to school. Perhaps he is a prince in disguise and this cruel test is a part of his preparation. He does not feel he is the son of his mother and father, and wonders who knows of his royal descent. His smile spreads: he notices it and stops smiling. However he may dream the fact of the seven days is hard and real. Yet still he cannot quite believe that he is to be sent away from his home, from Nanny and the nursery, from the garden, the high trees – all he knows and loves so dearly.

He jumps up, dresses, and soon it is time for breakfast. One of the budgerigars, belonging to Leo who is staying with his friend Tim, has laid an egg. For some reason this curious occurrence excites Vere.

When breakfast is finished he goes downstairs to the dining-hall. The front door is open and the flames of the spirit-lamps under the dishes on the sideboard wave and splutter in the gusts of air. His father is standing by the Chinese chest, glancing through his letters, and Vere kisses him good morning, then begins to step in and out of the sunbeams that cut across the oak boards of the floor. Smells of bacon, coffee, clean silver and hair lotion mingle in the room; envelopes are ripped; a maid moves along an upstairs passage and the kitchen door bangs.

Vere, silently, on his rubber-soled sandals, continues to play his intricate game until little by little he becomes aware of the prolonged hush that has fallen. He pauses, interpreting the sounds that are now important – Edith leaving his mother's bedroom, Mrs. Lark in her morning tantrum – then looks at his father. As if conscious of the attention focused upon him, although he does not raise his eyes, his father says, 'These are my call-up papers.'

Without understanding what his father means but sensing it is something bad and painful – frightened by this, yet at the same time flattered by the confidence, Vere blushes. He gazes at his father, wishing he could think of something to say. There is a steady silence.

'I've got to report in ten days.' His father speaks in the same surprised and injured voice, staring at the yellowish paper he holds in his large hands. There is another pause and then he raises his eyes.

Leo's birthday, Vere thinks with a start, before the picnic . . . When his father leant on his stick, watching and smiling sadly. Now as he gazes into the blue unhappy eyes he feels an identical sympathy, affection and tenderness. Nothing has changed – nothing ever changes. He is carried back to that other day, that forgotten moment. Yet everything is changed. His dreams and horrible awakening, his illusions and his disillusion – everything is eclipsed by the old and unexpected love that once more wrings his heart. He does not try to speak – he does not know what he should say – but his silence no longer seems to matter. He stands by the black and gold screen and the sunlight of a sudden seems to penetrate and warm his whole being.

His father moves. 'I'll just go and tell Mummy,' he says.

'All right, Dad.'

Vere watches his father mount the stairs in his restrained springing way, then goes through the open front door. The light makes him narrow his eyes. His unpredictable excitement has increased. He begins to skip over the lawn and to leap from daisy to daisy. He approaches the lily pool with caution, lies full-length on the paving-stones that already burn, and lowers his arm into the glassy water. He opens his hand and moves one finger. He wants a fish to mistake his finger for a worm and to swim close enough for him to catch it. He would not hurt the fish. He would only like to catch one, to examine it, to throw it high above the pool. How it would sparkle in the sun and splash as it fell! How grateful it would be! But perhaps the fall would kill it. Poor little fish!

He is filled with the desire to be bountiful. If he caught a fish he could give it back its freedom. He wishes he could think of something to give his father. But it is not only his father; it is everyone, everything – the pure air, the sky, the trees, the grass – the entire universe on which he suddenly yearns to confer his favour and his love.

His arm in the water looks broken and his finger – is that his finger? – really does resemble a worm. What if one of the ferocious carp were to think as he does? He struggles into a kneeling position and hoists his arm like an anchor. Rivulets bracelet his wrist, flatten and break up, and shapely beads of sunlit water hang on the tips of his brown fingers. He shakes his hand: the fish rise to the glistening shower: he jumps to his feet and the golden fish, with a fearful flashing shimmer, dive downwards and disperse. He runs round the pool, bounds up the steps and hops along the straight paved path.

Why is he happy? He cannot remember. When was he last as gay, lighthearted? Ages, years – a year ago, at least. Why is it, why? The sky was cloudless yesterday, the shadows equally sharp: the grass looked as green, the flowers smelt as sweet, the trees bowed as low and cast as fresh a shade. Today his father got a letter, that is the reason. What did the letter say?

He stops so abruptly that he stubs his toes against the ends of his sandals. What did that letter say, what does it mean? He sees old Harris by the summer-house, chases across and halts behind him.

'Morning, Mr. Harris!' he exclaims.

'Master Vere, you give me a start,' Harris answers, leaning on his long-handled edging shears.

'Mr. Harris, Daddy got his call-up papers this morning.'

The gardener adjusts his stiff tweed hat with a bent thumb and fore-finger. 'Ah, war's a terrible thing, Master Vere,' he says. Diamonds of sunlight, cut by the leaves of the trees, cluster on his rough clothes.

'Why?' Vere asks.

'Your Daddy'll have to leave his home.'

'Like going to school?'

'That's right, Master Vere.'

'He's only got ten days.'

'Yes, that's war.'

'Why do people have to go away?'

'I couldn't say, Master Vere.'

'I've got to go away, Mr. Harris.'

'Yes, we'll be missing you round the place.'

'I'll be missing you too.' Vere picks up the weighty shears and starts to clip ineptly. Harris opens a blade of his knife with his strong dark thumb-nail. The leaves rustle overhead and the diamonds glint and rearrange themselves. 'Daddy doesn't want to go away,' Vere says.

'He wouldn't want it.'

'Why do people have to do things they don't want?'

Harris, who has been scraping the bowl of his pipe with the knife, looks up. 'I don't know, Master Vere, that's just how it is.'

'I'll be gone in a week,' Vere says. Then he lays down the shears, thanks Mr. Harris and walks away.

Scamp the dog has followed him into the garden. She sits at a distance in her square Sealyham way, regarding him with deep indifference. Once or twice she sniffs, trying to point her rectangular muzzle; then she lowers herself stiffly onto the ground and starts to roll, emitting languorous growls and waving her fat broad paws in the air.

'Oh Scamp,' Vere says mournfully as he kneels beside her. 'Oh Scamp, oh Scamp.'

The startled dog rolls onto its four short legs and stares at Vere resentfully with its black eyes half-hidden by fur.

'Oh Scamp,' Vere says.

The dog growls. Vere tightens his grip of her head. He recalls nervously her evil nature – she once ate her puppies – and the fact that he has always particularly disliked her: and laughing at himself for his foolishness, he releases her suddenly and jumps away.

He continues to laugh and dance about the garden. He feels as if he is tearing off, layer by layer, an accumulation of thick hot clothes. He feels light and free; he fairly tingles with energy; and seeing Mal on the lawn outside the schoolroom windows, taking her regular twelve deep breaths of morning air, he runs towards her, calling 'Quel joli jour, quel joli jour!' and laughing now because she winces at his French. 'Let's have a game of croquet, ma petite,' he cries, and Mal joins in his laughter.

'I will beat you!' she chants as she lumbers indoors.

'Oh ma petite, ma petite,' he repeats, collecting a mallet and the croquet balls, whilst Mal stands in front of the glass adjusting her Robin Hood hat with the long feather.

He rolls the balls through the door, then runs and swings at them wildly. They spin over the smooth lawn, shining in the sun, and he dashes after them, waving his mallet and shouting to Mal to be quick.

She appears on the lawn – her mallet like a toy in her hand – addresses the black ball, sings out 'Vive le sport!' strikes the ball powerfully and pursues it as if nothing has happened.

Vere's eye is splendidly keen today. He seems to sense the track which each ball should follow, the speed and the angle, and he accomplishes feats which make him gasp and giggle. He is so happy. He loves Mal's cries of 'Croquet,' her quick aim and decisive shots, her snatches of song and vast good humour. Sometimes, watching her, he is overcome by that passionate tenderness the large woman is apt to provoke in him. Then he rushes at her fiercely, calls her 'ma petite', seizes her round the waist and tries unsuccessfully to lift her.

'Joue, chéri, joue, joue!'

The balls click and roll cleanly, into the shadow under the trees of the grove, out to the sunlight, through the hoops, against the stick; the heat levels over the lawn; the breeze abates.

'Vere! Where are you? Vere!'

'Mummy?'

Their voices carry and overlap.

'Mummy!' – 'Will you come here a minute, darling?'

He drops his mallet and runs to the far corner of the house, where his mother is closing the iron gate from the backyard. She kisses him and asks him why he did not come to say good morning.

'But Daddy had his papers,' he tries to explain.

'It doesn't matter,' his mother says. 'Darling, something's happened about school.'

For a moment he looks at her uncertainly, then he thinks: I am going to receive my reward. She will tell me I can always stay at home.

'I want you to answer me truthfully, darling,' his mother says.

Yes, he thinks, I will speak the truth, I will explain everything, when she tells me I need never go to school . . . And he gazes at her with his optimistic eyes.

'Tim's caught measles, can you believe it, and Leo's in quarantine.' She pauses, watching him.

'Oh,' he says, and waits for her to continue.

'It's awful, darling, but we couldn't foresee it.'

He does not understand.

'Leo won't be able to go to school until fifteen days after the term's started. I want to know whether you'd mind going alone too much.'

He looks away and immediately says 'No,' in a high polite voice.

'Are you sure, darling?'

'Yes.' He even smiles.

'I'm afraid it's rather a blow, isn't it? You could wait here and go with Leo. Would you like me to try and arrange it?'

'No, really, Mummy.'

'It means you'll be alone for your first fifteen days.'

'Yes.'

'Are you certain you don't mind?'

'Yes,' he repeats politely.

His mother is talking. 'Leo will have to come home today and you won't be able to see him, darling, I'm afraid. I've rung up Flora and she'd love to have you to stay. You could go down this afternoon.'

'Why can't I see Leo?'

'Because he's in quarantine, I've told you.'

'And I've got to go away this afternoon?'

'You haven't got to, darling.'

'To stay with Flora?'

'Well, I thought – '

'And go to school from Flora's?'

'Yes.'

'Does Nanny know?'

'Yes, I've just been talking to her.'

'All right, Mummy.'

'Wouldn't you like to think it over?'

'No,' he replies.

'It can't be helped, darling, these things will happen . . . I'll tell Flora you'll be coming.'

'Thank you, Mummy.'

They separate. He opens the iron gate and closes it behind him. The latch falls with an oiled metallic click. He places his foot on the first rung of the nursery fire-escape, grips the cold metal with his hands and drags himself wearily upwards. When he reaches the window he squeezes through it awkwardly and drops onto the floor. He lands on his heels – there is no spring in him now – hobbles towards the day-nursery door and enters the sunny room.

Nanny is sitting on the low chair by the fireplace, dressing Faith, and she says as soon as she sees him: 'Well, Vere, have you heard the news?'

He nods, shuffles to the sofa and sits down.

'Are you going?' she asks.

Again he nods.

'I told your mother I thought you probably would.'

'But Leo, Nanny . . .' His lip trembles.

'Well,' she says in matter-of-fact tones, 'you'll be on your own and you've always liked that.'

He stares at her with surprise and even resentment. Faith leans sideways, holding out her hand, and he closes her small fingers round his thumb and notes with a certain satisfaction that his lip is once again trembling.

'I'll have to go today,' he says.

'Only to Flora's,' Nanny answers, unclasping Faith's hand. 'And you'll be there a week. And you know how you enjoy being with Flora. You've been begging to stay there ever since she got married.'

He smiles weakly, feeling as he did when he dreamt one night that his little toe was being run over by a steam-roller. He begins to laugh – he cannot stop himself.

'Come along now, pull yourself together, Vere,' Nanny says, rising to her feet.

'But I'm going this afternoon!' he cries.

'Well, be a man about it,' she advises him. 'Are you coming out?'

'No,' he answers, suddenly injured. But the compliant laughter bubbles up inside him and he calls, 'Yes, all right, I'll come, but wait, Nanny, wait!'

He wobbles along the nursery passage, his knees bending in every direction and his arms swinging limply at his sides. He thinks of things like his bones – the bones in his feet which are surely incapable of supporting him, his blood which at any moment may refuse to flow and his flesh that he has heard is mostly water. He feels he is being dissolved by his frightful laughter, but the grisly humour of this thought makes him laugh louder than ever.

From the bottom of the stairs Nanny inquires, 'Have you thought what you'll want to take to Flora's, Vere?'

His laughter ceases. He catches sight of Faith's round eyes and open mouth, giggles painfully, then says 'Oh dear.' As he descends the stairs and follows Nanny towards the back door he repeats 'Oh dear' several times, feeling very miserable.

'Have you thought, Vere?'

'How could I?' he replies testily.

Nanny continues unperturbed. 'You'd better take your stout shoes because you're sure to be going farming. And what about your bicycle?'

'I can't take that,' he says. 'It's got a puncture.'

'Well, you can have it mended in Long Cretton.'

'No, I can't.'

'Why not?'

'Well . . . I won't use it if I do take it.'

'How do you know?'

'I just do, Nanny.'

'You take it, Vere, and then you can see.'

They cross the yard and pass through the garden gate. Faith runs under the apple trees, Nanny sits in a cane chair and starts to knit. After a time Vere throws himself onto the warm grass at her feet and says in the gloomiest voice he can muster, 'I suppose Rod might let me have a shot with his gun.'

'I expect he might,' Nanny agrees.

'It belonged to his father,' Vere informs her briefly. Later he says, 'Rod found some cartridges the other day, they're not made any more.'

'You'll have to ask him to let you have a shoot.'

'Shot, Nanny, shot!' he corrects her.

Time passes. Every so often Faith becomes absorbed in a piece of grass or a fallen leaf, picking it up and muttering to herself. Twice, her eyes shining destructively, she makes a dash for the flowerbed and Vere has to run and catch her. But she accepts the restraint with an innocent smile and toddles away as purposeful and unsteady as ever.

'Rod knows where some barn-owls have nested.'

'Does he, Vere?'

'They snore, you know.'

'No, I didn't know that.'

Nanny changes her knitting from one hand to the other.

'Nanny, would you like an apple?'

'Are they ripe yet?'

'The green ones off my special tree are lovely. Shall I get you one?'

'No, Vere, thank you. But get one for yourself.'

He goes over to the squat tree that clings to the crumbling red brick of the garden wall. His eyes follow the outstretched branches and fasten on a plump half-hidden fruit. His mouth waters as he reaches up between the leaves and begins to twist the apple on its stem. At the third twist it falls ripely into his hand. He carries it by the stalk so as not to disturb its subtle yellow-green bloom and runs back to Nanny.

'Look, it hasn't got a mark,' he says, dangling it in front of her.

'It's awfully green, Vere.'

'Oh but it's sweet and juicy, and really hard, Nanny. Are you sure you wouldn't like one?'

'Quite sure, thank you. You enjoy yours.'

His mouth and even his eyes water as he sinks his teeth into the crisp apple, and its sourness makes him catch his breath. Sucking, swallowing and smacking his lips, he munches for some minutes, then, turning the apple in his wet fingers, he questions, 'Nanny?'

'Yes, Vere?' she replies.

He nibbles. 'It doesn't make much difference, about school, does it?' he asks.

'What do you mean?'

'Going alone?'

'Leo went on his own.' He nibbles thoughtfully. 'You must fight your own battles, Vere. You don't always want Leo to look after you.'

'No, I don't,' he says.

'You're quite well able to stand on your own feet. Other boys have to and Leo did, so there's nothing so terrible about it. I'm sure you'll get along fine. Just work hard and persevere and then you'll succeed. And I've no doubt you will, Vere, none at all.'

He smiles with pleasure at her praise.

'Besides,' she adds, 'you've a nice week with Flora before you go.'

He finishes his apple. Nanny returns to her knitting, left elbow tucked against her side, right arm moving, eyes raised now and again for a glance at Faith who runs and tumbles harmlessly amongst the broken shadows.

'Was the apple good, Vere?'

'Yes, it was,' he answers, throwing the core over the garden wall. 'Nanny, I was playing croquet with Mal when Mummy called me and I never told her what had happened.'

'You'd better go and explain then.'

'All right, I will. Goodbye, Nanny.'

'Goodbye, Vere.'

Mal listens approvingly to Vere's edited account of what has taken place, then suggests that they finish their game of croquet. This reminds him of the time that must elapse before his departure, and he hesitates, wishing he could go at once, in his present brave mood. All the same he follows Mal onto the lawn, where the shadows of the white hoops shorten as the sun swings up into the sky, and, compared with Drake, plays out the game.

He leaves Mal and enters the house. Upstairs in his bedroom he finds Nanny kneeling on the floor in front of a small open case, and he helps her to pack it with the clothes and objects that suggest only the delightful life he will live at Little Lodge. At length however he forces himself to inquire about his school clothes.

'They can come down on the morning you go,' Nanny says.

'But you'll bring them, won't you?' An anxious tremor passes through him. 'You'll bring them down, won't you? I'll see you again, won't I, Nanny?'

'Yes, Vere. Quarantine or no quarantine, I'll see you off. So don't worry.'

His mother appears on the scene and asks if he would like to lunch downstairs. Because he has expected to lunch in the nursery and is unable to adjust himself to any fresh change in his precariously balanced plans, his face falls, and his mother, wrongly interpreting his expression, withdraws her invitation, looking away. She tells him she has ordered the car for three o'clock and speaks of the lovely time he will have with Flora. But before she leaves his room she kisses him, placing her hand at the back of his head and touching his cheek with her cool lips.

His father also puts in an appearance. He sympathises, whistles, admires himself in the long glass and asks vague questions, while his nailed boots crunch on the nursery linoleum.

'What on earth's that, old boy?'

'It's a hollow stick.'

'Why are you taking it?'

'I'm going to get Rod to fill it with lead.'

'What for?'

'Hitting people on the head and things.'

'Good God!'

Although his father does not refer to his own departure or anything Vere feels satisfied and relaxed, and is sorry when the unnecessary excuse is made and the boots crunch away down the passage.

Luncheon arrives. Vere has little appetite. As soon as he is able he goes out and says his various goodbyes, shaking old Harris by the hand and mentioning – unwisely – that they will meet at Christmas. Then he hurries up the cinder path. At the nut-hedge he pauses, remembering his purpose, and starts to study the ground with concentration.

It is here – here – that the fire burnt on Leo's birthday last year. That is where his father stood: here the ice-cream was churned: there is the bank on which he lay so happily. He stoops, stroking the green and gold moss. The branches of the nut-trees move and the moss is sprinkled with sunlight. How like that other day – how different! He wanders on.

He follows the drive – right and right again, directing himself as he used to direct Flora when she wheeled him in the Bath chair. Over there in the big field – far over, probably out of sight – he dropped his salt tears amongst the clover and discovered the nest of the friendly hare. He mounts the terrace, disturbing the noisy rooks in the grove, finds his secret path by the summer-house, pushes his way down it and arrives at the overgrown corner where his house once stood. A few dry stakes remain, pieces of plank, a mound of earth, earth with weeds – weeds everywhere. But there is the canvas satchel in which he used to carry provisions and string – there on the ground, rotten, discoloured. How did he come to leave his satchel here? He touches it with his foot. Why did he never build another house? One day he will.

He clambers over the wall and walks to the back drive. In the dust he can see the tyre-marks of Mr. White's motorbicycle. Beyond is the field where Contact galloped, and his father shot the pigeon in the green and misty wood. A cock crows at the farm. The heat seems to stifle all sounds, to slur them as it does the outlines of buildings and trees. The white doves coo and settle, an instant's trancelike afternoon peace descends, then the bell is jingled from the nursery window.

With his heart full of fond memories Vere climbs the fire-escape for the last time. After bidding Edith and Faith goodbye he picks up his case.

'Can you manage it?' Nanny asks.

'Of course I can.'

He heaves it into the passage and re-enters the nursery.

'There's the car,' says Edith, looking through the window.

'Now Vere,' Nanny instructs him, 'your mother's in her bedroom, so call in and say goodbye to her. And you'll get your bicycle tomorrow. I think that's everything. Well, you'll have to go.'

He glances at Edith. 'Nanny, is my yellow tie packed?' he asks.

'You won't want it, Vere.'

'Yes, I will.'

'It's too late now, I'll send it down.'

'No, Nanny – ' he begins to hop about with impatience – 'I must have it, I can't go without it!'

'Oh heavens, child.'

He leads her into the bedroom and whispers tensely, 'I couldn't say goodbye in front of Edith.'

They both laugh and she kisses him. 'So that was it. All right then, child – goodbye, and I'll see you in a week.'

'Goodbye.'

'Give Flora my love.'

'Goodbye, Nanny.'

He carries his case along the passage, dumps it at the top of the front-stairs, and goes and knocks on his mother's bedroom door.

'Vere? Come in.'

He opens the door. The blue blinds are drawn and the room is in semi-darkness. He says guiltily, 'Oh sorry, Mummy, I didn't know you were resting.'

'Come in, darling,' she repeats.

He feels his way round the screen and stands at the foot of his mother's bed. 'Did I wake you up?' he asks.

'No. Are you ready, Vere?'

'Yes, the car's outside.'

'Mary and Karen have been brought home from school . . .'

He waits for his mother to continue, then says, 'Oh, have they?'

'Well, darling . . .' There is an undecided pause. 'Have you said goodbye?'

'Who to?'

'Nanny?'

'Yes.'

The blinds flap softly and unnoticed lights – on a picture glass, across a mirror – shift and catch the eye. Through the gloom Vere can now distinguish his mother's head, sunk in a high square pillow, and he addresses it in a puzzled voice. 'I think I ought to go.'

'Yes, you must.'

He moves round the bed and kisses his mother. Her cheek is wet! He is so surprised that he starts and steps backwards. Is she crying – is that what it is – is her cheek wet with tears? But why? Why should she be unhappy?

'Goodbye, darling,' she says shakily. 'Let me know how you get on.'

'Yes, Mummy, I will.'

'When you arrive.'

'Of course, Mummy.'

'And darling . . . Goodbye then.'

'Goodbye, Mummy.'

He turns and tiptoes from the room, closing the door quietly behind him.

'Vere!'

'I'm coming!'

He pauses on the landing and takes a few deep breaths, then he picks up his case, relieved to be able to exercise his taut muscles, swings it lightly down the stairs and goes with Mary and Karen to say goodbye to Mrs. Lark, Ethel and Bella. Mal and his father are waiting in the front-hall when he returns.

'Goodbye, chéri, and good luck!'

'Goodbye, Mal.' He kisses her.

'Goodbye, old boy. Look after yourself.'

He kisses his father and looks freely into his eyes.

'You'll be leaving, Dad, in ten days, won't you?'

'Yes, we're in the same boat.' His father smiles gently.

'Goodbye, Dad.'

'Goodbye, monkey.'

They go out. Vere gets into the car, Mary and Karen jump on the running board.

'Gosh, I envy you – going to Flora's!'

Albert starts the engine.

'Tell me about the budgies' egg!' Vere suddenly calls.

'Ready, Master Vere?'

'Let me know about the budgies – whether the egg hatches, won't you?'

The car moves. Mary and Karen run beside it. Vere puts his head out of the window.

'You won't forget, Karen!' he shouts. 'Goodbye, Mal! Goodbye, Dad, goodbye!'

Scamp chases the car, barking. The cries of the girls grow fainter. The car gathers speed. Scamp is out-distanced. With a pang Vere sees her stop, sit down and heedlessly scratch herself. Then, intent on the happy life that is no longer his, he sees his father turn and re-enter the house, Mal and the girls make for the croquet lawn. The car dips down the incline. Only the upper windows of the house are visible, only the stone-tiled roof and the sky, only the arching green trees of the drive . . . But Vere continues to peer in the direction of the scene he can no longer see.

When the car stops at Little Lodge and Albert says, 'A week from now and bright and early!' Vere answers, 'That's it, Albert,' in a passably brisk voice.

After the car has backed down the lane he opens the gate in the wire-meshed fence and drags his case which again seems heavy up the short dusty path to the porch. The front door is open and he enters and calls, 'Flora?'

'Is that you, Vere? I'm out at the back.'

He follows the passage with its sharp left and right turns and emerges into the sudden light of the glass-roofed shelter behind the bungalow. Flora comes out of the coal-shed. She has a shovel in her hand and her cheek is smudged, and she smooths her hair when she sees him and smudges her forehead.

'Oh Flora,' he laughs.

'Did you shut the front gate, sweetheart? Chinky'll be off otherwise.'

He laughs again, as always pleased by the ceaseless Little Lodge activity, runs through the house, sees the mongrel Pekingese disappearing down the lane, pursues it and picks it up. Flora is in the kitchen which also serves as living- and dining-room when he returns, and he sits on the good end of the sofa and talks to her while she riddles the oddly-shaped range with its ovens and hobs. They speak of Chinky, of Rod who is harvesting, of the picnic tea they must prepare and take out to him, of the things they must first go and buy in Long Cretton. They do not speak of the circumstances of Vere's arrival. The room is shaded by the trees of the lane and the windows are open. On the high mantelshelf stand a clock with a loud tick, a photograph of Flora's wedding in a chromium frame, a Toby jug filled with used newspaper spills. Flora bustles away with the coal-scuttle. Vere chases after her with the shovel. They laugh; he unpacks his case and looks for Chinky's lead.

He calls to Flora when he finds it and she joins him in the porch, her scrubbed face shining and a basket with money in the bottom over her bare freckled arm. They lock the door and hide the key under the mat, forgetting the open windows, then set out for Cretton, Flora with her quick walk – toes a little turned in, knees a little bent – Vere pulled along by the dog

'What a thing about Leo, sweetheart, isn't it?' says Flora soon.

'Yes, I know,' Vere answers, and he tries to tell how everything has happened.

Talking, interrupting each other, sometimes laughing, full of relief and information, they walk in the centre of the tarmac road which blisters darkly in the sun.

But just before they reach the High Street Flora asks, 'Did you mind leaving, sweetheart?'

Oh Flora, why that question, he thinks. He looks straight ahead of him and does not reply. He cannot lie to Flora, cannot satisfy the demand for a brave answer the question has always contained: and he has learnt not to tell the unwanted truth. He meets Flora's eyes reproachfully. And they hold no demand, no pressure at all, no threat.

'A bit,' he says, and the admission as if by magic seems to remove an habitual burden from his shoulders.

'Yes, you would,' says Flora simply.

He longs to tell her more, really to tell her everything, and he recalls an impression he has attempted to blot out, of the group of figures which dispersed unfeelingly as he was being driven away by Albert. Breathing shortly, partly from distress, partly because of his daring desire to speak the whole and exact truth, he says, 'Mary and Karen went to play croquet with Mal when I was leaving.'

'Did they?' she comments, and her quiet continuing interest is like attention to his hurt – to all his hurts – soothing at last and healing too.

'Of course they got the afternoon off from school because of me.' His generosity surprises him. 'But I did mind awfully all the same,' he adds, smiling suddenly and feeling brilliantly happy.

They turn the corner into the High Street.

He asks her what she has to do. She fixes her eyes on some faraway object as she tells him; this, and that, and oh yes, the next thing. Then they exchange a look – one of those looks he only exchanges with Flora, wide and searching, often ending in laughter – and he goes and buys two ice-cream cornets. He licks one of them, meanders about contentedly, finds Flora and presents her with the other.

'Oh Vere, you shouldn't have,' she says.

'But Flora, you love ices.'

'I have got a sweet tooth.'

'Yes, you have,' he says.

They return to Little Lodge and prepare the picnic tea. Then they sally forth again, down the lane, over the meadows, up to the field where the yellow sheaves of corn are being gathered and stooked. Rod comes to meet them. They collect some sheaves and sit in the sunlight, eating their new-bread sandwiches, fresh doughnuts and cream-buns, and drinking their warm sweet tea out of individual bottles. Rod, his heavy forearms thatched with golden hair, uses the whole of his hand to grip his sandwiches and takes careful tearing mouthfuls. Vere copies him.

When tea is finished Rod and the other men rise to their feet, and roughly brushing off crumbs and calling to one another, resume their work. Vere carries the sheaf of corn on which he has been sitting and leans it against one of the nearby stooks. Flora shows him how to make a stook of his own and he starts to gather the sheaves, to stumble into line with them and to settle them on the ground in the correct fashion, shaking their heads together so that they hold and stand firmly. The stubble scratches his ankles, he itches all over and sweats, but he races backwards and forwards, fetching the sheaves he is scarcely able to lift.

Mr. Durrant the farmer appears in the field, wearing breeches and gaiters and kicking out his short bowed legs when he walks. He thanks Flora and Vere for their help and invites them to come to tea one day.

'Bring Rodney up,' he calls, strutting away with his hands clasped over the protruding flap in the tail of his coat.

Vere stooks the last rustling sheaves in his line and looks round. Flora is speaking to Rod, who pushes back his sharp-peaked balloon-like cap and frees his spiky upstanding forelock. The other men are moving towards an adjacent field, where the horse-drawn reaper clatters and turns. Some of them pause in the gateway and swig at their half-empty bottles of tea: one shouts and chases a rabbit.

Vere signals eagerly and runs ahead. Evening shadows are beginning to slant and sprawl, but the sun is still strong, he notes, determining to work for hours, until it is dark, even by moonlight. Rod and Flora join him. They gather and stook in unison, silently smiling at each other from time to time, while the reaper circles and slices the wedge of standing corn in the centre of the field, the sun slowly sinks and the sky changes colour.

But now Vere stops to watch the rabbits that bounce clumsily over the stubble, works for a spell, then stops to watch again. The insides of his arms and wrists are badly scratched. He tries to lift a final prickly sheaf, fails, sits down on it instead, and surveys the indistinct scene.

'We've done enough, sweetheart, come along home,' says Flora.

'Have we?' He smiles at her wavering outline, then shuts his eyes tightly and shakes his head. 'Flora, pull me up.'

He says goodnight to Rod.

'You ought to get paid for what you've done,' Rod observes in his quiet amused voice. 'We'll have to see about that. Night-night, Vere.'

Flora carries the basket, Vere swings a bottle in either hand. They wander between the stooks, sometimes separating, sometimes together. When they reach the stile they stop and look back. The reaper clatters across the red-gold fields, men faintly shout, but these sounds mingle with the nearer hum of swarming midges and the buzzing of flies.

'You're dropping, sweetheart, come along, come along.'

They trail up the lane and let themselves into the house. Vere enters his small room and puts on his pyjamas. Flora brings him a glass of milk. He sits on the edge of his hard mattress and drinks without opening his eyes. The sounds that he noticed when he stood by the stile still ring in his ears. Flora lifts his aching legs into the bed. She kisses him and draws the curtains. He does not hear her close his door.

After that moment at the top of the High Street when he told Flora how much he minded leaving his home, it never occurs to Vere to wonder if he is happy. The life that he leads absorbs and satisfies him; and because it is complete, because there is nothing false or discordant about it, he does not feel the need to withdraw or dissociate himself. The short days pass in a haze of activity, the nights in dreamless and unnoticed sleep.

These days at Little Lodge assume a pattern. Flora does not call him in the mornings. Rod has already left for work by the time he gets up and he breakfasts alone in the airy living-room. Then he helps with the housework and bicycles into Cretton to buy things for Flora. Rod returns for the midday meal. The afternoons and evenings they spend together in the fields.

On the few occasions that Vere is able to sit down and rest his stiff limbs during the days, he is overwhelmed by a powerful circulating drowsiness he cannot resist. One morning he nods at the breakfast table. This racking but pleasant tiredness surprises him, for he grows capable of longer and longer periods of heavy work, and by the third day is not more tired in the evening than he was when he awoke.

Although Vere accepts his life with Flora and Rod unthinkingly, certain aspects of it he knows that he loves in particular: Flora's forgetfulness, for instance, and the extra work this causes her, or the conscientious way in which Rod tackles the simplest task, or their harvesting, their picnics, the exhausted walks home. He loves the breezes that steal through the ever-open doors and windows of Little Lodge, the smell of frying sausages that makes the hour before luncheon a torment, the transparent red jelly that sets in the shade of the porch: and then the salt that is always damp, bread which crackles when it is cut, clear and icy water from the well – all these things Vere particularly loves. But perhaps without knowing it what he loves most of all is the deep sense of rhythm that these halcyon days engender. The tributaries of his hopes, fears, sorrows and joys are at last united, and the fulfilled stream flows peacefully, smoothly, irresistibly forwards.

On the sixth day of his stay there is a change in routine. No picnic tea is prepared, and at four o'clock Flora and Vere leave the harvesters and return to Little Lodge. They wash and tidy, then set out for Park Farm where Mr. Durrant lives with his sister.

The weather has continued perfect and this afternoon it is hotter than ever. They go by the road. Flora wears her crumpled white linen hat and carries a branch of elder against the flies. Vere walks beside the burnt grass of the verge, reminded of what awaits him on the following day and feeling for the first time restless, apprehensive and occasionally sad.

Arriving at Park Farm they ring the bell in the porch that is encrusted with ivy. Miss Durrant comes to the door and immediately leads them away to look at her aviary, her bees, her garden, her geese, and her brother's horses and greyhounds. Vere cannot concentrate on these wonders and is glad when they meet Rod and Mr. Durrant, enter the house and sit down to tea in the low oak-panelled dining-room.

When the many plates on the thick oak table have been cleared, Rod leans back in his chair and says smilingly, as if he expected everyone to laugh, 'Are you going to give Vere and me a treat, Mr. Durrant, and let us see your racers now?'

The farmer grins and gets up, and without apparently answering Rod's mysterious question, pulls out his watch, holds it in the hollow of his hand, studies it for a moment, then says, 'Right-ho, Rodney, yes, that's the time.'

'But where are we going?' Vere whispers to Rod, as they follow Mr. Durrant out of doors.

'You wait and see.'

They approach a black-and-white striped shed that stands in a grass field at the side of the house. A tremendous burbling, cooing, fluttering noise seems to rock this raised shed. In order to make himself heard above it Mr. Durrant shouts, 'Ever seen any racing pigeons before, Vere?'

'No!' Vere shakes his head.

'These are my beauties! Time for their fly-round! You stay with Rodney!'

He mounts the wooden steps and sidles through the door into the loft, closing it quickly behind him. The burbling increases. Suddenly a hatch in the side of the loft swings open. A cloud of pigeons, some brown, some nearly white, some grey, with their pale underwings and jewelled throats – a feathery swift cloud issues from the hatch and, swooping low over the field, begins to rise steeply into the sky.

A shiver runs down Vere's spine. The pigeons space out and lift magically above the tops of the elm trees. Turning, they begin to describe huge high circles round the farm. A white one is leading, a dappled one succeeds it, then a grey one, then another white. Dipping and soaring, each pigeon flying wildly, rapturously, they disappear from view behind the roof of the house.

'What did you think of that?' Rod asks.

'Oh they're lovely!' Vere cries, catching some of the soft feathers that swing in the still air.

Mr. Durrant opens the door of the loft and looks upwards, puckering his thin lips. He asks Rod to fetch some water, then turns to Vere.

'They'll be over Cretton by now,' he says, jerking his head towards the reappearing pigeons.

'Already?' Vere calls. 'But what are they going to do?'

'They'll be back shortly.'

'Here?'

'That's right.'

Vere moves into the field and sits down. He hears a bucket clink and the voices of Rod and Mr. Durrant, but although the sun makes him sneeze and blink, he cannot tear his eyes from the speedy circling birds. Mr. Durrant warns him to sit quietly, as the pigeons will soon be starting to home, and he and Rod position themselves beside the shed. Round and round fly the pigeons, in tighter and tighter circles, then with one accord they dive and skim across the field. The air rushes in Vere's face: he swivels, laughing, and sees the pigeons lift again over the elm trees. But now they are flying in a different way, stretching their long wings fully, allowing them to curve and droop, tumbling suddenly and twisting, then climbing almost vertically into the sky. They near the loft, playfully sheer away. The flock scatters. Pairs of pigeons rise one above the other, drop like stones, once more sweep up.

'Oh, oh!' cries Vere.

The pigeons begin to settle. Two are left, a white one and a brown. Sometimes their wings beat together as they soar and circle, sometimes the sun catches their pale feathers or colourful necks. High into the blue sky mount the two pigeons, then with a shudder they descend, flap hastily, alight. They enter the loft and the hatch is closed.

Vere leaves Park Farm, after thanking Mr. Durrant and his sister warmly, in a changed mood. Before going to bed that evening he eats a cream-bun and drinks a glass of milk in the living-room. Flora sits at the other side of the table, Rod on the sofa with his hands placed together and gripped between his knees.

'Do you remember the cream-bun I once ate, Flora,' Vere says, 'the day my tooth fell out?'

'Do you remember the bee-sting?' She laughs and covers her face.

'Do you remember when Nanny caught me smoking?'

Chinky lies in the passage, nose in a patch of rosy sunlight that streams through the open front-door. Faint sounds from Cretton, of a bus on the hill and the town clock, accentuate the busy quiet surrounding the bungalow.

'Do you remember that nurse when I was ill?'

Midges congregate outside the windows and juggle up and down.

'And the oranges with sugar?'

'And Mr. Bruise?'

'What happened when you were caught smoking?' asks Rod, who is never tired of hearing these stories.

Vere and Flora reminisce, their eyes shining retrospectively, their lingering laughter filling the silences, while Rod tilts his head and listens. Now and again Vere glances about him, imprinting the scene on his memory, treasuring each of the slowly-ticking minutes that seem to contain the whole essence of his stay at Little Lodge – all the love and the joy, all the friendship, all the freedom.

'Look at the time, sweetheart.'

'A little longer, Flora.'

'Come again, Vere.'

'I wish I lived here.'

'Come in the winter, then we'll take the ferret out.'

'We never shot with your father's gun.'

'Christmastime we will.'

'And you never showed me the owls.'

'They've flown now.'

'Have they?' says Flora, staring out of the window.

'There'll be some more next year.'

'Bedtime, sweetheart.'

The atmosphere alters. Vere imagines he can see his essential joy, so fragile, so marvellously strong, flit through the sunlit doorway. Perhaps because they have spoken of a future he cannot assume, of omissions now beyond remedy; perhaps because he became aware of it, or perhaps simply because of the relentless advance of life – that sweet mood passes.

Attempting to recall it, he says, standing up, 'Do you remember Leo's birthday?'

'You did enjoy that, didn't you?'

'Yes.' But then he thinks of his old criterion of happiness. 'I liked being here more,' he says.

He shakes Rod by the hand, bidding him goodbye, and goes to get ready for bed.

Everything is clear, everything complete. Even the passing of his gently joyous mood has left him with a sense of rectitude and peace. But now his desire for clarity turns on his arrangements for the following day, and when Flora comes to say goodnight to him he questions her closely. She explains that Nanny is arriving at nine o'clock in the morning with his school clothes and that therefore he had better breakfast in bed.

'Then you'll only have to dress the once.'

He asks what time he will have to go.

'Round half-past nine,' she tells him. And he will motor all day with Albert, picnicking on the road, and arrive at school about four o'clock.

'How will Nanny get home?' he asks.

'She'll take the bus.'

He kisses Flora goodnight and composes himself for sleep. Soon his interior flutterings become suspended, detached. The next thing he knows is that his curtains are being drawn and the early sunshine is flooding his room.

The moment Vere wakes he recollects the significance of Flora's action and his heart sinks. But something good inside him, something sound and solid, seems to act like a shield: and this sudden sinking of his heart, this awful descending feeling of dread and uneasy excitement, is miraculously arrested.

Flora brings him his breakfast tray and he eats hungrily his boiled egg, crisp toast, butter and jellied marmalade. Every so often he thinks of what is going to happen, stirring up feelings of dread and testing the strength of his extraordinary shield. As one after another these feelings are withstood and even repulsed, his uncertain spirits improve.

As soon as he has finished his breakfast he jumps out of bed and begins to run about the bungalow in his pyjamas. It is a fine September morning. The sun shines on the dewy grass, from which rises a thin low mist. Fresh breezes move the curtains at the sides of open windows, and the tiles in the passage are clouded in places with moisture. Vere is chasing Chinky towards the front-door, shouting and laughing, when he first catches sight of the big black car parked in the lane. He stops dead, and a great shaftlike shiver of fear plunges in the direction of his stomach. But once again his inner shield preserves him. The shiver seems to bounce off it and to shatter into harmless fragments. Shaken but unscathed, he calls to Flora and approaches the porch.

When Nanny sees him she says, 'Go in, Vere, go in for any sake – you'll freeze to death, child, without anything on.'

He laughs delightedly, tells her how tough he has become, and leads her into the living-room, where she and Flora embrace awkwardly. Then he takes his case from Albert, fetches Nanny, and with her assistance begins to dress.

For the last week he has worn only sandals, shorts and open-necked shirts, and the long black trousers he now climbs into, the socks and lacing shoes he puts on, and the stiff shirt that fastens with a stud – these unnatural clothes oppress him. But he has so much to say to Nanny that he scarcely notices what he is doing until the time comes for him to fix his starched Eton collar.

'Have I got to wear that?' he exclaims.

'Of course, Vere,' Nanny answers.

Together they tug and pull, bruising their fingertips, and eventually manage to attach the collar to the studs. Nanny slips on his black waistcoat and short jacket, and he goes to the mirror to brush his hair. And his heart sinks with new and horrible violence. His shield seems to bend beneath the blow. He cannot believe it will withstand this sickening onslaught, yet out of a curious perversity he continues to stare at his dreadful reflection, to look out of the window at the waiting car, and to strengthen the very forces he is trying to overcome. But his valiant shield holds. His horror and his fear retreat.

Nanny, who has been fetching his toothbrush, re-enters his room and regards him oddly. He is not surprised. He feels pale and ill, and wonders what would happen if his heart should sink again in such a way. For his interior armour now seems to disintegrate. In its place – in place of his protective shield – is something large and battered, raw, swollen and extremely sensitive.

Flora comes and asks how they are getting on, admires Vere's appearance and says she has coffee ready in the kitchen.

Before leaving his bedroom Vere looks round and says, 'The first night, Nanny, I went to sleep so quickly I didn't hear Flora close my door.'

'You must have been tired,' Nanny observes.

'That was when we started harvesting. I soon got used to it.'

'Well, it's hard work.'

'Feel my muscle.' He crooks his arm.

She squeezes it and says, 'Good gracious me.'

'You can't feel it properly because of these clothes.'

'Come along, Vere, let's go and have our coffee.'

They move into the living-room which Flora has tidied, and sit down. Flora pours the coffee out of the saucepan into three yellow cups, and Nanny says, after rummaging in her bag, 'While I remember, Vere, here are letters from your mother and father.'

He opens his mother's first. She encloses a pound note, which pleases him, and writes on thin paper in a small delicate hand, 'Darling, here is a little something for you to spend at school! Nobody's caught measles yet, luckily. I hope you have liked being at Flora's. I will bring Leo to school in two weeks, so it won't be long before I see you. This term is quite short and then it will be Christmas. Don't be too unhappy, darling. Fond love, Mummy.'

His father encloses two pounds, unevenly folded, and writes on one side of a double sheet of crested paper: 'Dear old boy, I've got to go off in a few days so probably feel a bit like you. No news here. The horses are being sold tomorrow. Most of the men have got to go into the army. I wonder what'll become of us all. Here's a bit of cash. Must close now – Daddy.'

Vere puts away the three pounds, lifts his cup of coffee which Flora has placed on the floor beside him, and takes a sip. The hot liquid seems to scald that sensitive lump in his diaphragm. He chokes, spilling a few drops of coffee, reaches for his handkerchief, remembers it is not in its usual pocket and begins to say, 'How silly –' But noticing Nanny's odd, watchful and almost stern expression, and Flora's wide tender look, he stops and rubs at the spots on his knee in silence.

'We had tea with the Durrants yesterday,' says Flora.

'Oh yes?' Nanny raises her cup, left hand spread beneath it.

'Vere went with Rod to see Mr. Durrant's pigeons.'

'Did you, Vere?'

'Yes. There were two . . .' He has so much to tell Nanny. The thought of it overwhelms him. He says, 'They were lovely,' and is thankful because of an unruly depth in his voice, a breathless quality he is afraid may betray him, that he attempted to say no more.

For a little longer they talk in polite strained tones. Then Nanny looks at the clock on the high mantelshelf and says, 'Well, Vere, you've a good drive ahead of you. I suppose you'd better be going.' And she stares at him solemnly through her spectacles.

He wishes he could instantly depart, but Nanny has risen and begun to unfold a black overcoat which has lain across the back of the sofa.

'Whose is that?' he asks, knowing quite well but wanting to say something light and possibly funny.

'It's yours, Vere. I'll help you on with it,' Nanny replies seriously.

'I won't need it,' he says.

'Yes, you will – it's sharp out.'

'But I was in my pyjamas! ...' The memory of that happy time in his pyjamas hurts him. He adds savagely, 'And look at all I've got on now!'

Flora says, 'But sweetheart, the front of the car's open and Albert's wearing a heavy coat.'

He turns and sticks out his arms behind him. While Nanny helps him into the coat he studies a corner of the ceiling. Then he says, 'I'm absolutely boiling as it is!' and looks round with a smile that trembles, still trying to make light of his impossible situation. But both Nanny and Flora now regard him solemnly and remain silent, so he returns to his study of the beamed ceiling and says in a deep jerky voice, 'The coat goes under my collar, Nanny.'

'Vere, I don't think it does,' Nanny answers.

He waits a second before saying, 'I've seen Leo with it under his collar a hundred times.'

'Are you sure, sweetheart?'

'Yes!'

'Well, we'll try it, Vere.'

He knows he is not believed. The insupportability of this further disagreement causes the sensitive lump inside him to swell. As Nanny struggles with the collar which already covers his waistcoat and jacket, and the tightness round his neck increases, the cruel pressure seems to bear directly on that lump, enlarging it moment by moment and paining him more and more. Yet he does not protest. He is certain he is right. And to give way over the collar would be to give way completely, to everything.

'There you are, Vere,' Nanny says finally.

He turns. Suddenly, because the collar is too tight, because he realises he has been wrong, because of the fond earnest glances that he meets, and the expectant hush, and all that has gone before, he is overpowered by violent anger, antagonism and resentment. He starts to say something. Burning damaging words rise to his lips. He makes a single unintelligible sound, then everything changes. His rage and hatred leave him. The whole edifice of conflict, control, containment of his grief, topples to the ground.

'I can't breathe,' he says.

'It's all right, child, it's all right now,' Nanny says quickly, removing the coat from beneath his collar.

'I can't go,' he says.

'You must, Vere.'

'I can't, I can't!' He clings to her hands.

'Say goodbye to Flora.'

Now it is Flora he clings to. He feels her lips on his face, sees her blue eyes. Nothing is distinct.

'Goodbye, my sweetheart.'

'Oh Flora, I can't.'

He seizes her jersey and her hands. Then it is Nanny he is kissing and holding.

'Don't!' he cries, meaning, Don't make me.

'Yes, child, you must.'

There are her spectacles above him and her straight eyes. He cannot move, speak, see or feel. He is robbed of every sense by his paralysing sobs. And he does not care about school. All he minds is being parted from Nanny and Flora.

'I can't, I can't . . .'

He does not know where he is, what he is doing. There is Chinky – the tiles in the passage – the porch.

'I can't!' he cries.

Please, Vere . . . Sweetheart . . . Child . . .

'No, Nanny . . . No, no, Flora!'

Albert helps him into the car. Nanny and Flora stand by the gate in the wire fence.

'I'm so sorry,' he tries to say.

'Be a good boy, Vere . . . Be good, won't you?' Nanny repeats.

He nods. Everything becomes blurred: Nanny, Flora, Chinky chasing the car, Little Lodge, a curtain blowing through an open window, the trees in the lane, the bright morning sunlight. He lowers his head and abandons himself to his sobs.

Very slowly, after a stretch of time which he cannot estimate, Vere pulls his handkerchief out of its new pocket. He wipes his eyes that are damp and sandy, and his face, hands and overcoat that are wet. Then he lays his hands with the fingers splayed on his knees to dry, and attempts to concentrate on the spasmodic movements of the needles of the black dials set into the dashboard. But he believes that he feels too miserable, too lethargic: therefore he sits hunched, blows out his hot swollen lips, allows his vision to become fixed and obscured. And again time passes.

'Sixty-five miles an hour!' states Albert unexpectedly.

'Really?' says Vere, looking out of the window.

Albert says no more, yet his single comment and the start of latent interest it has aroused force Vere to admit to himself that for some little while he has felt neither miserable nor lethargic, but strangely tense and excited.

He tries not to think of his strange excitement and continues to look about him. Birds swerve out of the thickset hedges, horses canter in a misty field. The car halts and a flock of sheep scuttles by. Vere returns the salute of the grave shepherd, watches his active dog, savours the warm smell of the animals, observes their yellow eyes.

And suddenly it seems to him that the world is not as it was. He cannot postpone realisation any longer: each object of the once more moving scene deepens his ache of wonder and of joy. For everything is changed. He thinks of Nanny and of Flora, then of sheep, shepherd, trees and pale blue sky, of all he sees, all he has known and may ever know – and he is not afraid.

'All right now?' Albert asks.

'All right,' Vere answers.

TUG-OF-WAR

ONE

It won't be any good unless I tell the truth.

I should have begun with the date: Saturday 14 April 1973.

God alone knows the whole truth, or if I'll be able or even if I want to churn out my version of it. The book I have in mind could finally wreck my relations with my family. Committing it to paper would constitute a threat, for the alteration of a few proper names never fooled anybody: a number of people, supposing it fell into their hands, would suffer still more damage. I definitely don't want that. And I don't want my private preserves to be trespassed and trampled on.

Why am I sitting at a writing table in a pub in Wales? What's the use?

An old-fashioned tale of love, kind modern readers might comment on the finished article. Having spent twenty-five years in publishing, at Nash and King, I'm acquainted with the fate of amateur authors like my present self, middle-aged idealists with a single story in them, the story of their lives, over which they've toiled for decades. Novels aren't popular nowadays. Confessions, however true, are hard to sell. As a rule they're rejected, not printed at all; or mocked in a brief paragraph by ambitious youth in a newspaper office, or, worse, ignored altogether.

I must remember my one month in which to write one book, and keep to the point. Years ago, twenty-five years ago, before I was married, in this very room, I anticipated my success in literature, in art, on my terms. My optimism was pathetic. I was quickly disillusioned. Everything's different now. My aim is not to snatch at victory but to mitigate defeat, or simply rid my system of the poison of the past.

Health in the sense of living for the moment, of clarity, a clear view of the future, and freedom – does it exist?

★ ★ ★

I'd written the above in an hour, in other words too slowly, when Mrs Elliott brought me in a cup of coffee. I hadn't asked for the coffee and at first resented the intrusion. But I realised that sooner or later her curiosity and mine would have to be satisfied.

I thanked her.

She stood in the doorway – thirty-ish, neat and fresh in her plastic apron, brightly eyeing my papers – and inquired if I was connected with this part of the country.

No, I said; I wasn't Welsh; was she?

Her husband's mother was, she replied; but she and Mr Elliott were Londoners. She'd been brought up in Kilburn, not far from Ravelin Road in West Hampstead, my home.

Since when had she been in charge of The Dellamere Arms?

Only for six weeks, since February.

She hadn't by any chance taken over from an elderly couple called Roope?

She shook her head, questioningly.

I explained that Mr Roope had been the landlord in the days of my previous visit.

'Oh – you've stayed here before?'

'Yes, once – it was after the war.'

'In the same room?'

She meant: is that why you reserved the room with the bow window?

'Yes,' I admitted. 'I came here after the war to be quiet and to write. And I've come again.'

'Are you a writer?'

'Not exactly. I'm a publisher. But I've some writing to do in the next four weeks.'

'Fancy!'

She was impressed by my literary pretensions, as those who never open a book are apt to be.

'Tell me,' I said: 'Llanwyn House – is it lived in?'

'Oh yes, by the boys – it's a school, Evelyn's Prep School.'

'I see.'

She bustled off, apologising for having interrupted me. Everything's different: Mrs Elliott's different from Mrs Roope who was so motherly and informative. My room's undergone changes: the wash-hand stand has been replaced by a washbasin with a point for an electric razor, the open fire is blocked and painted over, there's a red fitted carpet and a functional armchair. Out-of-doors the elms have grown – away to the left the Post Office and the cluster of cottages on the corner are scarcely visible through the sprouting green of the branches.

Evelyn's School would account for the goalposts in the water meadow. The lane outside the pub and below my window joins the Oswestry road by the Post Office. The water meadow is situated just across the lane. Enclosing it are the river Wyntrude on my right and, in the distance, the little stream of the Wyn. The Wyn flows down the hill, in a channel in the drive at Llanwyn, by the garden wall and under the chestnut trees, purling over the brown stones – or used to. It disappears beneath the Oswestry road and emerges amongst the roots of the ancient yew in the churchyard. Silver willows overhang the valley pool formed by the confluence of the Wyntrude and the Wyn.

Yesterday evening I unpacked and hunted through the telephone directory in vain, and walked along the river bank in the dusk, from Pub Pool by the hump-backed bridge to Wyn Pool.

Remembering is easier than to put my memories into words. I'd forgotten, or perhaps never knew, how reluctantly thoughts shape themselves into sentences, how creakingly rusty the brain can seem to be. Is it worth the effort, seeking my salvation at such prodigal expense, my own and others'? Yet I haven't the heart, I'm not humble enough to abandon my plans of literally years and allow that I was wrong. The various pressures on my month in the country, and the isolation and indeed the boredom, must be withstood.

I must hurry on, not wasting any more time in reflection. At least the weather's filthy – damp has clouded the lenses of my binoculars. The weather isn't tempting as it was in the spring of 1948. And boredom could be creative: Mr Nash said to authors from whom he wanted another book, 'Barricade your door and disconnect your telephone – you'll write in self-defence.'

Moreover the mention of Nash and King has a concentrating effect, like the prospect of imminent death. I'd rather be here than in my office. I'd rather be here than at Ravelin Road. Men and women need a break from matrimony, a holiday composed of a day off for each of the years they've been together: an arrangement that would entitle me to twenty-five days, plus a bonus of about a week for good behaviour. Especially as they approach middle-age, they require a period of peace in which to consider their situation minus their children, the shared solitude stretching ahead.

I've never been unfaithful to Mary, nor am I ungrateful. Her charge or her suspicion that my return to The Dellamere Arms represents the climax of a sort of prolonged mental adultery is a piece of feminine exaggeration. I'm trying to write a book. What climax is possible? She refuses to understand my acedia – isn't that the disease to which monks are said to be prone? Routine, repetition, even the repetition of rites that were once my pleasure, and playing safe and self-denial became unbearable. For instance, one night in March, a month ago, I went into our bathroom; Mary had rolled the empty portion of our tube of toothpaste round a patent gadget; I cleaned my teeth – and couldn't bear it.

I got into bed, switched out the bedside lamp, lay on my back and gazed at the squared pattern of the thermoplastic tiles stuck on the ceiling to cover the cracks. Mary in her bed was reading or looking at a fashion magazine, leaning on her elbow and with her free hand rubbing grease into her neck.

'I can't go on like this,' I said.

'What?'

'I can't go on like this.'

She stiffened slightly and asked in the lower register of her voice, pent-up, reproachful, if with a tinge of exasperated humour: 'For heaven's sake – what's the matter?'

'I don't know –'

'It's your indigestion.'

'Is it?'

She exclaimed emphatically, 'Yes!' as though she would have liked to strangle me.

She wasn't to blame for having rolled our tube of toothpaste. It wasn't her fault that she was tidy, housewifely, economical, enamoured of patent gadgets and repressive of my more extravagant fancies. She couldn't be expected to grasp the significance of feelings strange to both of us, which we refused to discuss. I'd never before noticed or minded the condition of our toothpaste tube. Yet it struck me as the last of many last straws, absolutely the final straw. She switched out her lamp; and the space between our twin beds seemed to widen into an abyss.

Perhaps indigestion was my trouble. Perhaps it was and is my age, the awkward age for men, she tells me – forty-six. Certainly I've been run down, and my nerves are in a bad way. One morning, again in March, I was talking to an American publisher and an American literary agent in my office. A bell or a buzzer sounded in the street outside, the note of which was precisely that of our alarm clock at home. I jumped and felt faint, sweated, and had to make an excuse and retire. The alarm clock was a wedding gift from Mary's younger sister Nancy Singleton, then a girl of fifteen, now the mother of four teenage children. It's always stood on the table by Mary's bed, and on approximately eight thousand occasions has roused us on the dot of seven-thirty. The similar ring in the street wasn't merely a reminder of my struggles to wake, it resembled a knell. Leaning over the lavatory in the washroom, not sure if I was about to be sick, I was forced to acknowledge that each of my days, my remaining days, had deteriorated into an endurance test and an ordeal.

I couldn't go on, embarrassing important American clients. I couldn't face the summons of the alarm clock and began to wake earlier and earlier, dreading it. From breakfast with Mother, Mary and my daughter Jean, from the race to catch my bus in West End Lane and the grind of my work at Nash and King, from arguments with Tom, my son, and evenings in my family circle, I had to escape. The worst of it was, on the one hand, my conviction that I couldn't continue as before, and on the other that I had no obvious overwhelming cause to discontinue.

The truth was buried in a remote fold of the Welsh hills. In a room in a lonely pub, at a writing table in a bow window, I may or may not be able to disinter it.

It's time for lunch.

Yes, notwithstanding my guilt and my regrets, I'm relieved not to be at Nash and King or at Ravelin Road.

Lunch consisted of sausages and mash and a bought blackcurrant pie, and was served by Mrs Elliott at a table in the single bar-room: the former division into saloon and public bars has been scrapped. Mrs Elliott had warned me that since nobody else was staying the food would be plain, a helping from whatever she cooked for her husband and two small boys. I was informed by Mr Elliott, a smart fellow in horn-rimmed glasses, that he's the licensee and not the owner of The Dellamere Arms – the Roopes must have sold out. Naturalists and mountaineers had booked for the Easter season, starting next week, he said. His trade today consisted of three old-age pensioners, sipping meditative half-pints, and a bland businessman from Oswestry.

Strictly speaking, I suppose it was the death of my father that once more set me on the road to Wales. He died on Tuesday 2 January 1973, as he had lived, bothering no one and with the minimum of fuss. He expired in the chair in his surgery in Root Street, Guildford, and was buried on Saturday 6 January in Shere churchyard. After the funeral I locked the doors of Deane End and took my mother home with me.

I saw him last, apparently in pretty good health, on the Tuesday preceding the day of his death, Boxing Day 1972 – not four months ago. Our family practice has been that we should spend our Christmases alternately at Thrushton with Mary's widower father and at Deane End, in spite of my mother's protests that it was unfair, I being an only child whereas there are four Singletons. Mary, Tom, Jean and I were at Thrushton, which is anyway adjacent to Deane End. On Christmas Day itself we had lunch with my parents, and entertained them to supper, according to custom. Then on Boxing Day we trooped through the garden gate to a tea party that was also an advance celebration of my father's achievement of his three score years and ten.

He'd be seventy on Monday 1 January. Mother had invited me to come down for it. But Jean, aged twenty, was being courted by Roger Smithson, a farmer and horse-coper aged thirty-two. The following afternoon, 27 December, she was to ride one of his horses in an informal steeplechase, and the plan was that we should watch her, collect her from the farm and motor on to Ravelin Road. Jean had already persuaded me to postpone my departure for London for twenty-four hours in order to meet Roger. I couldn't afford to be absent from the office on both days. 'Of course,' Father agreed, when I said I was sorry – he was the least possessive person. And Mother compromised by putting seven candles on her Christmas cake.

I've no recollection of the weather. The traditional sequence of events seemed assured and unremarkable. A sense of gastronomic surfeit had rendered me loath to turn out in the twilight for another meal, even to give Father his present and wish him well. Mary's elder sister Virginia, Virginia's husband Alan Band, Mary's father Henry Singleton, and Mary and I trod delicately through the mud of the gateway, while the children walked ahead of us, Martin and Annabel Band and Tom and Jean. On the steps by the Deane End lily pool Mary squeezed my arm, thinking sentimentally of our childhood and the rest of it in the connected gardens.

The french window was opened, and Mother and Father stood there smiling – Mother a solid figure with reddish hair, Father tall and bowed, benign, his spectacles glinting. He wore his threadbare tweed jacket and a new pair of grey trousers that appeared to be a bit loose round the waist. But I can't pretend that I paid particular attention.

Once, at the party, I registered the fact that he and Tom were chatting amicably at the top of the dining-room table. The back of Tom's long-haired brown head was towards me: over his shoulder I noted that Father was smoking a forbidden cigarette, a sure sign of his enjoyment. His right arm encircled the shoulders of Annabel Band, who was ten or eleven and standing by his chair, in his left hand with the broad cushioned fingertips he held his cigarette. His almost chubby face, a surprise considering he was so thin, was outlined against the oak panelling and the carved quadrangular motto above: 'This is the house that James and Vera Bartlett built in 1935.' He used to call it his worst joke, that untypically flamboyant motto, which for forty years he'd intended to have removed.

I reflected, or it crossed my prejudiced mind as Mary would say, that Tom's case might not be hopeless if he could still appreciate his grandfather, the apostle of moderation and tolerance.

Later, after the cake had been cut and eaten, Father went to his study to fetch his stethoscope for Annabel. We'd all loved to play with it, listening to the beating of one another's hearts and the rumbling of our stomachs, I and the Singletons, Tom and Jean.

I joined him for a private word. He was rummaging amongst the papers and the sample packets of pills in a bottom drawer of his desk.

I asked: 'Isn't the stethoscope still in the top drawer, Father?'

'No, I shoved it in here specially,' he replied. 'I'll have to tidy up this place.'

Mother's shopping and flower baskets and empty cardboard boxes were stacked waist-high against the walls. There was barely room to manoeuvre round the desk and wooden swivel chair. The bright overhead light emphasised the uncomfortable muddle.

'Mother's encroaching.'

'Yes.'

He smiled at our catchphrase, descriptive of countless invasions of our personal territory, countless interruptions of our bygone games of cricket on the lawn.

'Yes, but I'm as untidy as she is. I never have time to sort anything out.'

'Listen, Father, I hope you understand about your birthday. Jean's determined to ride in the steeplechase, she's mad on these wretched horses, and she wants us to provide moral support. I'll have to work all next week.'

'Don't worry. Festivities at my age are ridiculous, and not my idea of fun. Besides, we'll be seeing you tomorrow, we'll come along to the steeplechase, if it's fine.'

'I don't altogether approve – you know that, don't you? Who is Roger Smithson? And Jean's very young.'

'Yes, well – wait a bit. Wait until you've met him. She's a good sensible girl. They're good children.'

'Do you think so?'

He found the stethoscope. He straightened and, extending a veiny hand, supported himself on the desk.

He remarked, not answering my question, in an interior sort of voice: 'I shouldn't bend over, should I?'

Although he didn't mention the dizziness or whatever it was that I guessed afterwards he must have been feeling, I was suddenly a trifle anxious and therefore irritated – he was growing old.

'You shouldn't smoke.'

'No.' He gave me his inimitable look, raising his sparse wiry eyebrows above the white frames of his glasses, wrinkling his brow, as if startled by the acuteness of my logic and the wisdom of my advice. 'No,' he repeated, disarming me with his boyish agreeable smile and half congratulatory, half teasing pat on my shoulder.

We returned to the party. Sounds of conversation and laughter had filtered through the open study door: our exchanges had been less significant than my record of them suggests. I can't recall our goodbyes. He didn't come to the steeplechase. In seven days he was dead.

Yesterday I packed up at six o'clock. My hand ached from holding my pen. The rain had stopped; the clouds over the valley were like an inverted monochrome landscape of hills and rills; and I took a walk, not towards Llanwyn but turning right outside the pub, across the bridge and up the eventually steep incline to Penyboth. A few spring birds sang cautiously, as they do in woods, surrounded by their enemies. Ghosts not only of my father seemed to lie in wait for me round every bend in the road and behind every tree-trunk.

At dinner I compared Mr Elliott's smooth and impersonal service at the bar with Mr Roope's rubicund joviality in his tan-coloured knee-length apron, and Mrs Elliott's dingy frozen chop and tinned peas with Mrs Roope's fresh country fare. In my room, which smelt of beer, I was overcome with homesickness, with penitence as well as relief. But I resisted the urge to ring Mary.

Father's death was a break in the rhythm of my existence, anyway a break. I was in the exposed position common to those who have cared for and lost a parent. The brutal theft of our chance to resume, to carry on with our perennial talk, to see each other again and say hundreds of things, was my main preoccupation. Since death intervened, invariably in that unexpected manner, it seemed, priorities had to be reviewed and kept in order. If I'd understood before it was too late, I wouldn't have sacrificed Father to Jean and thus missed his birthday. And as far as my own schemes were concerned I couldn't procrastinate.

Death makes us egoistic. I grieved – that is, I was sorry for myself and resolved to waste no more opportunities. Additionally, although so fond of Father, I was aware of the removal of a restraining influence: I couldn't have fled from my family to The Dellamere Arms if he were alive. I loved him – but was forcibly initiated into or reminded of the complexities of the emotion. Loving and being loved, being depended on not to hurt or disappoint, is a type of repression, a gentle tyranny. Our single clash of wills, from which Father emerged the victor twenty-five years ago, was remembered. Whether or not he was right, I wanted to try to reverse that decision.

Inevitably resentment enters into love. But mine was confined to his dying, it was a development of the irritation which the signals of his getting older had summoned – nothing else. He was the most admirable man I've come across, the most patient and cheerful, a model husband and an excellent dutiful doctor. His faults were minimal and contradictory: a certain rigidity and a human readiness to yield in the interests of peace in his home.

Poor Mother! She was brave at the funeral. Her helplessness, her gratitude to Mary and me were touching; and we couldn't have left her alone at Deane End. She was sixty-nine, had known Father for close on fifty years and been married for forty-seven – happily, by marital standards. Her activism, which had suited him or to which he had adjusted, was quenched by tears, unlikely tears shed in unlikely spots, for instance at the sink in the scullery where I discovered her sobbing one morning. But after three or four weeks at Ravelin Road she – in a word – encroached.

The difficulties that arose from my having my mother and Mary having her mother-in-law in the house are the stock subject of music-hall jokes. Life can be horribly hackneyed. Mother's energetic, has a strong personality, was accustomed to battling on behalf of her charities, and was now unemployed; Mary hasn't much energy, she's unworldly and inclined to be inarticulate, was busy, busy and house-proud, and at an extra disadvantage in that she's been bossed about by her so-called Aunt Vera since she was a child. Their predictable wrangling and mutual complaints I was more or less able to ignore, until Jean announced her engagement to Roger Smithson.

Partially to explain or excuse my conduct, without delving into the distant past for the key to my relations with my parents and wife and children, I ought to mention my physical exhaustion. For six or seven weeks I'd been going to Deane End, spending the Saturday night there, packing clothes and books, docketing furniture and organising, preparatory to the sale of the place. Either Mary or Mother had accompanied me: but they were respectively self-pitying and self-righteous, and equally reproachful; and they could have spared me their assistance, I often wished.

It was a Friday evening early on in March. I got back to Ravelin Road at seven o'clock after a gruelling stint at the office. Mother was in the kitchen on the ground floor, cooking, basting a large expensive joint of beef rather grimly.

'Tom's popping round to dinner,' she said; 'so I told Mary I could cope.'

The implications of her non sequitur were ominous, and, into the bargain, I was immediately annoyed that she should have bought beef for the delectation of Tom. But I held my tongue and climbed the stairs to the sitting-room, where Mary was waiting for me. She was bitterly angry against Mother who, she claimed, was using her money to bribe and alienate the affections of our son and daughter. She'd ordered a nice meal for all of us, she added, and had been banished from her kitchen.

For some contrary reason I inquired: 'Does it matter?'

'You're on her side,' Mary accused me.

I retorted, 'Oh for God's sake!' – left her crying, continued upstairs and ran a bath.

I wouldn't have been so unsympathetic but for the accumulation of difficulties. I seethed and quivered, arming myself for the crisis in store, and was hardly calmer when I descended the stairs to the kitchen at a quarter to eight.

Mother was tinkering with the pots and pans – she was always a noisy cook. Mary was laying the table. Tom had arrived. He wore a purple T-shirt and his bleached patched jeans, and lolled in a chair, the ankle of one leg hooked on the knee of the other.

He greeted me with a wave of his hand. He addressed the company – aged twenty-two. He was going to buy a bigger and better car, tour Spain in the summer, and was thinking of chucking his job: a friend of his had asked him to teach English to Spaniards in Madrid.

I pointedly offered him a drink, having noted the full glass of whisky by his elbow.

'I've got a drink,' he replied, avoiding my eye.

His job in an estate agency, which paid nearly as much as mine at Nash and King, was an old bone of contention. The idea of his chucking it, the idea of his teaching anybody anything, his ingratitude, selfishness, rudeness and arrogance infuriated me. Moreover his inconsistency was beyond the pale, his eager participation as a socialist in the joys of capitalist society and his intention to visit and even work in 'fascist' Spain.

Mary, to protect him from my wrath as usual, tried to change the subject: had he brought along the dirty washing from his flat? Mother reverted to his new car: if and when Deane End was sold, she'd like to contribute to the cost of it.

These unfortunate interjections corroborated my view that Tom was thoroughly spoiled and again in need of corrective treatment.

Jean came in. I'd recognised her brisk light footsteps in the street. She threw open the kitchen door and stopped in the doorway.

'Sorry I'm late – I'm engaged.'

My memories of the ensuing scene are confused. There were exclamations. Kisses were exchanged. At length Jean stood in front of me.

'Well, Pa?'

'Well, darling!'

I too kissed her.

Soon we sat down to dinner. The beef was placed on the scrubbed deal table. I was about to carve – Jean and Mary were on my left, Mother was on my right, and Tom was pouring out wine.

Tom said: 'Have you fixed the date for the wedding?'

'No, but Roger doesn't believe in long engagements.'

'Doesn't he,' I began: 'doesn't he?'

I don't know what I felt. Mary assured me afterwards that I was simply jealous. I don't know what it was I expected to gain – or not to lose – by ruining everything. But I was driven on by the events of the evening, the day, the preceding three months or indeed quarter of a century. Jean with her sweetness and freshness seemed too young to marry, at any rate to marry Roger Smithson, who hadn't made a good impression on me at the Christmas steeplechase.

'I'm afraid I can't agree,' I declared.

Tom dared to challenge me. He trotted out some hoary adage about the freedom of the individual. By freedom, I countered with excessive warmth, I took him to mean his freedom to do exactly as he pleased and say whatever was or wasn't in his head, regardless of the consequences. I dragged in his drinking of my whisky, his allowing his mother to wash his clothes, his pocketing superfluous subsidies from his grandmother, and his trip to Spain, and the convenient flexibility of his socialist principles.

'Honestly, Pa,' he protested, very flustered and red in the face – his expression was startled, a travesty of his grandfather's inimitable look, pitiful but also pitying, pitying me because I was a reactionary has-been: 'honestly, Pa, I don't have to listen to this.'

'No! You're free not to. But surely according to you I'm free to speak my mind. I'm free to disagree with Roger Smithson. It's a free country, as it wouldn't be after your bloody idiotic revolution!'

He pushed back his chair and stalked out of the house, slamming the front door.

We'd had rows before, but none so serious or with such a melodramatic conclusion. When the hubbub had subsided, I asked who was hungry, harping on the melodramatic note.

'I'm not,' Mary exclaimed, and then, in an outburst as unnecessary as mine, glaring across at Mother: 'I couldn't have eaten that meat – ever!'

'What a waste,' Mother responded levelly.

'Well, it started the rot, didn't it?'

'Mary, are you trying to be unkind?'

I banged the carving knife on the plate, but without effect.

'No, I'm sorry, I don't like the tone of Mary's remarks. I feel I'm not and haven't been welcome here.'

'Oh Mother, really!'

She turned on me: 'No – you're not kind. You're not kind to your children. What would your father say?'

'Shut up, Mother!'

She left the room. Mary shrilled that she hoped I was satisfied and followed her – by definition quarrels are unfair and platitudinous. Jean and I were alone.

She put her elbows on the table and, half-clenching her fists, rested her forehead on them. She was wearing one of those high-necked cotton pullovers; it was pale blue; and her hair, gold and brown against the blue, fell forwards across the side of her face.

'Darling Jean –'

'Don't, Pa,' she said. 'Don't!'

The episode as a whole was absurd: the groaning board, the general exodus. I apologised to Jean and withdrew my objections to her engagement. I apologised to everyone, ringing up Tom at his flat to beg his pardon. Later, reunited, the family consumed beef sandwiches in the sitting-room. But for me, secretly, Jean's three words of denial, which repulsed and repudiated, were comparable with Father's death.

I realised in the sleepless stretches of that indigestible night – with increasing certitude I realised it: the straightforward path was blocked, impassable.

Another painful phrase is associated with Jean's in my heart, uttered by Mary. Again we were in the kitchen at Ravelin Road, Mary and I, she standing with her back to me by the window, I sitting on a chair by the deal table. It was three weeks ago, a fortnight after the great row, seven-thirty or thereabouts.

In spite of having rehearsed my speech I hesitated and stuttered: 'Listen, darling, I've been thinking – I must have a little holiday, I must get away.'

She swivelled and said, wistfully smiling, misapprehending me: 'Oh yes! Oh yes – where shall we go?'

Mary was unable to acknowledge and accept my desire to be on my own. When I confessed to the booking of my former room at The Dellamere Arms and that the dates of my projected holiday coincided with those of last time, she grew angry.

'Don't bother to come home,' she cried.

She was just as tired as I was, she argued; she longed to get away; but what would I have said if she'd decided unilaterally to leave me in the lurch? I was more selfish than Tom. I was to be permitted to gratify my whims, which were adulterous, childishly unreal but adulterous, while she remained faithful and approving? – No, thanks! She'd always let me off too lightly. Since I was deserting her, and Tom would be in his flat, and Jean mostly with the Smithsons on the farm, and my mother at Deane End, she considered herself at liberty to alleviate her loneliness as she chose.

Her practical problem was that she couldn't alleviate it at Thrushton. Although reconciled with her Aunt Vera, whose return to Deane End to complete the packing was more sensible than sulky, she was averse to a month in the house next door to her mother-in-law. Eventually it was settled that during my sojourn in Wales she would stay with her sister Virginia Band, near Plymouth. I personally telephoned Virginia in order to dispel any suspicions that Mary and I were parting.

By then George King at Nash and King had been tackled. No doubt he was alarmed by my unwonted assertiveness. I was released from my duties for four weeks. A directorship in the firm was hinted at. But none of that's important.

Seven days ago, last Sunday 8 April, I was at Ravelin Road. Mary handed or threw at me a yellow wallet of snapshots – we were in the sitting-room upstairs. The Bands' joint Christmas present to Henry Singleton had been a camera with a flashlight. He'd had his snaps developed and sent copies to his daughter. I flicked through blurred garish pictures of Thrushton and the tea party at Deane End, of Annabel Band with the stethoscope in her ears and Father blowing out the candles on the birthday-cum-Christmas cake. In another picture an elderly stranger in glasses was fiddling with a paper hat. I was on the point of asking Mary to identify him, when I recognised myself.

Objectively and in comparison with recent sorrows and shocks, it was nothing, a laughing matter. But I looked so haggard, lined, worn and faded – literally a stranger, a used envelope in which my soul with its untapped ardour had been sealed by accident. I remember sitting motionless on the sofa, sitting and staring at the likeness which wasn't like me, and sweating with fear and misery. The message of the snapshot was that life had already or almost passed me by. Father was buried, Jean would belong to Roger Smithson, and Mother, Mary, Tom and my routine were no defence against the prospect of impending annihilation. Alternatives to my pilgrimage to Wales were obliterated by my sense of panic.

Yes, it's Sunday again, my second full day of writing, ten o'clock. At six this evening I broke off and slept on my bed. On waking I washed and had supper, and went for a short walk along the Penyboth Road. The exercise and the night air were refreshing.

Up there amongst the trees, in the resonant spring silence, it occurred to me that each of the reasons I've advanced to account for my presence at The Dellamere Arms was negative. Turning at the top of the hill, facing across the valley of the river Wyntrude, I wanted to add a positive coda to my explanation of why I happened to be in a dark Welsh wood.

My desire or my obsession was to recreate exactly the circumstances in which I once fell in love. By writing the story I might fulfil a life-long ambition and ease some of the frustrations of my previous visit.

Well, I've begun my book – and the cost of it all has seemed to be too high. Concern for Mary, concern for our marriage – remorse has led me to try to justify my actions. Have I injured Mary and Jean irreparably, and detached myself from my family for ever? A host of second thoughts has congregated round my writing table, compelling me to prove the impossibility of any course other than that pursued.

The impossibility was relative: in truth I could have soldiered on. But my priority, what came first with me, was a certain ideal of love, of art, my single book – or, in less pretentious or less childish terms, the time that my father said he never had in which to sort things out. Walking downhill towards the pub I surrendered to the exclusive yearning to recapture the mood that's haunted my imagination for twenty-five years, my experience of beauty and my youth. Through the branches of the trees, under the line of the horizon opposite, I'd caught a glimpse of the lights of Llanwyn House.

TWO

I was born on 10 May 1926 and brought up first in the terrace house in Root Street, Guildford, where my father had his surgery, then from 1935 onwards at Deane End. In Root Street our neighbours on one side were called Singleton, Henry and Mabel Singleton and their children Harry and Virginia, Mary who was my age, and Nancy who was two years younger. Henry Singleton was my father's friend, a solicitor, a tall bulky man with fine straight brown hair which he oiled and brushed back and which formed points and spikes above his collar. In the war, in an air-raid at night, I saw him with his hair disarrayed: I feared the country was done for.

Henry and my father, James Bartlett, prospered in their legal and medical practices. Round about 1930 they bought a piece of cheap land on the Hog's Back, overlooking Guildford, and, splitting it, each built a house there, Thrushton in the Georgian style and Deane End more in the Tudor. They were follies, those houses, even if they've trebled or quadrupled in value; at least ours was far too big for the three of us and our maid of all work Amy Shift. Henry needed additional space for his family and might have had the odd delusion of grandeur. But neither he nor Father would have spent so much money except to mollify their wives.

Mabel Singleton was extremely energetic until her illness and death in 1963. She reared four children, was the motive force behind Thrushton, entertained, served on committees, raising funds for charity, and competed with my mother. She had a broad catlike face and commanding eyes, brown and deep, and a curling catlike mouth. Mother was her junior by an undeclared number of years, not without her attractions, I imagine, although somewhat ungainly: her heavy legs distressed her, and her soft waxy skin. Her auburn hair grew tight against her head and was cut very short, and her manner of speaking was sibilant and indistinct.

When Mary and I were apprehended in our infantile crimes, Mary's mother would say, 'No, I'm sorry, I won't have that,' and fix us with her feline gaze, whereas mine would hiss and nag, 'What the devil are you up to? Destroying my flower beds? Smoking? You ought to be ashamed of yourselves. I've been watering those flowers for weeks. I'm sure you stole those cigarettes. You little beasts . . .' and so on.

Mabel was the daughter of a local landowner and had married beneath her station; Mother had been a nurse and my father's receptionist and married correspondingly above hers. The five years that it took to plan and complete their houses were the blue period of the rivalry. Beginning when I was four and continuing until I was eight or nine, it reinforced my earliest intuition that Mother had better things to do than to study my welfare and entertainment. She wasn't maternal, she admitted in my hearing. I don't blame her – I wasn't paternal towards Tom; and I was doubtless a dull boy; and preferred Father.

We used to spend hours, days in all weathers, on the site of Thrushton and Deane End, Mother and Mabel, Mary and I, and often Nancy Singleton in her pram. If we children became friendly with any of the workmen, we'd be told not to hinder. The waiting, the cold and wind and rain and mud, and the edgy altercations with architects and town-clerks depressed me. Yet if I asked to be allowed to stay at home, Mother said she was afraid I'd only play with Amy Shift and learn to speak with an accent; besides, I should be interested in the progress and proud of our new house.

At some stage it was discovered that I was shortsighted and would have to wear glasses. Mother wasn't particularly sympathetic. She was competitive – snobbish – in every conceivable direction. She called me her mole and her bat, referred to my goggles, and broadcast the joke of my never having known where the drainpipes went. Strangely enough my glasses improved my moral as well as my physical vision. I felt she ought not to draw attention to my disability: from which, nonetheless, I derived the satisfaction of thinking that it made me more like Father.

My joys at home in the order of their importance were the company of Father; any sign of condescension from Mary's elder brother Harry Singleton, whom I hero-worshipped; and playing with Amy Shift. Amy belonged to the race of solitary troglodytes of indeterminate age who used to be absorbed into middle-class households. She was a small ugly spinster from Mill Hill, London – her accent was

Cockney: a bit of a simpleton, but adept at mortifying her mistress. After our move into Deane End, when Mabel Singleton at Thrushton employed a maid in a white cap, Amy in her aggressively soiled apron and down-at-heel slippers would march into the drawing-room and scream out that supper was ready. She insisted on addressing Mother as Mrs B. They squabbled for thirty years. In the end she had a stroke and was incapacitated for eighteen months. Mother, although of course she cursed her luck, fed and tended her invalid retainer throughout, refusing to commit her to the sort of institution she would have loathed.

With Amy I manufactured peppermint creams and baked miniature pies for my tea. I saw Father, at most, for an hour each weekday – he was a popular and conscientious GP; and Saturdays and Sundays were associated with the sudden cancellation of treats, because he had to visit a patient. I just sensed that he wished he could spend more of his time with me. I loved his large hands with the cushioned fingertips, his faint clean smell of surgical spirit, his calm, his knowledgeable reasonable conversation, and the fact that reserve was unnecessary between us, and the accolade of the surprised delighted expression which he bestowed on my accomplishments.

I loved to bask in his favour. Our annual family holiday, usually by the sea, occasionally on his brother's farm in Bedfordshire, was the happy climax of the year. But the happiest day of my boyhood was devoted to a fishing expedition from Root Street. We set off in an autumn dawn, Henry Singleton and Harry, Father and myself aged about eight. We motored through a clearing mist into the sun and arrived at the gravel pit that had been flooded and stocked with fish. Under shady trees, where we had a snack of coffee and cake, Henry Singleton amused Father by saying: 'Well, James, not a white elephant in sight, thank God!' – the mysteriousness of which allusion to Thrushton and Deane End impressed it on my memory. We cast our lines and settled down to watch the floats. Russet leaves dropped from the overhanging branches, swaying through the air, alighting on the still water. Whether or not we caught any fish was beside the point of our being together and out of range of encroachment.

Soon afterwards I started school. Father intended me to go to a state day-school, but Mother picked Treadles, which had the advantages in her eyes of being more expensive and smarter; and it boarded the boys. I passed two uneventful years there. Then a talented master, Mr Grinling, joined the staff. He was a dry dusty bachelor and perfectionist. He taught me to work and to enjoy working. He introduced me to the rewarding sensation of development through my own efforts. The upshot was that at his instigation I sat for an open scholarship to Eton College.

I won the scholarship. Father was congratulatory, but seemed to have reservations about my claiming my place at Eton. I was disoriented by my achievement, impatient to pluck further laurels, and influenced by Mother. She was thrilled: Harry Singleton had been average at his lessons. She'd stolen a march on Mabel – her son would be at the smartest school in the country. She was quite dazzled by the reflection of my glory, as I was by her adulation. The strength of her personality, the unpredictable kindness which later on rendered her protective of Amy, her reluctant reliability and her activism which was both relentless and jolly, were switched on me like a spotlight. Instead of being suffered, I was praised and courted. And I realised what I'd missed.

The process was slow and obscure. I and no one else failed to avail myself of the opportunity of Eton. Yet, homespun psychology apart, a few unenthusiastic reports on my career as a public schoolboy confirmed my suspicion that Mother cared more for success than for me. She showed her disappointment in my low marks in exams and lack of prizes; and the withdrawal of her confidence, in which I'd revelled temporarily, stirred up a resentment attaching to past and present.

The effect was my almost deliberate unwillingness to try. I wasn't prepared to be loved for the uncertain quality of my scholastic performance. I wished to please by being, not by trying. I as it were rewrote the whole story in terms of her carelessness and my humiliation, and deduced that she was in my debt, she owed it to me to please, rather than vice versa. We didn't see our respective responsibilities from the same angle. She nagged me to do better, with the result that I did worse.

Father remained neutral. Once he remarked in private: 'You've proved you can if you want to, that's what matters.' But I felt he wasn't entirely on my side. His detachment towards my Etonian experience discouraged me. He was right in his belief that the scholarship would sever valuable links with my background. My intellectual abilities weren't stretched by any other master; and I was poorer and less versed in the ways of the wide world than my schoolfellows, while, thanks to them, more sophisticated on the surface than my former friends at Deane End. In defence of Mother, I'd add that her reactions to my ups and downs were idealistic, inasmuch as snobbery is the common or garden form of idealism. But such sage opinions weren't forthcoming at the time. The declaration of war in 1939 suited my mood.

The secondary effect of my resentment, my isolation, was an addiction to reading. Books were my escape from my circumstances – books and my identification with the bold beloved heroes of the printed page. Inevitably, when I should have been working, I composed poetry; and having scraped through my School Certificate, a disgraceful business considering I was meant to be a scholar, enlisted in the army.

That was in 1944. I trained for a year, fought nobody, was never even posted abroad, and waited for my demobilisation in 1947. One day, during a spell of intensive training at a camp in Shropshire, I was given a map reference and ordered to get my platoon to it cross-country. We tramped over hills and dales in the heat of a summer's afternoon and reached our destination, a sequestered ivy-clad pub by a cool river, The Dellamere Arms. Its setting in a golden valley on the Welsh border, the geniality of its landlord, the frothy potency of its beer, and the river fringed with reeds nearby, gushing and gurgling under the humped bridge, stuck in my memory.

The idea was already dawning on me that I could be a professional writer. Romantically, also, in the course of a weekend's leave I was kissed by Mary Singleton. She was a member of the group of my Guildford friends from whom Eton had cut me adrift. After finishing at school, she learnt to type and took a job in her father's office. At intervals I met and talked to her – we were next door neighbours – but in a spirit of patronage. I was an Old Etonian, she was a secretary; I was a literary man in the making, she was blissfully ignorant of literature.

But the glamorous girls I hoped to seduce were either occupied or in the services or engaged to be married, and I fell back on Mary. We went to cinemas, swam and played tennis, lay on the lawns of Thrushton and Deane End, listening to records, and in the winter we tobogganed with other Singletons: Nancy was always around. Mary was nice to look at, of medium stature, brown-haired – she had lovely thick wavy brown hair; and her prominent sharp nose didn't detract from the sweetness of her smile. Her skin was white, the veins underneath were visibly blue, and her voice was high and quiet, and she was shyly poised. She was conscious of her dignity and wore neat crisp clothes perhaps more fitting for an older person.

My animal impulses, verging on the incestuous, for she might have been my sister, were stifled. I hoped to share my secrets with her, not seduce her. I counted on her allegiance, as in the days of our companionable childhood. Her nickname in her own family was Granny. I teased her: she was my Granny. Such was roughly the state of our relations when I invited Mark Connors to stay at Deane End for a pay-party in a large house in the vicinity, Yarrow Grange.

It was in November 1946. Mark Connors was my brother officer. He, Mary and I were twenty; Nancy was now eighteen. Mark was to be Nancy's escort for the evening. But at dinner he chatted to and flirted with Mary. He drove her over to Yarrow in his two-seater Morgan, while I drove Nancy in Father's Rover, and at the party he danced with her non-stop. I was most put out. At length, catching her alone outside the cloakroom, I told her she must choose either to come home straight away or carry on at the party and cram herself and Nancy into Mark's car.

She chose the Rover, in which we proceeded to have a stupid argument. She had behaved badly, I said. She repudiated the charge.

'My behaviour! You ignored me and drank too much.'

'I did not drink too much! And you ignored me!'

She exclaimed: 'Fiddlesticks!' in the lower dismissive register of her voice.

She'd never so defied me before. I was boiling with rage, which actually seemed to amuse her. We argued the point from Yarrow Grange to Thrushton. I braked to a violent halt by her front door.

'Good night!'

She laughed at my tone, leant across and with her left hand patted my cheek, coaxing me to face her, kissed my lips, stepped out of the car, waved gaily and entered the house.

I sat in the Rover, stunned by her action. She'd reversed our roles by seizing the initiative – contradicted her shy prim character – ceased to be my sister. The factor of alteration between us was infinitesimal and enormous. I was pacified and roused simultaneously, and on a deeper level steadied by our exchange. Mary had been revealed in her true loving colours: she was my fate.

I was a virgin emotionally, if not technically. Love for me had been a poetic sighing that didn't interfere with my life, lurid nocturnal fantasies and a nervous practical episode or two, from which I'd recoiled in puritan disgust. The novelty of my feeling for Mary was its being grafted on to our friendship virtually from birth. She was the girl next door, neither a tinsel fairy on a Christmas tree nor an elusive instrument for the satisfaction of my lusts – and it simplified our romance. I couldn't forget her any more than I could forget my home. I trusted her to be at Thrushton when I was at Deane End. I trusted her to respond to my caresses as to my summonses to sunbathe or play tennis. Her future was inseparable from mine.

The army transferred me to a barracks in Yorkshire for the last twelve months of my military service. In my exile I corresponded with Mary: although we could have loved each other all along without knowing it, lovers have to get acquainted. I was delighted by her ungrammatical replies to my letters. During our reunions I was bowled over by her prettiness, schemed in order to be alone with her and sued for permission to hold her hand. My imperiousness waned, hers waxed. Her original overture had been half humorous, and she continued to extract some feminine amusement from my subordination – she teased and laughed at me with increasing assurance.

Then in December 1947 I was demobilised. A week after my return home Mr Nash was asked to dinner by my parents. He said he'd heard of my literary tastes and offered me employment in his publishing house. A few days later I eavesdropped on a conversation between Mabel Singleton and Mother, in which my marriage to Mary was discussed.

My involuntary inward answer was: no!

I'd pined for my freedom, to see Mary, compose poetry, and decide at leisure what I was going to do. But my destiny had been mapped out by others. And I rebelled. With regard to the job at Nash and King, I said I must have time to think about it. I pleaded for a peaceful interim at Deane End and broke the news that my ambition was to be a writer.

Father was calm and reasonable. He mentioned the obstacles in the way of a career in the arts, especially for someone without financial resources. He propounded the deceptive doctrine that I ought to have a second string to my bow, a secure profession that wouldn't prevent my writing. Mother, having declared it was a dreadful shock, temporised by following his lead.

Admittedly my ambition in the context of my family's middle-class history of doctors and nurses, pillars of society, earnest upright husbands and respectable wives, represented an extraordinary departure. My speculation in literature, when I should have been getting to grips with reality, was bound to be a blow to my parents. But it wasn't aimed at them – consciously. My conscious aim was to establish my independence, cling on to my liberty for a little longer – not to be dictated to, not yet to be pressed into their mould.

I produced a few stories, which were rejected by the editors of newspapers and magazines. Mother began to encroach: it was one thing for her to be able to boast that her son who would become a literary celebrity was home from the wars, and another to have to support a hulking hungry twenty-one-year-old in apparent idleness. The honeymoon period of her cautious pride in my undertaking was over; and I realised that inadvertently I'd recreated the circumstances of my schooldays. If I were to succeed she'd care for me. As it was, she didn't.

Furthermore I could no longer afford to fail – I couldn't exact that revenge on her conditional affections. My bulwark against pressure, my sole justification would be to sell my stories, to have them printed; and I was paralysed by her antagonism. Our disputes ranged from the disorder of her kitchen, sullied by my cooking, via my obdurate attitude to Mr Nash, to my ineffectiveness at Eton and her mockery of my shortsightedness.

In the evenings she was apt to remark: 'I understand Harry Singleton's already earning fifteen hundred a year as a stockbroker,' or: 'Two or three hours' work, just reading and writing – couldn't you combine it with a decent occupation?' More aggressively she might demand: 'Well, have you made up your mind?'

Success in her philosophy, in the short term, was my being paid to publish books. I was dreaming of the fame that would accrue from writing them. But, partly owing to the various distractions of Deane End, I couldn't write, and was frustrated and sensitive to the slightest criticism. I'd insist that literature wasn't my hobby, that her approach to it was amateur and philistine and would never be mine, stealing glances at Father, trying to bring him round to my point of view. He smiled and said nothing; and because I suspected him of using Mother to express his doubts as to my vocation, I'd vent my wrath against his benevolent implacability by quarrelling with her.

Mary helped to force the issue. As I was flattered in a sense by Mr Nash's offer, so was I to have overheard Mother and Mabel Singleton canvassing my marriage: my love was raised on to a higher plane of seriousness. But when I told Mary of my artistic aspirations, she treated them lightly. I led her into my inner sanctuary, to the marvels of which she was blind. She was worse than blind, she was bored, uninterested, as she had been before she confused me with her kiss. One evening I expatiated on my bookish subject and complained that she wasn't listening.

'You don't listen to my office gossip,' she retorted.

We'd seen, and saw, too much of each other. The relaxed quality of our courtship worried me: the most disturbing feature of our landscape was its familiarity. Naturally she was fond of my father. She greeted my bulletins about the conflict at Deane End by hinting that he knew best. Once she observed: 'At our ages we shouldn't be living with our parents.' It struck me that Mary, who dismissed art, at least my art, and was proposing how and where we ought to live, could be conspiring with my enemies.

I retreated. The more I did so the more she advanced. Yet the assurance that had attracted me was undermined. Her telephone calls were reminiscent of her former wheedling appeals to please come out and play; and I wished that Thrushton wasn't adjacent. Alone together, although we were seldom alone for long – it was winter and chilly, and indoors we had our families in attendance – our kisses were a reprieve from the complications of conversation. She kissed me instead of saying: 'Write to your heart's content – I approve, I support you – be free!' I kissed her instead of saying: 'Marry me.'

One morning she delivered a note in which she asked me across for supper, adding in a postscript that the house would be empty, except for herself, overnight.

Early April 1948 must have been the date. Since my demobilisation we hadn't had a similar chance. Our kisses had drawn us to the edge of the sexual precipice. What would happen after dinner in the empty house was a foregone conclusion. Making love would commit me to her. Marriage would necessitate my having a job. The trap was baited and set.

I wouldn't walk into it. The game was too dangerous – and too tame. Latently my rebellion had been not against the usurpation of my prerogative to shape my destiny, but against my drifting into the wide well-trodden thoroughfare, from which I wouldn't easily be able to deviate. Marrying the right girl, siring typical children, slaving for a weekly wage, renouncing all for Mary – a life of her devising, without surprises, middle-class, middle-brow, mediocre – in my tender youth was I to be condemned to, was I to run the risk of such a harsh sentence?

That evening Mother and I had our fiercest quarrel. A relatively inoffensive rebuke of hers sparked off a disproportionate tirade from me. I swore that as a result of her policies I'd felt unwanted from the day I was born. She obviously hated me, except insofar as I gratified her vanity. And I was clearing out, leaving Deane End for ever.

Father, returning from his Root Street surgery, came into my bedroom.

'Your mother's in tears.'

'Is she?'

'What have you done?'

'What have I done? Shouldn't you put your question to Mother? What has she done?'

'It's always a mistake,' he said, 'making people unhappy.'

I agreed with him hotly. His closing of the parental ranks had irritated me for years. I listed the causes of my unhappiness and repeated that I was clearing out – I'd been driven out of my home. My decision was to invest my gratuity from the army in a visit to a pub in Wales.

He regarded me through glinting glasses and replied: 'So be it.'

At supper at Thrushton I also reduced Mary to tears. She begged me for explanations that I could only give in terms she was unable to accept. She accused me of being cold, heartless, horrid to everybody, mean and mad. I compromised to the extent of a pledge to reconsider my position in Wales, and attempt to remould my character.

Back at Deane End Father was reading in his study. I knocked on the door and entered. He was sitting in the swivel chair by the desk. I told him I was in a muddle and had to have a proper shot at my writing.

'Sorry, Father.'

'I'm sorry too,' he said in a tone that was either sad or steely.

He spared me no word of encouragement or forgiveness.

'Apologise to your mother.'

'Yes.'

'Good night.'

'Good night.'

I remember arriving at The Dellamere Arms in the middle of the week, say on a Wednesday, Wednesday 14 April 1948, having taken trains from Guildford to London and from London to Oswestry and a taxi on to Llanwyn.

It was perfect weather, freakishly warm, although not hot as it had been on the occasion of my introduction to the valley two and a half years before. As it were in the train winter had been outdistanced, and the sun, navigating between the high clouds, circular and scattered, shone on the slopes of the hills and the lush low-lying fields. Pines and firs grew on the hills, and beeches and ash trees bursting into leaf, red-green and grey-green.

I was predisposed to make the most of my literary holiday. From the moment I shook the Surrey dust from my feet, or indeed decided to, I began to enjoy myself. Youth may be tender; at the same time it's tough, resilient or shallow; and I was determined not to consider or reconsider anything for the present. The dissatisfaction that was brought to a head by Mary's assignation implies that I had an alternative in mind. My alternative can be summed up by the three syllables: adventure.

At Eton, at least, the snobbery I'd inherited or perhaps the snobbery that springs from inexperience was defined. I absorbed a view of the possibilities of a life of leisure, of choice, that could be gracious and spacious; and neither envy nor guilt, nor the destructive theory that society should be levelled downwards, bothered me as they might have nowadays. While reacting against my mother, I yearned for circumstances different from mine, to rise above circumstances, as she did. My nebulous ambitions, my honour would be satisfied by some sort of adventure.

After all my twenty-one years had been distinguished by their drabness. Reading was my substitute for life: my imagination was stirred by the imaginings of others. I'd never offended against a social convention or infringed a family law, or contemplated an act that wasn't an obeisance to somebody else's will: of my scholarship, the single exception to the drab rule, Mr Grinling was the begetter. Thus The Dellamere Arms was uniquely mine and mine alone. Coupled with literature – that is to say, my imminent apotheosis – it was my reply to my parents, Mr Nash and Mary.

The unusual fact that it didn't disappoint me reinforced my faith in my independent judgement. Memory hadn't deceived: the ivy-clad pub by the humped bridge was snug as ever. Mr and Mrs Roope, the genial landlord and landlady, he with a silver watch-chain across his waistcoat, she in an ample white apron, welcomed me and showed me to my room with its bow window, looking out on the water meadow in which cattle chewed the cud and drowsed in the rosy twilight by the river's bank. There was a table in the window. A coal fire had been lit in the grate. My dinner of roast meat, apple tart and that strong local beer was served in the Roopes' parlour behind the saloon bar: I was the only guest. At half-past nine, having chatted to Mr Roope and drunk more of his beer, I retired to bed in a haze of intoxication and excitement.

The next day I settled down to write. I boarded the vehicle which was to convey me to the land in which I'd love and be loved in strict accordance with my desires. But in spite of Father's dictum that I could if I wanted to, my optimism was privately balanced by a pessimistic estimate of my powers. Authors were heroic in that they endured indifference and ultimately conquered their foes: how might I become one? My horrid conduct at home and towards Mary was an excusable aspect of my call to be an artist: but what was art? What was an artist precisely? On the other hand my presence in the pub, and the obstacle course negotiated in order to get to it, almost entitled me to inspiration.

I kept on thinking of the torrent of persuasive words shortly to be poured forth, which would soften even my mother's heart. The floor was paced, cigarette stubs multiplied, while surrealistic visions of my glorious future were evoked. The weather contributed to my excitement: after lunch I went for a walk, crossing the lane and the stile into the meadow with the cows.

A scarcely marked path formed a diagonal line between The Dellamere Arms and Llanwyn Church. I followed it for two hundred yards, crossed another stile into the churchyard and, picking my way through the leaning slate gravestones, rounded the altar end of the building. A lych-gate, shaded by the branches of an ancient yew tree, gave into a road; and a stream, the Wyn, gushed out of a drain and swirled amongst the exposed red roots of the yew in the direction of the river. Opposite me, on the far side of the road, were the stately wrought-iron gates of Llanwyn House, where Mrs Roope had been in domestic service.

It belonged to the Dellamere family, after which the pub was named, Mrs Roope had informed me. Apparently Dellameres still lived there. A drive flanked by a chestnut avenue, by the stream in a canal and by garden walls, inclined uphill to a gravel sweep where a car was parked. Because the boughs of the double line of chestnut trees met and twined together, I could see nothing below them except a bit of the car and a sunlit flight of steps at a distance of about a hundred and fifty yards. The iron of the crested gates was rusty, and bracken and weeds sprouted from the canal through which the Wyn flowed. A small door in the garden wall on the right, veiled by ivy, seemed to be falling off its hinges.

I turned left and after a quarter of a mile came to a crossroads. Flaking paint on a wooden sign indicated that Oswestry lay behind me and Llanrhad ahead. On the left-handed corner – to Penyboth and the pub – clustered half a dozen cottages and the Post Office which was also the village store. The sign to the right bore the intriguing legend: The Forest. But the steepness and narrowness of the rutted cart-track weren't very inviting; and I carried on along the road to Llanrhad.

Again on the Friday morning I worked or dreamt at my writing table in the bow window, and at three o'clock went for a walk over the humped bridge and the wooded hill to Penyboth. I bought an ice-cream for tea in the Penyboth shop and at six was swinging down the lane to The Dellamere Arms. The Forest and Llanwyn House were across the valley. The sun was sinking in the sky above Llanrhad. The songs of the birds were somehow in tune with my sentiments. I was brimful of ideas respecting literature and life, perhaps nearer than ever before to burning with the hard gemlike flame.

On the bridge I heard a peculiar swishing sound and felt a sudden acute pain in my upper arm. I stopped – the tugging acuteness of the pain stopped too – but in a second it was renewed, it was agony, and the tug actually pulled me to the low parapet of the bridge on the pub side. I cried out, looked at my arm, afraid that I'd see a wasp or a hornet fixed to it; but no insect was discernible on my fawn-coloured jersey – I wasn't wearing a coat. Meanwhile my cry had been answered by the barking and yapping of dogs and by a man's voice.

Ten yards below me, where the river widened into a pool – Pub Pool, a fisherman was standing on the sandy stony shore. He had a red complexion, a white moustache, his tweed cap was pushed back, and he was staring up. I'd clapped my left hand to my arm, and now my fingers discovered that what was fixed to it was his hook: I hadn't noticed the transparent gut of his line on my jersey. I stepped forwards to shout at him, to curse him, but, leaning further over the parapet, saw a girl sitting on a boulder.

Her face was raised. She was beautiful. What can I say? Her beauty was more of a shock than having had a fishing hook stuck into me. She was blonde, blue-eyed, all gold and sapphires. She wore a straw hat with a wide brim and a dress of flimsy whitish material, and sat elegantly on her boulder, clasping a small open book, like the model of a masterly canvas of the age of romantic sensibility. In her free hand she held the leads of a pair of Shetland sheepdogs.

The fisherman was saying: 'Good God! My dear boy!'

The girl scolded the dogs: 'Be quiet, will you? Quiet!' She called to me: 'Hullo – what's happened?'

'I've been hooked!'

The feathery fly part of the hook wasn't visible, but I could feel it through the loosely knitted wool – and by twisting my head see the spreading stain of blood.

'Where? Where have you been hooked?'

'In my arm!'

The old fisherman was climbing the bank of shale towards the lane. The girl, climbing after him with the dogs, muttered distinctly: 'Daddy, really!' The Roopes emerged from the pub.

'Evening, Roope, evening, Mrs Roope!'

'Good evening, sir. Good evening, Miss Laura.'

'Hullo – we've had an accident.'

At the sight of the blood Mrs Roope exclaimed: 'Oh Mr Bartlett! Oh my word!'

The girl asked: 'May I look?'

Yes, I replied.

She could look at me, but, apart from a sidelong glance, I couldn't look at her.

'Daddy, have you got your pair of scissors? Mrs Roope, have you got a knife?'

'Yes, of course,' her father puffed co-operatively, depositing his fishing-rod on the gravel of the forecourt. 'Don't you bother, Mrs Roope – here we are!' He produced from his waistcoat pocket one of those unfolding pairs of scissors.

Mr Roope was saying: 'We might be needing a doctor, Miss Laura,' and Mrs Roope: 'Dr Hughes is with Mrs Rogers' mother – I was speaking to Mrs Rogers on the phone just a minute ago.'

The girl, Laura, commented: 'What luck! Ring again, Mrs Roope, and tell the doctor to hurry.' She touched my arm and snipped the line. 'You're free!'

'Thank you.'

'Are you feeling faint?'

'Slightly.'

My knees had started to tremble and seemed to be in danger of giving way under me. My main trouble wasn't the pain or the blood, it was her weakening proximity and her touch.

'Do you want supporting?'

'No, thanks, I'm all right.'

'Would you have a drink, sir?'

'No, thanks very much.'

I wobbled indoors and up the stairs to my room. Almost at once I heard the sound of a car: Mrs Rogers was in charge of the Post Office on the corner, only five hundred yards from the pub. The car halted, a door slammed, voices and footsteps approached, and Doctor Hughes came in.

He introduced himself and examined my jersey; and suggested that we drive to his surgery in Llanrhad, where he had more facilities.

'I'd rather not.'

Having wished to avoid Laura, to collect myself, I was now overwhelmed with the terror of being separated from her.

Doctor Hughes deliberated. He might require assistance. Would I object to Miss Dellamere acting as his nurse?

I replied: 'No,' but trembled, while I realised with an additional snobbish tremor that Laura was Laura Dellamere, a member of the family living at Llanwyn House.

I sat on the chair by the writing table. The doctor went to the door, called, returned and opened his black bag and began to search for instruments. She entered the room which was in shadow – the sun was behind the pub – and filled it with radiance. She'd removed her hat, exposing her short bright gold hair.

'Hullo!'

'Hullo!'

'Can you bear me to witness your sufferings? – Mrs Roope couldn't.'

'Can you bear to witness them?'

'Yes,' she said, smiling, but a trifle tensely.

Doctor Hughes, apologising for the damage he was about to do, slit the sleeves of my shirt and jersey with his scissors, cutting in a circle round the bloodstain. Laura helped to draw my clothing over my head. The pieces of material were eased from under the shaft of the hook. The gash in my arm was half an inch long, untidy, probably due to that second tug on the fishing line, and the hook's curved and barbed point was embedded in my flesh.

Doctor Hughes explained that he'd have to insert several stitches in the wound. He had a numbing freezing spray in his bag, but unfortunately no local anaesthetic. Wouldn't I prefer to drive to his surgery for a completely pain-killing injection?

Laura was standing in the embrasure of the window.

My eyes met hers, which were luminously blue, glistening, compassionate, curious – they seemed to me to say: 'Would you dare? Do you dare?'

'No,' I replied to the medical question. 'No, honestly.'

Preparations were set in train. Mrs Roope provided a kettle of boiling water, a bowl, a tray and towels, crooning 'Oh, poor sir' through the doorway. Doctor Hughes poured some water into the bowl and washed his hands with the rest in the basin on my wash-stand. He threaded a needle and placed it on the tray, for which Laura had cleared a space on the table. My arm was swabbed and dried and squirted with the spray. The hook was extracted.

Doctor Hughes reached for the needle and thread. But the numbing effect of the spray didn't last long enough, and an injudicious squirt from Laura froze his fingers. I think we laughed – it was quite funny; and the attempt to anaesthetise me was abandoned. She resumed her former position, leaning back against the angle of the walls between the bow of the window and the room. When the pain was at its sharpest, my eyes, watering involuntarily, again sought hers, which flooded at once with sympathetic tears.

After the operation she said admiringly: 'You were very brave.'

'You were,' I countered, meaning that she'd comforted me, not flinching, meaning that I had more to admire in her.

'No, no!' She shook her head and coloured ever so delicately. 'Does it hurt?'

'Not much.'

I remember another snatch of our conversation.

'Mrs Roope tells me you're a writer,' she observed. 'Are you?'

'I hope to be.'

'And you're here to write and be alone?'

'Yes.'

'How nice that sounds!'

While Doctor Hughes was packing his bag she said something about us all having a drink. But I was embarrassed by my partial nakedness and had to dress, and I refused.

'Can I come and see how you're getting on tomorrow?'

'Yes,' I agreed, meaning: please, please!

'I'm so sorry. My father's so sorry. We –'

'No, please,' I interrupted her, 'don't mention it.'

She laughed at the phrase.

'I'm sorry I wasn't more efficient with the spray.'

'You were fine.'

She was carrying the kettle and the tray and nodded her goodbye. I thanked and said goodbye to Doctor Hughes, who arranged to take the stitches out in five days' time. His appearance, what he looked like, remains an absolute blank in my memory.

Yet I remember vividly the scene of the Dellameres' departure. Doctor Hughes had driven off in his car. The Roopes were waving from the forecourt of the pub. Father and daughter crossed the stile into the water meadow. He walked along the path to the church, his fishing-rod in the crook of his arm, bald-headed, his tweed cap bulging in his jacket pocket. Having bent down to unleash her dogs, laying her hat and book on the ground, she hurried to catch him and took his hand. Soon they emerged from the lengthening shadow into the sun. One of the dogs stayed at Laura's heels, pausing occasionally with a tiny paw lifted, the other skimmed over the shining grass, barking at the cows by the river in the distance. Her white dress, the floppy straw hat, the golden halo of her hair, her affectionate gesture and the valley in the evening light enchanted me.

It was the happiest moment of my life.

THREE

EVEN when I was with Laura, I always had to verify her beauty. Perhaps beauty is attested to by its incredibility. At any rate I could never believe in hers unless I was looking at it. In that sense she was like a person in a dream – my dream – whose supernatural comeliness eludes our wakeful recollections.

And after a quarter of a century, notwithstanding the notes and memoranda accumulated during it, I can only describe her in terms of statistics. She was tall, at least as tall as her father, five feet seven or eight, well developed, as they say, and my senior – she was twenty-six. Her bones weren't small, but her proportions were excellent – she seemed to be slenderer and slimmer than she was. Her arms were strong yet not muscular, and she had a rare attribute, noticeably elegant elbows and wrists, neither angular nor fleshy.

Her brow was wide and vertical, not sloping, and her nose straight, firm and sensual. Her upper lip was full and protruded over her lower one; it might have been the childlike fullness of her exquisitely curving upper lip that imparted such charm to her expression. Her smile caused the skin under her eyes to swell a little. Her smile had a poignant quality, suggesting that her laughter wasn't far from tears.

Her colouring rather than her features was responsible for the visual shock I received on the bridge – and repeatedly afterwards. On occasions in later years I experienced it – that shock, the administration of which is the birthright of beautiful blond youth, girls and boys: but it was never so intense. She was golden, composed of varying shades of brightest burnished gold, although with nothing metallic about her – she glowed like the flame of a candle in a dark world. Her magnetism, her allure and appeal were dependent on factors still harder to pin down, for instance vitality and warmth, a desire to please, and her clear voice, her natural regard, her ways of moving and tilting her head.

On the whole her manner throughout the fish-hook incident was robust: when and how did I get the idea that she was balanced on a knife-edge between joy and sorrow? There was humour in her rebuke, 'Daddy, really! '– and her mode of addressing me was direct. Possibly the tantalising enervating scent she wore was labelled: Availability. But if I felt the normal barriers were broken down by our abnormal situation, my pain and her concern, I was also aware of her reserve, her womanly reticence amounting almost to inhibition.

I suppose the statement about my happiness, while watching her walk across the water meadow, requires qualification. All the expectations sown in childhood, in adolescence, which had grown and spread in the forcing house of my room at The Dellamere Arms, were fulfilled. My belief in magic, in my potential translation into a new being and an altogether superior sphere, was confirmed. My vagueness as to why I was in the pub vanished: I'd been waiting for Laura. I'd been waiting for her on the site of Deane End and Thrushton, at Eton, in the army, and recently. She was my adventure. She was my inspiration and muse. Moreover my responses to her white figure in the field were totally disinterested. I asked no more of her than the scenic proof she was giving me of her existence. My pleasure in the present was unalloyed.

It was the first irrecoverable ecstasy of love, a certain sort of love, recognised and unrecognised, beyond analysis, momentary.

As soon as Laura and her father and dogs had disappeared from view behind the church, melting into the obscurity under the yew tree, I dressed and descended the stairs to talk to Mrs Roope.

Yes, the elderly gentleman was Colonel Dellamere, she informed me, stepping in and out of the parlour with my supper. He was the owner of Llanwyn House and the land round it, and the fishing rights in the Wyntrude: he often fished for an hour in the evenings, in Pub Pool by the bridge or Wyn Pool, along where the Wyn joins the river – he and his crony Captain Charrington were great fishermen. He was a widower; his wife had been killed in a car smash.

'When would that have been?'

'Oh, long ago, before the war, 1935 or '36.'

'How many children did they have?'

'Only Miss Laura.'

'Were you working at Llanwyn in those days, in the nineteen-thirties, Mrs Roope?'

I was eager for her reminiscences, to which previously I hadn't paid sufficient attention.

'Oh no. I worked for the Colonel's father – I was his cook – until Mr Roope and I were married in 1926. Mr Dellamere, he was stern, but a good master; he passed on in 1928, and the Colonel inherited the place. Of course the Colonel and Mrs Dellamere came here for visits, like, from London. But my Mr Dellamere, well, he couldn't take to his daughter-in-law. She was such a lot younger than the Colonel, and such a gay spark.'

'How much younger than the Colonel was she?'

'Fourteen years, she must have been. He couldn't ever do enough for her. He let her have her head: that's how she was killed, driving to London in the middle of the night. And it's the same with Miss Laura.'

'Does she live with her father?'

'Gracious, no!'

'Where does she live?'

'Mostly in London, like her mother. She'll spend a few weeks here in the spring and the summer, weeks or days, she's usually here for the holidays, and then we won't see her for months at a stretch. The war and her job in England spoilt it for her – Llanwyn, I mean – and she can't settle. Well, it's dull with the old people, when she hasn't any of her friends to stay.'

'Who are the old people, apart from her father?'

'Her aunt, the Colonel's sister, she's a lot at Llanwyn, and Miss Tufton always is – she was Miss Laura's governess.'

'And her friends?'

'Mr Sawrey and the others, they keep her company.'

After a slight depressed pause I observed: 'She's terribly pretty, isn't she?'

Mrs Roope agreed.

I might have asked more questions, I can't remember. Upstairs in my room I drew the curtains and gazed out into the April night. Over the lane and the water meadow, to the left of the square tower of the church, through the branches of chestnut trees, glimmered the lights of Laura's home. I sat by my writing table, loving her and already hating her friends. I wished she weren't so beautiful or that I alone appreciated her beauty. Would she call in the morning? Had she been serious? Should I telephone?

⋆ ⋆ ⋆

She arrived at eleven.

Perhaps in parenthesis I ought to say that time has distilled my recollections into essential scenes: on the bridge or in the water meadow, or of Laura standing by the bow window with her hands behind her back and tears in her eyes while my arm was stitched. The rest is reconstruction. Granted, a story has to have some linking passages. But the truth was to have been my guiding principle. I'll try again to stick to the point and the facts: which shouldn't be too difficult. For the chief characteristic of my association with Laura was its absence of adequate reflection. Reflection in any depth belonged to a more protracted period in the future.

I hadn't slept much, but on that Saturday morning wasn't tired. I was racked by indecision, and revisited the bridge and the boulder, and attempted in vain to work, still wondering whether or not to telephone.

Laura arrived on her bicycle, without her dogs. I heard her voice in the forecourt of the pub and dashed to the open window.

She called through the quiet air: 'Hullo!'

She was wearing trousers, blue trousers and a white shirt or smock.

'Hullo!'

'Are you better?'

I'd forgotten my arm, but replied: 'Yes!'

'Am I luring you from your labours?'

'No,' I cried. 'No, no! Will you wait there?'

I hurried down the stairs. She was straddling her bike, leaning on the handlebars, the chromium of which sparkled in the sun. She was like the spirit of morning, like spring itself, except that her trousers revealed the taut ripeness of her figure.

'We've been worrying about you,' she smiled. 'Are you really better?'

'Yes,' I repeated breathlessly, trying to control the trembling and knocking of my knees.

'It was so nasty, wasn't it? It was nasty for you – and for Daddy. He's been utterly stricken.'

'Do tell him not to be.'

'Will you? Will you tell him? That's partly why I called on you: will you come and dine this evening?'

'At Llanwyn House?'

'Yes.' She laughed at my confusion, as if to say: where else? Dinner would be at seven forty-five, she added – not changed.

'Thank you very much.'

I feared the interview was over – I was in receipt of her messages. Yet she seemed to wish to prolong it.

'Isn't the weather heavenly?'

'Yes, but not for work – it's hellish for work.'

She inquired almost flirtatiously: 'I'm not helping, am I?'

'I didn't mean that.'

'Truly?'

'Truly.'

'You wouldn't like to walk to the corner with me?'

'Yes, I'd love to.'

She dismounted and turned her bicycle. I noticed the golden sheen of the skin of her hands, gripping the handlebars, and that the nails of her long fingers were bitten. The unexpected flaw in her perfection constituted another attraction in my eyes. I was reassured by her soft pink fingertips, implying that she also was nervous.

Her wheeled bicycle ticked as we walked along the lane.

Why had I chosen The Dellamere Arms for my retreat? How had I discovered it?

I described my day in the army two years before.

As it were in inverted commas she queried: 'Did you vow to return?'

'No, not then. But after I was demobbed I found out I couldn't write at home. It wasn't any good – so I'm using my gratuity to buy a little peace and privacy.'

'When did you get to the pub?'

'On Wednesday.'

'And it's Saturday now: you haven't had much peace, what with the accident and my interrupting you this morning. I got here last weekend. How long are you staying?'

'Oh, a month – until my money's gone.'

'What will you be able to write in a month?'

'Probably nothing. But I may learn whether or not I'm a writer.'

'Supposing you learnt that you weren't one, what would you do?'

'I'd become a publisher. At least I've been offered a job in a publishing firm.'

'Which publishing firm?'

'Nash and King.'

'Oh yes.'

'Do you know it?'

'I know of it. I've worked for publishers, proof-reading and reading manuscripts. There's a manuscript I ought to be reading at the moment.' She shrugged her shoulders. 'I'm a bookworm. But publishing's a business – as a rule its connection with literature is purely incidental.'

'That's what I think!'

We were by the shop on the corner presided over by Mrs Rogers, whose mother was the patient of Doctor Hughes.

Laura smiled up at me: 'Dare I ask you to stroll on? I could show you round the gardens.'

We duly strolled – past the cottages, entering and emerging from the light ante-meridian shadows of trees on the road. Each step seemed to be leading me deeper into a virgin country of sympathy and intelligence, a million miles from Deane End and Thrushton.

I reverted to her remark about publishers, seeking to convey my astonishment both that she should share my interests and in a sentence had provided me with a rationalisation of my resistance to Mr Nash's offer.

I mentioned my feeling that if I accepted his offer I'd never write another line.

'No, you wouldn't,' she agreed absent-mindedly. 'All the same it's brave of you to spend your money as you are spending it. You were brave yesterday evening, when you were having your arm operated on, and you're brave to commit your resources to your writing. You're obviously a brave person. I'm a coward.' In a different tone, a sudden strange tone, she said: 'But it's necessary to have courage. One must have courage.'

I was gratified. Although courage wasn't a quality on which I'd prided myself, or for that matter contemplated either subjectively or objectively, I was gratified by her praise. In the course of our short walk the range of her dominion over me had been extended: it was intellectual, moral, as well as emotional. The charm of her voice and manner didn't disguise their authority, their claim to which I was happy to yield that she was older, more experienced, wiser. Her being employed by publishers to pass judgement on manuscripts, as a literary expert, might have had something to do with it.

Anyway, simultaneously, whatever it was that was so gratifying, our literary communings or her invitation to stroll on, or her golden closeness in the silver setting, I registered the oddity of her declaration that one must have courage. Latent awareness not merely of her beauty, of her individual existence and the fears that existence is heir to, was implanted in me, even while, despite her bitten nails, I rejoiced in her outward serenity.

We'd reached the gates of Llanwyn and were standing in the heavier shadow of the yew tree in the churchyard. Her reiterated reference to courage was accompanied by a playful appealing flirt of her head: she seemed to be shaking off care and apologising for having allowed her preoccupations to intrude amongst mine. Her direct smile, her shiny white teeth caused my heart to miss a beat or two – and similarly served to create a pause in our conversation.

'Where are your dogs today?'

'I never take them on the road. I'm terrified of their getting anywhere near a road. They're so disobedient, Sven in particular.'

'Sven?'

'They're called Trilby and Sven: Sven for Svengali.'

'Svengali – wasn't he a character in a book? Wasn't he a hypnotist?'

'Yes,' she replied dismissively.

She wheeled her bicycle through the gate and dumped it against the trunk of the first chestnut tree, by the channelled stream of the Wyn, where it disappeared underground; and moved towards the dilapidated door in the garden wall.

'Incidentally,' I said, 'that sign at the crossroads, pointing to The Forest: I saw it the other day – it amused me: is there a forest up the cart-track?'

'No.' She was dismissive or curt. 'No, the cart-track leads nowhere, except to woods, the pine woods above the house.'

I followed her through the door. The whole of this garden on the right-hand side of the drive was walled. For a walled garden it was huge, a square of about a hundred yards across. A rectangular pool or lake, deep in the middle, Laura told me, and filled with water-lilies and green snakelike weeds that broke the surface, occupied the bottom part. Between it and the road, the Oswestry road, reared a line of tall ragged cypresses; and beyond the lake, on the far bank, was a summer house with greenery sprouting from its thatched roof and on its verandah a pair of deck chairs with faded canvas seats. An unkempt path of yellow sandy gravel, gently sloping uphill, led past the lake and the summer house on our right, and winding through an orchard of gnarled fruit trees and a wilderness of ornamental bushes opened into a space of weedy flower beds and insecure trellises. At the upper end of the garden was a wall some twenty-five feet in height, red brick again, a bleached crumbly red, from which overgrown apple and pear trees sagged disconsolately.

Here Laura turned left through another door by a potting shed. We were immediately below Llanwyn House, in the gravel sweep for cars, the drive and chestnut avenue behind us. The steps visible from the main road mounted to a railed terrace and a central porch barred and largely hidden by creeper. Three wings including the porch wing jutted out on to the terrace, thus forming the letter E, the initial of Queen Elizabeth I in whose reign they had been added on to the original earlier residence. The stucco of the front, peeling in places, was grey, a mature variegated grey in the sun; the windows were outlined in stone, sashed on the ground floor, otherwise latticed; the wings were steeply gabled; and woodland trees and pines, presumably The Forest, rose above the regimental ranks of chimneys.

I listened to Laura, explaining the system of lawns in terraces to the right of the house, and watched the gestures of her hands and tapered wrists.

I listened, I admired, and asked: 'But how do I get in when I come to dinner?'

'That's a good question!' She laughed. 'The wistaria on the porch ought to be removed. But it's taken such ages, growing – and you can't imagine how romantic it'll be in a few weeks. I love this time of year, spring, the beginning of spring, don't you, before anything's over?' More practically she indicated a door in the angle of one of the wings.

We crossed into the kitchen garden, also with its line of cypresses at the bottom. But the rear wall of garages and stables enclosed it at the upper end, and a fence and farm buildings on the Llanrhad side. Having wandered round we returned to the gravel sweep.

I thanked her for my tour – it was half-past twelve.

'Forgive me for ruining your work.'

'No, no – I mean yes, I do forgive you.'

'See you later.'

'Yes! Oh – your bicycle!'

'Don't worry, I'll leave it in the drive.'

'Shall I wheel it up this evening?'

'If you like. That'd be kind.'

'Goodbye.'

'Goodbye.'

I walked away from her, under the arch of chestnut branches, resisting the temptation to turn until I was by the gates. She must have gone indoors. I took the short cut to The Dellamere Arms, by the churchyard and water meadow, had lunch and managed to get through the rest of the day.

I collected her bicycle in the dusk, which was deeper, virtually night, in the avenue of trees. At the top I propped it against the flight of steps, and then on the terrace, after casting about in the gloom, found an insignificant door with a bell-pull hanging by it. A squeaking and creaking, a faint delayed tinkle and a prolonged pause followed from my tug at the bell; and my hand was rusty, I noticed. Bats were circling overhead, flittering in the paler patches of sky, woken from their winter sleep by the warm weather. Eventually I heard someone approaching, although no light was switched on, and the door opened and a ghostly figure greeted me – Morgan the butler, I gathered later, who was inclined to drink and to go in for gothic effects. He conducted me along a passage, towards and into a windowless panelled staircase hall decorated with antlers and lit by a dim glow from a landing above, and ushered me into the library, which had no bookcases in it.

The room was spacious and L-shaped. On the same blackish panelling hung black family portraits of irregular sizes. But it was better lit by lamps with crinkling parchment shades, and cosy in a threadbare way. A log fire burnt in the hearth, round which were arranged a pair of sofas in cretonne covers, easy chairs, needlework stools and occasional tables. Colonel Dellamere and two ladies were there; he rose from his armchair, wearing his green tweed fishing suit with a waistcoat and gold watch-chain, and introduced me. One of the ladies was his sister Miss Dellamere, Miss Angela Dellamere – in her sixties, taller and thinner than he was, whose voice crackled drily; the other was Miss Tufton, Laura's ex-governess, pink-cheeked, rotund, with innocent china blue eyes.

Colonel Dellamere's bumpy bald head gleamed in the lamplight and his white moustache curled crisply back on itself. He was so glad I'd come – asking me to dinner was the very least he could do. How was my arm? Pub Pool was always an awkward spot, he huffed and puffed – casting into it was awkward, but in fifty years he'd never hooked a passer-by on the bridge. He begged my pardon sincerely. Would I have a glass of sherry?

Miss Tufton volunteered in her bland voice, on a childish note of wonder: 'You caught a big fish, Colonel,' and Miss Dellamere, eyeing me dispassionately over her spectacles, grated: 'Yes indeed.'

Laura entered, preceded by her dogs, Trilby and Sven, barking. Her loveliness surpassed my recollections of it, as usual – it reduced everybody and everything else to dross. Her apparel was as striking as her white dress of the previous day – it was the long loose violet-coloured housecoat she often put on in the evenings.

Miss Tufton in her grey flannel skirt and twin set objected.

'Oh Laura, you're over-dressed, you will overdo it so!'

But Miss Dellamere approved: 'That outfit's rather fetching,' to which Laura replied gratefully: 'Darling Aunt Ange!'

We sipped our small glasses of sherry, Laura kneeling on the turkey carpet in front of the fire.

And she pleased me by saying: 'Daddy, you know you'll have to buy Arthur' – she stopped and smiled and inquired if she might call me by my Christian name – 'a new shirt and jersey?'

I was pleased by the slip of her tongue, not the new shirt and jersey.

'Quite right, my dear, you must buy him what he requires.'

'We'll make a shopping expedition into Oswestry.'

After protesting feebly that I required nothing, I said thank you with all my heart.

Dinner was announced by Morgan, a thin-lipped man with wiry grey hair and startling black eyebrows, wearing a grubby tailcoat.

We moved into the other part of the L of the room and through a second door into the dining-room – or converted main hall of the house, behind the wistaria-covered porch. A wide extra curtain of tattered green velvet was drawn across the porch's inner doors. Panelling again lined the walls, its sombreness scarcely alleviated by the single lamp on the sideboard and the shaded candles.

Laura had linked arms with her aunt. Miss Dellamere's costume was autumnal, unseasonably so, stiff and sere, a sort of husk. She and Colonel Dellamere had an expression in common, in his case martially straight and apoplectic, in hers unswerving – unnerving, too – and sceptical. If she resembled a type of insect, a grasshopper or a stick insect, he was more like a bumble-bee.

At the table father and daughter sat at opposite ends. Miss Dellamere was next to the Colonel, I was between Miss Dellamere and Laura, and Miss Tufton faced me. Lukewarm soup in soup plates, slopping over the edges, was served, and meat and a pudding. When Morgan poured out the wine I noted the shaking of his hand, especially as he tried to detach the last drop from the lip of the decanter.

Miss Dellamere addressed me reflectively at some stage, no doubt during the meat course: 'Lucky it wasn't your eye that was hooked. Your glasses could have saved you. Still, I've heard of eyes being hooked clean from their sockets.'

Laura laughed and protested: 'Aunt Ange, don't – not while we're eating!'

Miss Dellamere continued: 'How long before you have to have your stitches out? Stitches can bite into you, if you're not careful.'

Five days – no, four – on Thursday, I replied, at the Doctor's surgery in Llanrhad.

Laura offered to drive me over in her car.

'You haven't any transport of your own?'

'No.'

'Well, I'll look after you.'

She was wonderfully friendly, proprietorial, humorous and gay.

Miss Tufton at dinner concentrated on her victuals. The pink of her cheeks turned to dewy digestive red. She interrogated me about Mrs Roope's cooking, which she'd apparently enjoyed for a brief period in the war.

'Does she make you those darling little pies?'

'Darling pies?' Laura scolded her. 'You oughtn't to think of darling pies, you ought to be thinking of salads and cheese.'

'But I'm not fat, I'm not! You're cruel to me,' Miss Tufton wailed.

'I don't want you to blow up.'

'How can I blow up with food rationing and' – she lowered her voice – 'with Mrs Wipps in the kitchen?' Mrs Wipps was the present cook at Llanwyn. 'Mrs Wipps hasn't any idea of how to bake crisp pastry and cakes.'

Miss Tufton had either had a Swiss parent or spent her youth in Switzerland, and was bilingual in English and French: which might have accounted for her precise childish style of enunciating her words.

'No – Colonel, you remember,' she said, 'it was that winter when Mrs Wipps was ill. We had our lunch at The Dellamere Arms. We had pies and suet puddings. We gorged ourselves.'

Laura exclaimed: 'Oh Pixie, you're hopeless!'

Her pet name for her governess, who was far from ethereal, whose flesh was all too solid, tickled me.

She excelled at a spirited tender teasing, for instance inquiring of her father, who ate silently and slowly and was delaying the progress of the meal: 'Daddy, did you know that Queen Victoria chewed every mouthful eighty-seven times?'

She forced him to laugh, giggle, really, in the unwonted and somewhat pained manner of old people: he was seventy years old. Her teasing of Pixie Tufton, and the accusations of cruelty and the wails, were evidently a traditional joke, which caused even Miss Dellamere to emit dry cackles of laughter.

They lived together but separately, the trio of the Colonel, Aunt Ange and Pixie – in separate worlds from which, as it were, they released occasional irrelevant signals into the ether. Thus Miss Tufton would observe: 'I like cabbage chopped and with a white sauce; but if I say so to Mrs Wipps she loses her temper,' and Miss Dellamere, who did the crossword puzzle: 'Bobs, that fish thing in thirteen letters must be ichthyosaurus.' Bobs was her brother's nickname, an adaptation of Robert. He would announce: 'We're planting firs in the Seven Acre,' or: 'Jenkins' leg's coming along splendidly.'

Laura cemented the union of our youth, and gave a comic twist to such statements, by means of the speaking glances she cast in my direction, indulgent or satirical. Yet she wasn't arrogant: she showed no lack of respect for her elders and betters, or sympathy with their concerns. Sometimes she'd investigate an obscure allusion, asking her father which Jenkins he was referring to and what on earth was happening to Jenkins' leg. As a result of her interventions the talk round the table, in fact rustically sedate, seemed to me lively to the point of scintillation.

It was the same in the library, to which we adjourned after an inspection of the dust-sheeted drawing-room beyond the dining-room. Laura again knelt or sat on the carpet, gracefully supporting herself on an outstretched arm, while Miss Dellamere polished her spectacles and resumed her crossword puzzling, Miss Tufton with her plump fingers laced across her stomach sank into a post-prandial stupor, and Colonel Dellamere smoked an ancient stubby pipe. Trilby and Sven had played their part in the evening's entertainment, barking to begin with and being fed surreptitiously with titbits from Laura's plate, a practice at which Miss Tufton cavilled: 'You spoil them – they'll become spoilt itchy lapdogs!' Once or twice in the dining-room I'd been surprised by having my lowered hand licked or touched by a cold nose. At about a quarter to ten the dogs, which were well-behaved in spite of Pixie's prognostications, left their baskets and joined our fireside circle.

'They're rude,' Laura exclaimed: 'they're suggesting that it's time you said goodbye and they were let out for their run.'

'They're right – I should be going.'

'No – you're not to be bullied. You're not to surrender. Trilby isn't bad, Trilby isn't the culprit, it's Sven. Sven! You're not to be a bully, Sven!'

The dogs' flowing brown and white fur and silky black muzzles appeared to be identical. Trilby was five, Sven three and slightly larger. Laura had bought Trilby from a local breeder; Sven had been a gift, she told me. Yes, they complicated her life in London, needing lots of exercise and being of different sexes. When Trilby was in season she had to spend a month at Llanwyn, and Sven sulked and punished his mistress.

'He's a horrible character, horribly strong and selfish – he's a proper male.'

Trilby, true to Laura's description, sat on her haunches and neat forepaws at a distance of two or three yards, politely enough. Sven positioned himself at my feet, lying down but with his head raised, and stared at me with liquid black eyes set slopingly in his narrow elongated skull.

'I think he actually is trying to stare me out of the house.'

'Yes, that's his method.'

She reproved him. On being addressed he half-rose hopefully, wagging his tail, but, catching the drift of her reproof, subsided and renewed his ocular pressure. When I shifted on the sofa he tensed his muscles, poised for action – and re-settled, as if heaving a canine sigh of resignation. His fixed unblinking wilful eyes were decidedly hypnotic.

'I can understand why you called him Svengali.'

'Yes. Trilby's in his power. So am I for that matter.'

'Which of the dogs do you love best?'

'Guess.'

'Trilby?'

'No! No. No,' she said, 'I'm afraid not.'

We'd been laughing. Laura's answer to my last question changed the tempo of our dialogue – and, it emerged, the mood of the party. It was like her declaration in the morning that one must have courage, like lifting the curtain on an interior stage on which some strange secondary drama was being enacted. But in the event I was probably conscious of no more than a pause, her pausing and switching her attention to Miss Dellamere, who obliged her by reading aloud a couple of clues to the puzzle.

We pondered the clues in the hushed room. For Laura's benefit I put forward solutions that were intended to be funny: they elicited none of her quick appreciative smiles.

She murmured, taking me too literally: 'You'll have to ask Aunt Ange. Could that be it, Aunt Ange?'

The fire fell and flared, and the dogs waited. Colonel Dellamere and Miss Tufton were more or less asleep. A grandfather clock somewhere in the house chimed ten. Its whirring and mellow chiming made me jump.

I got up.

The others followed my example. Colonel Dellamere, when I said goodbye, invited me to come again soon. Laura escorted me into the staircase hall, turning on a light in the passage.

I remarked on the light, which hadn't been turned on for me earlier.

'It's a trick of Morgan's,' she replied. 'He likes to keep people in the dark. He's sinister.'

She opened the door and shivered. The dogs rushed into the night.

'Thank you so much.'

'No, thank you, thank you for being so forgiving.'

She meant: for having forgiven her father for the fishhook. But it crossed my mind that she wasn't only thanking, she was also asking for my forgiveness. She seemed to be sorry for her access of reserve, against which she'd waged a losing battle.

Although I wished to propose a plan for the next day, I couldn't – she was unapproachable – and said lamely: 'Well, good night.'

'Good night.'

'Your bike's by the steps.'

'Oh, thanks!'

I descended the steps and crunched across the gravel sweep into the tunnel of trees. It was black as pitch, I remember; and at the end of the drive I hesitated cravenly, fearful of the churchyard and the water meadow with cows in it, and more inclined to walk round by the road to The Dellamere Arms. But this was the very spot on which courage had been advocated, and I gritted my teeth and passed by way of the lych-gate beneath the funereal branches of the yew.

The final half-hour of the evening was different from the rest: I noticed no more. Laura had withdrawn into herself: why shouldn't she? I didn't feel to blame for her withdrawal. Perhaps her superiority in every respect had persuaded me that nothing I could say or do would have the least effect on her. Temporarily my humble attitude, my hazy happiness eclipsed between them the sentence or the sentiment that disturbed her: the admission that she loved Sven, who was horrible, better than Trilby. I assumed she was tired or wanted her father to get to bed. The mystery, if there was any mystery, added to her fascination.

In the morning she rang me. Was I hurrying off to church? – She wasn't. Would I have lunch at Llanwyn? Could I fit in a walk beforehand? Audibly she'd recovered her spirits, and, when I arrived, was throwing a ball for Trilby and Sven on the lawn on a level with the house, above the twenty-five foot wall in the flower garden.

The weather was too heavenly for work, we agreed, laughing; and we strolled across the lawn with its central cedar tree, up some steps on to a higher terrace which was cut into the hillside, a sort of promenade of mown grass, and up still more steps to a woodland path. We now overlooked the roof and chimneys; the library chimney was puffing a transparent column of smoke into the blue sky. The path wound down to the farm buildings and cottages and round to the stables.

'I never offered you a lift home last night,' Laura said. 'I could have run you back in the car. I'm sorry – it was thoughtless of me.'

I replied that I'd been glad to stretch my legs.

'Were you?'

'Yes.'

'Did you go by the churchyard?'

'Yes. Why?'

'Weren't you frightened in the churchyard in the dead of night? I would have been.'

'Well, so was I.'

'But you weren't deterred.'

She was complimentary and rueful.

As if she'd tested my bravery by which she set such store, and to reward me because I hadn't disappointed her, she continued: 'You were nice to everyone yesterday.'

'They were nice to me.'

'Yes, they were – they liked you – and in my opinion they're very nice. But Daddy and Aunt Ange aren't what they used to be. Daddy's older, older and slower, Pixie's greedier – you know – and Llanwyn's falling apart. I hate changes, don't you? They depress me. Do you understand?'

My response was an eager affirmative. I imagined she was simply explaining and offering her explicit apology for the end of the previous evening. I was touched by her filial solicitousness, touched and flattered that she should confide in me, and keen to comfort her. The proof of her feeling heart conferred fresh lustre on her beauty, if possible.

In fact, in my innocence and at my age, I didn't begin to understand her. My greatest mistake was believing that anything she ever said to me was simple. But I mustn't anticipate.

Indoors we met the others in the library, where I was introduced to Captain Charrington, the Colonel's crony, according to Mrs Roope. Laura had told me that he lived in a cottage near Oswestry, on a small private income and with a housekeeper, and had been a friend of the family for years. He was younger than I expected, a youngish sixty or sixty-five, spry and talkative, and dressed in smart twill trousers, a loud check jacket and a spotted bow-tie. His first name was Esmond.

He embraced Laura warmly, calling her Loll.

'How long is it since I've seen you? How long is it since I've kissed you, Loll? I'll be putting in for compensation – look out!' He swivelled her into the sunshine that flooded the room and said: 'Come here, let's examine you. Any lines yet?'

She laughed and coloured, she struggled and exclaimed: 'No, Esmond! You're a devil, Esmond! Get away from me!'

He was full of merciless banter aimed at the ladies. I thought he might be a misogynist, but after lunch Laura said that I couldn't be more wrong: 'He's just retired.' – 'Retired from what?' – 'From being a womaniser.' His smile was certainly a bit wolflike, and his laughter reminded me of port and walnuts.

In the dining-room he remarked: 'What a civilised crew we are – three spinsters, two widowers and a bachelor – not a husband or a wife, not a single traitor amongst us! Isn't that so, Bobs? You and I know what we're talking about. If we weren't decent fellows we'd show our matrimonial scars. But why ruin the roast beef? We wouldn't be popular with Miss Tufton. Celibacy sharpens the appetite – I mean for the flesh of dumb animals. Women should marry, men shouldn't – and to hell with the consequences or the blessed dearth of consequences! Ange, you should have married. I can't say the same for you, Loll. I don't suppose you've had the chance.'

Miss Dellamere, having cracked a wintry smile at these pleasantries, grated out: 'I never married, Esmond, because the men who wanted to marry me were always like you.'

Captain Charrington chuckled and retorted: 'You never married, my girl, because you always scared men to death with answers like that one.'

He kept it going through the meal, his paradoxical flirting, then was taken by the Colonel to see the farm and to fish. Miss Dellamere and Miss Tufton agreed to sit in the sun on the terrace, and Laura, Trilby, Sven and I went for a longer walk.

At least I believe we did; surely we were together for most of the Sunday and indeed the Monday, Tuesday and Wednesday subsequent to our encounter on the bridge on the preceding Friday. I remember mounting the terraced steps to the woodland path and, turning right instead of left, following its looping course parallel to the river in the valley and up to the top of the ridge of hills behind the house. We rested on the summit, under some windswept Scotch pines, on a soft brown bed of pine needles, and skirted The Forest in our descent to the stables. We duly motored into Oswestry in Laura's car, an open scarlet two-seater MG, to buy my shirt and jersey. And we sauntered through the garden, the flower garden, and reclined in the deck chairs on the verandah of the summer house by the lake.

The mornings and late evenings were misty. On moonlit nights, crossing the water meadow, I'd be gazed at by legless and even bodiless cows, only their heads emerging from the layers of mist. At night and in the dawn the river was a misty white ribbon threading through the landscape. But the heat of the sun soon dried the air, and summoned the spring blossom and green buds of trees: the sticky buds along the languorous branches of the chestnuts were in leaf. The state of nature – the growing confidence of plants and song birds – was also mine.

It was almost mine. The checks in my relations with Laura, infinitesimal as they were, were almost forgotten. Yes, our friendship advanced straight and true, like an arrow from a bow, shot into the empyrean blue of the phenomenal weather. I can't recall in detail what it was that we discussed. I can't recall what we didn't discuss. Random pieces of information and echoes of our laughter float back to me. For instance, Esmond Charrington lived with his housekeeper, Mrs Blenkinsop, in every sense; but he imprisoned her in his cottage; he really was a cynical devil. Llanwyn was entailed, it and the estate would pass from Colonel Dellamere to a distant disagreeable cousin; whence Laura's reluctance to pester her father to repair the place. Her flat in London was in Aberystwyth Mansions; its nominal connection with

Wales eased her nostalgia. She loved her country and her home – she loved them all the more in the capital of England.

We laughed at indescribable incidents. The circumstances we found ridiculous have escaped me. But I can hear her saying: 'I haven't laughed properly for such a long time!' – and visualise the poignant swelling of the skin under her eyes, her eyes awash with sweet tears. Often she was serious, although seriousness doesn't describe her capacity for fervently glowing. My ambition to be a writer, my apprenticeship to literature which would never be done, the renunciatory aspect of the work, the self-denial and dedication, and the likelihood of disillusion in the final analysis – thus she'd ascend, as if by the rungs of a ladder, to an idealistic plane far above mundane matters, where she was somehow at peace.

Her sacrificial view of my career could get me down. Once she opined judiciously: 'As a rule good books are written by authors quite a bit older than you are.' Despite my own enthusiasm for the ideal, notably the ideal of her interest and herself, I ventured to remonstrate: what was the literary point of my presence in Wales in that case? Was she saying my cause was doomed? Was the struggle worth it? She answered in oracular fashion: 'Oh yes – struggles are!' She added or inquired on a cogent pleading note: struggles by definition were worthwhile, struggles to develop, weren't they?

She'd read and she knew much more than me. The establishment of her as my intellectual mentor relieved me of the need to examine or cross-examine her theories. Again I listened, I admired; and hoping that her forecast of my career wasn't accurate, concentrated on the rise and fall of her voice and her moving lips, her full expressive outward-curving upper lip and moist white teeth.

On the Tuesday or the Wednesday I told her my story. We were sitting on the verandah of the summer house; she was wearing dark glasses to protect her eyes from the glare; therefore it must have been morning, before the sun had circled and sunk behind the chestnut avenue – from mid-day on the rotting summer house and the lake in shadow were gloomy. In those surroundings and in her company the reasons why I'd sought refuge at The Dellamere Arms seemed to be positively fictional. Deane End and Thrushton, Bartletts and Singletons and Nash and King were figments of my imagination, and pressure to marry and support Mary had been exerted on someone else ages ago. I remember replying to Laura's questions unwillingly, not because of the private intensity of my feelings but because they were already so dim, and, even if I was unaware of the subtleties of the situation into which I was being drawn, because of the banality of my past in comparison with present realities.

Whether or not I loved Mary or ever had loved her, I curtailed and glossed over the story of our association, its conventional plot, in order not to bore Laura. Possibly it was during my recital that I recognised her restlessness. Although she sat still, I sensed the effort that was being expended to obtain her stillness. Except when she was promulgating her ideas, rising to the challenge of literature, soaring and glowing impersonally, there was an element of self-control in her – she was like someone with train fever who is resolutely refusing to look at the clock. Am I exaggerating? She could be gay and seemed to be equable; but the appeal of her laughter lay in its undertone, its melancholy; and she said she was cowardly; she was tense and nibbled her fingernails. At any rate, by the lake with its reeds and lily roots snaking out of the water, my secrets however hackneyed and her responsive murmurs carried our friendship a stage further.

On the Wednesday evening I dined at Llanwyn. Esmond Charrington in a brown velvet suit and velvet slippers to match was dining also. He'd probably had a drink or two in his cottage, and he tossed back several glasses of sherry, and wine and port in the dining-room; and afterwards in the library, while Miss Tufton blinked soporifically and Colonel Dellamere smoked his stubby pipe, he engaged in a duel of words with Miss Dellamere and Laura.

Laura was fond of him, I realised, but uneasy in his presence, nervous no doubt of what he would say next. His subject was women; women who would have a great deal to answer for at the last trump, he asserted; whose object in life was to render as many members of the opposite sex as unhappy as they could – haughty icy-hearted creatures such as Angela Dellamere had been, a regular Boadicea, slicing her lovers to pieces with her chariot wheels, and goddesses with feet of clay, naughty disingenuous girls like Loll.

He was provocative and aggressive. I recall the concluding exchanges which were definitely hostile. Laura, on being called naughty, flushed uncomfortably and glanced at me.

Captain Charrington advised her: 'Leave your young man out of it.'

Whereupon she blushed, her colour deepened, and she rounded on him: 'You make me feel sorry for Mrs Blenkinsop!' – and Miss Dellamere chipped in: 'As usual you've gone too far, Esmond. Run along home – we've had enough of you.'

He was disconcerted, but recovered himself and laughed. He informed the Colonel that his sister and his daughter were harpies.

'They say they've had enough of me, Bobs – and I can take a hint.'

Everybody now laughed. The party was over. Captain Charrington tried to kiss Laura, who pouted and repulsed him.

'Come on, Loll, don't sulk – see me off the premises.'

It would have been difficult to refuse. Moreover Sven was nagging Laura to be let out. Covertly she glanced in my direction.

Through the evening her glances had seemed to celebrate our closeness. After all I'd confided in her, and she was confiding in me to the extent of suing for my protection. I said my goodbyes – I wouldn't allow her to be embarrassed by unwelcome overtures and kisses. The colour that lingered in her cheeks, the fugitive movements of her eyes had stirred my chivalrous instincts; and I wondered at her excessive sensitivity to a few rather harmless jokes, at her overdoing it, in Pixie Tufton's terminology. Into the back of my mind was creeping the suspicion that Esmond Charrington's charge of naughtiness and Laura's reaction were signs of a certain intimacy between them.

We progressed along the passage and emerged from the side door on to the terrace, Captain Charrington with his arm round Laura's waist, I and the dogs following behind. The dogs disappeared into the night. Captain Charrington muttered in an undertone or whispered in Laura's ear, and attempted to embrace her. She, as she wrestled with him, reminded me that I'd forgotten my book.

The reminder was genuine: she was lending me Turgenev's *First Love* – Turgenev was her favourite author: earlier she'd brought the book downstairs.

'Oh yes!'

'I'll fetch it,' she said.

Captain Charrington swore under his breath, and he and even Laura laughed.

'Well, I know when I'm beaten. Good night, darling – don't be cross with me. Good night, sir, and good luck!'

I replied: 'Good night!' – and he retreated round the corner of the wing of the house.

'That man,' Laura burst out: 'he's got a viper's tongue!' She turned, touched my hand, squeezed it gratefully. 'Thank you for coming to the rescue.'

My heart began to thump. I pursued her along the passage, back towards the library. On a table, visible through the open door, was the copy of *First Love.* She entered the room.

'Laura,' Miss Tufton inquired, 'when are you expecting George?'

'On Friday.'

'Friday! Isn't that the day Penelope Wessel arrives at Foresters?'

I was waiting in the passage. She collected the book and thrust it at me. We returned to the side door and we parted. I might or might not have received the impression that she'd relapsed into her strained unapproachable mood. I was too excited by the touch of her hand to notice anything much, apart from my own feelings.

I was surer of the miraculous possibility of her loving me.

The next morning at ten o'clock I rang her.

Morgan answered the telephone.

'Oh, Morgan, could I have a word with Miss Laura, please?'

'Miss Laura's gone away.'

FOUR

I was astonished.

'What?'

'Miss Laura's gone away, sir,' Morgan repeated.

'When did she go?'

'Early, sir, soon after eight.'

'But where?'

'I wouldn't know, sir,' Morgan replied primly, as if to say: that's no business of yours or mine.

'When's she coming back?'

'Coming back, sir?'

'Yes!'

'She should be back tomorrow evening.'

I rang off, relieved, temporarily relieved, having imagined for a moment that she'd gone for good. It was another of Morgan's tricks to suggest spitefully that I'd never see her again. She must have been summoned somewhere without warning, to London, to attend to her flat in Aberystwyth Mansions, or to talk to the people for whom she was reading the manuscript, or for medical reasons: but I couldn't believe she was ill. We hadn't planned to meet – but precedents had been set in the last week; my consequent assumption was that we'd spend at least a part of the day together; and the touch of her hand on the terrace was tantamount to a promise. I convinced myself that Miss Dellamere or Miss Tufton would telephone an explanation, or a regretful note would be delivered shortly. Nothing happened, except that I remembered my appointment to have my stitches out in Llanrhad.

It was for twelve o'clock: it was already eleven. In the absence of Laura, whose promise to drive me over had been broken beyond any doubt, I consulted Mrs Roope. The Llanrhad bus would stop at Mrs

Rogers' shop at eleven-fifteen, she said, and the afternoon bus for Llanwyn and Oswestry left Llanrhad at four. Of course I could take a taxi or try to, but that would cost more money. No, I answered, wishing at once to economise and obscurely to punish Laura by piling on the agony, I'd catch the bus – and I sprinted along to the crossroads.

The bus was late – I had to sweat and kick my heels for a quarter of an hour. In Llanrhad I had trouble in finding Doctor Hughes' surgery, and the removal of my stitches was painful physically and morally, reminiscent as it was of the beautiful fortifying eyes into which I wasn't gazing. Lunch in a pub consisted of cold pie and indigestible ale; and then I hung about, smoking and thinking too much, for the bus to carry me home.

Not a word from Laura awaited me at The Dellamere Arms. My disappointment was the more acute both because of the assurances of her hand the previous evening – what had that intimate squeeze signified? Had I misinterpreted its message? – and because I was unaccustomed to such cavalier treatment. At least Mary wouldn't have abandoned me, let me down, sacrificed me to a whim, behaved so ruthlessly. For the first time since saying goodbye to Mary I dwelt on her virtues; but they recalled Laura's which weren't secretarially scrupulous, which were on a bigger scale. I was halted in the mental tracks of my resentment by the recognition that if Laura hadn't been mysterious, capable of flouting the rules and upsetting me, I wouldn't have cared for her. I might have been attracted, I would have admired her fleshly attributes, but not cared, not respected and looked up to her, as I did or I had.

Towards six-thirty I descended from my room to chat to Mrs Roope. In the bar, the saloon bar, through which I had to pass in order to reach the parlour, was Morgan. He wore a shiny blue serge suit. His black homburg hat and a glass of whisky were on the counter.

He greeted me. I returned his greeting with mixed feelings. A number of equivocal incidents, the latest of which was his manner on the telephone that morning, had inclined me to agree with Laura that he was sinister – and he might be drunk. At the same time I jumped to the conclusion, largely because of his use of the saloon rather than the public bar, remarkable in view of his butler's training in class discrimination, that he was the bearer of news.

He'd appeared to be on the lookout for me.

Yet all he said was: 'Another fine day, sir.'

As far as I was concerned it couldn't have been more frustrating. But

I allowed that it was fine, and, rallying my forces, asked outright: 'Have you heard from Miss Laura?'

'No, sir. Have you?'

'No. No – she seems to have vanished into thin air, doesn't she?'

'Yes, sir. That's her way, sir.'

I winced. He had a throaty voice with a Welsh lilt. His eyes under his bushy black eyebrows, which curled upwards and almost met his shock of grizzled hair, were watching me attentively; his eyes were small and black. Could he have come to The Dellamere Arms not to give but to get news – to study and if he could to add to my frustration?

'Will you do me the honour of accepting a drink, sir?'

'Well – no.' I wanted neither to talk nor to be beholden to him. I felt more than ever that he was deliberately transgressing against a social code. I sensed beneath his obsequiousness, in his inquisitive eyes, the strain of his malice. 'It's kind of you, Morgan, but Mrs Roope's expecting me to have supper.'

'Then I'll wish you health and happiness, if I may, sir.'

The hairs on the back of the red shaky hand that held his glass were black.

'Oh, thank you – same to you, Morgan.'

'Good evening, sir.'

'Good evening.'

In the parlour I mentioned Morgan to Mrs Roope.

'Yes,' she said; 'he was inquiring for you.'

'Isn't he a peculiar man?'

'It's the bottle.'

I agreed: Morgan must have been tipsy. Yet I'd been right in believing that one of the objects of his visit to The Dellamere Arms was to see me; another, probably, was to insinuate his drop of poison in my ear. Laura's way, what did it mean – not keeping faith with her friends and more than friends? Had she done it before? And to whom? The meaning of his wish for my happiness was that he wished me to be unhappy: why? Was he in love with Laura? I'd led a sheltered life, had never at school or in the army or anywhere been at the receiving end of malevolence, gratuitous malevolence, no less. The metaphor that sprang to mind was biblical: the serpent had crawled into the Garden of Eden.

My mystification and depression deepened in the next thirty-six hours, that Thursday night, Friday and into Saturday morning. I talked to Mrs Roope, who told me Morgan was nearly seventy: I was additionally shocked that at his age he should entertain evil intentions towards me. He'd been with Colonel Dellamere for ever, since he was the Colonel's batman in the 1914 war, and was a bachelor, but supposed to have an understanding with Mrs Wipps. Laura had introduced me to Mrs Wipps, a widow, a stringy female in glasses with elastoplast bound round the nose-piece; she and Miss Tufton quarrelled constantly and she persecuted her kitchen-maid, a slob of a girl called May. Her fiery temper could have driven the butler to drown his sorrows, including a jealous passion for his employer's daughter.

I recollected my own spasm of jealousy of Esmond Charrington. Repeatedly I reconsidered the events of the evening on which he'd accused Laura of naughtiness. His charge had been that she was naughty and disingenuous: was her sensitivity to it overdone because of her guilt? Yet surely Miss Angela Dellamere was never like Boadicea. Captain Charrington had gone to absurd lengths in order to provoke her – and, by inference, her niece. On second thoughts the wrath of Laura, who wasn't naughty in any accepted sense, was righteous; and she soon laughed and swore at her traducer in a manner that was normal in the circumstances. No, Captain Charrington in spite of his viper's tongue wasn't the serpent in our paradise. And his slightly immoderate conduct couldn't be the cause of her taking flight – flight or fright.

What else might have frightened her? She herself, voluntarily, had squeezed my hand: I was passive and therefore not at fault. We'd returned to the library for the copy of *First Love,* and she'd been asked a couple of questions by Pixie Tufton, about somebody's arrival somewhere. I interrogated Mrs Roope. She knew of no one's arrival in the neighbourhood. She was sorry, she couldn't help. The triviality of those indistinct questions had quite erased them from my memory. Yet reflection persuaded me that a minute later, when Laura and I parted by the side door, she was in her withdrawn, her abnormal state, preparing possibly to flee from the scene of her sudden unaccountable discomfiture.

Of course it wasn't much – I'd have noticed more at the time if it had been. She seemed to pause, lose her thread, interrupt her rhythm, shy off into introspection: she'd done so by the gates of Llanwyn, where she insisted on her cowardice and on the need for courage, and again when she confessed that she loved Sven best. Such episodes assumed more weight by being tacked on to her disappearance. There was a duality in her – her birthday was a month after mine, on 2 June: her sign of the zodiac was Gemini, The Twins. She was the original Laura of the operation to extract the fish-hook, whose advances were comradely, direct, frank, and another Laura with a separate emotional existence, a creature of ambiguities and retractations.

My conclusion was a conscious statement of the obvious. A girl as outstandingly beautiful and intelligent as she was wouldn't hover in a sequestered Welsh valley in anticipation of the union of her destiny with mine. At twenty-six she couldn't be an innocent unattached angel. The illusion fostered by our exclusive association was too good to be true. The world and its claims, and the implications of my love, to wit that she was exceptionally lovable, refused to be kept at bay. Besides, without false modesty and discounting the subservience of my feelings for her, realistically, I wasn't her equal in age or experience, physically, socially, in any department. I was a raw youth, penniless by her standards, not handsome, bespectacled. All of value, or perhaps of value, that I had to offer her was the romance of how and why I came to be at The Dellamere Arms, and my heart.

Clearly it wasn't enough.

On Saturday morning Laura telephoned. The sound of her voice immediately cancelled my resentment and reversed my hopelessness. She explained – superfluously, for the slate was wiped clean by the magic syllables of her hullo – she explained or exclaimed that she was aghast to think of my trailing into Llanrhad to have my stitches out alone. She'd only remembered her promise yesterday, Friday, driving down to Llanwyn. Was I cross with her as I had every right to be? Would I ever forgive her?

'You're always being asked to forgive some member of my family. But I'm truly sorry, Arthur. Please don't hold it against me – and tell me how you are.'

Yes, I forgave her, naturally, I replied, and I was pretty well.

She said she was glad. She invited me to dinner. She also said she was in a rush, unable to speak freely for the moment.

In the evening I crossed the water meadow. Spring, apparently, had resumed its sanguine sway. The birds were singing as before in the chestnut avenue and the gardens, and bats were swooping and squeaking in the twilight above the terrace. I entered the house without bothering to ring, according to recent custom. In the library Miss

Tufton was standing by the fire with a tall fair-haired man in a dinner jacket – George Sawrey.

So that was it. That was the name, George, which had eluded me. George Sawrey – hadn't he been cited by Mrs Roope as one of Laura's friends? The fantasy of my love was shattered by the facts, represented by this broad-shouldered, straight-backed, immaculate and mature interloper. Laura in her car had fetched him from London, Miss Tufton grumbled – driven hundreds of miles, reached Llanwyn at midnight – wasn't it silly? But I didn't have to be told. I recognised my rival at once, who was successful, who had anyway profited from my losses. I was no longer able to dodge the full force of my solitary deductions. Yes, Laura's separate existence was emotional, yes, she was lovable: she must have been and must be loved by crowds of men, from amongst whom she'd chosen George Sawrey.

I could see why. I wasn't surprised by the man of her choice. Part of me wasn't surprised by the revelation of our actual positions, which simply justified my worst fears. But I remember feeling thinner and paler and, next to George, in my tweed jacket and grey flannels, in a defeatist spirit, that I was the interloper. He turned out to be the second son of Lord Netherhampton, the Earl of Netherhampton. His elder brother was called Lord Stotebury: because he was Laura's friend and Laura was literary, when he first referred to Stotebury, 'Stotebury says this, Stotebury wouldn't approve of that,' I thought he was quoting from some esoteric influential author, another Gibbon or Macaulay. It was a foolish mistake, illustrative of my condition, for George was scarcely literate, although educated at Eton and Oxford. In the war he'd served in the army, winning a Military Cross, and now aged twenty-eight was demobilised and looking for a job.

He reminded me of old-style athletes in sepia-coloured photographs at school or in discontinued magazines, Bloods, Blues, fabled captains of winning sides, wearing tasselled caps and sweaters to their knees emblazoned with badges. He was a few inches taller than me, well over six feet, with a rectangular face and strong round neck, and very good complexion, powdery pink and white, and slightly tanned. His hair was blond with red in it, parted high up, brushed across rather than back from his forehead, flat and yet thick. The hand I shook was huge; but his hands were nicely shaped with large hard shiny nails. His nose was Roman, his teeth behind his unsensual lips were regular, and his manner was faultless, unassuming and unspoilt.

Colonel Dellamere and Miss Dellamere joined us in the library, and eventually Laura. Her beauty made me catch my breath – as usual, I was going to write: I mean more sharply than usual. Her beauty in which I'd have to renounce my interest seemed to surpass itself. She kissed me, crying, was she forgiven? – and then stood in front of the fire with George. The novelty of her kiss, which had been dreamt of, but not in public, not a pitying kiss, and the picture she completed of an ideal couple, all robbed me of breath.

Morgan announced dinner. As he served the soup he unsettled me further by mumbling into my ear: 'Good evening, sir,' as if to say: Well, I warned you, it's her way. Laura, seated between George and myself, gently teased her father and scolded and was scolded by Pixie. She fed her dogs and rallied her lover, who even had a jolly sense of humour. He discoursed on jobs and having to have them disarmingly.

'Colonel, how the hell does one earn one's living?'

Miss Dellamere cackled with mirth, evidently she had a soft spot for George, and said he should have stayed in the army.

'You're so right. I can't think why I ever left it. Why did I leave it, Laura?'

He went on in the same vein: 'The aristocratic principle won't wash. I'm dead against the aristocracy. We younger sons have the run of houses like Llanwyn and Netherhampton, and are trained to believe that meals grow on trees, and when we've become idle and effete, and our backbones are thoroughly decayed, we're cut off with a shilling and expected to compete for our slice of daily bread.'

Miss Tufton volunteered: 'The bread's no good nowadays. You couldn't keep body and soul together with a slice of modern bread.'

'Well, cake, Pixie, cake,' George laughed.

He was very much at home.

Later in the library, where the subject was reverted to, Laura inquired: 'What does Stotebury advise?'

Her ironical tone initiated me into the joke of his previous references to his brother.

'Ah, Stotebury! – Stotebury has spoken from the mountain top, from which he surveys his rolling acres. He says I'll have to marry an heiress or prepare for a pauper's grave.'

'A pauper's grave wouldn't suit you.'

'Exactly; but Stotebury says I'm digging it with my teeth.'

'Come, come, George! You're not as poor as that. I bet you're nowhere near as poor as Arthur.'

I was startled thus to be drawn into their conversation. Laura referred to my total investment of my resources in my writing. It shamed me to be championed mainly on the score of my poverty.

George must have shared some of my feelings: the comparison of his situation and mine showed his complaints in an inconsiderate light. For when the dogs had bullied us at ten o'clock, and I'd said good night and been kissed again and asked to lunch on the next day, he escorted me to the side door.

On the terrace he remarked, smiling down benignly, more than ever like the Captain of Games in a school story: 'That's a spiffing notion of yours, taking a room in a pub in order to write a book.'

'For the time being the book's only a notion, I'm afraid.'

'I'm sure you'll pull it off.'

'Thanks very much.'

'No – I mean it.'

He was a most engaging fellow. And I was pleased to revise my estimate of his chances. He and Laura might be lovers; but they'd been acquainted for years and were at ease with each other, which didn't tally with my experience of her separate existence. The tensions that divided her attention and impelled her to vanish into thin air argued a relationship more highly strung than at least the outward habit of theirs. Come, come, she'd corrected him. She could have punctured his conversational balloon because she was piqued by his contemplation of heiresses or coolly critical of his materialism. But her coolness ruled out her pique – and if she was in love with him would she have ventured to criticise? If he was in love with her, would he have offended against his code of kindness and tact by quoting Stotebury's advice? Why had she dragged in my name, to flatter and mollify me because she was sorry not to have nursed me through the removal of my stitches, or to mortify George?

Overnight I tended confusedly to the view that the probable bond between them was a scratchy old friendship, not a past or present love affair. On the other hand she'd driven hundreds of miles for his benefit; and he was such a paragon, her peer in many respects, that I couldn't count on her resistance to his suit.

The next day was Sunday, Palm Sunday, the Sunday before Easter, and in the morning the bell in the tower of Llanwyn Church rang across the water meadow. From the bow window of my room I watched the congregation arriving in twos and threes. They emerged from under the yew tree into the sun and followed the path round to the porch. I reached for my pair of binoculars with which I'd intended to study the birds of North Wales. I saw Colonel Dellamere and Miss Dellamere, he stumping along, she stiffly striding. Behind them was Miss Tufton in a blue beret, and behind her were Laura and George Sawrey, arm-in-arm. She had on another white or pale-coloured dress, and a hat with a floppy brim. His clothes were grey, light grey, festively light, and he wore a flower in his buttonhole.

It was like their wedding.

Having absorbed this last shock more or less, I partook of lunch at Llanwyn. Esmond Charrington was my fellow guest, and afterwards we found ourselves on the upper terrace, the promenade on a level with the first floor of the house and the top of the cedar tree in the centre of the lawn. He'd suggested a stroll: I think he and the Colonel were waiting for the brightness to fade before they started fishing. Our meal had been unproductive of any memorable incident. Captain Charrington had known George Sawrey since boyhood. The decanter of port had circulated, I seem to recall; and money was discussed once more.

Perhaps it was under the influence of the port that George declaimed: 'The best method of making money these days is to inherit the bloody stuff.'

Anyway the hour was about three. The sky was cloudless and the air warm, as warm as summer, in spite of the hint of a breeze. A net had been rigged up on the lawn, a volley-ball net, over which Laura and George had begun to throw a rubber ring. Miss Dellamere and Pixie Tufton were sitting on deck chairs on the lower terrace, between the porch and the shuttered drawing-room, in the sun and out of the wind. The Colonel was pottering somewhere.

Esmond and I strolled: he'd insisted on my using his Christian name. He said that if he'd settled with the ladies and listened to their chatter, 'which was like a sleeping-pill', he would have been out of commission for the rest of the day. He compared the raised promenade with the poop of a sailing ship – 'not that I've ever been on a sailing ship, let alone a poop.' He was fanciful, communicative, wryly amusing and relaxed. There was an angular promontory in the middle of the grass walk, with a rickety seat in it, constructed from the knotty branches of trees, to which he proposed that we should entrust our weary limbs.

The blue valley, the meanderings of the river marked by aspens and willows, the willows of Wyn Pool, The Dellamere Arms away to the right, above the tips of the cypresses in the kitchen garden, and the wooded opposing line of the hills were visible from our vantage point.

Down below us, George had divested himself of his grey Jacket and tie, and Laura of the cardigan she'd been wearing and her shoes: the clothing lay in heaps on the lawn, striped by its first mowing of the season. A game was in progress with the ring – it sped flatly over the net, or twisted elliptically, and was caught and returned. George stooped and reached for it with lazy grace, Laura was hampered by Trilby and Sven, who leapt and barked, pawing at her dress and tripping her.

Sometimes they caused her to miss or drop the ring, and Sven pounced on and ran with it in his mouth, proudly wagging his tail, and was pursued. She pretended to be ferocious, she ordered them to stop it and to come here, but laughingly – her game was as much with the dogs as with George. The flimsy skirt of her white dress flounced out as she tried to avoid or chased after them. Her ankles, not strained by the heels of her shoes, were sturdier.

'She's lovely, isn't she?'

Esmond had voiced my thought. I'd ceased to be jealous of him since the advent of George. His tone was detached and verged on the valedictory.

'Yes.'

That agreeable moment on the terrace, watching Laura, was one of the peaks in the graph of my feelings.

But for more than a moment I couldn't forget the evidence of the morning, outside the church, or again below me, provided by the symbolic ring – I couldn't divorce the bitterness from the sweetness of my love.

'Loll's a lovely girl, yes. Lovely girls have ruined my life.' He laughed or rather snorted complacently. 'They were my weakness, lovely helpless girls, damsels in distress, always in distress. I was born with the fatal gift of being able to understand women: fatal because to understand all is to forgive all. I made excuses for them. Once excuse a woman because she's a woman and you're finished. Take it from me: the person to look for is a woman whose attitude and actions wouldn't disgrace a gentleman. You don't mind my rambling on?'

I replied in the negative, although near to being alarmed, as I'd imagined Laura was, by what he might say next.

'Women let me rail at them because they know I am or was in their power. They only get angry when I tell the truth. They see red when I tell them black's black and white's white. The fair sex is unfair. Most of them behave appallingly. But they'd quibble at my opinion. They'd murder me for entertaining it.' He paused and chuckled: his chuckle was rich and nutty. The grey hair at his temples grew upwards and flowed back, waving and curling at the nape of his neck. His long-sighted countryman's eye was untroubled. He was a grand advertisement for a ruined life. 'Pretty faces are ten a penny. Stunning figures are common as muck. Loll's different, isn't she? It isn't just that she wins the prize for loveliness. She's clever and she wants to be good.' Again he chuckled. 'That's the definition of a siren, did you ever hear it? – A beautiful girl who wants to be good. I'm sorry she isn't happier.'

'What?'

'Loll isn't happy. She hasn't been here for a few months. And she's worse than she was. Who's the villain?'

'I'm not sure.'

'She hasn't poured out her troubles to you?'

'No.'

'Not yet. She will.'

They were laughing, and the dogs were barking, on the lawn.

'She's got George,' I said.

'George? George Sawrey? He'd be about as much use to Loll as a sick headache. Oh, he's a nice chap, a proper toff. But he's expensive, he's a luxury. He's a man for the woman who has everything. What he needs is a gilded cage. And Llanwyn won't belong to Loll, you know.'

As I remember, my companion was summoned by Colonel Dellamere, decorated like a Christmas tree with fishing-rods and fishing tackle, or Laura called to me to take her place – she had to have a breather. Whatever the reason, at that point my talk with Esmond merges reminiscently with its twin, which occurred on the following Wednesday.

George Sawrey left Llanwyn after tea on the Sunday. Laura drove him into Oswestry to catch his train. But, thanks to Esmond, I was impervious. George's marital needs, George's niceness, and in particular George's departure combined together to make my goodbye almost affectionate.

I was as tentatively hopeful as I'd been depressed by Laura's still unexplained disappearing act. For two and a half days we met, spoke on the telephone, walked and so on, as if nothing had happened.

It was idyllic. But she seemed to have lost the knack of dispelling my confusion, of expunging the past, by the sound of her voice or the sheer sight of her. She'd upset me, injured me – I loved her more, I required more than idylls: and the nature of love is not to be content. Further, due to her disappearance, and to Morgan, George and Esmond, I'd changed inasmuch as I was alert to her changes of mood.

She'd informed me in advance, as in the case of George Sawrey she hadn't, that two friends of hers would be spending the Easter weekend at Llanwyn: David Skelton, a painter, and Guy Toller. She and Guy Toller had worked in the war in a government office at Brayle in Berkshire. The annual Dellamere tradition was that on Sunday, Easter Day, local people and their children were invited to tea and an egg hunt. On the Wednesday we went into Oswestry to buy eggs for everyone. But the process of shopping had a bad effect on her. She complained of the traffic and the crowds. The colour drained from her cheeks. And in case I was in her way, and because it was my idea to find her a small private gift, I suggested we should part for an hour.

She read my mind.

She sparkled with a kind of flirtatious pathos and said: 'Promise me you won't be foolish.'

'I don't know what you mean.'

'I won't have you wasting your money on me.'

'That's my business.'

'Please, Arthur, please don't.'

'The same applies to you.'

She laughed. We arranged a rendezvous for lunch. But then I felt that her relief was overdone, she was hurtfully relieved to be on her own.

We lunched and drove home mainly in silence – it was difficult to talk in her open car. Her relief at being on her own in the trinket shop would have hurt less if it had fitted into any pattern of her avoidance of my company. But, since Sunday, she'd sought me out – practically clung – indicated that she wished to see as much of me as possible. Amongst the changes that I'd noted were the queries in her eyes and pauses in which she might have been trying to reach a decision. Her social kisses were equally indecisive – or such was my impression. To a certain extent therefore, if tacitly, she seemed to admit that her trip to London couldn't be ignored, was a happening, as a result of which our relations were entering a new phase.

But her relief denied it. Consciously I no longer aspired so high as her love or her reciprocation of mine. Partly because of what Esmond had said I expected her to confide in me. The fact was that she owed me an explanation. Her silence wasn't only a breach of her usually charming manners, it was defaulting on a debt.

At Llanwyn in the gravel sweep I thanked her formally and said goodbye.

'Oh no! Don't desert me. Come into the garden.'

I followed her through the door by the potting shed and along the winding path to the summer house. She sat on the worm-eaten wooden boards of the verandah, leaning against one of its side posts, while I reclined on the ground at her feet. Sandy earth, worked by ants, showed between the tufts of grass, and small yellow stones. I picked out the stones and tossed them into the shadowy lake.

I was now sure that she was about to explain all. But the rural peace remained unbroken, except for the occasional hollow plop of the stones.

At length I couldn't stand any more of it and inquired: 'Laura, why did you go to London?'

She started, jumped, she must have been very tense – but I was tense too – and returned jerkily: 'I knew you'd ask me sooner or later.'

'Well, why?'

'I had to. I had to deliver my report on that manuscript.' She mentioned Macleod's, the firm of publishers for which she was reading it. 'And I wanted to check that my flat hadn't been burgled, and collect clothes and things.'

It could have been true. An explanation on those lines had occurred to me. Yet I wasn't satisfied.

'So it was planned, your going to London?'

'I'd thought of it.'

'Why didn't you tell me?'

She hesitated.

'I hadn't finished my report. I really took off on the spur of the moment.'

'You could have told me you were thinking of going.'

She paused and shifted on to a different tack: 'I hoped you'd quite forgiven me.'

'I have. But – but you weren't collecting George?'

'Good Lord, no! No, I gave him a lift. Was that wrong?'

I replied, 'I see,' rather glumly, I suppose, and she laughed with more confidence and challenged me: 'Are we having our first quarrel?'

In my turn I protested: 'No!' – and glanced over my shoulder. Her head was thrown back against the supporting post of the verandah, and her regard from under lowered lids was taunting and quizzical. I wasn't entitled to catechise her, and to mitigate my offence, and because frankly I'd lost my bearings, I blundered on: 'No, but I was worried, Laura. I've been worried about you. Esmond worried me.'

'Esmond? What's Esmond got to do with it? Have you been discussing me?'

'No!'

My lie made me blush: I'd discussed her not only with Esmond, but with Mrs Roope and Morgan.

She swept aside my negative and levelled the charge: 'Esmond was gossiping on Sunday, wasn't he, on the terrace?'

'Yes –'

'What did he say?'

'He's devoted to you.' I sensed or heard her gesture of impatience. 'He said you were unhappy.'

'Did he? Did he say why?'

'No –'

'How dare he?' She controlled the throb of pain or anger in her voice and assumed a lighter tone: 'What else did he have to say?'

'He said lovely girls had ruined his life.'

I'd meant to amuse her, but, instead, seemed to provide a neutral pretext for the release of her pent-up emotions.

Esmond was intolerable, she declared – the most selfish of men.

'He's ruined the lives of hundreds of girls, and he passes judgement and puts the blame on them! He keeps his mistress incarcerated, he refuses to take her anywhere with him, and he flirts outrageously with every female for miles round! Oh, I can't help it – sometimes I loathe and despise your sex!'

I was horrified: she was so seriously irate.

'I'm sorry.'

She relapsed into silence, which reminded me of the inspiration of the whole unfortunate scene.

'I'm sorry, Laura – but you weren't yourself today – and I hate it when you're like that –'

'It wasn't your fault.'

She'd interrupted me, but sounded better.

'When you went to London I couldn't understand your not telling me, and Morgan said –'

'What?'

'Morgan said, it's her way.'

She questioned me softly and sadly: 'Did you mind that?'

'Yes.'

'Had you been gossiping with Morgan?'

'No. Honestly! He was in the pub on Thursday evening. I believe he wanted to get at me. But he was probably drunk.'

'He wanted to get at me, not at you. He never misses his chance. We've disliked each other for years.'

'Why should he dislike you, Laura?'

'I've no idea.'

For the second time I wasn't completely satisfied by her answer. But whether or not her father's butler liked or disliked her, and why, was a peripheral problem.

She shivered. She was chilly: the summer house in the afternoon, by the deep cold water of the lake, was a chill spot. We rose and retraced our steps along the path, I having ostentatiously dusted my trousers in order not to have to meet her eyes.

'You shouldn't be sorry,' she summed up. 'I'm sorry for everything. I'm always sorry! One day I'll tell you more. Can we leave it there?'

I was quick to agree that we could.

We emerged from the garden into the sunshine of the gravel sweep and began to unload our packages from the car. Miss Tufton appeared on the terrace above and called: 'Oh Laura, I've spoken to Penelope Wessel. She's coming with John and Elizabeth on Sunday. And Dick's arriving tomorrow.'

Laura acknowledged this message vaguely. She said she could manage to carry the packages indoors. I said goodbye and looked at her. But now, as on the occasion on which she'd been accused of naughtiness, her cheeks were flushed. Her colouring was rendered more vivid by the addition of bright pink to the gold. The expression in her sapphire eyes was indecipherable. But her eyes seemed to hold some sort of anguished plea.

At The Dellamere Arms, when I was calmer, I remembered Miss Tufton's previous reference to Penelope Wessel. Hers was the other name that had eluded me, uttered with George Sawrey's on the night prior to Laura's disappearance. I asked Mrs Roope at supper if she knew of a Miss or Mrs Wessel.

'Mrs Wessel from Foresters?'

'Yes, that's it.' I remembered the whole of the sentence overheard through the library door. 'Yes, Foresters, where is it? And who is she?'

'It's in the hills behind Llanwyn, Llanwyn House, a ramshackle place, at the end of the cart-track that starts by Mrs Rogers' shop.'

'In The Forest?'

'The Forest isn't a real forest, Mr Bartlett, it's woods, pine trees, planted by old Mr Dellamere. But Foresters is where the forester used to live – he was a Mr Edmonds, he died many years ago. It was empty in the war. When Mr and Mrs Wessel were bombed out in London, Colonel Dellamere offered it to them. They stayed for twelve months; but Mrs Wessel was alone with her children for most of the time – he had to work; and since then they've taken it for the school holidays at Easter and in the summer. Mrs Wessel's here now, Mrs Rogers was saying, but I haven't seen her.'

'What's she like?'

'Oh, Mrs Wessel's a great favourite.'

Upstairs in my room I paced the floor and sat at the writing table in the bow window, peering into the gathering mist, attempting to peer through the metaphorical mist. My efforts were and had been unavailing. In retrospect the scene in the summer house was worse than useless. I'd requested information and received none – Laura had been brilliantly evasive. All along, incidentally, by being in a rush, by behaving as if nothing had happened, she'd evaded the issue of London. Granted, our conversation was more emotional and intimate than any to date. Her undertaking to tell me the truth one day constituted an admission that she hadn't told it and that there was a truth to be told: thus my inquiries were legitimised. What was the cost of these uncertain advantages? – A situation so fraught as to imperil the resumption of our former friendly relations, while ruling out new phases in the foreseeable future.

In the night, or the small depressive hours of the morning, I came to the conclusion: it could be impossible. Obviously she was attached to somebody else, a villain who made her unhappy, a representative of the sex she loathed and despised. What was the point of loving her in vain, from afar, frittering my opportunities and money, getting more and more involved and bewildered? Shouldn't I pack my bags forthwith and slink home to Surrey? But in the dawn I was woken by dreams of the anguish in her eyes, no longer angry and not disingenuous, mysteriously pleading, pleading for my patience, and the sound of her voice, saying: 'Don't desert me.' I regretted my clumsy indiscretions which had annoyed her. The difficulties ahead, the constraints and resentments in our respective selves, dissolved in the rays of the sun.

I rang her.

The consequence of my telephone call was another trip into Oswestry to pick up Guy Toller and David Skelton later in the day. Again Laura had asked me to keep her company. I felt that she was determined to avoid a recurrence of the trouble over George.

We drove to the station in the Colonel's Wolseley Ten, a characteristically stubby black car with room for four. She drove it there, I drove it back – she'd tested my driving in her MG. I was conciliatory, she was subdued, but not silent. We might have swapped more apologies, I can't remember. Guy Toller was a short foxy-faced hard man of thirty. David Skelton was younger, twenty-three perhaps, tall and thin, with close-cropped brown hair and a widow's peak, like an overgrown faun. Guy sat beside me, David with Laura, who became rather animated on the return journey.

For various reasons I was beginning to relax. The circumstances of my introduction to her weekend guests allayed my jealousy. She sat sideways in the back-seat, her elbow almost resting on and touching my shoulder. Once at a crossroads I got in a muddle with the gear lever, and she leant across and placed her hand on mine; and at Llanwyn she reminded me of the luggage in the boot, as if I'd been her servant or her spouse. Pleasure that she was herself again, happier for the moment, mingled with my access of confidence in my power to see things through.

She invited me into the house. But the others would have to be shown their rooms and so on; it was already six-thirty; and I refused. Miss Tufton joined us on the terrace, dressed to visit Mrs Rogers at the Post Office – I said I'd walk with her to the corner. Laura seemed to kiss me goodbye more warmly than ever before.

'Thank you for your help,' she said: she must have meant with the Wolseley.

A sudden optimism possessed me. The evening was still sunny, and vibrant with the chorus of birdsong in the gardens. Miss Tufton carried an ash walking stick with a rubber grip on the bottom, and wore stout flat shoes, a faded Burberry and her tight blue beret – apparently in winter she wore an antique mackintosh pixie hood, whence her nickname. The drive, down which she plodded determinedly, was slashed by sunlight, and the Wyn trickled and purled in its canal.

'Who is this David Skelton?' Pixie demanded rhetorically. 'I know Guy Toller. He's been to stay two or three times. He's a socialist, he likes to be waited on hand and foot in big houses.' She tittered childishly. 'Laura says Mr Skelton's going to be a painter. She's enthusiastic! Her mother was enthusiastic, too. She overdid it if she could.'

We turned to the right on the road, after Pixie had paused to poke her stick at the gates and to grumble: 'Look at the rust! The gates need a coat of paint. But Colonel Dellamere lets them rot because of the entail. He's more like an Irishman than a Welshman. I've told him the roof will fall in on our heads before long.'

'Was Laura's mother beautiful?'

'Everybody talks of beauty. I'm sick of beauty. Mrs Dellamere's pet name was Missy.' She tittered innocently. 'Haven't you admired her portrait in the drawing-room? Oh no, it's been closed, the drawing-room, but it's open today – you'll be able to judge for yourself. The artist fell in love with her. He gave her eyes like blue saucers. She led the Colonel such a dance.'

'Why did they marry?'

'Oh, he adored her.' Pixie drew out the word, satirising the concept of adoration. 'And she was a widow, she'd been married to Michael Blake, who was killed in the First War. She was a poor widow.'

'Were they happy?'

'Mrs Dellamere would never stop to think whether she was happy or not. Her name for Colonel Dellamere was Daddy – he was fourteen years older than she was. Missy and Daddy! She didn't have enough to do at Llanwyn. She'd come down here for two or three months and after three days she'd be off to London – and bring home masses of people. She used to have crazy parties. At one party she sailed across the lake in a copper pot for flowers. She was motoring to London on the night her car crashed.'

'Was she alone in the car?'

'No.'

'Did the other person die?'

'No, he recovered.'

'Was it someone she loved?'

'Mrs Dellamere loved Michael Blake, Michael Blake and Laura. She was fond of the Colonel. But she wanted life to be romantic.'

'Did Laura love her?'

'Oh yes. Poor Laura! She'd love to be like her mother. She thinks she can follow her example. But Michael Blake was killed.'

'I don't understand, Miss Tufton.'

'It's time she found a reliable husband, who'd look after her. It's time she had children and security. But Mrs Dellamere was a widow when she married the Colonel.'

We were by the corner shop. Miss Tufton halted. I gazed into her pale eyes, seeking without success for an interpretation of these cryptic remarks.

'I'm sorry, I don't understand.'

'No,' she agreed absent-mindedly. 'No – that's right.' She appeared to recollect that the purpose of her walk was to call on Mrs Rogers, and, bidding me an emphatic goodbye, she lifted her stick and thumped its rubber end on the shop door.

FIVE

A medical or biological theory is that our bodies contain the germs of every conceivable disease, one or other of which will assume clinical proportions in certain conditions, for instance when we're in a weakened state of health or under the influence of some catalyst. For all I know the theory is proved, no longer theoretical, and the likelihood is that as a layman I've stated it incorrectly. But it could be an accurate metaphor for experience in general.

Whether or not we're born with a compendium of consciousness in our heads and hearts, an encyclopaedia of life, the pages of which will be turned by time, memory persuades me that the moment I set eyes on Laura I was in latent possession of the facts of her situation, hers and mine. Although afterwards I was bewildered and often nonplussed, each succeeding event and stage in the process of elucidation, as my initial surprise subsided, called forth the comment: 'Of course!' I'm thinking in particular of the realisations, realisations rather than discoveries, that she must be loved by lots of men and that she was in love with one, who caused her unhappiness.

But exceptions to my rule immediately present themselves. As to how Morgan figured in Laura's affairs I hadn't a clue, and Pixie Tufton's intervention seemed to fall into a category of its own. I was sure of nothing: what Pixie had been trying to tell me – even if she'd intervened. Walking from Mrs Rogers' shop to the pub, my optimism was nonetheless converted into the blackest pessimism. For I extracted from her enigmatic utterances a warning to desist. Laura wasn't as free as her widowed mother had been to find a reliable lover to look after her. Was I cast in the role of the victim of her futile attempts to follow her mother's example? Was my lack of understanding in Pixie's estimation a reason not to take the risk of paying my court? What was there to understand, what were the insuperable obstacles in my suitor's path, productive of so much unsolicited advice to give up?

I rose contumaciously to the challenge – and sank back at once into my defeatist posture. Laura was too mysterious, too beautiful, and rich and rare, and clever and old for me, I repeated. She wasn't poor except in a special sense. She'd told me she had a private income of six hundred pounds a year from a family trust and earned another hundred or two. She had enough, in that uninflated age, to keep a single girl who lived for perhaps three out of every twelve months at her father's expense in the country. The additional four hundred pounds that I might receive from Nash and King would provide the pair of us with a modest sufficiency. But owing to the entail Laura had no expectations to speak of, and my parents were always struggling financially in order to maintain Deane End: we weren't going to make money by inheriting the bloody stuff, the method recommended by George Sawrey. And carrying the argument to its logical conclusion, our union liable to be blessed by offspring, the drudgery of it on a meagre thousand per annum, exclusive of white dresses and sports cars and artistic tastes and temperamental excesses, was unthinkable.

The veiled hints and allusions of Morgan, Esmond, Pixie Tufton and Laura herself were largely wasted on the obtuseness of my youth: I was discouraged without being enlightened. But at last and at least they guided me towards an independent assessment. My future would be grim or dull, grim if I stuck to my writing, dull if I didn't and opted for publishing – and Laura was equipped to cope with neither alternative. She was fired by the difficulties of the literary vocation, but would never sustain its actual ascetic rigours, which I envisaged the more starkly because of her dire prophecies and my creative failures at The Dellamere Arms and elsewhere; while her becoming the consort of the office boy at Nash and King was out of the question. She needed a stately home and secluded grounds to roam in, a Bobs Dellamere who would endow her with ample leisure to sympathise with the ambitions of artists, who would disregard whatever dance she might lead him.

It was impossible, our union, in practical terms.

The embers of the fantasy of the first week of our friendship were extinguished on that Thursday evening.

The next day, Good Friday, the start of the third week, and on Saturday and Easter Day, I returned to Llanwyn. I'd promised to – and since I was now on my guard against sentimentality, why not? As Pixie had said, the drawing-room was open. Laura showed it to me: a large rectangular room with several windows, including a french window, and plaster strapwork on the ceiling. The panelling was painted white: 'It was a crime, painting the panelling, committed by Mama – but she hated the darkness.' I don't believe Laura had referred to her mother before.

The portrait hung above the fireplace. It was of a woman in her forties, swathed in semi-transparent draperies, with eyes absurdly big, like the saucers of Pixie's description. The head was held high in a striking pose, the neck long and curving, the slightly smiling face heart-shaped and elfin. She was attractive, not beautiful, despite the painter's manifest efforts to flatter her. An elusive quality, suggestive of a shy swift wild creature, was reminiscent of her daughter; also, behind those wide blue eyes and the proud curl of the mouth, a somehow frantic look.

I could have imagined the look almost of desperation. I had to equate the refined lady in the picture with the crazy party-giver and the sailor in a copper pot across the lake. No doubt the contact of her temper and that of the Colonel, of her restlessness and his regularity, contributed to her overdoing it. Perhaps she despaired of herself because she had to defy him, strain his steady affection and squander his money prodigally, or, in a more female down-to-earth fashion, because she loved and had lost Michael Blake and her second marriage was a secret travesty. Or was it that I happened to see Laura's desperation in her rather than her desperation in Laura?

Desperation is a strong word. Mrs Dellamere had an adoring husband and devoted child, a home, position, security. To my knowledge neither she nor Laura had anything concrete to despair about. Michael Blake's death, Mrs Dellamere's death, were sorrows for each of them, admittedly. Yet sorrow with its repose wasn't the common denominator that concerned me.

And speculation apart, and allowing for my tendency to exaggerate and anticipate, Laura's mood or variations of mood were extreme, to put it mildly, throughout the Easter weekend. Her Thursday animation in the car turned into a sort of fierce good humour. Pixie Tufton complained of her spirits: 'Laura, why are you laughing so loud? They'll hear you at the Post Office!' I remember a brittle interchange on a walk we took with Guy Toller and David Skelton, the looping walk parallel with the river and over the hill.

She asked me in an undertone: 'Are you all right?'

'Yes.'

'You've been quiet. You're not upset?'

'No!'

'Don't be. Don't be upset. Life's too short!'

On the Saturday evening, on which I dined at Llanwyn, we sat in the drawing-room. A fire was lit, and after dinner Laura knelt on the rug in front of it, beneath her mother's portrait. She was more solid in a complimentary sense than her mother, more sensuous. Her features were classically correct, although the severity of the classicism was alleviated by the idiosyncratic fullness of her upper lip: she'd inherited some of her father's cosiness. She caressed her dogs, sinking her smooth-skinned fingers into their fur, and chattered and joked with her guests. But every so often she seemed to falter, her expression frozen for an instant, her eyes unfocused, like a person spellbound, like a hunted animal, pausing with bated breath to listen for its pursuers. Then in a subliminal gesture so discreet that I was convinced nobody else could have noticed it, she'd shake her head, pull herself together, resume her conversation and plunge once more into the social fray, laughing louder than before.

When Sven had indicated that it was time for me to leave, she drew the curtains at the end of the room opposite the fire and opened the french window giving on to the terrace. There was a fine crescent moon, across which the shapes of bats flitted. She called to Guy and David, who joined us, admiring the landscape in the indigo light – and we wandered towards the lawn. That rubber ring was lying on the grass by the volleyball net. She picked it up and threw it over the net to one of us: we began to play a game in the moonlight. The ring was more or less invisible, and wet and slippery with dew, and we missed and dropped it, we slid and skidded and laughed.

The craziness of our sport on the lawn was worthy of Laura's mother. We must have played for half an hour. Pixie Tufton increased our amusement by screaming that we'd all catch pneumonia. At length we stopped.

'Look at your dress,' Pixie screamed – she was silhouetted in the window. It was a long dress: the back was stained with green and the hem was soaking. 'You're such a silly, Laura. And your father's fast asleep.'

'I love you, Pixie,' Laura retorted.

The dogs had disappeared.

She shooed her governess and the others into the drawing-room and kissed me goodbye.

'I'll get them much quicker if I'm left alone. Truly! They'll be by the rabbit warren. Pixie, do tell Daddy not to wait for me.'

'But you'll need a coat, Laura!'

'No, I won't. I won't be a minute.'

She strode round the corner of the house, heading for the steps to the higher terraces and the woods. I descended the steps to the gravel sweep and lingered under the chestnut avenue. I wanted to be sure she'd found the dogs, and was detained by her voice.

'Sven! Svengali! Sven, Sven!'

Her cries receded. Her cries in comparison with an occasional excited yelp were forlorn. The moon shone down on the brooding pile of her home and the black woods behind, a veritable forest tonight, a forest in a fairy tale, fit to engulf a princess.

'Sven, Sven!'

The gaiety of her laughter was exchanged for a note of – yes – desperation .

'Sven!'

Her single faint poignant cry inspired me to fancy that she was lost, she was hoping to be found by Sven, instead of vice versa. It penetrated my defences. But a dog barked and whimpered with joy – Trilby, I guessed it was. I heard nothing more and proceeded along the drive.

In the morning I went to church. A disinclination to have to watch the Llanwyn house party through my binoculars, jealousy again, and interest or self-interest, because I required help from any quarter, and finally the fact of its being Easter Day: these were my motives. I crossed the water meadow and waited by the porch, and eventually sat with Pixie Tufton and David Skelton in the pew behind Colonel Dellamere, Miss Dellamere, Laura and Guy. Laura had known of my plan to attend the service – I was to have lunch and assist with the preparations for the afternoon's entertainment – and greeted me with a cursory clasp of the hand. She wore a white dress and a wide-brimmed hat.

The interior of the church was barred by sun. Motes floated in it dreamily. Colonel Dellamere stumbled through the first lesson, and a Welsh patriarch with a walrus moustache and a weird accent read the second, and the parson, Mr Llewellyn, sermonised. In between times Laura seemed to me to pray very hard, kneeling on her hassock, bending her head and arching her neck, whereas the Colonel and Miss

Dellamere merely leant forwards in their seats. Her piety surprised me, as, for that matter, I was surprised by the presence of Guy and David, whose religious inclinations were no more credible than mine.

Needless to say, I'd been observing them closely in the last two days. I liked David Skelton. Given the chance, we might have become friends. He was delightful; funny, boyish, vital, if apt to suffer from physical exhaustion, being so tall; a genuine artist, I shouldn't wonder, although I saw none of his pictures – his saying that he couldn't work in the holiday atmosphere of Llanwyn salved my conscience to some extent. I remember his easy unforced tone and his appearance of a faun, bonily gangling yet graceful, and his eyes aslant under the widow's peak.

The sense of fun he shared with Laura was infallible. He relished the eccentricities of the old folk, the older Dellameres and Pixie, and without the trace of a smile would lead them on by means of polite questions – and unexpectedly glance across at Laura or at me, who would have to strive to contain our mirth. He nearly finished me in church by a nudge during the second lesson, intoned by the patriarch with the weird pronunciation, and again when Miss Dellamere lifted up her tuneless voice which was like the creak of a rusty hinge.

He was the son of a lawyer, of my class, and eked out his existence in the inevitable garret in London. At Llanwyn he preferred the library and the dining-room to the drawing-room: he differed from Laura's mother in his liking for dark ruinous rooms. He was charmed to think that the house was falling to pieces and congratulated Colonel Dellamere on not spoiling it. Early one morning I caught a glimpse of him through my bow window, knee-deep in mist by the river's bank, gathering a posy of spring flowers. He was always picking flowers and presenting them to Laura.

Undoubtedly he adored her, as Pixie might have put it. He admired her, commented on her clothes, the style and length of her hair, the shade of her lipstick and powder – they discussed such intimate details together. Indeed he aroused my jealousy by meeting her in the no-man's-land of her feminine preoccupations. But I hoped he was studying her beauty with his painter's thumb raised, judging it by pictorial standards, as if she'd been a model on a dais or an arrangement of apples and a pewter jug. And in spite of her evident affection for and gratitude to him, because he was undaunted by her notices to keep out, the idea that he wasn't a technical lover of women tended to assuage my fears.

My feelings for Guy Toller were more straightforward. His foxy face topped by a central wisp of hair, pale leathery skin, small discoloured teeth and tightly-knit aggressive figure weren't prepossessing. A disability – I never knew what it was – had exempted him from military service. He was educated at Winchester and Oxford, and since the war, which he spent in Berkshire, employed as Laura was in that governmental establishment, had worked in advertising. He was also a politician, nursing a constituency somewhere.

I'd laughed at Pixie's jibe at his socialist principles. But it seemed to contain several grains of truth. He did his best to be waited on hand and foot, he waived none of his rights as a guest of the Dellameres. For instance, on being offered the usual glass of sherry, he demanded gin; and I overheard Miss Dellamere muttering to Laura, 'Guy can't come down to breakfast at eleven o'clock – it's too hard on Morgan.' He annoyed me by borrowing my cigarettes, having arrived without any and smoked those in the Llanwyn cigarette boxes. Otherwise he ignored me until he was informed of my Eton scholarship. His more friendly overtures took the form of condescending remarks. He said of the Colonel: 'It's a fascinating survival, isn't it, his paternalistic approach to running the estate?' and, more oddly in view of his aim to become a representative of the people: 'Thank God he hasn't sold off the valley for a caravan site!'

The trouble was that Guy was intelligent, in spite of his crudity and lapses of taste, and competitive. He and Laura discussed their wartime experiences, and people I didn't know, at whose expense he could be witty. He was responsible for the witticism on the subject of my situation: 'How lucky you are to sleep every night in the Dellamere arms.' He was as energetic and as articulate in his sharp worldly way as David was the reverse. And pride wasn't his problem. On one occasion he had the temerity to suggest that Miss Dellamere was dressed to kill; was rebuked grittily – 'None of your impertinence, young man!'; and apologised in an abject manner and in public, thus causing extra awkwardness.

By Easter Day I'd arrived at the opinion that he was an unlikely recipient of Laura's love. But my very complacence in respect of Guy and David, a complacence which in other contexts had been shattered more than once, inclined me to imagine I was probably wrong. For David was out of the ordinary, and Guy proprietorial, he claimed Laura's attention, he held her hand and stroked her, and in private he might be sweet. Wasn't he competing, hadn't he competed in the war years, for her favours? What was he doing in church?

Afterwards, after matins, walking back to Llanwyn, he started to argue that Jesus Christ was homosexual.

Laura said: 'Oh shut up, Guy!'

She was angry. Her voice was exasperated. We were in the drive.

He laughed and led her across to the canal. Apparently his apologies were accepted and a reconciliation occurred; and the incident wasn't noticed by the others. But I was depressed to realise that my defences, sapped the previous evening, when I stood in the moonlit pool of the gravel sweep and listened to her despairing cries for Sven, were now weaker than I wished them to be. That she should sternly check Guy was gratifying, that he should so quickly reinstate himself in her good graces dismayed me. I was dismayed by the proof that they were at any rate close enough to quarrel.

I reformed my forces, my resolutions to be impersonal, but unsuccessfully. As soon as we reached the house, on the terrace, the distribution of Easter eggs began. Laura brought out a basket full of them, one for each person. The cardboard eggs, tied with ribbon, contained fishing flies for her father, embroidery scissors for her aunt, and chocolates for Pixie, who was forbidden to eat them all at once: the flies and the scissors I'd helped to buy in Oswestry. Inside Guy's egg was a miniature copy of Wordsworth's poems bound in red leather, inside David's a similar copy of Shakespeare's sonnets, and inside mine a copy of the sonnets of Keats.

She hadn't differentiated between us. Guy and David kissed and thanked her for their tiny books and retired indoors to fetch their presents. While they were absent and, as I remember, only Pixie remained on the terrace, I seized my opportunity, such as it was, for I'd longed to be alone with Laura for our first exchange of gifts, to produce mine.

It was in a small cardboard egg – it had fitted into my jacket pocket.

She opened it and saw the silver snuffbox bought on that day in Oswestry.

Her exclamations of curiosity deteriorated into cries akin to those of the night before, with a ring of desperation.

'Oh Arthur! How could you?'

'Don't you like it?'

'Yes, but – you shouldn't have. You promised me you wouldn't.'

'I never did.'

'You did! What am I supposed to say! Thank you! But I'd much rather you hadn't.'

Pixie, who was shown the box, aggravated matters. 'It's an expensive toy. You must be very rich. Laura'll lose it, she loses everything. Easter eggs are a waste of money.'

The box had cost four or five pounds. Apart from being a token of my sentiments, it was an inadequate recompense for the hospitality I'd enjoyed at Llanwyn.

'It wasn't expensive,' I protested: 'and think of the meals I've eaten here!' – although the meals were beside the point. 'Please, Laura!'

She shrugged.

But she was still agitated: her cheeks were pink and her eyes fugitive or frantic.

Guy and David returned with their presents, a chocolate egg and a comic woolly chick. Pixie had to mention the snuffbox. Their admiration of it increased our embarrassment.

Guy remarked: 'Well, well!' and typically, addressing Laura: 'Well, it must be nice to be loved.'

She changed the subject by crying out: 'Have a drink!' and carried the box and the basket into the drawing-room.

Even allowing that my egg was more valuable than it should have been, her agitation was disproportionate. Her extreme responses, her egg which wasn't preferential, agitated me. Was it Guy from whom she'd been careful not to distinguish me? Was her clash with Guy in the drive the tip of the iceberg of a deeper disagreement between them – which could account for the despairing episode of twelve hours before?

The advent of Esmond Charrington, followed by lunch, didn't dispel my sense of impending crisis. I was aware of Laura's discomposure in every gesture and every word she spoke. Although she reappeared on the terrace for a glass of sherry, smiling, especially in my direction, as if pleading for pardon and to console me, I half feared that her hesitancy and a particular abrupt movement of her head – marked – not subliminal any more – would provoke comment.

But Esmond, who might have picked on her, was teasing Guy. They were acquainted, had met in the course of their former visits to Llanwyn, and immediately entered into a political dispute which continued through the meal. Esmond accused Guy of being a champagne socialist, or, he corrected himself, a sherry socialist; Miss Dellamere observed that any politician who pretended he could alter things for the better was either a damned fool or a charlatan; Pixie Tufton blamed the socialists for food rationing; and Laura confounded my confusion by seeming to agree with the opponents of her lover.

At about two-thirty she rose from the table: we had to prepare for the party. It was one of two annual Easter celebrations, I understood, the other being the tug-of-war between the Llanwyn House and Llanwyn Estate teams, due to take place next Sunday. She fetched a second basketful of eggs and, while Esmond and Guy, Miss Dellamere and Pixie took their controversial ease on the terrace chairs, and Colonel Dellamere pottered towards the farm, she and David and I set to work. The names of grown-ups and children were written on labels attached to each egg, which we hid in the flower beds, in holes in the trunk of the cedar tree, and on the higher terrace, in crevices in walls.

Occasionally Esmond's cynical crow or Miss Dellamere's cackle of laughter was heard.

At some stage I said to Laura: 'Guy's getting the worst of it.'

'Guy deserves to,' she replied in her terse exasperated tone.

Her terseness was another contradiction of my theory that she was suffering for Guy's sake. Perhaps she wasn't suffering, she just wasn't feeling her best. She issued her orders: 'Put an egg behind the aubretia – no, Arthur, that won't do.' But my attempts at conversation obviously tightened the screw of her tension or whatever it was. In a sort of agitated version of her winning way, she jerked her head instead of tilting it, she shied from me. Then she'd bite her upper lip and force herself to answer and smile, or talk to David.

By three the eggs were all concealed. We rejoined the others. Morgan was collecting the coffee cups. He suggested to Laura that tea should be laid out-of-doors.

'Wouldn't it be a bother, Morgan?'

'No, Miss. The trestle table's handy – we'll be needing it for the tug-of-war supper.'

'The party today isn't smart, Morgan.'

Again her tone was exasperated.

'No, Miss, I know.'

'Oh well – if you don't mind.'

'Thank you, Miss.'

Laura, Miss Dellamere and Pixie went indoors to get ready. The deck chairs were pushed into the bay between the porch and the extension of the drawing-room wing. On a board balanced on trestles a white cloth reaching to the ground was spread. Through the french window Morgan bore trays of plates and cups and saucers and glasses for orangeade which he arranged symmetrically on the cloth. Esmond and Guy had been detailed to find the Colonel. David and I strolled on the lawn.

The weather was decidedly hot – we were in our shirtsleeves. The blue wistaria across the front of the house was almost in bloom. But a certain sound recreates for me the atmospheric conditions of that Eastertide and my spring season in Wales: the shrieking and twittering of swifts and swallows round the eaves of Laura's home and down by the river, where they obtained the mud for their nests. They were flying in for their summer stay, and provided a constant accompaniment to my love during the hours of daylight, as the squeaking of the Llanwyn bats was an obbligato on the same theme at night.

An equally evocative sight lingers in my memory: that of the farm labourer who used to trudge past my window at The Dellamere Arms in the morning mist. Invariably at mid-day he returned to the pub for a pint of beer to drink with the sandwiches which he carried in a gas-mask case. His gas-mask case was slung on a piece of string across his chest: it was a symbol of peace. He carried his tankard of beer over the road, placed it on the lower step of the stile into the water meadow, and sat on the top bar, surveying the valley. I forgot to ask the Roopes or Laura who he was and where he worked and how he happened to be within walking distance of his beer in the middle of every day; and can't recall his countenance, never having had more than a bird's eye view of it – and he wore a cap with the peak pulled low. Yet time and I together have translated him, notwithstanding his bulky hunched shoulders and red hands, patched coat and mufflers and cap, into one of those naked cherubs on antique maps, benevolently puffing out vernal zephyrs.

The honking of a car's horn announced the arrival of our guests. Rudely, playing tunes, three short honks and a long one, the V-for-victory signal, the horn blared in the drive. David Skelton and I, Colonel Dellamere, Esmond and Guy and the ladies congregated above the terrace steps. An American station wagon was pursuing a Baby Austin, honking at it: both cars parked in the gravel sweep. All the doors in the station wagon opened at once, and the Deeps family tumbled out, laughing, honking with laughter. An elderly couple, Charles Winter and his wife and their only child, a boy aged ten or eleven, got out of the Austin.

Deeps surrounded Winters. There were two Deeps adults and some five children: the children were like a litter of puppies, constantly on the move, scrambling over one another, ragging, fighting, and impossible to count. Charles Winter was a dignified estate agent with smooth grey hair perfectly parted, hardly the man to be honked at; but Billy Deeps was no respecter of persons. He was a landowner and farmer, heavily built and bursting with exuberant health and good humour. He and his plump wife Molly and their issue had a common characteristic, apart from their exuberance and corduroys: loose oily wrinkly skin, like the skin of a Labrador dog. Metaphorically speaking they barked and yapped and pawed and wagged their tails at, and licked the hands of Mr and Mrs Winter, who gallantly withstood the onslaught, sheltering their cringing little boy between them.

The groups of guests and hosts met, and introductions were effected. Another car, a sedate Ford Pilot containing the Wessel family, rolled up the drive. Except for David and myself, everybody seemed to know everybody else. Guy had come across the Deeps and Winters at Llanwyn, and had been a colleague of Dick Wessel's in the war: Dick Wessel had worked in Berkshire too. The Wessels' period of residence and then their holidays at Foresters had drawn them into the social life of the county.

Mrs Wessel was a junoesque woman, taller and broader than her husband, who was a German refugee, surely Jewish: his name hadn't suggested he was a foreigner. She was forty or so, handsome although worn, with a mass of untidy blondish hair and sticking-out teeth. He had receding black hair, curly at the neck, a wide flat mouth, large even teeth, and an aloof or defensive manner.

The Deeps were creating havoc. The Wessel children, John and Elizabeth, were hugged, kissed, patted, punched and pulled in different directions by the Deeps children of both sexes. There was an extraordinary amount of activity: Deeps bodies squirmed and wriggled through the crowd, bumping into people, and Deeps voices shrilled and boomed. Esmond Charrington's remark: 'My God, Billy, you're a noisy crew!' was greeted by gales of laughter. Penelope Wessel, who was such a favourite, was embracing or being embraced by Guy, Pixie, Molly Deeps. Laura, looking wan, wanly beautiful, was trying to organise the Easter egg hunt.

Eventually, having called for silence, shouted for silence, she explained the rules of it and pointed to the territorial limits of the hunt.

'Go!'

The Deeps, including Molly and Billy, thundered across the paving stones of the terrace, followed by the Wessel and Winter children. Mr and Mrs Winter sauntered after them, chatting to Colonel Dellamere and wondering where their eggs could be. I remained on the lawn with Pixie, and Esmond and Miss Dellamere, and Guy and Dick Wessel, watching the busy searchers in the sunshine, supervised by David and Laura. Penelope Wessel was over by the tea table, talking to Morgan who had appeared with plates of sandwiches and cakes.

Pixie observed with her innocent titter: 'Morgan'll be happy now. Tea out-of-doors is for Penelope's benefit. He's in love with Penelope!'

Colonel Dellamere hailed Dick Wessel: 'Afternoon! You know my sister, don't you? Ange, you know Mr Wessel, don't you?'

'Yes indeed,' Miss Dellamere replied drily and resumed her conversation with Esmond.

The Colonel, more polite, continued: 'Is the water working at Foresters?'

'Thank you, yes.'

'I was afraid you'd all die of thirst.'

'Thank you, Colonel – no danger of that while the pubs are open.'

'No!' Colonel Dellamere was kind enough to laugh at the ponderous joke, a would-be anglicism. 'Only down here for the weekend, I suppose?'

'Yes, sir.'

'But you'll help us with the tug-of-war a week from today?'

'Certainly – my son will help you.'

'Splendid!'

Laura passed us, leading a child, one of the younger Deeps, towards the flower bed above the retaining wall of the garden.

She called to Dick Wessel: 'You shouldn't be standing there, you should be hunting for your egg!'

'Oh?'

'Have you been introduced to Arthur Bartlett? Arthur's a writer –'

The child, a true Deeps, dragged at her arm.

Dick Wessel and I shook hands. His hand was small; at close quarters he was smaller and neater than he'd seemed to be – perhaps five feet six inches in height. He wore grey flannel trousers with a sharp crease and a conventional tweed jacket, and struck an outlandish note in his English clothes. I couldn't imagine his being any use in a tug-of-war. But he himself had said that his son would help.

His teutonic accent was marked. His attitude to the Colonel had been a trifle smarmy. His brown eyes flickered up to and across mine. He had soft brown eyes, thin-lidded and suspicious, flickering as if not to miss any sign of prejudice or persecution.

'What do you write?' he asked ironically or even sarcastically.

Oh, nothing, I was a beginner. Was he interested in books?

'Yes.'

'Do you write them?'

'I have written a book.'

He was uncommunicative and inattentive.

I floundered, feeling stupid, and inquired: 'What type of book?'

'I'm ashamed to confess it was a book of poetry.'

'Why are you ashamed?'

He smiled, but not at me, his flat lips parting over his large teeth, and, producing a silver cigarette box from his pocket, lit a cigarette without offering me one.

I added with a tinge of asperity in my voice, resenting his rudeness: 'I wouldn't be ashamed to have written any book. Are you writing poetry nowadays?'

'No. I'm neither youthful nor wealthy, so I don't write.'

I'd been snubbed and I blushed.

He added quickly, with another smile, penitent and more direct: 'No – I wrote a book of poems in German when I was a student: student's poems! As you can see, I've become a family man. Families and poetry don't mix.'

We were interrupted. Children were dashing to and fro on the lawn, yelling. Dick Wessel was defensive: he was small and a refugee. But in fact my questions had been stupid, tactless and disrespectful of his seniority – he was about the same age as his wife. And he was sorry to have snubbed me; he was self-possessed, not to be patronised, and a poet; and I was sorry not to have made more of our talk. His eyes were rather tired than anything else.

Before tea or while it was being consumed, I can't remember which, I overheard Esmond Charrington saying to Angela Dellamere: 'You're a hard-hearted hussy,' to which she retorted: 'I have my likes and dislikes.'

The winner of the prize for the first person to find the egg with his or her name on it was Molly Deeps. She uttered a wild hulloo on the upper terrace and plunged down the steps, her matronly excrescences swinging and swaying. Soon afterwards the eggs of the other grown-ups were found, thanks to hints from Laura and David, Laura going so far as to tell Esmond and her Father where theirs were hidden. Tea was served: the Deeps lined along the trestle table as if it had been a feeding trough and devoured the dainty fare. At tea-time Trilby and Sven were allowed to join the party.

An hour went by: it was getting on for six o'clock. The Winter child, the Wessels' Elizabeth and a couple of Deeps were playing a game with the rubber ring and the volleyball net. A solitary Deeps, Laura's erstwhile charge, was clambering on the steps by the drawing-room windows. The adults had split into groups. Pixie was with Penelope Wessel and Morgan on the paved terrace; Dick Wessel and Guy were standing near them on the lawn. Dick was a chemist, Guy had informed me during tea – that is to say a director of an international chemical firm, a success in his line, Jewish, yes, and clever as a wagonload of monkeys. Sven had taken a fancy to him and was lying at his feet.

I was with the main group by the cedar tree. Out of the corner of my eye I saw the oldest Deeps boy climbing on to the wall above the flower garden at the end farthest from the house. He advanced along it, balancing with arms outstretched, and toppled and landed in the bed of flowers two or three feet below, on the lawn side of the wall. The drop on the other side, into the garden proper, was considerable, I vaguely recollected, and the balancing act must be dangerous. But I didn't interfere. Another Deeps boy climbed on the wall, emitted a scream of mock terror and flopped into the flower bed, giggling; and John Wessel wanted to have his turn.

He was younger than these Deeps boys, ten or eleven, small like his father, with small delicate bones, and dressed in a clean blue Aertex shirt and grey shorts: he had that unmistakable cosseted aura. He climbed up and stood there, leaning back against the wall supporting the upper terrace, with which the garden wall formed a right angle. He inched a sandalled foot forwards, put his weight on it, but was obviously frightened and began to wobble.

I broke off my conversation, I think it was with Mrs Winter, to exclaim: 'Listen, you on the wall, mind out!'

Simultaneously there was a piercing cry, 'John!' – and Penelope Wessel ran past me – she ran from the tea table right across the lawn, a hundred yards, pursued by Dick.

They were bad runners, she was unathletic and clumsy, his style was cramped by Sven's cheerful leaps and bounds to bite at his hand; but in their united parental anxiety they were impressive.

John Wessel wobbled worse than ever and fell amongst the flowers.

He was clutched to his mother's breast. He was fussed over and scolded by both parents.

Everybody now gathered round. We invaded the flower bed and peered over the wall, avoiding the roses trained to grow on the middle bit. The drop into the garden was at least twenty-five feet, and anyone falling the wrong way would have been mangled by the branches of the fruit trees underneath, lurching forward from their original fastenings. The prospect was horrific. But the Deeps boys seemed to disagree. Casting pitying glances at John Wessel, mollycoddled by their standards, they surrounded their father, enthusiastically whispering, trying to persuade him to have a shot at the feat.

I hadn't seen Laura since she introduced me to Dick Wessel. She was on the path between the flower bed and the lawn, no longer wan – with hectic spots of colour in her cheeks; and her eyes were shining brilliantly.

She announced to the company: 'No, it's not quite the thing for a child, although I used to do it. But someone ought to be able to get from here to the house, to the railings by the house, not touching the ground. It's not impossible – I promise you I've done it – it wouldn't be too difficult for a grown-up. Billy, be brave!'

I was startled on several counts, by her feverish eyes, by the hardness of her voice and her speechifying, that she should issue such a challenge, and particularly by that final word of hers – brave – which in the past she'd applied to me: she might be devising a new test of my bravery.

The excited children chorused: 'Oh Laura, please! He will if you ask – ask him again – please, Laura!'

The party had already convinced me of her attraction for and power over children of all ages: they were mesmerised by her beauty.

'Well, Billy?'

Pixie was furious: 'Laura! The poor man! Are you mad?'

But Molly Deeps, sportingly or because she was in a difficult position, for the honour of her family, said: 'Go on, Bill, kill yourself – what do I care?'

The children clapped and screamed advice, while Billy Deeps heaved himself on to the wall. But he mounted it right foot foremost; he hadn't any space for his left foot and was facing across the garden with his back to us; he couldn't swivel in order to start his walk, he was too heavy; and after some cumbrous gymnastics, and mortified bellows of laughter, he had to step down. David Skelton, the next candidate, progressed along the wall for a yard or two, then laughed so much that he couldn't continue – he complained of having come over spastic.

Laura said in her hard voice: 'What about you, Dick?'

'No, no!'

She jerked her head.

'Guy?'

Guy was more businesslike than the others. He removed his coat and re-tied his shoelaces and nimbly got on the wall. I'd accepted the idea that I too would have to have a shot, was resigned to it, and really wanted him to fail, not to rob me of my chance of succeeding. He was so competitive that he aroused my competitiveness, although what exactly we were competing for I wasn't sure.

He reached the half-way mark, where the roses grew. Thorns tangled in the bottoms of his trousers. In attempting to yank his trousers free he lost his balance.

'Arthur, you're my last hope!'

As soon as I was on the wall my ambitions wilted. The top of it was at most eight inches wide. The wall at a right angle behind me, against which I tentatively leant, stopped between my shoulder blades – I partly leant on air – with the result that by scrabbling at the bricks for a secure hold I grazed my fingers. From the level of my eyes to the dry stony earth of the garden on my left, under the hazard of the fruit tree branches, it was a good thirty feet, a lethal distance; and it was hundreds of feet, nearly the full hundred yards' length of the lawn, from where I was standing to the iron railings enclosing the gravel sweep. My scorn of the ineffectiveness of Billy and David changed into instant admiration, while Guy was a hero, to whom I should and happily would have yielded the palm.

I'd underestimated the danger of the exploit. Moreover its publicity, the audience on my right, the gaping faces and chatter of the children, Billy Deeps' wrinkled brow, Dick Wessel's flickering gaze, and the obsessiveness of Laura, were the opposite of relaxing.

After a long motionless minute I said: 'Listen – it's not on.'

The children disagreed vociferously, jeeringly, I suspected. Guy was talking to Dick, telling him I'd never get anywhere, no doubt. Laura offered to walk along beside me.

'All right,' I said, quelling the uproar, and, drawing a deep breath to steady my voice, added: 'Laura, would you tuck my trousers into my socks?'

She did so – her touch was encouraging, as was the proximity of her golden head and my knees. I raised my arms like a tightrope walker and, fixing my eyes on the faraway railings, not daring to lower them, edged forward. On the path she kept pace with me, her left hand stretching out close to my right hand, to be snatched at in emergency.

The roses covered the wall for fifteen or twenty feet. Guy had tried to insinuate his shoes in between their shoots and tendrils. But I obtained Laura's permission to tread on them. My method worked well for the first ten feet. But unfortunately I trod on a tendril that was green and whippy, slipped, slipped to the right, towards the flower bed, and through my efforts to recover myself lurched in the other direction and was sickened by a glimpse of looming fruit trees.

I didn't fall. I didn't even have to have recourse to Laura's hand. I arrived safe and sound at the railings.

My audience cheered and clapped, it had been following alongside. I jumped across the flower bed on to the path, sweating and trembling. The children thumped me on the back.

'Thank you, thank you,' Laura was saying.

And she kissed me.

SIX

SHE'D kissed me before, hullo and goodbye for ten days, more or less warmly, but not like this, with melting spontaneity in front of everyone. The expression in her shining eyes ceased to be obsessive or compulsive, her complexion regained its overall gold shade; and my mystic feeling that for some reason it had been vitally important for me to walk the wall was reinforced by her air of triumph. She was triumphant and released, although why, considering we'd only played a party game, if a dangerous game, not that she'd cared about the danger any more than Molly Deeps, I didn't know. To tell the truth I was overwhelmed by the combination of delayed strain and her active ostentatious gratitude.

Drinks were served in the drawing-room. Guy congratulated me grudgingly: 'You've got good nerves.' The Wessels and the Winters took their leave, and the Deeps bundled into their station wagon. I retain an impression of the windows of the station wagon being wound down and children hanging out, panting, of wrinkly faces and raucous honks of laughter and on the horn: 'Goodbye, Laura!' But that scene could belong with my memories of the Sunday of the tug-of-war.

At The Dellamere Arms, for twenty-four hours, I swung between detachment from and attachment to Laura. It was a novel sort of indecision: to contradict myself in terms, an indecision of a more committed sort. I wasn't as detached as I'd determined to be before the weekend. Her desperation, round which description of her mood I perhaps ought to put inverted commas; her crying for Sven in the night; and on Easter Day her relations with Guy, and our mutual displeasure with our presents, and my anticipation of a climax which had occurred sure enough at the party – I was impervious to none of it. I'd become almost as tense as she was. I never would have been able to meet her challenge in cold blood.

Yet, notwithstanding her kiss, I hesitated to throw in my emotional lot with hers. She'd proved she was elusive. By rushing to London and refusing to explain why, by her retractive manoeuvring in innumerable small ways, she'd sacrificed some of my potential trust in her. Furthermore I had absolutely no firm evidence that she might love me; on the contrary, all the evidence pointed to her loving another. The entrancing notion that I'd jumped from the wall into a futuristic phase of our friendship, literally into the Dellamere arms, was disqualified by my inability to recall just what had happened in those critical moments.

Thus I attempted to be realistic. But the realities definitive of my former caution, my decision that our union was impossible, now escaped me. They'd been sucked into the vortex of events.

On Monday morning, Easter Bank Holiday, David Skelton walked across to the pub to say goodbye: he and Guy were returning to London in the afternoon.

I asked after Laura and was told: 'You should have stayed to supper yesterday – she was in great form.'

We wished each other luck with our work and agreed to try to keep in touch.

'What time's your train?'

'Oh, five or five-thirty.'

At five o'clock sharp Laura arrived at The Dellamere Arms in her MG. I'd remained in my room, waiting for her, and ran downstairs and out-of-doors.

She greeted me, sitting in her open car and raising her eyes – and the angle of our interlocking glance reminded me of the one we'd exchanged the previous evening, when I was standing on the wall, by the railings, and she was on the path below.

Her expression was the same – it was different from any I'd seen prior to the end of the Easter party – released, calmer, more submissive, melting.

I didn't kiss her. I was no longer keen to kiss or be kissed, except spontaneously and intensely. Our not kissing was more intimate than the usual social peck.

'I was hoping you'd come and call.'

'Yes,' she said.

'Didn't you have to take Guy and David to the station?'

'No, I packed them off in a taxi ten minutes ago.'

'Would you like to stroll a little?'

'Yes.'

We strolled by the Wyntrude – or over the bridge and up the hill opposite Llanwyn, or to the shop and along the road to Llanrhad, or across the water meadow to the church. I can't remember: we strolled in so many directions in that week. The weather, meteorological and moral, was set fair: it seemed to get better and better. Laura called on me in her car or on her bicycle – she'd ring her bicycle bell as she approached the pub, and in the forecourt, straddling the machine with a foot on the ground, raise her velvet eyes to mine. My superior position, on the wall or in my bow window, or when she was in the MG, has its significance. But I rejoiced thoughtlessly in the easing of the tension between us.

Sometimes she forgot her bicycle. I'd walk with her to Llanwyn and back to The Dellamere Arms, and later on pedal round to dinner. If, at night, her bicycle was by the terrace steps, she might suggest that I should borrow it to freewheel home. Once or twice I availed myself of the offer for sentimental reasons, in order to preserve a tenuous contact with her through the inanimate object. Meals in her family circle – for me – were the more enjoyable because I was the only guest. Esmond Charrington was absent on the Tuesday, Wednesday and Thursday; I had no visible rivals and could concentrate on Laura; and the staple diet of our conversation was enriched by the complex undertones and overtones of recent experience.

Colonel Dellamere could be said to provide the continuo of the quiet harmony of our quintet. He was a living exposition of the phrase: the even tenor of a man's days. But I may be mixing my metaphors; and my knowledge of the owners of large estates and people connected with the land remains limited. Perhaps they have to cultivate not merely their acres but an essential imperturbability, subject as they and their neighbours are, more subject than the rest of us, to drought, floods, diseases and every manner of accident.

The Colonel rose early in the morning considering he was in his seventy-first year, at seven o'clock. He had two hairy tweed suits with waistcoats, a green and a brown, and a grey suit yellowing with age for use on Sundays. He had two or three pairs of brown shoes with bulbous toes and clusters of nails in the soles, and a cracked black pair for best. After breakfast he and his bailiff, called Jago – a Huguenot name – supervised work in the farm buildings beyond the kitchen garden and in the fields, or drove to Llanrhad market in the Wolseley Ten. As a rule in the afternoons, when he wasn't fishing or participating in Easter egg hunts, he pored over papers in his study, a room in the third wing at Llanwyn, aligned with the drawing-room and porch.

He appeared punctually for lunch and dinner, drank a glass of sherry and another of wine, and endlessly munched his food, dabbing at his moustache with his napkin. At tea his beverage was whisky and soda – a glass, a dwarf decanter and a bottle of soda-water, the latter manufactured in an antediluvian apparatus in the pantry by Morgan, would be laid before him. He ate several slices of bread and butter and jam and two slices of Mrs Wipps' fruit cake. His fingers were crooked and stiff – he had swollen outdoor hands and horny concave fingernails. He always sat between his sister and Pixie, since no females were invited to formal repasts, at any rate in my time.

He was a picture of contentment – not entirely attributable to his being a landlord. His adventures in the army and misadventures in marriage were hard to imagine, although I couldn't believe they'd deflected him by a hair's breadth from the precision of his routine. He resembled a tree, a blasted oak, dying but by no means dead, faithfully doing its seasonal duty. Yet he had his humanity and he had his views. Once I was cursing the system of taxation, idly, for I hadn't any money and wasn't a victim of it. He cleared his throat and corrected me: 'We have to pay for our privileges.' He wasn't priggish, he was sincere.

Laura had linked her arm in his in the water meadow after the fish-hook incident. She'd bend over and press her lips to his bald pale forehead, as he smoked his stubby charred pipe in the library. He was undemonstrative, so much so that he seemed to me passively to tolerate her gestures of affection. But I didn't understand. He was replying to them in the subtle language of love. When she entered the room his eyes under his wiry grey brows would open wider, and he'd square his shoulders, as if her presence infused his system with fresh sap and vitality. When she spoke, his ruddy countenance would assume a scarcely perceptible receptiveness: he was ready to laugh at her least joke.

His joy in her added to mine in the week following Easter. Probably the development of my love enabled me the better to appreciate his. It was a brief period of peace, without a history, a lull after the storm – or before it. Miss Dellamere stuck to her astringent opinions and Pixie Tufton grumbled placidly; but they too could have shared in the sense of release and of our unity. The demands of the library fire, the dogs, the grandfather clock, the rustle of the newspaper with its crossword puzzle, and the scratch of Miss Dellamere's needle against her thimble as she stitched at her piece of embroidery, filled our rare companionable silences.

I was glad that the portrait of Missy Dellamere hung in the other room. Some of the restlessness of the mother might have transferred itself, reactivated that of the daughter – and I loved to see her kneeling composedly on the turkey carpet, Trilby's pointed head in her lap, and to think of her as unique. Tension was unravelled like Miss Dellamere's skeins of coloured wool and silk. Again I gloated over Laura's beauty. The inclination of her head above Trilby's, for the purpose of murmuring an endearment, 'Such a good dog, such a good sleepy dog,' caused her hair to fall forward across the side of her face. It kept in enviable condition, her sleek hair, neither oily nor frizzy. When she turned away from me to talk to her Aunt Ange, I traced the gentle indentation of her temple and the outward curve of her high cheekbone.

Unaccustomed poses and tricks of light revitalised the shock effect of her beauty on my eye that beheld it. At a distance, in the glare of the sun, her hair was green; and her lips were white by moonlight, blanched by moonbeams. Out in the sun, if she was wearing a hat, the shadow of its brim would flow over her facial contours, exposing and accentuating the redness of her lips. I became more conscious of the outlines of her figure, her breasts and the inverted V of her diaphragm, the tender swelling of her stomach and the strong flat arch of her thighs as she knelt and caressed Trilby.

Something other than my performance of a foolhardy feat must have happened at the party, something mysterious: for at last my manhood stirred. My love and its apologies for achievement, her handclasps and kind kisses, had been theoretical, an exercise in pursuit of the ideal – and ideals, I would recollect repressively, were unattainable. I sighed for Laura as for literary fame. Admiration and innocence inhibited me and enjoined chastity. Yet on the wall the sensation of her hand tucking my trousers into my socks brought about an overdue change; and jumping off it, a pungent whiff of her scent which was labelled Availability summoned a suitable response.

I was astonished that it hadn't done so before. My attitude had been aesthetic, humble and respectful, plain obtuse and I'd missed the point for seventeen days. But while I blushingly wondered whether she'd been aware of my slowness in the uptake, a crowd of factors that mitigated it sprang to mind. Her beauty was supra-physical, had stunned me, petrified me, and inspired a sublimated type of desire. The stateliness of her home, her class, and family and friends, and literary expertise, and social occasions, and her moods and my jealousy, had so distracted me that I hadn't had a chance to think of her in that way, as the saying goes. Moreover, if she'd been available, her availability was mental.

Yes, her scent had been an appeal to an ideological or spiritual communion. A consequence of her desperation and its climax at the party was to alter it – our scents are supposed to express our various emotions. For, I argued, if she hadn't altered, would I have changed? My subordination would never have permitted me to grow excited, inconveniently, in public and in danger, without her sanction.

She melted towards me on that day and the next, when she drove to The Dellamere Arms for a stroll. As the week progressed she wore down my hesitancy with her charms of one sort and another. Intermittently she induced, for instance in the library, by standing in her revealing housecoat in front of a lamp, a feeling of utter defencelessness. Our kisses good night were at once lingering and shy, abbreviated, and our voices breathless.

Or was I mistaken? It would be a mistake to over-react to her admitted desirability as previously I'd under-reacted, and subject her to attentions that wouldn't be welcome, in the style of Esmond Charrington. Indeed a further argument in favour of her having initiated the present state of affairs was that I still lacked the power, I was still waiting for her, to take charge. My being younger than she was, only twenty-one, English, an ex-public-schoolboy and a sexual ignoramus could excuse my craven coldness. But I'd plead on my own behalf the irreversibility of the commitment on the brink of which I assumed myself to be.

Laura and I discovered the ducks' nest on the Tuesday evening. The ducks – or duck – were mallard: the drake had head feathers of every shade of green and blue and purple feathers in his wings. We or the dogs scared the pair from the lake a couple of times, then we noticed some twigs scattered on the emergent roots of the lilies, a few feet from the water's edge just below the verandah of the summer house. In the morning, Wednesday morning, we collected fallen branches and stole sweet-pea-sticks from the potting shed and built a hide, a low hedge of sticks away to the left, sufficiently far from the nest in order not to alarm the ducks and sufficiently close to allow a good view.

We reached our hide, having shut Trilby and Sven out of the garden, by stalking to behind the summer house and crawling left-handed along a dip in the ground. The hedge formed a three-sided enclosure, two or three feet high, with natural gaps and peepholes between the branches. Because the ducks flying in would see into the enclosure and anyone lying there, Laura produced a fawn-coloured blanket to serve as a roof. We had to wriggle on our bellies over the tussocky grass to get beneath the blanket.

The nest was in fact nearly complete. It wasn't on top of the water-lily roots but amongst them, snugly sited on an island of black silt. The twigs were the foundation and outer covering of a downy grey hollow. The ducks must have strayed from the river – Laura said she'd never heard of ducks nesting on the lake. She was thrilled by the whole business. She threw herself into the externalised activity of the hide's construction and christened the ducks Emerald and Crispin, names from which we derived a childish amusement, childish or perverse, for Emerald was the drake, so-called because of his green-blue head, and Crispin his mate, the female of the species.

Crispin was brown, a housewifely brown except for her purple wing feathers, which were like a brooch on a sensible dress: a trim crisp avian personage, indefatigable and resolute in the accomplishment of her intentions. Emerald merited his girl's name by virtue of his vanity. He floated about amongst the lily leaves, a spoilt darling of the duck world, wiggling his tail with its jaunty curl and lifting his beak to quack, so that the jewelled tints of his head and plump breast flashed and shimmered.

They copulated in the water. Crispin would swim towards Emerald demurely – she was not without a sleek allure even by human criteria. To catch his attention which was inclined to wander, she'd snap her beak and nibble at his, and paddle by as if love were the last thing that concerned her. He'd paddle in pursuit, seize her by the scruff of her neck and clamber on her back, while she sank squawking in protest beneath his weight and passion. She then surfaced, looking outraged or at least flustered, and hurried home to the silt island, where she flapped and preened herself, contributing the feathers that she shed to her nest.

Emerald also preened on the island. Crispin rescued his discarded feathers, which she incorporated in the downy hollow by standing in it and turning round and round, a process of stroking and nudging. She began to sit in the nest on Thursday. No more than her head and the tip of her tail showed above the twigs. I had my binoculars in the hide: we studied her eye. It was black, beady, alert, yet with an introverted brooding expression, uncompromising and fulfilled. Laura admired Crispin for knowing and for having got what she wanted.

Meanwhile Emerald dozed on the bank of the lake, balancing on one yellow webbed foot, the other retracted and out of sight. He waddled inland and slept amongst the tussocks of grass, once so close to the hide that without binoculars we could observe the intricate workings of his double eyelids: Crispin's eyelids never closed. Waking, he stretched and seemed to yawn, and half-heartedly took to the water. Sometimes he fed by the nest, tipping himself up, head underwater and tail in the air, or he appeared to put on a comical act for Crispin's benefit or because he was so bored, swimming towards her with his beak on the waterline, dibbling, like a boy blowing bubbles in the bath. But soon he'd navigate to the part of the lake where the lilies didn't grow, quacking in a comforting solicitous fashion, in short deceitfully, and with a sudden splash and in a crystal spray fly off – for a bit of fun with the other fellows on the Wyntrude, we decided.

I don't know how long we spent in the hide, perhaps two hours each day: but the ducks filled our lives. We discussed them and described them at meals. We anthropomorphised and fantasised about them. The Colonel came to have a look at them, and Miss Dellamere and Pixie were conducted with much shushing to the rear of the summer house. They poked their noses round the corner for a glimpse of Crispin – Laura was afraid that if the bird was disturbed it would desert the nest.

Pixie said she could see nothing.

Miss Dellamere, when we'd retired to the area of apple trees, inquired: 'Was that your hide? Do you get under that blanket together?'

Laura replied in the affirmative.

Miss Dellamere remonstrated: 'My dear!' – at which instance of her Victorian prudishness I started to smile.

But Laura flushed guiltily.

She had no real need to. There was adequate room under the blanket for us to lie side by side, not touching: and we were equally careful not to touch. On the other hand excitation doesn't depend on contact. Our propinquity behind the hedge, in the semi-darkness, our whispered dialogues and efforts not to laugh aloud at the ducks' antics, and the bare extended forearms on which she supported herself, her sensitive fingers fiddling with a stalk of grass or brushing against mine as she reached for the binoculars, her actual as distinct from her moral scent, her stifled smiles and warm breath and blue and white eyes – naturally they tantalised.

The potency of her inclusive attraction was established in the hide. She couldn't climb in or out save by means of suggestive contortions and the exposure of her underclothing or naked flesh, a pink thigh above her stocking or the undulating small of her back, because her shirt had parted company with her trousers. If she wore a skirt, she'd modestly insist that I should be the first to enter and the last to leave – an embargo probably more stimulating than the peep of knickers I might have obtained. Again, the reason why the ducks had sought the sanctuary of the lake constituted a stimulus.

Laura was capable of humour on the subject. When the ducks copulated, she eased my embarrassment by whispering with a grimace: 'Poor old Crispin!' – who was squawking and sinking beneath the burden of Emerald's ardour. She giggled and made me do so at her clothes' disarray. Laughter removed another layer of our shyness. It and our preoccupied peering through the hedge helped us to relax. And relaxation, at least in my case, fixed my interior vision on the pleasures of the present, blurring the periphery of past and future: the questions posed by the Easter party, by a catalogue of erratic conduct, by the advice I'd received and the prohibitions of my own invention, remained unanswered.

At moments I was almost physically paralysed by my feelings. Or the temptation to kiss her golden neck or her ear, within an inch or two of my mouth, would have to be contended against. Observing her as she observed the ducks, her undivided interest in their doings and the fervent glow of her face, I came to the familiar conclusion that she was simply irresistible and adorable – however Pixie might scoff at the concept of adoration. Yet still I resisted her. I restrained myself or she restrained me. I sensed that she too was waiting and holding back.

She melted – she melted me – but managed to retain her dignity in circumstances not always dignified. Even as I was persuaded that she or fate had vouchsafed the signal, and I could and should gamble my all on a throw for complete happiness, she'd seem once more to falter and pause – and I followed her example. For a few hours after her Aunt Ange's exclamation 'My dear!' she was distant towards me, dejected, or unsettled perhaps by the fancy that Emerald and Crispin, like siren birds, were luring us into a wilderness of love. She resembled a magnet in her ability to repel, to keep me at a distance, as well as to attract.

On the Friday afternoon, before the arrival of George Sawrey and Guy Toller for the tug-of-war weekend, we were sitting in the dip in the ground, the gully behind the hide. Emerald had flown off, Crispin was on the nest: we could talk in low voices without fear of disturbing them. The date was 7 May – Laura had referred to my twenty-second birthday on the subsequent Monday 10 May.

'We'll have to celebrate it,' she said.

'Oh no, please don't.'

I was constrained by the threat of more hospitality which I couldn't repay.

'I should have got you a present, but I haven't. We've been so busy, haven't we, with our pets?' She nodded in the direction of the lake. 'We'll drive into Oswestry on Monday, when we're alone, for a wild shopping spree.'

'No, Laura, honestly, I don't want you to buy me a present – please don't.'

'Why shouldn't I? You bought me one. You spent your precious money on my silver box. I love that box, you know. But it was too expensive. You should have remembered that Pixie was my governess.'

She meant that Pixie's economical doctrines had been inculcated in her.

I laughed and proposed a postponement of the matter until Monday.

'Yes.' She agreed and she sighed: 'How ancient we are!'

She was mournfully joking, but serious underneath – she hated any reminder of the passage of time. She was reclining in the gully, her arms raised and her hands behind her head, against a background of the bleached planks of the side of the summer house. I laughed at the idea that she could ever grow old.

'Were you at Deane End for your last birthday?'

'Yes – on leave from the army.'

'Was there a coming-of-age party?'

'Sort of.'

'With Mary Singleton?'

'Yes.'

'Tell me.'

Her request was exceptional. Since the day on which I confided in her in the same setting, by the lake, she hadn't mentioned my family or

Mary. But then I'd forgotten them. I was ashamed of my forgetfulness, and found it difficult to have to try to reconcile my two lives.

I described my cake, my parents' gift of a wristwatch, the Singletons' gift of my pair of binoculars, and so on.

At the finish of the recital she remarked: 'Your home sounds nice and secure.'

'Do you think it does?'

'I'd like to meet your father.'

I replied: 'Well, you easily could,' although the prospect daunted me I couldn't visualise Laura at Deane End, in its mock-Tudor rooms and with my mother in the offing.

She lowered her arms, turned and leant on an elbow, and began to pluck at a blade of grass.

'Arthur, how long are you going to stay at the pub?'

It might have been a nerve of mine, that blade of grass. 'I'm not sure.'

'What about your writing?'

'What about it?'

'Have you done any?'

'No.'

'Is it my fault?'

'No!'

'And your money – is your money holding out?'

'Yes,' I lied.

In fact my funds were nearly exhausted.

She inquired half teasingly: 'Will you wish you were at Deane End on your birthday on Monday?'

'No, certainly not.'

'Will you miss Mary?'

'No! No!'

'Do you promise?'

'I promise!'

We both laughed. She looked straight at me and stood up: the summer house screened her from Crispin. Before I joined her on the path to the potting shed I glanced at the lake. It was in the shadow of the chestnut trees. The coils of green weed writhed amongst the water-lilies – the subaqueous weed wasn't visible when we were lying flat in the hide. The tips of the cypress trees lining the road were gilded by sunlight, but, below, their dense foliage was black. My first impression of the place as gloomy, gloomy and ominous in the afternoon at any rate, was reinforced – in the three days since the discovery of the ducks' nest I'd been too busy, too enamoured, to care. Her interrogation checked my progress: could she be introduced into my family? Would my financial resources hold out until she loved me? I loved her, yet had inwardly flinched at my denial of Mary. What had we said? What had not been said? There were riddles between us, moral problems, which the sweetest kisses wouldn't solve.

SEVEN

OUR conversation in the gully was less effective than her flight to London or those warnings to desist, insofar as it put a brake on my progress. My misgivings even at their strongest didn't embolden me to try to catechise Laura and not to take no for an answer. I wasn't prepared to swallow another dose of the unpleasant medicine of her evasiveness.

No, I preferred to keep my illusions, if they were illusions, intact. But our situation wasn't like that on the eve of the tug-of-war weekend, or seemed not to be.

We strolled in the direction of the house, and, having had tea, drove in Colonel Dellamere's car to fetch George Sawrey and Guy Toller from the station. On our return journey we stopped by the gates, and Laura led the way through the lower rickety door in the garden wall and by a roundabout route to the summer house, so that George and Guy could view the ducks. I can't remember if I stayed to dinner; but I spent most of the next day, and of course Sunday, at Llanwyn.

A change in Laura had already occurred in the car. Her comparative calm disintegrated. In the period between the Easter Bank Holiday Monday and the Friday before the tug-of-war, she wasn't calm in the sense that Pixie and the Colonel were – she wasn't stolid. She overdid her attitude to Emerald and Crispin. If her father was like a tree, she was more like a leaf, never still – inwardly, I mean.

I should explain that the beauty of her form was an expression of a perhaps rarer loveliness within: a capacity for responding vividly and in proportion to events. It's a paradox, granted, at this stage of our story. I've largely traced the lack of proportion, the illogic of her behaviour. But I wouldn't have been able to measure her divergences from her individual norm if she hadn't been normal. Normality's not quite the word. She fulfilled for me the universal hope that nature is equitable and we're born with a clear idea of right and wrong. She satisfied my conscious or unconscious yearnings for order and balance.

Intuitively I was satisfied: whence my dissatisfaction on a less metaphysical level with her tension and her unaccountable excesses. I believed she wasn't being true to herself, to either of us. Loving her I suffered with her, and dreaded a repetition of the Easter mysteries, and was disappointed and jealous. On the Friday evening, suffice it to say that I sensed another alteration in her inner rhythm. Her mood, her animation and humour, her eagerness to show off our pets, became precarious. I regretted the fact that I hadn't prosecuted my inquiries into her feelings for her friends.

For I ascribed the latest change in her to George or to Guy. They said they were pleased to see me again and I returned the compliment. But Guy was scornful of the hide and its purpose: 'You've been staring at a broody duck from under that moth-eaten blanket? Tastes differ! But as an occupation I wouldn't have called it sensationally rewarding.' And although George was amiable he confessed that he'd rather not take a closer look at Crispin at the cost of dirtying his clothes. They didn't laugh at Laura's names for the ducks.

She contradicted my assumptions by not being influenced: surely, if she'd been in love, she wouldn't have bothered to bird-watch any more? But I resented George and Guy for renewing my confusion. Actually her guests' disinterest seemed to work in Emerald's and Crispin's and my favour. On the terrace Laura whispered in my ear, secretly smiling and lowering her tawny eyelashes: 'Behind the summer house at eleven tomorrow morning.' On Saturday and Sunday, at a coded glance, I'd absent myself from the company and steal towards the lake, and, soon, hear Sven's whining by the garden gate and be joined by his mistress.

She was conspiratorial. We conspired together not only to watch, also to guard the ducks, Crispin especially, sitting so admirably tight that we were nervous a fox might snap her up. Once, in the hide, Laura murmured: 'I wish I could invite Emerald and Crispin to stay' – an implied criticism of George and Guy. At meals, on communal walks, she was unmistakably restless – impatient, I presumed, to be with me, debating more important matters, for instance how many eggs had been laid in the downy hollow and whether Emerald was still playing truant. She'd run on tiptoe to the summer house and wriggle under the blanket, disregarding the proprieties, in her anxiety to see that all was well.

Yet having got into the hide she'd want to get out again almost immediately. Her protective attitude to the ducks, while increasing to the point of obsessiveness, was no longer steady or single-minded. I blamed the distraction of her hostess's duties and the division of her time and loyalty. I blamed the weather, which was changing too, at last.

Its change had coincided with hers on the Friday. A haze spread across the sky, which had been extraordinarily clear for three weeks, and clouds massed at the Llanrhad end of the valley. On that evening and the next, Saturday, the sun set amongst semi-circular banks of clouds, their greyness emphasised by their gilded edges and haloes of rosy rays – like a crown of thorns. An oppressive stillness descended on the countryside, in which some solitary blackbird sang in an enervated voice, peacefully but as if nostalgically, trilling and whistling for a breath of air.

The mornings continued to be fine. But instead of the gentle hygienic breeze that had helped to disperse the dawn mists in the water meadow, a fitful wind blew until about mid-day, then subsided completely. In place of the pure whiteness of the mist in the fields, and following the winding river, a sickly pallor overcast the heavens. The sun glared, a blind round orb. Shadows lost their outline, sounds were distorted and muffled. Perhaps the weather was responsible for my unease in the garden, my reappraisal of its gloom, after Laura had elicited my promise that I wouldn't miss Mary on my birthday.

I'd shivered by the lake, although the temperature rose from Friday onwards. The wind in the morning was cold as well as hot, cold in a draughty sense, but the afternoons were sultry and muggy. Hands were never dry, clothes stuck clammily to bodies. Guy Toller sweated and even George Sawrey's noble forehead shone; and in the evening in the drawing-room at Llanwyn the fire wasn't lit and the french windows were thrown wide. Swallows and housemartins flew low over the lawn outside, a stormy omen, another of which, according to country lore, was that the cows in the water meadow were now inclined to lie down.

On Sunday I was woken by the red sky at sunrise: shepherd's warning, as the adage has it. Ruby pinpoints of light glowed in my curtains, and burning shafts smote the wall by my bed. For forty-eight hours there had been a lot of talk of the storm: would or wouldn't it spare the tug-of-war? I was pessimistic. Anyway the needle of Laura's personal barometer was moving anticlockwise; her restlessness was infectious – I was beginning to be tired of our tentative relations. The state of my finances, on which all depended, worried me; and my worries were exacerbated by her visitors, whose demands for attention conflicted with mine and with those of Emerald and Crispin.

The bad start to the day brought home my general apprehensiveness. Strains united in unholy alliance, and shocks that had seemed to be absorbed recovered their force. Moreover I had a headache. When I drew my curtains, and the sky had paled, been bled of its unhealthy colour, as it were, the nagging wind intruded into my room, scattering the papers on the writing table. If I opened the window the room became at once chill and humid, and, if I closed it, fetid.

I didn't go to church. At eleven, when the bell tolled, I watched the Llanwyn house party, and at half-past I collected my binoculars and a tweed overcoat and crossed the water meadow. Laura and the others were singing a hymn as I walked through the churchyard – profanely it titillated me to think of her at her devotions, kneeling and praying, and the sensuous curve of her naked neck. The hinges of the lower door in the garden wall had been oiled: I entered the garden silently and stalked round to the hide. An effect of the atmosphere's humidity was that the grass within refused to dry. I therefore covered the tussocks under the blanket with my overcoat.

Crispin was on her nest, Emerald not to be seen. The wind had dropped; the surface of the lake was unruffled, glassy, and the towering black cypresses were motionless. In the quietness I could hear the congregation coming out of church, voices, Guy's voice, banging on about the service as he had a week ago, and steps on the gravel of the drive. Before long, according to our plan, Laura slid in beside me. She was laughing, amused by the spectacle of my feet protruding into the gully. She wore a whitish dress.

'Hullo!'

'Hullo!'

'You looked funny, lying there with your feet poking out.'

'Don't make too much noise.'

'No,' she agreed. 'Is Crispin all right?'

'Yes.'

'Where's Emerald?'

'I think he's buzzed off.'

'He's wicked, isn't he?'

She studied Crispin through the binoculars.

I whispered: 'How are you?'

She whispered in reply: 'Isn't it a horrid day?'

'The sky was red first thing this morning.'

'Yes, I know. I couldn't sleep. I hope we don't get the storm before the tug-of-war.'

'Same here.'

She commented on the overcoat.

'Thank goodness you remembered it – Pixie wouldn't have forgiven me if I'd mucked up my dress.'

I was feeling better, when she said: 'I must fly. I must buzz off like Emerald. Do you want a glass of sherry?'

I'd counted on having her to myself for half an hour, for a quarter of an hour, and refused sulkily. I hadn't been asked to lunch because Mrs Wipps was overworked, preparing the food for supper.

I offered to walk her to the door by the potting shed, but she told me not to budge. She'd return to the hide at five, before the crowd arrived, she assured me.

Her restlessness now combined with the climatic conditions and other factors somehow to justify my anticipation of disaster.

In the late afternoon the weather went slightly mad. Not a leaf stirred, yet, the haze having vanished, the sun blazed through gaps in large high clouds with dark centres which sped across the sky. There appeared to be a gale blowing in the stratosphere. Beyond Llanwyn the valley was blocked, dammed, by a solid menacing cloudy barrier.

I was back at the hide by half-past four. Mrs Roope had been cooking pies for the party since early in the morning, Mr Roope had ferried them along with barrels of his beer to Llanwyn – they were in a rush to finish in time for the tug-of-war. I'd escaped from the pub with a book in my pocket, Laura's copy of *First Love,* which I hadn't got round to reading. I walked by the Wyntrude, flushing various duck, including one that might have been Emerald, and swerved left by the Wyn and skirting the herd of recumbent cows reached the churchyard, where I sat on a flat gravestone. But I still couldn't read.

Dazzling light and intense shadow hunted each other over the landscape. In the wood on the hillside opposite, opposite Llanwyn and towards Penyboth, trees resembled open green fans. An ornamental cherry in the garden of The Dellamere Arms was alternately bright pink against a sombre background and almost white in the sun. May trees in the hedgerows were a dusty red and the willows by the river suddenly silver. I sat and smoked: if the cigarettes were good for my nerves they were bad for my headache, which extended to my neck and shoulders.

At length, after a final glance at my watch, I passed under the branches of the yew and crossed the road, the lych-gate clicking behind me like a pistol shot in the silence. The stream in its canal had become a soundless trickle. Above, in the foliage of the chestnuts, a lethargic humming of bees and flies was just audible. The heat or the heaviness of the lukewarm air was overpowering. But it was cooler by the lake. I transferred the book from my jacket pocket into that of the overcoat in the hide, and clambered in to peer at Crispin.

At ten past five Laura hadn't arrived. My feeling that the day was fated, would go and had already gone awry, gained ground. Then she called me.

'Arthur! Arthur!'

I jumped. Her cries, although distant, had a desperate ring. They were reminiscent of her crying for Sven in the night.

I didn't dare answer for fear of disturbing Crispin, but withdrew from the hide and strode up the garden path. She must have called from the lawn, over the wall on which we'd played our dangerous game of the week before. In the gravel sweep I mounted the steps to the terrace.

Everybody was there: the family, George and Guy, Morgan, Mrs Wipps and her scullery-maid May, a gardener, Thomas, a man from the farm, Williams, and assorted females who had been recruited to render assistance. Most of them were talking, arguing, arguing with Laura, whose cheeks had a tinge of hectic colour. They were all perspiring more or less freely – for the moment the sun was beating down.

'Arthur!' Laura cried, extremely excited. 'We can't have people wandering about the garden, can we? They'll frighten the ducks. They'll let in the dogs who'll eat the ducks. I won't stand for it!'

Pixie, her chief opponent, was saying: 'But the people always go into the garden before supper. It's a tradition. Why shouldn't they? Drat your ducks! You're so unreasonable!'

'Please, Arthur! Daddy, you won't allow it, will you?'

She sought support in her anguished voice.

But when Guy suggested in an undertone that Pixie was probably hoping for a fresh duck's egg for breakfast, she giggled, cancelling my previous painful impression of the soreness of her plight.

Meanwhile she was engaged in an argument on another front. She wanted to have supper out-of-doors, on the terrace, as arranged. Morgan was determined, because of the uncertainty of the weather, to lay the trestle table in the dining-room.

'We can't carry the table in, Miss, once things are on it, cutlery and glasses, if the rain starts.'

'The rain won't start – look at the sun! And parties out here are much nicer. At Easter you told me so yourself. You've changed your tune! Besides, if the worst comes to the worst, you won't have to carry the table, we'll carry it in a minute.'

'I'm sorry, Miss, but I doubt that.'

'Well – take my word, Morgan!'

She was unnecessarily sharp. Their subterranean enmity had erupted. But I didn't understand any of it. How upset was she? What was upsetting about these weekends?

Class solidarity complicated the issue. Mrs Wipps declared in fiery style that she wouldn't have the food spoilt, May simpered agreement, the assorted females clucked their disapproval, and Thomas and Williams scowled radically in their best suits. As usual Pixie berated Laura. Guy Toller propounded to me the egalitarian theory that servants were impossible. George Sawrey urged, forthright and disarming: 'Oh come on, Morgan, let's have a flutter on the weather – if it rains, we'll cope, don't worry.'

Eventually Miss Dellamere conferred with the Colonel, who ruled in Laura's favour. I was handed a key with which to lock the garden door, the top door, that is. When I returned to the terrace the trestle table or rather tables, long enough to accommodate twenty-five chairs on either side, had been erected in front of the porch. Morgan and his minions had compromised – supper would be eaten out, weather allowing, but served in the dining-room. White cloths were being unfolded and spread. Mr and Mrs Roope had arrived.

Mrs Roope had on her tug-of-war hat, a livid green stetson with a false strawberry plant on the brim. She bore a pie-dish under a napkin in reverent arms, as if it had been a baby's coffin. Mr Roope was lugging extra crates of bottled beer through the drawing-room french windows.

'You got all your cooking done, Mrs Roope?'

'Yes, thank you, Mr Bartlett – I've brought along the last of it!'

She entered the house by the side door, accompanied by Mrs Wipps, May and their aproned assistants: who would emerge later on in party attire. Thomas and Williams arranged the chairs, collapsible wooden ones from Llanrhad village hall. Laura and the others were on the lawn, untangling the rope, and cars were turning into the drive.

The Deeps' station wagon parked on the gravel sweep, and faded battered old cars containing farmers and their friends and relations although I half expected to see a pig in the back seat, and the Winters' Baby Austin and the Wessels' Ford. Some couples came on foot: the parson and his wife, Mr and Mrs Llewellyn, walked from the vicarage on the Oswestry road, and Mrs Rogers and her ailing mother from the Post Office. Trilby and Sven barked frantically at a snarling blue-eyed collie shut in a car.

Colonel Dellamere, Miss Dellamere and Laura shook hands above the terrace steps. The Colonel wore his grey suit with waistcoat and watch-chain; Esmond Charrington, Dick Wessel and Charles Winter were in their tweed jackets, while Billy Deeps, George, Guy and myself had removed ours. The agricultural contingent was soberly suited in three-piece worsteds, much creased under the armpits and behind the knees. The village children were ceremonially dressed, unlike the Deeps in tattered shirts and grubby gymshoes; and the women from the village were decked out in flowered frocks, matching colour schemes, snappy bags, brooches and hats.

I knew some of them, Mrs Rogers for instance, and Mrs Wipps, and was greeted by a few of the men, whom I'd either been introduced to at Llanwyn or seen in the bar of the pub. Jago, the bailiff, pumped my hand, and Billy Deeps and Dick Wessel said how do you do: also Esmond Charrington. Dick Wessel struck me as more foreign, and tireder, than he had a week ago. The labourer who ate his daily sandwiches under my bow window, sitting on the water meadow stile, wasn't present – or perhaps, minus his cap and mufflers, I failed to recognise him.

Each new arrival was ushered towards the drawing-room and the dining-room beyond, where Morgan, the Roopes, Thomas and Williams were dispensing drinks. The men with pint glasses of beer, the women with glasses of sherry and the children with orangeade re-formed in groups on the terrace. It would have facilitated the flow to open the front door in the porch, leading straight into the dining-room; but the wistaria trailing across it was in full bloom. Pixie Tufton marshalled the two-way traffic: 'Come along, Mrs Jenkins, don't dawdle! Tell them not to hang around in there!'

A sheepish drift on to the lawn was taking place. The Deeps children were playing with the rope, which was thirty or more yards in length and lay on the grass parallel with the garden wall: under it, in the middle, a strip of white tape was pinned to the grass. Empty beer glasses with frothy stains inside were put on the trestle table. Colonel Dellamere and Mr Owen, the patriarch who had read the lesson in church in a weird accent, began to organise the contestants. I can't remember what the weather was doing: in the commotion I ceased to notice the state of the weather, of Laura, and my own headache.

The adults of the village team were stripping off their coats, revealing their braces and elastic sleeve-bands. The smallest child had to be nearest the tape – the largest and beefiest warrior, called the anchor-man, at the other end of the rope. Our anchor-man was Billy Deeps; next to him was George Sawrey and I was next to George; then in the order of their size came Jago, Guy, a sixteen-year-old Deeps, several younger Deeps, the Winter child and John Wessel. Hands were spat upon, heels were dug in. Colonel Dellamere invited Mr Owen to give us the signal to start. 'Right, boys,' he quavered – and we heaved and tugged.

In the first of the six rounds we pulled the villagers across the tape with such despatch that we fell in a heap. But they might not have been ready, or were too polite to exert their superior strength. For three times in succession they won easily. Two chances remained for us, the fifth and final rounds of the match, to level the score.

The audience was becoming more vocal and partisan. Wives and mothers, who had observed the proceedings from the path alongside, surged on to the lawn. Refined wishes of good luck and maidenly titters were converted into vulgar exhortations: 'Don't be so wet, Billy – pull! Go it, Dai! Show 'em, Dai!' Colonel Dellamere and Mr Owen shouted instructions to their teams. Little girls danced about and hurled insults at one another. Penelope Wessel was standing over John Wessel, begging him not to strain himself. Dick Wessel, who had refused to participate, was talking to Esmond Charrington by the cedar tree, Sven at his feet.

We managed to win the fifth round – the sixth would decide the match. A breather was taken, during which Laura, from somewhere behind me, called to Dick to be a sport and join in. He shook his head – anyway the Colonel declared that teams were not to be added to at this stage; and I intercepted an unfriendly glance aimed at Laura by Penelope Wessel. Once more the rope was seized and duly and inconclusively tugged. Molly Deeps was screaming advice or abuse at her husband and her sons. In a transport of zeal she clasped Billy round the waist and lent her weight to his efforts. But, amidst protesting laughter, the village team hauled her as well as the rest of us across the tape.

Colonel Dellamere proposed three cheers for the victors. The members of the teams mingled, swapping congratulations and discussing their experiences. We converged on the terrace for more drinks – it had been thirsty work, as a villager with a scarlet face and a sly grin remarked; leaving the children to their junior tug-of-war. Ties and jackets were donned, even by Billy Deeps, and hands washed and hair combed. The time was roughly seven-thirty. Pixie was shepherding people towards the drawing-room french windows, saying supper was ready.

Generous portions of Mrs Roope's chicken and ham pies, topped with short brown pastry and containing exactly the right mixture of tender meat and clear savoury jelly, and of Mrs Wipps' potato and vegetable salads, reposed on plates on the extended table in the dining-room. There was a mountain of slices of crusty bread and butter on a platter. Mr Roope was drawing jugs of beer from barrels propped on kitchen stools; Mrs Roope, from jugs on the sideboard, was filling and refilling glasses with beer and orangeade. Morgan and a detachment of females were out-of-doors, distributing knives, spoons, forks, and big bowls of fruit salad and whipped cream from the farm along the trestle table.

When the entire company was ranged behind the chairs, staff included, Colonel Dellamere made a short speech. He explained why the garden was closed; he said he was glad the tug-of-war hadn't been won on a disqualification – Molly Deeps laughed loudest at the courtly quip at her expense; he thanked those responsible for the supper and hoped everyone would enjoy it. Mr Owen, while the children fidgeted, replied on behalf of the village, and Mr Llewellyn intoned: 'For what we are about to receive may we be grateful, O Lord' – a sentiment that called forth an impatient murmur of Amen.

We sat down to our victuals. The Dellameres were in the centre on the house side of the table. I was on the same side, but further along, nearer the lawn. I've forgotten my immediate neighbours; but Winters, Wessels and Morgan were on my left, the villagers in a line opposite, Esmond Charrington and George Sawrey, quite at their ease, amongst them, and Roopes and Deeps at the other right-hand end. Guy Toller must have been sitting next to Laura. Morgan, from crates of beer on the paving stones by his place, kept on doling out bottles.

The supper was scrumptious – the physical exercise had sharpened our appetites. Children ran into the house for second helpings of pie. The bottles of beer circulated. Dirty plates were stacked and removed, clean plates for the fruit salad and cream were passed. Faces grew redder and sweatier. Brows were mopped. The shyness partly overcome by the tug-of-war, between employer and employed, between Gentlemen and Players, gave way to good fellowship. George was nudging and being nudged by his companions, chunky farmers' wives, convulsed with merriment at his sallies.

Cigarettes were lit. The flare of matches was a reminder that it was almost dark. A great gust or scoop of wind whirled across the terrace. None of us had been paying attention to the weather. Now the party scanned the sky. The scudding theatrical clouds were lower, looming overhead, although here and there violet gaps still separated them. Over Llanrhad the clouds were an ugly black and orange. But no rain had fallen. Because our fun hadn't been interfered with, and might be at any moment, it became more furious.

Jugs frothing with the residue of the barrels of beer were brought from the dining-room. Miss Dellamere and Laura were drinking beer, entering into the spirit of the feast. Homely jokes, although obscure as far as I was concerned, were being cracked by Colonel Dellamere and his dependants: 'Is your leg in one piece, Jenkins? . . . What became of the brindled cow, sir?' – provocative of hearty laughter. I leant forwards to look at our host, his cheeks rubicund in the glow of somebody's cigarette. He laughed helplessly at the reference to the brindled cow. He loved and was loved by these friends of his who worked for him: so much for his paternalism, I thought.

Toasts were drunk. Guy Toller and Billy Deeps were trying to toast the village tug-of-war team, and vice versa. Esmond Charrington was reducing a buxom hoyden to near hysteria by clinking his glass against hers. I heard cries of 'Speech, speech!' without guessing to whom they were addressed. Then the clouds parted and the moon shone through, round and luminous. One of the children noticed the shape of a bat, flittering through its beams, and began to shriek. Several of the women were frightened and pushed back their chairs. George Sawrey called: 'Speech, Laura!' And she stood up.

'The bats won't hurt you,' she said. 'They won't get in your hair, they're good creatures – I've known them for years!'

Her appearance in the moonlight, in her white dress, more than her words of advice which weren't generally heard, interrupted the clamour.

George added above the titters of reassured laughter, in the hush that had fallen: 'Well – go on!' and voices chimed in: 'Yes, go on, Miss! Speech, speech!' and beer glasses were banged on the table.

She paused in the act of sitting down, stood again, caught in the fleeting effulgence of the moon. Everybody was gazing at her, the Winters on my left, Morgan, the people opposite and the wide-eyed children. Only Dick Wessel smoked and stared ahead – his face with its full flat lips was averted.

'Thank you for coming here,' Laura said. 'It's been a wonderful party. We've never had such a wonderful party, have we? Thank you all!'

A lot of things happened at once. Cheering and clapping broke out, and I realised that Laura wasn't desperate any more and that I too was cheering and applauding. Another great gust of wind blew; the moon clouded over – we were plunged in darkness; thunder rumbled; and sheet lightning flashed and was followed by a shattering thunderous crash. Morgan switched on the lights in the house and everybody rose and set to clearing the table and folding the chairs.

The headlamps of a car in the gravel sweep were also switched on. Tablecloths billowed in the scooping wind. Beer bottles were returned to crates, chairs stacked and the trestle tables dismantled, and the clatter of crockery in the dining-room mingled with the continual groaning and grinding of thunder in the distance. Lightning flickered in the black sky above Llanrhad.

Esmond Charrington and the Winters were saying goodbye. The parson and his wife and Mrs Rogers and her mother were in a hurry to walk home before the deluge, and the Deeps were collecting and swearing at their children. A closer flash illuminated the confused scene vividly, but had a blinding effect; and the subsequent crash deafened. I descended the terrace steps and started to slam the doors of cars and to direct their drivers. My hand was shaken by ladies fighting for their hats with the flurries of wind, and by the hands of their husbands which were like hams or agricultural implements.

'Goodbye, goodbye!'

Laura was with me, under the chestnut trees, stopping the cars to bid the occupants goodbye: rear-lights shone red in the dark.

'Goodbye! Good night! Wasn't it wonderful? Come next year, won't you? Yes, we beat the storm – just! Good night!'

The Wessels must have been amongst the first to leave. The Deeps in their station wagon were the last.

'Good night, Molly, good night, Billy!' Laura cried in her carefree voice, and the children echoed: 'Good night!'

We were about half-way down the drive, a yard or two apart. The rear lights of the Deeps' car outlined her figure. The car turned at the gates and disappeared from view. But I could still distinguish her pale form in the baleful flickers from over the kitchen garden wall.

'Laura!'

She embraced me – we embraced. She kissed me – our mouths met. She had her arms round my neck, I had mine round her waist – I felt her dress slipping on the silky stuff of an under-garment, her ribs, the outward curve of her hip bones – our bodies were pressed against each other.

Her lips opened – her full upper lip was sprung and coolly moist.

'You're trembling,' she whispered.

Perhaps it wasn't meant to be a reproach. The chestnut branches swayed and clashed in the wind. I struggled without success to control my passionate palsy. Huge drops of rain splashed on to the gravel.

'Don't,' she whispered, pleading with me to be bold, to be as brave as she believed that I was, and consistent and masterful – or so it seemed.

'It's raining,' I said.

She unlocked her arms, dropped them in a disappointed gesture, and drew a little away from me.

I repeated: 'Laura –' but not as before.

I was now pleading for her patience and forgiveness.

'You mustn't get wet.'

I couldn't see whether or not she was smiling ironically.

'No,' I countered. 'No, it's you – you mustn't.'

Rain drops spattered on the gravel.

'Good night,' she cried through the noise of the storm, possibly on a note of desperation or exasperation.

Lightning flashed and thunder cracked and roared almost simultaneously .

'You're right,' she added. 'We shouldn't be under the trees – really, it's dangerous! Please go! Good night!'

I replied. I obeyed. But I didn't know what I was doing or had done except that I'd failed her. I emerged from the tunnel of the drive, crossed the road, the churchyard, the water meadow, and, soaked to the skin, for the rain was pelting down, let myself into the pub by the Roopes' private door and reached my room.

It wasn't late, not more than ten-thirty. Customers were in the bar, drinking or sheltering there: I hadn't wanted to run the gauntlet of their eyes, or to have to talk to the Roopes, who might or might not be back from Llanwyn. I smoked cigarettes, spoiling them with my rainy trembling fingers. The stratospheric gale was at ground level, raging along the valley, lashing green leaves against my window panes; and the lightning had changed from sheet to forked – it zigzagged diabolically from heaven to earth, like an estuary of white fire or a terrifying diagram of arteries and veins.

I couldn't rest – I smoked and paced the floor. The turmoil of the elements was transferred into my brain. The thunder could have been exploding in the attic overhead. All my anticipatory feelings of disaster crowded in – the party had been a mere palliative. Was it disastrous? What was the extent of my failure? Were our kisses the climax and the crisis I'd been tired of waiting for? But they solved nothing! Suddenly I remembered my binoculars and my overcoat with the copy of *First Love* in the pocket, which I'd left in the hide by the lake.

I had to rescue them: at least I had an excuse for action. Time had elapsed – I don't know how much time. I retraced my steps, out of the pub and across the water meadow. The rain and wind were colder: it was the blackest night. A car was parked in the road not far from the yew tree – but I couldn't see properly. I opened the door in the wall and heard voices, crying or moaning, wailing in the storm. A prolonged flash of forked lightning rent the sky. Two people were on the verandah of the summer house. They were Laura and somebody else. They were Laura in her white dress and Dick Wessel. She was kneeling, kneeling in front of him. He was standing over her with his hands on her shoulders. She had her face in his crotch.

EIGHT

MELODRAMA as well as drama derives from life. Melodramatic episodes occur in the experience of most people. The night of the storm was uniquely such an episode for me.

Why, already soaked through, already wretched, I battled out into the rain again, to catch cold and to be devastated by the scene in the summer house, I can't say. The value I set on my binoculars and overcoat, my scrupulosity in respect of the copy of *First Love,* hardly account for my expedition. Simplistic psychology might argue that I wanted to punish myself for my failure to grasp the opportunity in the drive, for all my failures, and was indulging in a form of masochism as a result of those abortive kisses. Mystics would comment: it was written.

I couldn't sleep – I couldn't get warm. The thunder and lightning ceased in the early hours of the morning. Intermittently rain continued to pour down. At about seven-thirty, in the delayed white dawn, I dressed and sloshed across the water meadow, my purpose being to recover my belongings before George Sawrey and Guy Toller were driven to the station. I didn't want to run into anyone. I hadn't said good night to George and Guy, or Colonel Dellamere or Miss Dellamere, the previous evening: not that it mattered any more.

Crispin was gone. Although the level of the lake had risen, the nest was safe and apparently dry. But it was untenanted. By standing on the verandah and craning my neck, I could see that it contained five cold green eggs. I rescued my binoculars from the hide and my overcoat which was wringing wet. *First Love* in its pocket was soggy and wrinkled. Later in the day I toasted the book at the fire lit in my room by Mrs Roope.

I toasted myself, but couldn't stop shivering: my palsy seemed to have become chronic. The constituent parts of my sense or clinical state of shock were astonishment that Laura's companion on the stage of the verandah should have been Dick Wessel, and horror, the irreversible horror of having been the witness of the brutal intimacy and sexuality of their pose, whether or not they were performing an overtly sexual act. I was devastated by the speed of her compensation for my kisses, her carrying on from where they left off, and by her carelessness of Crispin.

But it was far more complex – nothing connected with Laura was ever simple. Dick Wessel was physically insignificant, ugly, a blot on the landscape compared with George Sawrey, and married, the husband of Penelope, a family man as he had once said. He might be clever and successful, but he was a poet who didn't write poetry, a casualty of the war in which he hadn't fought, an object of the charity of the Dellameres, a displaced person and pathetic refugee – I'd scarcely bothered to notice, let alone be jealous of him.

And Laura wasn't only beautiful in my eyes, she was a queen, a goddess, the touch of whose lips had turned my worshipful muscles to jelly. That she should kneel to Dick, that she should have sought him out like a bitch in season, was sacrilege. Her feet of clay had trampled on my illusions. Esmond Charrington had accused her of having feet of clay, of being disingenuous and naughty. Why hadn't I heeded his and other warnings?

Again, I'd desired Laura, dreamt of her in sexual situations, dwelt on our loving trustful tender union. The exchange in the summer house was beastly. It disgusted me.

Her face was in the crotch of Dick Wessel – how could she? The memory of her libertine mouth on mine made my flesh crawl. I sourly hoped that she was consoled, that in the end her lusts had been satisfied, even if her storm-tossed cries had suggested the opposite. They reverberated in my soul, broadcasting waves of pain, her cries or his, the moaning and wailing, perhaps the ultimate expression of her capacity for despair. She was desperate for Dick. She was oblivious of Crispin and of what Crispin had come to represent in our relations.

For days she'd carried her solicitousness as to Crispin's peace of mind to almost ridiculous lengths, locking the dogs out of the garden, never allowing anybody near the front of the summer house. The future of the ducks had entwined itself with ours. Their security had been our common concern. Yet she must have met Dick on the verandah. The wailing was done within a few feet of the nest.

On the morning after, as time dragged by, I began to suffer on another score. It was my birthday: on which she'd undertaken to drive me into Oswestry to buy my present. She didn't telephone. She didn't call at The Dellamere Arms. Could she have seen me in the garden doorway, spying on her, as she might imagine? That was impossible, for she was fully occupied for the duration of the lightning flash, and then I'd fled. Could she be as ashamed of herself as I was of her?

A letter from my parents and a card from Mary had arrived; but I hadn't read them. I speculated exclusively, crouched before the fire. Would Laura have taken George and Guy to the station? When would she be likely to return? Would she disappear, would she drive to London? There were three explanations of the affair with Dick: it followed from a random plot laid at the tug-of-war party; or was a chapter in a longer story of attachment; or was – legalistically – not proven. The storm was noisy and the lightning brief, and both the contribution of human voices to the former, and the revelations of the latter, were phantasmagoric.

I could be wrong. Laura and Dick could have met by accident, she tripped and fallen on her knees, he chivalrously stepped forward to support her. But while I endeavoured to cast doubt on my recollections of that instant in the garden, I remembered with unarguable clarity, with a clarity not clouded by emotion, the single averted head in profile during Laura's speech at supper. I remembered Sven: Sven had lain at Dick's feet throughout the tug-of-war. Sven had made a telltale fuss of Dick at the Easter party, jumping up when he ran across the lawn to succour his son. I remembered that Laura and Dick had worked together in the war.

Laura had also worked with Guy. But Guy and the others had receded from the forefront of my jealous mentality. In the course of the tug-of-war weekend I'd never felt the need to compete with Guy or George or anyone, for the ducks had quacked their false assurances of my special place in the list of Laura's suitors. Their quacking along with everything else had deceived me, except in its inspiration of the fancy that I was being lured into a wilderness of love.

Laura rang at twelve.

Mrs Roope's summons as it were answered many of my questions: instead of rushing downstairs to the telephone I paused involuntarily, wishing to postpone the moment of truth. Confusion had been my refuge. Definitions and solutions would soon be forthcoming. I was afraid it was finished between us. Therefore Laura could wait for me and waste a little of her time.

'Happy birthday,' she said.

I knew at once that I'd been right – the period of ambiguity and possible mistakes, sweet in retrospect, was past: she sounded faint and ill.

'Thank you.'

'How are you, Arthur?'

'I think I've got a cold.'

'Oh dear, I'm sorry. You were caught in the storm.'

'Yes,' I agreed. 'But how are you?'

'I'm all right,' she replied quickly and went on to say that her guests had only just left Llanwyn – she hadn't been able to ring before. And alas, in the afternoon, she had to perform various chores for her father: could we put off our trip to Oswestry?

Yes, I agreed again.

But I thought: lies!

'Forgive me.'

'It's not like that, Laura.'

'Will you come to tea?'

No, not tea – I couldn't have borne a social encounter; not tea, I said, for I too would be busy, writing; but was there any chance of seeing her afterwards?

'Yes.'

'Five-thirty-ish?'

'Yes. Where?'

'In the hide, Laura?'

She hesitated for so long that I queried into the mouthpiece: 'Hullo?'

'Yes, I'm here. Yes, in the hide,' she replied.

My anger was cruel. But my choice of rendezvous was impulsive, not deliberate. I wasn't acting on the tutelary principle that a dog should be shown its vomit. Besides, the cruelty cut both ways – I'd be rubbing my nose as well as hers in the hide's associations.

That afternoon I didn't write, I slept. I'd claimed that I was going to be busy because she'd claimed she was. But my tit-for-tat rejoinder had resurrected the idea of writing. I was at once the angrier with Laura for having seduced me from my literary duties, and reluctantly grateful to her for having provided me with a subject and a theme. I mustn't exaggerate: my gratitude was dim, my creative urges at an even lower ebb than usual. But already my intention was to jot down a note or two, some record of my deception and betrayal at The Dellamere Arms.

I woke with a burning face and drank a cup of tea. My throat was sore. The atmosphere out-of-doors was like skimmed milk. Clouds lowered, watery white, and white steam rose from the earth. I sweated and shivered in the chill clamminess. The birds seemed to have decided not to sing. I pushed open the garden door on its oiled hinges and saw Laura. She was sitting on the step of the verandah of the summer house, leaning against the side post that supported the extension of the roof, her feet on the ground and hands in her lap: very much as she had on the occasion on which I'd tried in vain to catechise her about her flight to London.

She was less tense – or was it that she was spent? In her dress of darker stuff than usual, blue, I think it was, in the drenched setting of the garden, she might have been the model for a Victorian picture entitled: Melancholy. A pale filter of mist alleviated the blackness of the lake. The garden was still and quiet – the wind had dropped at mid-day. The relative inaudibility of the rushing flood of the Wyn in its canal, over the garden wall in the drive, accentuated the quietness. I advanced round the water's edge.

She stood up.

But I said: 'Don't kiss me – you mustn't – my cold's worse.'

She commiserated and exclaimed: 'Arthur, where's Crispin?'

She smiled, but her tone of voice was tragic. I particularly noticed, when she smiled, the swelling of the skin under her exhausted fugitive eyes. She'd quite forgotten my birthday.

'The bird has flown,' I returned.

'Did you know she had?'

'Yes. I came along earlier to fetch my coat and binoculars.'

'You didn't warn me that Crispin had deserted when I telephoned.'

'No,' I admitted.

'She laid five eggs.'

'Yes.'

'She was frightened by the storm. She must have deserted because of the lightning and rain.'

'Not only the storm,' I corrected furiously, inwardly furious that Laura should be so dishonest.

'What do you mean?'

'I came to fetch my things last night.'

'What?'

'You frightened her.'

She sank down on the steps. A pause ensued, and she started to sob. Her forehead was touching her knees, her hands with their bitten fingernails covering her ears. She sobbed more violently – her strangled inconsolable sobbing and retching were awful in the surrounding white peace.

'Please, Laura, please,' I repeated continually, sitting by her, stroking and patting her.

Her tears washed the fury from my soul, and the accumulated deposit of my resentment against her. It appalled me that I was the immediate cause of her humiliation and extravagant torturous sorrow. I couldn't abide the reversal of our positions. I didn't want her to be overheard.

Eventually she accepted my handkerchief and dried her eyes.

'Don't look at me – smoke – have pity,' she muttered in broken accents, with a rueful attempt at humour.

I lit a cigarette. We sat side by side, staring out at the lake and the cypresses. Leaves and budding twigs floated on the surface. Sometimes she cried; but she controlled herself.

She said: 'I should have told you long long ago.'

'About Dick?'

'About Dick. Do you remember asking me why I went to London? We were here. We were by the lake. I should have told you then. You'd been frank with me. Why couldn't I be frank with you? I promised to tell you one day. I meant to tell you one day. But it's so involved – I hadn't the strength – and I'm such a coward! All I could ever do was to plead for forgiveness. And now I've got to plead with you to forgive me for everything!'

'Did you go to London to be with Dick?'

'Oh no. I went to London because Penelope was arriving at Foresters. I panicked and couldn't bear it.'

'Bear what, Laura?'

'Dick and I parted four months ago. We parted on New Year's Day. In April, after three months, I had to get away, escape from Aberystwyth Mansions. I couldn't be alone, not for another minute, pretending to work and feeling sorry for myself. I wanted to be in Wales, at home, with my family, my father – to stay at Llanwyn even for the rest of my life – and begin again. And I'd test my reactions, prove I was finally free, at Easter time, during the Wessels' spring visit to

Foresters. It's so involved! Dick would have avoided the place for my sake and his, if he'd had any choice in the matter. But his wife insisted. His children insisted. They were partly brought up here. They always came back for the holidays. Dick couldn't spoil their fun in order to spare the blushes of his ex-mistress. And Penelope's a determined woman with that jutting chin of hers.'

I prompted: 'What couldn't you bear?'

'What could I bear? I do dislike people who boast of their misery. But Llanwyn didn't seem to be the answer to any of my problems. Everyone was old and growing older, including me. I was lonelier, more miserable, and dreaded the confrontation with the Wessels. Then I met you. The gods had relented, I believed. You were young and hopeful, still hopeful, and as brave as I longed to be. You endured surgical operations without an anaesthetic, and were writing under pressure, against the clock, yet not unduly perturbed. I learnt from you and lived through you. For nearly a week you made me forget or almost forget. Pixie reminded me. I panicked on your account, in case I was leading you on or misleading you, and because I couldn't face Penelope - she was bound to call at Llanwyn on arrival – Morgan had the keys of the cottage. I had to gather my forces or collect my wits or whatever the expression is, and I retreated to London. Can you understand? How can I expect you to understand? I don't understand myself!'

'But Laura, hadn't you faced Penelope before?'

'Yes! But before, in other years, she'd had to face me – there's the difference! This year she was the winner – I'd lost. You see what a bad character I am.'

'But you invited the Wessels to the Easter party.'

'No! Daddy or Pixie invited them. Their attendance at the party was inevitable – it's a tradition.'

'You were desperate.'

'Was I? Was it obvious? Oh God!'

I think she cried for a minute or two – desperate no longer, beyond desperation – desolately.

'Laura! Laura, what happened at the party?'

'Did you realise something had happened?'

'Yes.'

'John Wessel was climbing on the wall. Dick ran across the lawn with Penelope.'

'And you were jealous?'

'I don't know! I lost my head or my temper. I said I was the loser, didn't I? I wanted you to walk along the stupid wall. I wanted you very badly to be steady and brave for me in public. I was so grateful! But I shouldn't have asked you to risk your neck.'

'It was lovely afterwards.'

'Yes.'

'With Emerald and Crispin.'

'Yes.'

She cried again momentarily.

'Until the tug-of-war, Laura.'

'Now you must tell me what happened,' she said.

'I was fetching my things from the hide. I was by the door, you were on the verandah.'

'Oh God! I would have explained today, I swear it! Dick and I used to meet in the summer house. I didn't speak a word to him at supper. There was no arrangement between us, truly. When the cars had gone, in the drive, it wasn't any good, was it – for you or me? I suppose I lost my head again. The dogs were missing – I put on a mackintosh and searched for Trilby and Sven. Dick was waiting for me.'

A note of wonder insinuated itself into her voice. Regret was modified by a sort of bemused gratification, because Dick was waiting, had responded to her telepathic messages, demonstrated that after all he needed her as she needed him, because of the fatal aspect of their reunion. The crisis of my love was dismissed in a single sentence.

I protested: 'We'd kissed each other half an hour before!'

'But that was why –' She broke off and added: 'I'm sorry.'

'Honestly, Laura!'

I meant: can you only apologise? Can't you do better?

'I've loved Dick for six years,' she said.

The baldness of her statement, her declaration of love for Dick which entitled her, she seemed to imply, to treat me anyhow, a declaration that shed a criminal light on her encouragement of my feelings, and in particular those six years, getting on for a quarter of my whole existence, a period of attachment infinitely longer than I'd bargained for, which negated the argument of the three and a half weeks of our friendship – provoked me to retort in impotent rage: 'Well, I hope you'll be happy.'

'Happy? No, you don't understand! I was happy yesterday – I was happy to be on the verge of happiness. No, no! Happiness isn't for me!'

She turned her head. Her eyes were red and swollen, tears coursed down her stained cheeks. Her lips were swollen.

In her agitation, her abandonment, she stood and continued: 'I wasn't able to escape. I thought I was free, I struggled to be free, but I wasn't, I'm not, and I can't struggle – what's the use of it? God knows what the end will be! I didn't mean to hurt you. Go back to Mary. You must be happy. Goodbye! Don't follow me, don't follow me!'

Twenty-four hours passed.

Mainly, setting aside for the time being the active consequences of our interview, I nursed my cold and rewrote in my mind the story of Laura Dellamere.

She was the source of the new material that had to be woven into events, which I've already narrated from my original point of view. Her revelations on the evening after the storm had been blurred by our mutual distress. The information she gave me was incomplete and garbled; and of course at my age, as she and others had reiterated, great gaps in my understanding remained to be filled. Nevertheless, by limiting the scope of my inquiry and with the aid of hindsight, I was able to work out a rough revised version of our dealings.

Many mysteries were now explicable by reference to Dick. If Laura hadn't been defeated by Dick or Penelope, or by Dick and Penelope, she wouldn't have retreated to Llanwyn in the first place, she wouldn't have buried herself in the country, or been seeking an alternative to her outward and her inward circumstances. She wouldn't have gone fishing with her father – she never went fishing on any other occasion. She wouldn't have seemed to be available. While I was having the fish-hook extracted and my arm stitched, she wouldn't have associated my physical pain with hers. In the embrasure of the window of my room at the pub, her eyes wouldn't have glistened so sympathetically, so movingly, with heraldic tears.

She was already exercising her talent, her gift for getting into untenable positions. Loving Dick, a family man, and launching forth unreadily on an attempt to love me, were essays in failure. Cynics, cynics more cynical than Esmond Charrington who appreciated the unusual charm of her character, would say that I hitched my wagon to the straightforward star of her beauty. I would repeat that almost at once her beauty was the least of it, that I fell under the spell of her impracticality. Below the surface she was unworldly and unwise, quixotic, good. Her mute appeal to which I rallied was: help me.

Her cowardice that put a romantic premium on my courage was

attributable to her uncertainty as to whether or not she was at liberty – whence, too, her reserve: whence her bitten nails. Perhaps she had indeed cut loose by coming to Llanwyn. But she looked forward to the trial of strength of the Easter party and the tug-of-war, to which by tradition the Wessels would be invited. Would she withstand the influence of Dick and resist the undertow of the six years of their affair? I was her insurance policy, her opportunity if she chose to avail herself of it to change her life: to become a wife, a housewife, with luck a mother, the better half of my possible literary success, a woman as secure as others, marching along the middle of the road.

I was the bearer of the glad tidings of chance, a second chance.

'One must have courage,' she said, pausing, interrupting our conversation, to take stock of her supply for the thousandth time.

It was insufficient.

When she was reminded that Penelope Wessel was arriving at Foresters, she sacrificed me and my appointment to have my stitches out to her panic. She enjoyed a vicarious triumph by willing me to walk the wall on Easter Day. But a week later, after the tug-of-war supper, what she actually and irretrievably lost was her nerve.

Our joy in each other had been a wasting asset. On that very first evening, watching her in the water meadow, arm-in-arm with her father while Sven skimmed across the grass, I was happier than ever before or afterwards because she was happier. Yes, love is a telepathic link, whatever the scientific pros and cons. And she was happier because I could be her champion: unaware of her past and undeterred by the future – swinging down the hill from Penyboth to slay the dragon of Dick and release her from the dungeon of the dark rooms at Llanwyn, where the grandfather clock measured the brevity of her empty interminable days and the transience of her looks.

But if, for love of her, I were to vanquish her adversaries, what was to be my prize? Would she ever be able to reward me adequately? Guilt set in. She was divided – moody, frustrated, restless, exasperated and so on. At dinner at Llanwyn, after the fish-hook incident, she was disturbed to have to admit to her preference for Sven: she was sad to say that she preferred Sven to Trilby: and Sven was Dick's familiar. Her progress in my direction was arrested. In her conscience her advances were translated from a legitimate exploration of her friendly feelings for me into an adultery of the heart, a more culpable adultery than that which our friendship might replace, and a victimisation of my innocence.

She paused, she faltered, pulled back by Dick, as if she'd been the rope in the tug-of-war. She had no confidence in my ability to haul her across the tape – and none in herself. She was therefore at fault in her dalliance with me. That was her way, according to Morgan. No, not again, she must have thought.

She was torn in two by her paradoxical principles. On another day at Llanwyn Esmond Charrington called her a naughty disingenuous girl. He was perceptive and guessed at her emotional predicament. He was accusing her of filling an idle hour at my expense. She couldn't shrug off the jest.

Charges from outside weren't as bad for her as those from within. My Easter egg, the silver snuffbox, overwhelmed her with guilt that resembled ingratitude. She was keyed up to face the Wessels after four months, preoccupied by her desperate determination not to weaken; and the waste of my money, in Pixie's phrase, represented my submission of an inconvenient claim, and a reproach she merited. She'd bought me no equivalent present; had been depressed in Oswestry to have to shop for meaningless trinkets – probably she remembered the presents she'd exchanged with Dick; hadn't been inclined to differentiate between me and Guy and David; couldn't requite my generosity – and never should have inspired it.

She jerked her head abruptly, a gesture indicative of shame, amongst other things. She was ashamed of having incurred another extraneous responsibility. In spite of herself she was ashamed of her infidelity to Dick and, simultaneously, her fidelity. She was frightened of causing and of being caused more pain. She was tormented by indecision. For the same reasons, in the hide on the morning before the tug-of-war, she was hasty, she had to fly like Emerald – fly from me. As a result, not far from the hide which had become unnecessary, her tension was relieved at last by awful sobs.

She shouldn't have: she'd said it. She shouldn't have evaded my questions, for instance about The Forest in which Dick had his lair, or why Morgan disliked her – incidentally why did Morgan dislike her? She shouldn't have skated over my doubts and hers on the precarious vehicle of the theory that life was too short.

Yes – but in her more constructive moments she yearned for her alternative association to follow a fresh path, a path without obstacles, without barriers, in the open, untainted. She didn't want to confuse one issue with another, ours with hers. Impractically, unselfishly, she yearned not to have to hoist her burden on to my shoulders.

And of course I should have understood – somewhere deep down I wasn't surprised by the turn of events. I should have identified the villain of Esmond's query. On the Friday of the Easter weekend Laura asked me to drive to Oswestry station not because she couldn't do without my company, not because she couldn't wait to introduce me to Guy Toller and David Skelton, but because Dick Wessel might be on their train. I was her charm against the evil eye of Dick or of Penelope who could be collecting him, and her protection against her untrustworthy self. That was why she anticipated my thanks for the pleasant jaunt by thanking and kissing me so warmly.

At the Easter party I should have realised that John Wessel was the catalyst. I either misinterpreted the signs or didn't connect them: Laura's desperation; Dick's strained state and snubbing remark to me; Sven's devotion to Dick; the attitude of Miss Dellamere who disapproved of her niece's seducer – Miss Dellamere must have been in possession of the facts of the case. When Dick and Penelope rushed to the rescue of John, united by their anxious parenthood – banging and bolting the door of their marriage and shutting out danger and thieves – Laura couldn't bear it. Her general challenge to the grown-ups was aimed at Dick, who wasn't the type to walk on walls. She wished to taunt him, terrify Penelope, ridicule and punish them.

She wished to demonstrate that she also was loved – and foolhardily and regardless of risk. I was the agent of her proud and bitter mockery of the Wessels.

Again at the tug-of-war she issued her challenge: 'What about you, Dick?' She was publicly stigmatising his poor sportsmanship, his spoil-sport traits, his physical feebleness and his defensiveness. Considering his clothes which were more English than any Englishman's, she was hitting him in the sore spot of his ambition not to be a foreign outsider. She could have hoped to undermine his and Penelope's children's respect for their father.

She was more or less beside herself, loathing and despising Dick, at any rate at the Easter party. Yet her hopes as they applied to me had a positive aspect. My feat of daring brought them to a finer pitch, persuaded her that we could complement each other. She kissed me in front of everyone. She loved me for loving her. I was her saviour, her slave to command, as she was almost mine.

The domesticity of the ducks was additionally persuasive. If only we could bind our destinies together sexually, naturally, like Emerald and Crispin, if she could concentrate on the fulfilment of her feminine role, how happy she might be! If she were to forget for ever with my assistance, and build and tend her nest in some secluded spot, what unwonted satisfaction might be hers! She went so far as to mention my father and my home – Deane End which must have seemed as remote from her experience and therefore safe, as the lake did to the ducks. She elicited my promise that I wouldn't miss Mary on my birthday.

On the Sunday of the tug-of-war she summoned me from the hide to support her in her arguments on the terrace. Her fears had revived. For the sake of Emerald and Crispin, that is to say for her fond dreams associated with them, the garden had to be out of bounds to guests. Her wilfulness with regard to the whereabouts of the supper was a clue to her uncertain estimates of the power of her will. She was compelled to prove she was stronger than Morgan who was in love with Penelope; she was proving she'd be stronger than Dick.

In church, that morning and the Sunday before, Easter Sunday, she must have prayed for strength. It was on the eve of Easter that she climbed into the woods to call Sven. Those woods extended up the hill behind Llanwyn and merged into The Forest which contained Foresters: perhaps, then, she'd weakened to the extent of wanting her cries to carry to the ears of Dick – my impression had been that she rather than the dog was lost. She herself had used the word: lost. Her anguished pleas to me were that I should find and keep her, so to speak.

Pixie in her parable of Missy Dellamere had hinted at Laura's difficulties. Missy had loved Michael Blake and married Bobs Dellamere. She'd managed to switch her allegiance, her craziness hadn't confined her within the prison of her feelings for Michael, or stood in the way of her opportunity to become Bobs' adored wife. The difference between the mother's and the daughter's situations was crucial: Michael Blake had been killed in the war and Missy was a widow, whereas Dick was alive, her neighbour in London and at Llanwyn, the friend of her friends and her family.

Laura was afraid she couldn't – that to sanction my adoration wouldn't be fair. She hesitated, she teetered, and, swayed by her, so did I. After the tug-of-war supper, and her speech in the moonlight beneath the wistaria blossom, when the cars had departed and she hadn't succumbed to Dick, in a spirit of sudden elation she fell into my arms. The drops of rain dissolved our scruples. The wind swooped on our discretion and scattered it abroad. Why did my knees have to tremble? It wasn't any good in the drive, not really, as she said.

Her hopes of me and of herself were shattered. She returned to the house, and left it to look for the dogs. The past lured her to the scene in which she'd loved wholeheartedly and been loved once upon a time. She didn't worry about the ducks which had let her down. She was in revolt against the falsehood of our sessions in the hide.

Dick was waiting for her.

All of us had failed: I to learn my lesson from Emerald – I to seize Laura by the scruff of her neck and masterfully make her mine; Laura to be free; Dick to honour his pledges; Penelope to hang on to him. I'd failed in my writing. Crispin had failed. The gods had failed.

Or in the last analysis had I got everything wrong? Against the odds, the argument could run, despite the firmest and the most rational resolutions, and by means of the miraculous coincidence of that stormy meeting in the summer house, true love had succeeded.

Laura's object throughout could have been to recapture Dick.

If so, she'd won.

NINE

My father had written my birthday letter, Mother adding affectionate messages. After the tearful scene with Laura I read it. Father offered a hundred pounds to enable me to continue with my work.

I could stay on at The Dellamere Arms. But the emotional and literary inducements were nil; and my parents' kind gesture effectively blunted the revolutionary edge of my ambition to write. Since they seemed to have swung round in my favour, I swung round in theirs. I was in an extraordinarily muddled and contrary state. I telephoned Deane End to say I'd be coming home on Thursday.

That was on Monday, my birthday, in the evening after the tug-of-war and the storm. I dined alone; gave notice of my departure to the Roopes; wrote a card to Mary in reply to hers, putting a cross beside my signature; and retired to bed, coughing and sneezing. I was homesick for my family, homesick for unequivocal people who cared for me. On the Tuesday I remained indoors, making notes of my experience at Llanwyn and reading *First Love,* the toasted pages of which crackled and were apt to stick together.

I'd looked into the book already. But its mere story hadn't prevailed over my preoccupation with life. Now the mystery of the heroine Zinaida, loved by Turgenev's narrator whose name I can't recall, absorbed my attention. She was beautiful and unpredictable, like Laura. When the youth lurks in the garden at night, ready to stab his rival with his penknife, and recognises the figure of his father, I received a double or treble shock. For his riddle was solved brutally, as mine had been; his father was his least likely candidate for the role of villain of the piece, as Dick was in my case; and it struck me that I'd been lent and was reading – but too late – a cautionary tale.

The intention must have been that I should identify Zinaida's situation with Laura's, and at least be warned. Laura had repeatedly urged me to read *First Love:* she said she wanted to talk about it. She'd required an oblique peg on which to hang some references to her own adulterous love affair and the fate of youths who fall for mysterious girls. Turgenev's story, its relevance revealed, filled in another corner of the jigsaw puzzle of her attitudes.

The more I pieced together her various attitudes, the more I had to admire her sense of proportion. She overdid it; had done so all along; but had been responding to a secret set of circumstances, in the context of which her behaviour was surely reasonable. She'd begun to confide in me, in accordance with Esmond Charrington's prophecy, and to convince me. Esmond had volunteered an extra word of warning. What was it? – 'Once excuse a woman and you're finished.'

Certainly I excused her later on. I accepted her explanation: indeed her motives took on a moving transparency. She'd been fighting her private battle with Dick also for my benefit, in order to be free to love me. But at moments, during those final hours of cogitation or revision at The Dellamere Arms, my memories of her disingenuousness played devil's advocate.

The fact was that Laura had got Dick back, I argued. Their decision to part could have been reached either jointly, as she suggested, or unilaterally – it could have been his idea which she'd desperately sought to reverse. Llanwyn could have been the battleground not of the establishment of her freedom from Dick, but of the re-establishment of her dominion over him. Would she have stayed in her father's house, while Dick was at Foresters with his wife and children, to test the abstruse theory that her nerves were proof against his proximity? Wasn't her visit simply a feminine design to see him again? In the drive, before the storm, when she was saying goodbye to everybody, she could have proposed the assignation in the summer house: why else had she traipsed through the rain to look for her dogs in the garden? She knew the top door was locked – and that the dogs frequented the rabbit warren.

But then, I retorted, she wouldn't have kissed me under the chestnut trees. Her kisses weren't lascivious, a sort of appetiser for the more luscious meal she was counting on, they were climactic or anti-climactic, they were anyway critical. She wasn't cut out to scalp-hunt or plot, she was too impractical. In the summer house, if she'd been celebrating the success of her wily manoeuvres, would she have wailed on the verandah? And on the following day, Monday, she wouldn't have sobbed inconsolably, as though her heart and her will – her will to escape from abnormality, to lead a normal life with its chance of happiness – were both broken. She wouldn't have been so guilty and ashamed.

Perhaps my bewilderment boiled down to the question: what was love? The pure beauty whose guileless eyes had met mine when I glanced over the parapet of a rustic bridge had slipped through my fingers, like a handful of the water of the Wyntrude. An adulteress, a scarlet woman bathed in tears, who had encouraged and discouraged me, whose kisses were the precursor of her passionate intercourse with another man, had replaced her. Emotions that could so transform, with such destructive force, were beyond me. Love was friendship leading on to legal marriage, not agony and ruin. Although the drama of Laura's destiny was perversely exciting, my remaining illusions and my middle-class upbringing with its ideology of comfort rebelled against it.

Mary Singleton was my answer. Laura Dellamere and Arthur Bartlett – even our names were ill-assorted. Laura was too old, sullied, used: there had never been any future for us. Deane End, Guildford, not wild Wales, was my homeland. I'd return and recover, recuperate from the infections contracted in the environs of the pub. The weather would be less extreme, and the twittering of the swallows in the softer southern atmosphere wouldn't make me wince.

I went to bed on Tuesday at about eight o'clock and woke on Wednesday with my curtains glowing. The sun shone, it was dispersing the white blight on the landscape, and I felt better.

At nine-thirty or so, the earliest opportunity, I rang Laura. I couldn't desert her, not as things were. Residual optimism or renewed resentment might have changed my mind. The waste of her loveliness on Dick Wessel was intolerable. I hoped to save her soul, if not my own.

She thanked me humbly for ringing: 'I didn't think you would.'

I was overcome with relief to hear her voice: she hadn't gone away.

'I had to talk to you once more.'

'Once more? Why – are you leaving?'

'Yes, probably.'

'When?'

'Tomorrow.'

'Oh.' She paused. 'Talk – talk on the telephone, do you mean?'

'I wondered if you'd like to have a walk.'

'Yes, I'd love that.'

'At two o'clock?'

'Yes.'

She asked after my cold. I told her it was all right. We agreed that the day was finer.

She inquired: 'Where shall we meet?'

'In the churchyard?'

She replied, 'Yes,' without hesitation.

She seemed to approve of my latest choice of meeting-place.

We were together for approximately four hours. We walked, talked and had tea. We trod the long looping path through the woods behind the house. Her monologue that took up most of the time had a quiet conversational coda. She was waiting for me, sitting with Trilby and Sven on a gravestone in the sun, as I crossed the water meadow.

In due course I said: 'Are you happier?'

'No. But I'm not hysterical. I'm sorry I was hysterical. No, I'm not happier.'

'Haven't you got what you want, Laura?'

'I don't know. I don't know what I've got. I haven't got anything. And I don't know what I want.'

'You knew on the night of the storm.'

'I suppose so.'

'You knew I wasn't important enough, that Dick was more important.'

'Maybe.'

'You were jealous of Dick. Was Dick jealous of you?'

'He is jealous.'

'Was I your way of arousing his jealousy, your defence against Penelope?'

'No, never, I promise!'

'Was I your revenge on Dick?'

'No – please! Don't think so badly of me!'

'What am I to think, Laura?'

She allowed that I had every right to ask her. She owed me much more than an explanation. But, again, she'd do her best to explain.

'I'll have to begin at the beginning. Words can't tell the truth about life. That's why I wasn't able to be frank with you, because whatever I said would be incomplete and untrue. But I was cowardly – and wrong. If words are one kind of lie, silence is another. Besides, I long to speak the truth just once – I never have before; or to try to speak it or find it out.'

We'd set off on our walk, along the drive, on to the terrace, round the corner of the drawing-room and into the woods by the flights of steps, down which Molly Deeps had plunged with the first Easter egg of the Easter party.

'Well, to begin with, my childhood was happy. I loved my mother. I miss her still. She had vitality as distinct from energy, although she wasn't lacking in energy. I understand exactly why my father was so fond of her, for I've inherited bits of his temperament, the dutiful dogged bits. I'm a creature of habit and routine, too – and women need to be adjustable and flexible. She lifted us on to a different plane where everything was less serious, less fraught, easier, more vivid, and the letter of the law didn't matter. Not that she was amoral – far from it – or always such fun: I hate people who are always fun. No; she gave us a special sense of security: we depended on her to charm us out of our ruts. She was killed when I was thirteen.

'The next year I was sent to a boarding school. I'd never been away from Llanwyn – Pixie had taught me, or rather hadn't taught me – and cried nightly for my home and my mother. The shock of her death was delayed: gradually I realised that a whole dimension of my nature was shrivelling up. But I stuck it at school. I had to be educated somewhere and at least learnt to read – I formed the habit of reading books. Then in the summer of 1939, aged seventeen, I stayed with Aunt Ange in London, and took part in the social season.

'I'm a divided sort of person, as you've discovered to your cost. My birthday's on May 22nd. If I'd been born two or three days earlier my sign of the zodiac would be Taurus, not Gemini – I'm on the cusp between The Twins and The Bull. Popular astrology may not mean much. But you see what I'm driving at? Duality and stubbornness, bull-headedness – they're a rotten combination. In London I realised I was pretty; was flattered and courted and so on; and was genuinely surprised – it was like coming into a fortune.

'I was as gregarious and frivolous as I'd been solitary and glum. Music, parties, compliments, flirtations, I revelled in the novelty of it all. What did I care that the war was approaching, while I danced and slept late? What do dizzy girls care about? When the fighting started, Llanwyn was turned into a convalescent hospital for soldiers. I joined the staff as a VAD nurse, that's to say I carried trays and mopped floors for a year; but didn't like the work or being cut off from my friends. I took a shorthand and typing course and, in time, largely through Guy Toller, a job in that unit of the Civil Service at Brayle. I met Dick Wessel in 1942. I was twenty.

'Fortunes are notoriously difficult to manage. Millionaires moan that it's harder to be rich than poor, I've heard them. Yet millionaires, however hard it may be, seldom want to get rid of their money. I was delighted to be told I was pretty. The drawback was that men not only paid compliments, they pestered me – and I was bad at dealing with their declarations and propositions. I couldn't say no as firmly as I should have done and allowed foolish situations to develop.

'My power to damage others was a worry. It was horrid when admirers I hadn't been very nice to were wounded and killed in the war. I can't pretend I was sorry to have that power, that fortune of my appearance. But it altered me: I grew more careful and guarded. Perhaps it corrupted me. The search for someone to love was complicated by my idea that he'd have to be worthy of the gift I could bestow on him. There are always prettier girls for men who like pretty girls, and, equally, better and more attractive men for girls who are in a position to pick and choose. I was as restless as the rich are, thoroughly muddled by the wealth of my opportunities. I needn't add that women distrusted me.

'An old-fashioned social circle which includes an older generation has its advantages. It sets standards and provides a degree of protection; and the majority has to be protected. My experience of such a circle ended in 1939. From the age of seventeen and a half I was on my own. Even at Llanwyn I got into hot water with soldiers in the hospital and stationed nearby. At Brayle I was billeted in a dreary bedsitting-room in a house in a strange village. The result was that I accepted invitations to go out with men and sooner or later felt persecuted. I didn't wish to be a total failure. I just couldn't cope with success. I'm explaining, not swanking or complaining: you do see, don't you?

'I thought I'd been in love often – who doesn't? But none of my loves were satisfactory. I'd read too much. Books really are forbidden fruit. Having been unhappy as I was at school is forbidden fruit. I mean that reading had made me simultaneously more romantic and more discriminating and selective. And I was afraid to care and run the risk of crying nightly. Everything had heightened or deepened my choosiness.

'You've only met Dick twice, haven't you, at the Easter party and the tug-of-war? On both occasions he was under stress, not himself. I can imagine your reactions to his size, his smallness and plainness: mine were similar. But his secondary effect on me was disarming. Since I couldn't take him seriously as a man, and the question of his being worthy of my emotional interest didn't arise, I dropped my defences. He was extremely polite. He was respectful and diffident. He invited me to lunch.

'We lunched three or four times in two months. We discussed books – he'd read a lot. He was thirty-four and had a responsible job in the chemical warfare department of our unit; and I bowed to his superior knowledge of literature and life. My critical faculties were subordinated to his. But he wanted to know my opinions. He was amazingly quick and clever, responsive and sensitive, and different from anyone I'd ever come across. He was the first man to pay the slightest attention to my mind.

'I waited for him to become personal, but he didn't. He lent me books and sent me cuttings of the reviews in magazines. His patience wore down mine: eventually I talked about myself. In return he confessed to having a wife and two children in London. I was startled by this piece of information, although Guy or someone had mentioned his marriage. He'd been no more than a disembodied intelligence in my eyes. Possibly, without admitting it, I was depressed by the news that he belonged elsewhere; and my competitive possessive instincts were involved.

'The innocence of our friendship had fascinated me. I was fascinated by the differences between us. We dined together once or twice. He was foreign and fussy and told the waiters in restaurants that he couldn't eat the food. He was definite and dynamic: his sign of the zodiac was Scorpio. He was so clumsy that if the books we swapped had to be carried to or from a car, I'd do the carrying. He was so warm. I could tease him – I was at ease with him; and he was as amused by his eccentricities and mispronunciations as I was. We laughed at his inferiority complexes and his being a midget in a land of giants.

'One evening, after dinner, we walked along the towpath by the Thames – Brayle was by the river. I suppose it was our ninth or tenth outing; the month was July. He spoke of his youth in Germany, and his parents and sisters and cousins who had been caught by the Nazis and thrown into concentration camps – he hoped for their sakes they were all dead. He loved his family. He was eloquent on the subject of family life. He described his wife and children. She was an admirable wife and devoted mother, and had staunchly stayed in London in the blitz because they couldn't afford to sell their house. He wasn't free, he said. And now he was going to America for several weeks on business.

'I pitied his German relations, but was otherwise unmoved. His reference to freedom passed me by. We shook hands like comrades. When and how, in his absence, I fell in love with him, I can't tell you. The process was gradual – and relentless. He was coming back to Brayle in August. I left a note at his lodgings, asking him to get in touch with me. On the night he arrived, that was what happened.

'I was amazed. Amazement was and is the refrain of our affair: but I hate the word affair, don't you? I was amazed by Dick, by myself, and that we should be lovers. At the same time love seemed a foregone conclusion, predestined and inevitable. I can give you any number of reasons why I wrote my note. I'd missed him. I'd had an alarming reminder of my loneliness at school. In the oddest way Dick was a reincarnation of my mother, for he also had vitality, he was able to loosen my knots and soothe my anxieties. He opened new perspectives and restored my sense of an extra interior dimension.

'I was perfectly aware of what people would say: beauty and the beast and so on. But not to be hanging round for the always more attractive man who would sweep me off my feet, not to be reserved for a suitable match, not to be at the mercy of the conventions – to swing in the other unconventional direction and shower the gifts I had at my disposal on the poorest of my friends, like the Fairy Godmother in a pantomime – that was my achievement and reward. Dick settled me, settled my restlessness. His tributes to my looks were more gratifying than anybody else's. They were an appreciation of my moral virtue, my generosity.

'But reasons never accounted for love. I can't account for mine. Dick's marriage didn't matter: we met on two or three evenings each week. And now I was pleased to be alone, to be able to think, and spend weekends at Llanwyn when he was visiting Penelope. The organisation of my retirement from the social scene called for considerable tact. But we hid our lives, as the philosophers advise us we should; and discretion's definitely on the side of love. Not even Guy had any inkling of our secret.

'I was on the crest of the wave that had borne me along since I launched forth into the world. Nothing had really troubled me. Dick and I were happy for the last three years of the war. Sometimes I despised myself for dreading the prospect of peace. But my happiness was present and not concerned with the future. I actually might have believed in my conquest of happiness.

'In 1944 the house in Islington in which Penelope and her children were living was bombed flat – no one was hurt.

'I ought to explain: Dick had escaped from Germany in 1932, when he was twenty-four. He'd written and published a book of poetry at a prodigious age *Lieder Ohne Worte,* Songs Without Words. He translated the poems for me. They were composed according to mathematical formulae and above my head. But our love was a song without words. Life and nature imitate art.

'Dick couldn't write in English. His childhood ambition was to be a poet and author. He was already establishing a literary and incidentally a political reputation in Germany. Politics drove him from his country and spoilt his career. But if he'd stayed he would have suffered the fate of his Jewish relations. He renounced literature. He had degrees in mathematics and chemistry, and got a job in the chemical industry, and married in 1935, and he and Penelope produced John and Elizabeth. She was an upper-class girl – her maiden name was Penelope Masterson-Buller. The traditions of old families, their security, meant a great deal to Dick as a homeless refugee.

'Anyway, the bomb exposed in me a novel emotion: guilt. The consequence was that I offered Foresters to the Wessels, who had nowhere to go. They accepted – and I was introduced to Penelope. She couldn't thank me enough and Dick was very grateful. But the truth was that I'd been guilty of a shocking wish.

'Penelope stayed at Foresters for a year. At weekends and in the holidays Dick and I travelled together from Berkshire to Wales and back again; and in order to snatch an hour of each other's company, we met in the summer house and various places. Not only Penelope's jealousy intensified. I hadn't minded Dick's visits to his unknown wife which fitted in with my visits to Llanwyn. But, here, he was cohabiting with my declared rival in cramped quarters within a few hundred yards. As soon as the war was over, Brayle closed down. The Wessels bought another house in London, at Kew. Dick moved in and resumed his civilian work.

'He said he loved me. He loved his family. What could he have done? He'd warned me he wasn't free. His pet phrase was that we should never act drastically, violently, so as to get blood on our hands: Penelope's or his children's blood, that is. His love for me was ideal. He couldn't associate me with his view of marriage: his wife would have to be his cook, his secretary, his children's nurse, and the rest of it. In 1946 Penelope had a severe illness. Afterwards her health was suspect – he was bound to her more tightly. And she became a Roman Catholic: with apologies for my cynicism, she was thus ruling out divorce.

'I'm not complaining – I'd no complaints. Except for the business with the bomb, and uneasy moments during the Wessels' residence at Foresters, my happiness had been unblemished. Dick had spared me the sorrow of his marital problems. I leased the flat in Aberystwyth Mansions and looked forward to the continuation of our love. If the worst should come to the worst, not that it would or could, I wasn't married. I was twenty-three and had many happy years with whoever it was in front of me. My fortune, my good fortune to date encouraged my complacence. I was convinced that men who suited me must grow on trees.

'So the crusade against circumstances began. We advanced into the fray like the soldiers in epic films, in spotless uniforms, with flags fluttering and bands playing – or I did. Soon we were all covered with blood, in spite of Dick or because of him. And his and my blood, at any rate mine, was shed for a lost cause.

'We ceased to meet. No, that's an exaggeration. We saw each other on average for five hours every week. Five hours a week equals approximately two hundred and fifty hours a year, or ten days and nights, ten twenty-four-hour days out of three hundred and sixty-five. I've practised my arithmetic.

'Often for weeks I wouldn't catch a single glimpse of him, when he was abroad or at Foresters. Penelope clung on to Foresters – and I couldn't evict her. She was defying me with those spring and summer holidays. She was daring her husband and her husband's mistress to behave badly at the expense of the children and their welfare. We didn't dare. There wasn't room for the three of us in Wales. I was more or less banished, although I insisted in my turn on patronising the Wessels at the Easter parties.

'Dick and I compensated by sneaking off for a couple of days to hotels in the Midlands or Scotland. But he'd have work to do. We occupied separate rooms. It was squalid and a sad change from Brayle.

'We had the telephone. I detest the instrument. It was my lifeline. But the wrong person would ring up, or Dick would ring when I was out, or we wouldn't be able to hear properly, or he'd be at home and not to be contacted, or my number would be unobtainable. A tone of voice could wreck a whole fortnight, if, for instance, he was going abroad on business. Misunderstandings, miseries multiplied on the telephone – and I'd have to wait for Dick to remove them at his convenience. We had letters. But love by post was a pathetic substitute for our previous liberty.

'I waited and I read. Once you asked me how I'd managed to read so widely. You have your answer. I was amazed by my situation, by its alteration, classical as it was. I read better books than at school, stories of men and women paying the price of their happiness, their adultery, through the centuries, romances with a familiar flavour; and was consoled by the message that, historically, I wasn't unique or quite alone. But I was still lonely. Believe me, courage is the most essential quality. For cowardice seems to create the very predicament we're afraid of, or tempt providence to create it. I was as lonely as, after my mother's death, I'd fearfully determined never to be again. I was lonelier, more homesick for Dick.

'Jealousy was my chief companion. I didn't demand much; I acknowledged that Dick couldn't discard his family; I tried my hardest not to add to his difficulties; and was uncertain of my ability and my desire to translate myself from his mistress into his wife. None of it arrested the growth, the growing tumour of my hatred of Penelope. Once I went to the house at Kew – she was away. Shortly before, Dick had brought me a present of an overcoat from America. In Penelope's bedroom with its double bed, its bed which was sinister even if Dick had a room of his own, I noticed an overcoat of the same type, but made of more costly material. I felt sick. I was as angry with Dick as I could be. But my wrath was deflected on to the person of Penelope.

'It sickened me that my gratifying sense of my generosity had deteriorated into the pettiest meanness. I was humiliated by being demoted from a lady bountiful, handing out charity to the Wessels, into a beggar at their back door. I was angry with Dick – and terrified of taxing his nervous and physical strength beyond endurance. I swallowed slights, controlled my quarrelsome instincts, yet had to watch him getting smaller and thinner, tireder and more distracted, partly on my account. My fancy was that we were drowning, Penelope included, in a sea of mutual concern. And I was responsible, the passenger responsible for having sunk the boat.

'Clearly it couldn't go on. Dick and I first broached the subject of separation eighteen months ago. We were realistic, we were optimistic. We'd remain the best of friends. I was reassured by the dowry of my appearance and cast about for somebody to share it with, who would restore me to my former state of happiness. I accepted invitations. But no one was like Dick. I'd go out to dinner with a man and spend the evening wishing I hadn't. I'd ask a man to Llanwyn for a week and after two days leave for London. I always reached a point at which I recoiled in horror. The emotion that defeated me, more potent than any of its predecessors, was regret, a regret beyond description or belief.

'What's the use of talking? Years of absolute devotion can't be summed up. Our separation was circumstantial, arbitrary, not natural or heartfelt. The divisions in me blurred the issue: to be torn between sense and sensibility was morbidly satisfying to my temperament. I was inflexible; Dick was my habit; loving Dick however remotely was my routine; and bull-headedly, doggedly, like my father, although I strove to surrender and give him up I couldn't. You haven't had my experience – how are you to understand? How were the men I flirted with to understand? Love that's intense and frustrated, and will be curtailed, without a future as they say, tends to throw a tragic light over everything. I hoped, but was more at home with hopelessness. My suitors' views and mine never coincided.

'I misled them guiltily, knowing I probably couldn't keep my promises. Guilt was my disease. Happiness, lovable men, weren't to be picked at my pleasure. Despair, it seemed, wasn't only my state, but humdrum, universal, amongst adults. Dick's occupation of the forefront of my life had become impossible. Yet the alternative was impossible: to carry on as before, and the slow strangulation of our love, the complications which were certain to get worse, the disabilities of age, age and ugliness, and the chances I'd have missed, and the end of Llanwyn, the extinction of my family, poverty and the void. Our feelings were interchangeable – we were trapped between our separate impossibilities.

'Love isn't blind; it's desire that's blind; and sexual desire's a trifle, beside the point of my sort of love, Dick's and mine, which might be called obsessional in this cold country. I thought of my mother, identified myself with her as girls will, or tried to. For she married twice, Michael Blake who was killed in the 1914 war, then my father. I'm not sure how well it worked for her, her second marriage, but it existed: she succeeded in the transference of a good many of her affections. One day, in the course of another agonising futile conversation, talking to Dick who was acquainted with the story, he said the final solution was that he should die like Michael Blake.

'He was thinking of me. Everybody was thinking of everybody else:

unselfishness can be idiotic. But he was jealous too, jealous and possessive, although he struggled not to be, not to be a dog in the manger. We'd entered a region of general extremity, extreme emotions, extreme opinions – moderation had been left far behind. We overdid it. But the introduction of death into the picture was chastening. His idea of dying in order to release me, of death that was preferable to our divorce, shook us into seeking a less catastrophic way out, the horrible obvious way – for I suppose it was obvious. We decided to part. We decided on a clean cut – no telephoning, no communication.

'That was in January, four and a half months ago. To begin with I fared better than expected. The vacuum within me seemed to fill. I'd no more cause to be in Aberystwyth Mansions and returned to Llanwyn. My sole loyalty was to my father, Aunt Ange and Pixie, whom I'd neglected. I wouldn't be scared off my territory by the Wessels. At Easter the extent of my emancipation from them would be measured.

'The rest you know.

'I was courageous because you were. For three weeks I borrowed my courage from you. When your courage wavered, my cowardice took over. The sight of Dick's face at the tug-of-war supper, so tired and grim, stabbed me to the heart. We met in the summer house, not by arrangement – no, as if we'd been summoned there supernaturally. And I was amazed for the last time.

'Truly I didn't mean to betray you or myself. But I've learnt the lesson that my motives are inexplicable and incomprehensible. I'm not happier – no! But, again, happiness has hardly any connection with love. Love's nothing unless it's an inner need, an imperative need just to care for another person, against which common sense and every other practical consideration are powerless.'

Laura's narrative was related in her own style and in reply to my questions. She interrupted it to summon the dogs. She apologised for its length and for her egotism. I remember her level voice, at once drained of expression and with its vibrant undertone, and the proud lift of her concluding sentiment.

After our walk we sat on the rustic seat on the upper terrace, where Esmond Charrington and I had watched the game with the rubber ring between Laura and George Sawrey. On the lawn below us the volleyball net sagged: the stay-rope stretching from one of the posts to a peg in the ground was loose. The house on our right, the flattish top of the cedar tree on our left, framed the view clear across the valley.

From my pocket I produced the copy of *First Love*.

'I'm sorry it got wet.'

I offered no further explanation. And she appeared not to be interested. Perhaps she guessed that her book was also a casualty of the storm.

'Did you read it?'

'Yes, eventually.'

'Did you like it?'

'Yes, very much. Laura, did you lend it to me because of its subject matter?'

'To put you on your guard against girls who aren't what they pretend to be?' She smiled. 'I might have done. But it's exquisite, isn't it? And Turgenev's my special hero. He loved an opera singer who was married all his life. He could have understood me.'

A pause ensued – we paused for reflection. Trilby and Sven were playing below, chasing each other round the trunk of the cedar.

'I was very dense,' I said.

'No, you weren't. I was deceitful. I was deceived. It was my fault.'

'Was I the only person not to be in the secret?'

'Daddy doesn't know, thank heavens. But Aunt Ange does. She disapproves. She won't ever speak to Dick. And Pixie knows. They were cross with me for encouraging you.'

'Anyone else?'

'No.'

'Not Morgan?'

'Morgan has his suspicions.'

'Is that why he dislikes you?'

'Well, he's mad on Penelope – yes.'

'Where do George and Guy and David Skelton fit in?'

'They accept me as a friend and nothing more.'

'You asked them here because you feel safe with them?'

'Precisely.'

'They made me feel the opposite of safe.'

'Forgive me.'

Pixie was calling Laura's name – it was five o'clock, teatime.

'You'll stay to tea, won't you?'

'Would you like me to?'

'Please!'

We strolled along the upper terrace and down the steps. Trilby and Sven, growling and biting gaily, ran towards us.

'Sven knows, of course,' I added.

'Yes, Sven knows.'

'You told me once that you loved Sven better than Trilby, do you remember?'

'Yes.'

'Why were you depressed, what was depressing in that?'

'Dick gave me Sven.'

We paused by the drawing-room french windows.

I inquired: 'Is Sven like Dick?'

'A dominating personality, you mean – my Svengali? Yes, he's rather like Dick.'

'I see.'

We entered the house. At the dining-room table Colonel Dellamere in his hairy tweed suit was sitting with his whisky and soda in front of him. Miss Dellamere supplied us with clues to the crossword puzzle and Pixie Tufton munched steadily.

After tea I announced my departure on the next day.

Pixie said, extending her plump hand for me to shake: 'I'm sorry you're leaving, I was beginning to get used to you.'

Miss Dellamere grated: 'Good luck with your writing – better luck than you've had at Llanwyn with so much going on.'

I thanked Colonel Dellamere for his hospitality.

He invited me to stay.

'You'd be more than welcome, my dear boy.'

'Thank you.'

Laura led the way into the dark panelled hall. She ran up the stairs with the copy of *First Love* and in a minute reappeared with another book. She preceded me along the passage to the side door.

'Arthur –'

On the terrace she hesitated, seemed to change her mind, as if she wished to postpone the finality of our goodbye, and said: 'Do you think Crispin could have returned to her nest?'

For reasons similar to hers I replied: 'Shall we have a look?'

We descended the steps, crossed the gravel sweep, let ourselves into the garden by the door I'd locked on the evening of the tug-of-war, and tiptoed to behind the summer house. The nest was empty. I hadn't expected it to be otherwise – probably neither of us had.

But our disappointment or the sad associations of the place now urged us to finish quickly. The lake with its writhing weed and water-lily roots was in shadow.

Laura, standing on the bank between the lake and the summer house, handed me the book.

'I want you to have this. It's not new, it's mine, but I want you to have it. It's by Turgenev, too – and there's a sentence on page 203 that might help to explain things. No, read it later. The point is – not that it'll be much comfort to you – I'm not upsetting any more people. Never again!'

As I understood her, she was dedicating herself to Dick.

'But Laura –'

I protested against the waste of it all.

'No, not again,' she repeated; and tears started into her eyes and her lower lip and a nerve in her chin quivered. 'Please don't thank me. Thank you, thank you for always being kind. Goodbye!'

We embraced.

I walked round the lake to the other door and turned back. She was on the verandah and she waved.

I was more moved by her restraint than by her sobs of two days before.

At The Dellamere Arms I found the relevant sentence on page 203 of *Smoke,* her parting gift.

It runs: 'One cannot love twice – another life has entered into you, you've let it in – and you can't get rid of the poison ...'

On the following Thursday morning I said goodbye to the Roopes and travelled home. I was reunited with my parents and with Mary. Mary and I spent most of the Friday, Saturday and Sunday of that week together: on Sunday evening we were alone at Thrushton. In about a month we were engaged to be married.

TEN

My story's done, in the words of the nursery rhyme – or nearly. I began to write it on Saturday 14 April 1973 and finished yesterday, Monday 7 May. I've produced a shortish book in twenty-four days, very much faster than the average professional author. I was afraid that once again I wouldn't be able to: doubt and my sort of despair, and my need of an antidote to them, drove me on. At last I've reached my literary destination – and am still not satisfied.

Perhaps the trouble is that I'm exhausted. The day after tomorrow, Thursday 10 May, is my forty-seventh birthday. My birthdays at Llanwyn seem not to be lucky.

The cause of my dissatisfaction isn't just vanity. I didn't write in order to be published and praised, and couldn't afford the luxury of perfectionism. I wrote in the hope of ridding my system of the poison of the past and recovering my emotional health in the present. It hasn't happened. No decision in respect of my marriage has been arrived at: have I taken a month's break from Mary or are we on the brink of divorce? Laura Dellamere – the ball-and-chain of Laura, which I've dragged after me, hasn't been removed from my leg or heart or whatever it was attached to. My position is unchanged: as on the night of the tug-of-war supper, like Laura herself, I don't know what I want.

Moreover in my haste, although, again like Laura, I've tried to tell the truth, so much has been left out. In the two days following the thunderstorm, the Monday and Wednesday, when she sobbed in the garden and recounted her tale of woe, my imagination was partially and protectively shuttered. I'd had enough and imposed a limit on my receptivity. And my reactions on paper have been as selective as those of twenty-five years ago.

Time has extended the range of my sympathies. But I haven't conveyed it adequately. I haven't dwelt on Laura's beauty in sufficient detail. After the storm I shrank from her beauty. My ambivalence has persisted; and the gold of her hair and the brilliance of her complexion and colouring continue to dazzle me.

Faithful snapshots of her grace, her enchanting gestures, her fuller upper lip and the quiver of the nerve in her chin are stored somewhere in my memory. Repeatedly, in streets and shops, I've been arrested by the resemblance of young girls and children, especially children, to the original of the portrait engraved in the back of my mind. Their hair would be almost of that rare shade or texture, they would have her straight nose or sweet mouth, or their overheard laughter would echo hers. But they were never Laura. Again I was tricked.

Does it matter?

Even if my ambition to convert my life into sentences and paragraphs has been gratified in a technical sense, these pages merely corroborate the negatives and the negations of my previous visit to The Dellamere Arms. The price of my future in literature is beyond my means, not only intellectually, not only materially as my father once suggested, emotionally into the bargain. I can't stand the solitude or literally the perversion of natural instincts that is required. I won't deny the world in order to write about it. I've ceased to be an aspirant for the favours of a cruel muse, whose intermediary I became at Nash and King.

In the end I too was realistic twenty-five years ago. The split second of the lightning flash in the Llanwyn garden revealed my fate in the form of Mary Singleton and my job at Nash and King. Laura and Dick on the verandah, dreams, fantasies and romanticism were repudiated. My recriminations were no more than the death throes of my courtship. Love in Laura's monologue was uninviting, fearsome, not at all in accordance with my ideas, and Dick's role was unheroic, unmanly, in a word foreign, if enviable. In transit between Wales and Surrey I breathed a final sigh of relief at my freedom.

And I married Mary. Perhaps I didn't altogether intend to – how many men intend to marry? At the same time I was loath to interfere with the processes that had been set in motion. We had the children, Tom and Jean; we were poor and then better off; we bought Ravelin Road and began to prosper modestly; and whether or not we were happy by Laura's exacting standards, we were content. I had good parents, a good wife, good children, tolerable work to do and a house of my own. The stream flowed smoothly and busily for ten years.

A stone under the surface of a stream, a tiny pebble of an awkward shape, can catch a twig that is being swept by – have you ever noticed? Mud accumulates round the twig, a branch lodges in the mud, weeds sprout and enlarge the obstacle, and an impassable dam is created. Laura Dellamere was such a stone. I'd thought of her, but not very often. I discussed her with Mary. The twig she stopped in passing was my feeling of futility. Everyone was good: and I was bored, I suppose. I reacted against the rectitude of my conduct and, by inference, was less certain that Laura's had been wrong. I was thirty-two or thirty-three. Was I to sweat out my stable mediocre life until I was seventy?

Contentment deteriorated into a middling wretchedness, occasional at first. It expressed itself in indigestion and irritability. The would-be writer in me, re-emerging, clashed with the publisher that I was. I resented office hours which might have been devoted not to the merchandising of mainly bogus books, but to the practice of authentic art, at any rate my art, or to the reflective leisure from which it could have sprung. Along with Laura, I wanted a second chance. I mentioned my problem to Mary. She advised me to have a chat with my father and offered me a sleeping-pill.

I was privately aware of linking literature and Laura. A nostalgia for Llanwyn, curiosity as to how its inhabitants were and where they were, and further revision of the events of my month at the pub, filled my reveries. I was half desirous and half nervous of encountering Laura in London. One night Mary and I celebrated the fifteenth anniversary of our marriage by going to a performance of Chekhov's *The Seagull*. Yes, we'd been married for fifteen years – it was ten years ago: the time-scale of these developments is both a tribute to our compatibility and a comment on my sluggishness. We were in a sentimental mood and clasped hands as the curtain rose.

The young hero of the play, Constantin, yearns to be a writer, and Nina, the girl he loves in vain, to be an actress. She delivers the speech that he's written for her from the verandah of a summer house in the garden of his home: the summer house overlooks a lake, I seem to remember. The setting and the white figure on the stage were a terrible shock. Waves of uniquely intense feeling engulfed me. My hand in Mary's was wet with fear. The rest of the play, in which Nina commits herself destructively to an older man, was also evocative – and unhelpful. I left the theatre, limped out of it across the wreckage, as it were.

Ten more years elapsed before I actually returned to Wales. The influence of a single dramatic evening was resisted. At intervals I was content as before. But the reminder of Laura on the verandah by the Llanwyn lake, by Crispin's empty nest, waving goodbye, ratified my love. The terrible and terrifying thing was that the intervening period and all it contained might never have been, except that during it my unreasonable affections had deepened subconsciously. An extraordinary interior revolution had occurred: Mary, Tom aged fourteen and Jean aged twelve, Ravelin Road and Nash and King were translated into ghosts and shadows, while my companion of a few largely forgotten hours assumed a new and singular reality.

The situation was ridiculous: I deplored it. Laura had never cared for me and could well be married – she could be dead. I was blessed with so many advantages, and in danger of sacrificing them to what scarcely deserved the name of will-of-the-wisp. I clung to my daily round and kept my secret. The consequence was division: Mary who had been my best friend, sister and sweetheart, and had borne my children, and Laura who was beautiful, who was herself a work of art, Laura with her idealism and divine discontent, beckoned me in different directions. I was torn, regretful, guilty, desperate at moments, as she had been. I began to excuse her.

The more I understood the more completely I excused her – and it finished me. My objections to her love of Dick Wessel were overruled by my equally impractical attachment. In retrospect I wasn't disgusted by the tragic scene in the storm, and was no longer jealous. Simply having known her, just caring for her, fulfilled a need. I re-read *First Love* and *Smoke:* that two Russian books and a Russian play should have figured in our romance wasn't its strangest coincidence. Litvinoff, Turgenev's protagonist in *Smoke,* does love again, notwithstanding his decision that it's out of the question; after several years he cuts his adulterous tie to Irina and surrenders to Tanya's devotion.

If only I'd been patient, Laura might have done likewise. As I pined for her she could be pining for me – at least she could be liberated from Dick. A wild hope and a dread that every day was reducing the number of my opportunities combined to increase my restlessness. But now Dick and I had more than Laura in common: I'd become a family man and wasn't free. Besides, apart from my altered state which would once more restrain me from profiting from the possible alteration of Laura's, it was inconceivable that after twenty-odd years – not several: twenty – she'd be waiting and wishing to surrender to my suit.

I was too late. Sanity insisted that in physical terms I must have lost her. But the physical element had scarcely entered into our experience: loves on the lines of mine and indeed hers thrive on separation. And, to compensate, I found the driving force to tell the story – I'd recapture her by means of my memory. The literary impulse which was one effect of the tug-of-war revived. I found the faded notes jotted down at The Dellamere Arms.

The steps by which fate propelled me here, towards the same room with the bow window, have already been recorded. Father died, I quarrelled with my mother and my son. Jean announced her engagement to Roger Smithson. It seemed to me there were no more reasons to delay and procrastinate. I'd have my month by myself, a sabbatical month, which was perhaps deserved, which was essential.

I was wrong, not Laura – wrong to hurt Mary – wrong throughout for that matter. For Laura still eludes me, and my life has been stripped of purpose. On my writing table lie her Easter gift, the miniature edition of the sonnets of Keats, and the copy of *Smoke.* The pile of manuscript is symbolic of the waste of time, effort and emotion it describes. Who would ever publish it? People don't buy gloomy books; and in this country, this cold country, as distinct from Russia or France, the more extreme literary manifestations of love aren't popular. I'm exhausted – tired of making mistakes. I'll have to stop.

Oh God!

I should but can't be calm – my hand shakes – the pen slips in my sweaty hand. I wrote the above on Tuesday morning, yesterday, and in the afternoon, in two minds as to whether or not to tear it up, went for a long walk, getting back to the pub at six. I was in the bar when a man of roughly my age entered, wearing an open-necked shirt, grey flannels and white tennis shoes: tall and hefty, rather bald, with a loose tanned skin and a wrinkly forehead.

He ordered beer and sausages. He jingled the money in his pocket and declared that the day had been fairish. I hadn't noticed the weather – it's been bad for the last three and a half weeks. It hasn't tempted me from my labours. But, true, the sun had shone on my walk, although surely without its former warmth.

'I've played five sets of tennis since lunch,' the jovial customer declared; 'I'm starving!'

I was more convinced that the weather was good by his talk of tennis and his summery clothes than by any actual recollection of sunshine.

The bar-room, having frosted windows and a low ceiling, was dark. I was sitting at a table, Mr Elliott the landlord was behind the bar and the tennis player in front of it. No one else was present.

I racked my brains, trying to remember where and when I'd seen that loosely wrinkled friendly countenance: a faint bell had been rung by the starving man's appearance and voice. He bent to sup the froth from his pint of beer and greedily to eat a lukewarm sausage plastered with mustard. He was like an animal, an animal feeding at a trough, a pig or a hound, or an overgrown puppy – he was like a large Labrador puppy.

I crossed over to the bar and said: 'I beg your pardon, but is it possible that we've met?'

'I don't know,' he mumbled, smiling through sausage. 'My name's John Deeps.'

'I thought you must be. Billy Deeps must be your father.'

'That's right. I'm his oldest boy – there are quite a few of us – well, not exactly a boy!' He laughed and winked at Mr Elliott. 'Sorry, but I can't place you.'

'No. You wouldn't be able to. I met you and your parents at Llanwyn House.'

'Oh yes – we used to go to Llanwyn when the Dellameres had it.'

'You hunted for Easter eggs at an Easter party and we were in the same team for a tug-of-war. It was twenty-five years ago.'

'Oh, the tug-of-war, yes! The annual tug-of-war and supper afterwards, we enjoyed that. And the Easter party! By Jove, I've got it! Or have I? You weren't the chap on the wall by any chance? Does a garden wall at Llanwyn mean anything to you?'

'Yes. I'm Arthur Bartlett.'

'Well, blow me down! Arthur Bartlett! Certainly I remember!' He expatiated on my balancing act. 'How long ago did you say it was?'

'Twenty-five years, in 1948.'

'Twenty-five years! Heaven help us! Tempus fugit, doesn't it? What are you doing here?'

'I've been staying in the pub. I was staying in the pub in 1948, but became a friend of the Dellameres. I've been working, writing, for the inside of a month.'

'You should have given us a tinkle. Mum and Dad would have been tickled pink to hear from you. They're always pleased to natter about the old days. Listen – pop across – no need to ring – could you? They're in the farm at Llanrhad, same as usual, although I'm the farmer now. The rest of the family's scattered far and wide. But I converted a handy barn and dug in.'

He munched sausage and swilled his beer. I was wondering how to tackle the sensitive subject uppermost in my mind.

He lowered his glass mug and inquired: 'Have you seen Laura?'

'What?'

'Laura Dellamere? She's living in The Forest – the wood on the hill behind Llanwyn – she moved into a cottage there when Colonel Dellamere died.'

'In The Forest?'

'Yes. Foresters, it's called.'

'Is the Colonel dead?'

'If he wasn't, he'd be getting on for a hundred, I'd say.'

'Yes, of course, how stupid of me.'

'He died around 1950. He had a sister – she was often at Llanwyn, but she died soon after. Anyway the place was entailed, it was inherited by a distant relation, who sold it to Evelyn's School. Laura bagged Foresters.'

'And she's been living in it all this time?'

'Yes. At least I think so. She keeps herself to herself. She's a bit of a recluse. That's why I asked if you'd seen her.'

'I'd no idea she was in the neighbourhood.'

'She's not on the telephone, that I can tell you. Peculiar, not having a telephone, isn't it? If you want to look her up you'll have to call. But I ought to be running along.'

He drained his mug and declined my offer of another pint.

'Don't go,' I said. 'Laura never married?'

'No. I can't imagine why. It's lonely, the life she leads. And she was a pretty girl, wasn't she?'

'She was pretty, yes. One other thing: do you remember the Wessels, Dick and Penelope Wessel – they used to take Foresters for holidays – they had two children, John Wessel and Elizabeth?'

'Dick Wessel – wasn't he a German Jew?'

'He was a refugee. He was at Foresters when I stayed here in 1948. The Wessels were at the Easter party and the tug-of-war.'

'Didn't he emigrate? Didn't he push off to America?'

'Did he?'

'I've a notion that he invited us to a picnic in The Forest, a farewell do, before he left for America. But you ought to talk to Mum and Dad.'

John Deeps headed for the bar-room door, followed by me. A Land Rover was parked in the forecourt of the pub.

'What became of Esmond Charrington?'

'Poor old Esmond, he was loads of fun, wasn't he? He died twelve months ago. He was a great age. Laura turned out for his funeral. And Mrs Blenkinsop was much in evidence, if you catch my drift.'

He laughed loudly.

'Your father used to drive a station wagon.'

'Right again! You've got a hell of a memory! Our station wagon was a splendid bus, a Buick. Well, cheerio! I'll be in trouble with Jenny if I don't make tracks.'

He clambered into the Land Rover. A racket and a string bag of grey tennis balls were on the passenger seat. He explained that Jenny was his lady wife. Jenny and the four kids had been to a bunfight somewhere while he got in a game of tennis with the Winters – 'Adrian Winter – you can't have forgotten Adrian Winter!' And he had to fetch his family.

'Jump in! Join us for a spot of pot luck – I'll fix it with Jenny!'

I thanked him but refused. I had to be alone.

He started the engine; asked me a couple of polite belated questions – was I married, what was my work, and so on; referred to my walk on the wall and to his parents; and in a cloud of dust roared towards the Post Office.

Twenty-four hours have passed since then. It's Wednesday 9 May, five o'clock in the afternoon. The account of my meeting with John Deeps was written early this morning. But I'll try to keep to the sequence of events.

As soon as John Deeps had gone I mounted the stairs to my room, feeling faint with excitement. I wasn't in any condition, was too tired to withstand ultimate shocks. I couldn't eat Mrs Elliott's supper. I pleaded a sudden headache.

The night was fine, with a clear sky full of stars. Between nine and ten I walked along to the Post Office crossroads and up the cart-track. But after a hundred yards I halted, smoked a cigarette, and, utterly jittery, returned to the pub. How could I call on Laura without warning? Neither of us was prepared. The cart-track, which I'd never explored before, was steep and lined by high banks and thick silent hedges. The Forest frightened me.

I retired to bed, but couldn't read or sleep. Every feeling ever inspired by Laura seemed to be stretched to breaking point. The time wasted in writing, in not giving Deeps or Winters a tinkle immediately after my arrival in Wales, was the cause of fierce regret: I'd hunted through the telephone directory, but in vain. This month might have been like that one – with a less gloomy ending. I'd have found Laura, Laura at Foresters, in person, not on paper – we'd have found each other. For if the Wessels had emigrated to America, and so long ago that John Deeps' recollection of their farewell do was hazy, Dick's spell over her must be cancelled by now. I should have marched into the Post Office and made my inquiry and received the reply: yes, not five minutes from here!

Why hadn't we met? Except for my single stroll by the Wyntrude, from Pub Pool to Wyn Pool, I'd always intentionally walked in the direction of Penyboth, which was fraught with fewer associations. We'd both kept ourselves to ourselves, I to write of her in my loneliness, she, in hers, possibly to mourn a past that could have been redeemed. If only, if only! Years ago I should have sent her a letter, care of the Post Office, asking for her news in return for mine. I should have waited after the storm, not been in such a hopeless hurry. So much loneliness, so many mistakes – unnecessary, wasted!

The night was like those of once upon a time, clear and starry. Would the bats be squeaking above the terrace at Llanwyn? I stood in my pyjamas in the bow window and scanned the hillside for a glimmer of light. Although there was none, my heart pounded – she was close to me, in reach at last in her house of memories in which I'd have my place. I wouldn't fail her again, however I might tremble. But I couldn't settle on any course of action. Ought I to call on her? Should I employ somebody to deliver a note?

I wrote, but not to her. Frenetically, from dawn onwards, I wrote the account of my conversation with John Deeps. I paused for breakfast, vacated my room at eleven-thirty, and went out and across to the church. The sun was bright, the valley shimmered reminiscently. In the churchyard, not far from the stile, was the Dellamere family vault, a grandiose stone hut with crooked railings round it – Laura had told me that she'd be buried in its subterranean chamber. The door in the porch of the church was unlocked. By the altar a marble tablet, cleaner than the others fastened to the wall, bore the names of Robert Guard Dellamere, his beloved wife Marjorie Dellamere and his sister Angela Eveline Dellamere.

Dates were carved in the marble. I wasn't very interested, my attention was elsewhere – I was procrastinating. But the mementoes of death urged me to grapple with life; and through the ecclesiastical sunshine I seemed to see the tenderly arched neck of a girl kneeling, praying for strength to resist her lover. I retraced my steps, had a bite of lunch, and collecting my binoculars, the same pair that had been used to spy on Emerald and Crispin, sallied forth. I crossed the water meadow with its goal-posts and, via the stile and the lych-gate, emerged into the road at the bottom of the Llanwyn drive. The cypresses towered above the garden walls.

My theory was that I could approach Foresters from the side; the direct route didn't appeal to me. I therefore turned right towards Oswestry, proceeded for a quarter of a mile, turned left and skirted two or three fields, climbed through a hedge into the woods and intercepted the path looping to the summit of the hill. Amongst my fears was that of being arrested for trespassing. But nobody was about. Under the windswept pines I paused to get my breath – the roofs of Llanwyn, the cedar on the lawn, the chestnut avenue and the lake in the flower garden appeared to be unaltered; then, deviating from the downward slope of the path, continued along the ridge.

After tramping through bracken and brambles I came to a fence of rusty rabbit wire, beyond which was a plantation of firs and young beeches. A convenient grassy ride stretched ahead. Stepping over the wire I followed the ride. In the distance it was blocked by a fallen fir tree. I began to wonder if my assumptions were correct: was this The Forest? Where was Foresters? I negotiated the obstacle. The ground dropped sharply. Below me was the cottage.

It was situated on the far side of the cart-track which petered out at its garden gate, at a right angle to the track, on a little plateau in a ravine in the line of hills. I was above and behind and some fifty or seventy-five yards from it, in an exposed position at the end of the ride and on top of the bank or cliff. Immediately, stealthily, I took cover in the fir trees, as if to observe an enemy.

The sun hadn't penetrated into The Forest. The brightness and the apparition of the object of my search were dazzling. Gradually in the shade of the firs my eyes and my senses adjusted to the scene. I lay prone on the pine needles.

The cottage overlooked the valley, and was small, on two floors. I could mainly see the wall with the front door, which was open. A blue car, a Morris 1100, stood by the garden gate. There was a television aerial attached to a chimney. The garden was L-shaped and neat – the lawns mown and the earth in the flower beds dug. The place nestled in the lee of the hills, orderly and peaceful.

In the corner of the garden was a rose pergola. The general stillness was disturbed by a movement within; I stared through the screen of roses; in time the movement was repeated; I focused my binoculars. A woman was sitting in a deck chair, reading – I could distinguish her outline. Every so often she turned a page. She was wearing a straw hat. I don't know for how long I watched her. I lowered the binoculars, but at once raised them again. A dog, a Shetland sheepdog was trotting towards her across the lawn. Two more dogs emerged from the pergola to greet the first one. They started to play together, pretending to snarl and bite.

The woman stood up – I could hear the creak of the deck chair – and joined them. She was Laura. She knelt on the lawn and teased and caressed and spoke to the dogs – I recognised her figure, her voice, although her words escaped me. She was relaxed, otherwise unchanged: but her face was hidden. She was wearing a dress with a print of flowers and an apron with a pocket. She got to her feet, as if her period of recreation were over, and returned to the pergola, where she produced secateurs from her apron pocket and clipped at something in a concentrated way.

I heard another voice, a female plaintive voice.

Whose? Pixie Tufton's?

Distinctly Laura replied: 'Yes.'

She went on clipping for several minutes. Two of the dogs were missing, but the third, the one that had trotted towards Laura, I believe, crouched by her, nose sniffing and pointing in my direction. I gazed into his slanting black eyes through the binoculars and he gazed back at me – he was surely a descendant of Sven.

Laura addressed the dog.

Darling, she said.

She was walking into the part of the garden in front of the cottage. Her tread was firmer than it had been, more positive and decisive. She seemed to be busy, to have work to do. She disappeared behind the angle of the cottage walls.

I maintained my vigil for perhaps half an hour. But there must have been an alternative entrance – she must have gone in by a french window. At any rate I caught a glimpse of someone through the open door. When I glanced at my watch it was four o'clock; and I retreated.

It wasn't a complete anti-climax. No indeed! It was a climax, but of the most unexpected kind.

I lacked the courage of my convictions. History was repeating itself. Agreed! But the fact is that I've misinterpreted all my fears.

Even at this stage I'll stick to the sequence of events.

The moment I set eyes on the cottage my aspirations crumbled. They were like a perfect mummified corpse which turns to dust as the air strikes it. A charming woman in a straw hat, reading on a spring afternoon in a rose pergola, was still a subject of romance. Laura wasn't decrepit, quite the contrary. Her figure was instantly recognisable, it was wonderful considering she was over fifty, slim and shapely by any standards. Granted, I hadn't taken the passage of time into consideration. I hadn't fully realised that many of the actors in the drama of our youth were dead.

But, to begin with, her age and mine weren't to blame. No! She was happy. Foresters was her happy home. That was the impression made on me. And I'd imagined it totally different: as ruinous as Llanwyn, a refuge in the depths of The Forest, charged with memories, to be lonely in. It could be called a desirable residence with its trim garden and modern comforts. I'd been in love with Laura's unhappiness. Almost her only visible connection with the person for whom I'd pined was her dog.

Yet I wasn't sad. She was liberated from Dick, evidently; her peaceful surroundings, her purposeful activity proclaimed her liberation; and, once more, I was responsive to her influence. The pounding of my heart was partly due to the removal of an interior obstruction or constraint.

The twenty-five years of my commitment to the ideal, of our extravagant idealism no longer seemed to be wasted. In some mysterious manner she really had succeeded, either come to terms with her bondage or conquered her liberty, struggled worthily and won through; and by revisiting The Dellamere Arms, writing my book, running into John Deeps and reviewing my life from the point of vantage above the cottage, perhaps I'd done the same.

The binoculars were a kaleidoscope. I stared at one woman, who turned into another. Laura was relaxed, therefore I was; I was relaxed enough to be tugged towards Mary. No, that's not true. I haven't told the truth about Mary. I couldn't consider her if I was ever to accomplish my task. She's obeyed my instructions to the letter, not ringing up or communicating, not tugging me anywhere, leaving me strictly alone. Nonetheless, to my agitation of the last twenty-four hours and its crisis on the carpet of pine needles, she contributed more than I've allowed. Indecision heightened my feelings, indecision in respect of my marriage.

The cliff in The Forest was also metaphysical. I could descend it, slide downhill into legal divorce, or draw back. Although Laura was self-possessed and self-sufficient, we might have been able to start again. But I was in her position in the chestnut avenue in the thunderstorm: I couldn't. I didn't want to. No doubt age, habit, the habit of failure and my depleted resources of energy helped to restrain me. But the busy gardener below wasn't the passionate despairing girl whose image had haunted my marital experience. At last, in the absence of her tears, I was moved by Mary's.

I haven't described Mary. The omission has a certain significance: description requires disassociation. Laura was written out of my system before I saw her. Superimposed on Foresters was Ravelin Road, and on her figure in the luxurious sunlight that of my wife, who, thanks to me, has had no leisure to cultivate her garden. A vision of a face lined and ravaged in my service, a pang of the inner need that attests to love, paralysed me. Mary and my children had been deserted. Guilt had been my disease. But I was a free agent – and was choosing freely.

The shadowy form in the hall or front room of the cottage didn't mean much. I remained on the pine needles in order to study the scene in my mind's eye. I was surprised. I was amazed. Incidentally, during my strategic retreat to the pub, the amazing thing was my sense of physical restoration. Notwithstanding my literary and emotional excesses I wasn't tired any more. An actual eager impatience to soldier on at Ravelin Road, at Nash and King, stirred in me. Twenty-five years ago I was infected with Laura's divisiveness: as a would-be writer who loved her, and a publisher and husband and father, I lived a double life – whence my debility.

I'd return to Mary not on the rebound and in a spirit of compromise, rather with a heart somewhat lacerated, pounded into better shape, whole. By the gates of Llanwyn, near the door in the garden wall through which I once strayed into a world of rejection, I remembered her advice: 'Don't bother to come home.' I reinterpreted my fears. Why my cautious detour by the looping path, why my contrary trembling in repeated crises, if, underneath, I hadn't always been afraid that Laura might say 'Yes' and Mary 'No'?

I trusted her to retract. But Mary's had to strive against her ghostly rival for too long. She's been taken for granted for nearly forty-seven years. She'd have every reason and every right not to yield to my apparent acceptance of a second best.

My anxious impulse was and is to telephone her. But my story, like The Ancient Mariner's, detains me. Supposing Mary were to lift her ban, my compulsion to scribble the rest would be removed. And if she should say 'No', I could only guarantee to write: the end.

Seven-fifteen by my wristwatch, and my hand aches from holding my pen. I'll ring her in a minute. Will she be well? Yes, that's it. I've been so selfish, more selfish than Tom. Tom was resented unfairly, because he was the link between my drinking a glass of beer at The Dellamere Arms when I was in the army, and my wedding. Tom and that chain of events shackled me to a consequential reality far from Llanwyn and Laura. Jean represented the youth and the hope I'd lost. I loved her for herself, but desperately, possessively.

Is it too late? Is it too late to change? Tom's sweeping opinion is that the era of individualism and romanticism has come and gone. He reminds me of Guy Toller: he subscribes to current political fashions. But perhaps he has a point, in spite of his ignorance of invariable natural laws. Romanticism has damaged us all. Laura overdid her love of Dick, and I my love of Laura – and not only we, others in their innocence, paid the penalty.

In our defence, I'd put forward the platitude that life is harsh, and enjoins the attempt to be true to our individual selves. Laura loved Dick against her will and at great personal cost. She may love him still: who knows? She's kept her promise – never again! Dick wasn't able to injure Penelope irreparably and have her blood on his conscience. And my dreaming days are done.

The essence of my revelation on the pine needles can be expressed in a single word: death. Father was dead, and Bobs and Ange Dellamere and Esmond Charrington, and Missy Dellamere and Michael Blake. I hadn't understood. I'd never understood. Laura and Mary and I would die – and had to act accordingly. Choice in the context of my own or my wife's approaching dissolution was easier. Death defined for me, as for Laura and Dick, the truth of love. And truth alone is the agency of true happiness.

I've just spoken to Mary.

Tomorrow I'll spend my birthday with my family.

GENTLEMAN'S GENTLEMAN

TO CARLO ARDITO

ONE

WILLIAM KITCHENER BROWN died last October, between the ninth and the sixteenth days of the month, at the age of sixty-three or sixty-four or sixty-five.

He was always secretive.

For thirty-odd years he was the manservant, butler, cook, valet, general factotum, jester and boon companion of my old friend and fellow-writer Hereward Watkins.

You have to be famous to merit any sort of biography, let alone a biography embarked upon a few weeks after your death. The following anecdote is a measure of the fame of William Kitchener Brown, alias Bill, Billy, Kitch, for some unknown reason Terry, and Brownie.

A resident of Dundee, a retired nurse acquainted with Hereward, was introduced to a couple of young New Zealanders who were touring the British Isles. She had previously lived in London and said so, whereupon they exclaimed: 'In that case you must know Brownie!' She was amused by their assumption; referred to the millions of Londoners and thousands of Browns; but admitted that in the metropolis she had known one particular Mr Brown, often called Brownie; and having satisfied herself that they were talking about the same man, asked where they had come across him.

'In pubs,' they replied. 'He's a wonderful character. He kept us in fits of laughter with imitations of his boss.'

Hereward was not surprised to hear he was the chief butt of Brownie's jokes with strangers. He used to complain that he could scarcely look his neighbours in the eye because he was sure his reputation had been ruined.

But let me describe my hero – or rather heroes.

My friend is now in his early fifties, tall, thin as ever, not to say gaunt. Although his narrow face is remarkably unlined, his hair is grey and scanty. With his long inquisitive novelist's nose he resembles a benevolent heron. In those books of his which he narrates in the first person he pretends to be middle-class – actually a fib, or poetic licence, or an expression of literary tact in an egalitarian era, or inverted snobbery. If he had been middle-class, Brownie would never have worked for him for thirty years. Hereward, as his Christian name may imply, was born an aristocrat: he has given me permission to reveal the shameful truth essential to my present undertaking. He can trace his lineage to barbarous Welsh antiquity. His family home is Watkins Hall, a stately pile in the Brecon Beacons.

Nobody should wonder that he and his manservant got on so well together – extremes touch, after all. Brownie was reared in the humblest circumstances in the dark interior of South-east London. To begin with he reminded me of films of the Great War – the 1914 war – showing stunted, wiry, invincibly cocky and cheery private soldiers marching, cooking, fooling about and chatting up the local populace. He was the same Tommy Atkins type, the quick-witted Cockney personified, irreverent, amoral, ever ready to laugh at life and at death, eternally making the best of things. At that time, when I met him, he was thirty-ish. His head was more square-shaped than round – he had a squared top to his forehead. His fine straight hair was light mouse-colour: he parted what remained of it in the middle, brushed it flat and back, and had it clipped short, army style. His eyes tended to protrude. His features were fleshy and formless. He would have defeated an Identikit artist not only because his whole appearance seemed to be ordinary, also because he could change it at will.

Later he put on a lot of weight. His chins doubled and his belly burst out of his shirts. He cursed the manufacturers of his tight trousers: 'They cut them for queers nowadays.' But at a party in his white jacket he could still hold himself in and boast he was broad-shouldered and not broad in the beam. Strutting off for a weekend visit to relations, wearing a suit with knife-edge creases, brightly polished shoes, a spotless blue overcoat, a black trilby at a rakish angle, and carrying a rolled umbrella, he could play the part of a perfect gentleman's gentleman. His repertoire of roles was inexhaustible: he should have been a professional actor or comedian. He would don his oldest dirtiest clothes and shamble along unshaven to tell a hard-line tale to his Tax Inspector. He twisted doctors round his stubby little finger. As for his ordinary face, from one moment to the next it expressed rosy shiny good health, chronic sickness and debility, deep respect for his social superiors and radical scorn, a touching desire to please his master and long-suffering resentment of the way he was being exploited, simple-hearted frankness, wily sophistication, fastidious refinement, stunning vulgarity, and so on.

He was purest mercury and never to be taken too seriously. He was bored by woe, repetition, accuracy, sincerity. He really lived for laughs.

Yet he was a golden person as well as mercurial. His vocation, arguably the highest, was to look after others.

What could be more complimentary than those twin epitaphs?

Perhaps he was bound to fall foul of the occupational hazard of extremely kind sociable sensitive people and especially menservants: in short, drink. He fought against it. At least he said he fought against it. And Hereward was drawn into the fight, despite his appreciation of the irony of the situation – no doubt Hereward did most of the fighting. Thus, notwithstanding his natural abstemiousness, and indeed his asceticism on principle, he was engaged in a vicarious losing battle with drunkenness for three decades.

One day somebody consoled him: 'Don't worry – when Brownie's in heaven and you're knocking on the pearly gates, he may put in a good word for you.'

Whether or not Brownie has wangled himself the ultimately comfortable billet remains to be seen. And even if he was not famous in the full worldly sense, although two tourists from New Zealand were quite right to assume an ex-Londoner in Dundee must know him, he deserves to be commemorated – along with his jokes.

Moreover he meant to write his autobiography. My book aims to be a representative token of the esteem and gratitude of his boss's various guests, whom he welcomed and fed and helped to entertain unforgettably – and a second-hand or third-hand substitute for his.

Hereward has promised to supply me with the necessary biographical material, which he feels he could never be objective enough to use. He is resigning the copyright he inherited from Brownie in my favour.

Co-operate as we may, rack our bookish brains as we may, the trouble is that the title of our tribute will not be a patch on Brownie's.

He planned to call his reminiscences: *Bad Manners And Peculiar Habits Of The Upper Crust.*

⋆ ⋆ ⋆

His mother was Scottish and worked as a charwoman in Kent.

I am quoting Brownie: gentle readers should therefore abandon hope of consequential logic.

His mother married twice and produced hordes of children, Brownie being the youngest of the second family – I suppose she began by marrying an Englishman and that they settled in Plumstead in Kent.

But immediately the plot thickens. Although Plumstead is not within range of the sound of Bow Bells, Brownie qualified as a Cockney in many other respects. He was not merely the Tommy Atkins type, his native speech was Cockney, he was familiar with Cockney rhyming slang, he excelled at repartee Cockney-fashion – he was like Shakespeare's clever clowns with their pavement wit. Nevertheless his mother was definitely Scottish – and then he confided in Hereward that his father was Austrian.

'I should spell my name with an *a* and a *u* in the middle instead of an *o* and a *w*,' he stated rather proudly, for he admired the Teutonic race, its efficiency, its punctuality.

How an Austrian met and married a Scottish widow in Plumstead, and lived and sired children there during the First World War, when Austria was our enemy, I cannot imagine.

Brownie was no more than rather proud of his father. He was apt to dismiss the subject by saying: 'He died before I knew him.' He was a trifle uneasy about his parentage.

'One of us was illegitimate – or so they said. We were never sure which it was – probably one of my half-brothers or half-sisters. But they were all little bastards.'

'Could it be you, Brownie?'

'No, sir!' His pronunciation became military: 'No, SAH!' He emphasised the 'SAH!' in his old soldier's accents whenever he wanted to convey strong disagreement. 'No, sir! Would you like to see my birth certificate, sir? It's signed and sealed and above board – SAH!'

In fact he was tickled by Hereward's suggestion that he might be the little bastard, which was the more outrageous in the context of the severe working-class attitude towards bastardy. He revelled in outrageousness, even when he was on the receiving end of it.

But Hereward could have been closer to the truth than he knew. For Brownie was born in 1914 or 1915 or 1916. And supposing an Austrian called Braun married his mother, would not the said Braun have gone home or perhaps been recalled to his colours as soon as war was declared? If he had remained here, would he not have been interned as an alien, unless he was naturalised, in which case he would have served in the British army? Would he have been so patriotic for the country of his adoption as to christen his son Kitchener?

The circumstances of Brownie's paternity were characteristically ambiguous. His offer to produce his birth certificate was merely a red herring: the document would automatically include the name of his mother's husband, absent or present: it would not decide on which side of the blanket he had been conceived. Yet, while it is tempting to believe he was what he seemed to be, that is the Cockney offspring of a Kentish Cockney father who committed adultery in Plumstead, doubts again creep in with recollections of his square forehead and the roll of flesh at the nape of his neck, which would have fitted snugly under a *pickelhaube*.

To confuse the issue further, he also claimed he had gipsy blood in his veins.

'I'm part Romany. I like to eat roast hedgehog and I don't like hot baths. We Romanys are against baths because they wash off our precious body-oils.'

For that matter he claimed he was a rat-catcher – R.C. or Roman Catholic: which would reinforce the theory that he was half-Austrian.

At any rate I feel sure his mother was Scottish. After the death or disappearance of her second spouse whoever he was, she presided over her brood and taught it how to behave. Her justice was rough: at meals, should any child reach out rudely for food, she would spear the offending hand with her fork. She had to slave at her charwoman's work in order to provide for the fatherless family. She earned the respect of her landlord, who bought and brought her an occasional glass of stout from the pub.

Brownie, her last baby, possibly a love-child, and possessed of winning ways into the bargain, was her favourite. In return he revered her memory. Home was crowded, although some of the older children had already married and left it. Brownie shared a single bed with two teenage sisters, Evie and Ada, lying with his head between their feet until he was fourteen or so. He may have developed his antipathy to hot baths when he was forced to have them in a hip-bath in public in front of the kitchen stove.

He was a wild lad with a shock of fair hair and a terrible temper by his own accounts. One day in school he lost his temper, threw an inkwell at his schoolmaster, knocked the schoolmaster's eye out, and was sent to a boys' reformatory. He was pretty miserable there for an unspecified period.

Then fortune smiled on him for maybe the first of many times. Somehow he got a job as a page in a grand London club.

Meanwhile his mother was dying. She suffered from a rare ailment which she passed on to her ewe lamb. Von Recklinghausen's Disease causes fatty non-malignant tumours to form on the nerve endings. It is incurable, but not dangerous unless a tumour should inhibit a vital function. Apparently she got one on her optic nerve, and went blind and mad, owing to pressure on the brain, before it killed her.

Brownie would describe her death in such horrific detail that Hereward's initial sympathy was tempered by cynical suspicion. He was mourning his mother and protesting against her cruel fate, incidentally extracting a bit of black humour from his bereavement, and slipping a trump card up his sleeve. If he drank too much, he could plead the extenuating circumstance of fear of his heredity. He had a ready-made excuse in the shape of the ominous tumours bulging from his body.

Mrs Brown or Braun was buried in about 1930. She must have been kindly, brave in her poor widowhood, and appreciative of merit. Some of her children joined the Salvation Army. The others were sinners, according to Brownie's hints. He lost touch or quarrelled with all his siblings sooner or later.

He wore a page-boy's uniform at the Piccadilly Club in the street of the same name.

Once an old curmudgeon of a member complained that he had spied a page strolling along Piccadilly, whistling and with his hands in his pockets. Brownie was identified as the culprit and hauled in front of the club committee.

'What have you got to say for yourself?'

'Mr So-and-so made a mistake, sir!'

'What's that? Are you trying to be impertinent?'

'No, sir! But I can't whistle, sir. I never learnt how to whistle or spit. And my uniform doesn't have pockets – the side-seams of my trousers are sewn up to the waist!'

The case was dismissed. Brownie had scored another victory in the class war – or at least in his lifelong campaign against authority.

He was English through and through in his acute consciousness of class and his snobbery. He liked to work for, he felt he profited from being associated with, and actually enjoyed the company of gentlemen by his standards. He cultivated a manner of speaking that he believed was gentlemanly: as a result, unperceptive upper-class people thought he was a mincing homosexual when he mimicked their voices and airs and graces.

He used to tease Hereward by answering the telephone in his affected pretentious style: 'Hillow? Hillow – Mr Hereward Watkins' residence! . . . Oh, 'ullo, sir! It's you, is it? Yes, 'e's 'ere – 'ang on, I'll give him a shout.'

Either because he was intelligent, or because of the experience he gained at the Piccadilly, he arrived at an understanding of the interdependence of masters and servants. He was therefore never awed by his social superiors: he realised they needed him as much as he needed them.

'There are good 'uns and bad 'uns – they're like the rest of us, if you get to know them.'

On one level of his complexity he accepted the class system. On another it was material for his mocking jokes: 'Went to Eton, did he? I know – I can see it. He was eaten and brought up.' On a third he was poised to take cover behind the revolutionary barricades and open fire on the idle rich.

In spite of himself he was impressed by authoritarianism. Almost more than a lord, he loved an eccentric authoritarian plutocrat, whose bad manners and peculiar habits were amusing copy for the book he intended to write.

The Albanian oil millionaire Achmed Bogu was a member of the Piccadilly. He had as it were gone native in England and acquired a country seat, a pack of hounds, shooting and fishing, and a couple of dozen racehorses. In London he had breakfast in his club every morning. The ritual began by Brownie being despatched to buy a fresh peach and a fresh nectarine from Fortnum and Mason. Then at a quarter to nine sharp a Rolls-Royce drew up at the door and Mr Bogu's second chauffeur unloaded from it and carried downstairs to the club barber's shop the special chair in which Mr Bogu liked to have his beard attended to. At nine another Rolls-Royce driven by the head-chauffeur deposited Mr Bogu in person, who, after spending half an hour with the barber, appeared in the dining-room with his beard and his eyebrows trimmed and curled and his monocle in place. He sat at a table by a window and ate two kippers, several racks of toast and marmalade, followed by the peach and nectarine, and drank half a gallon of potent coffee and cream.

Naturally Brownie was chosen by Mr Bogu to serve breakfast: he had risen in the staff hierarchy of the club from page to waiter by this time. His boast that he was always chosen to wait on the most demanding members was probably justified: he was so quick, willing and eager to please, and his trick of remembering and indulging their individual fads was so flattering. Moreover he liked to practise the sport at which he excelled, as we all do: in his case it was taming fierce establishment lions and – nearly literally – training them to feed out of his hand.

For instance Sir Gervaise Such-and-such would eat nothing but a slice of paper-thin brawn and a baked potato in the middle of the day; the Marquis of Somewhere had to have pepper within reach to sprinkle on his strawberries; an apocryphal Count Nudel drank warm water with a meal, whereas Admiral Lord Hamish McNaught stuck to pink gins – none of them needed to remind Brownie of these requirements. The Earl of Grimlingham, notorious for his evil temper, a wife-batterer and a scourge of club servants, could not bear to have any waiter near him except Brownie: who decided His Lordship was lonely, which was to be expected, and quite sweet.

Of course the source of my information was Brownie himself. Paradoxically it was proof of his modesty that he published every compliment he had ever been paid.

'The Earl of Grimlingham said I was the only young feller with any sense he'd given an order to in the whole of his life . . . Admiral Lord Hamish thought I took the ship's biscuit.'

Whether or not he exaggerated the praises of the innumerable people he looked after is a moot point. But Hereward's opinion coincides with mine: such exaggeration would have been superfluous.

The Piccadilly seems to have had a more cosmopolitan membership than the other three clubs then in its vicinity, the Turf, the St James's and the Naval and Military. Brownie would say that Prince Everhazy, Duke Socci di Bocci, Graf von Twisch and Baron Rémy were members, as well as Count Nudel and Mr Bogu.

He adopted a heavy foreign accent when he reeled off the above list of names. He fancied himself as a linguist. His enunciation of the French title and surname, Baron Rémy, included the full glottal stops. He was partial to the glottal stop and inclined to introduce it into English words, pronouncing porridge por-h-ridge, for example.

The fact that the Piccadilly was a gambling club might have had something to do with its members from abroad. Brownie was excited by his turns of duty in the Card Room: he had no sociological objections to the size of the sums of money at stake. But it amazed him that the players talked and laughed and called for drinks in loud voices, while thousands of pounds were changing hands, whereas in the Billiards Room strict silence was the rule, although bets on a game were restricted to a maximum of five shillings.

One of his special pets amongst the members was Lord Charles Tatham, D.S.O. and Bar, known as Tatters. Tatters Tatham was a gambling man, a womaniser, an amateur jockey who had ridden in the Grand National, a celebrated wit and *bon viveur* in his day. He instructed his mistresses to telephone him at the club rather than at home, where they might get through to his wife. If – or when – a mistress rang and asked for Lord Charles, the telephone operator's drill was to say he was out, take a written message and pass it to Brownie, who would fold it carefully and carry it on a silver salver to the Card Room and slip it under his habitual tumbler of whisky and soda. Should Lord Charles really be out, Brownie would hang around in order to hand him his messages as discreetly as possible the minute he came in. The object of the exercise was threefold: to make sure Tatters was not interrupted at cards; to give him a chance to prepare his defence against the hysterical females he had treated in cavalier fashion; and to avoid the unpleasantness of his fellow-members' discovery that their own wives or daughters were compromised by being on the line.

Brownie told a good story illustrative of the wit of Tatters Tatham, who was temporarily engaged in an extra-marital affair with a certain Lady Grace Something-or-other.

He – Tatters – pulled a noticeably long face as he entered the club bar.

'What's up, old boy?' his cronies inquired. 'Have a hair of the dog that bit you!'

'No, thanks – nothing to drink – I've finally reformed.'

'What? You don't mean it! Reformed?'

'Yes – it's true – scout's honour! I've got religion. Nowadays I even have Grace before dinner.'

In the thirties, genuine English gentlemen and the would-be sort seem to have spent most of their lives with other gentlemen – at school, in the armed services, at work, in their sporting pursuits, and at mixed social gatherings in the evenings over port and cigars. Furthermore they gratified their apparently insatiable appetites for masculine company, or sought refuge from the opposite sex, in their exclusive clubs.

Yet historical documents attest that they distressed the ladies, and vice versa, as much as we do in our unisex epoch: where did they find the time?

The hall-porter at the Piccadilly, and his minions like Brownie, had to be careful not only about telephone calls. Wives and daughters who had run through their money out shopping would demand to see their husbands and fathers, or beg for a loan from the club's petty-cash-box. Importunate women would come and wait on the club steps for their elusive lovers. On several occasions an aggressively drunk girl with a grudge against a member tried to force an entry.

Brownie remembered a white-faced wife asking for her compulsive gambler of a spouse, and then sitting for hours in a car outside the club, her despairing eyes fixed on the front door. Again, he felt sorry for everyone concerned when some wretched young member was summoning the Dutch courage in the bar to go home and break the news to his family that he was ruined.

A little world so male-oriented was bound to be productive of homosexuality.

As Brownie put it: 'We had our share.'

He was convinced that he had been a pretty youth.

'Colonel Algy Poppin and Duke Socci di Bocci couldn't keep their hands off me,' he assured Hereward.

'Really? When did you lose your looks?'

'Thank you, sir. I never lost my looks – I just matured.'

'Well – when did you lose that mop of hair you say you used to have?'

'I shed my blood and my hair, fighting for king and country.'

'Who were the members that couldn't keep their hands off you?'

'Colonel Poppin and Duke Socci di Bocci. And Graf von Twisch – he was a holy terror.'

'Are you sure you've got those names right, Brownie?'

'Yes, sir.'

'They sound a bit funny to me.'

'They were funny gentlemen, sir!'

Colonel Poppin had lured Brownie into a telephone booth and

attempted to kiss him. And Mr Gregory Nickson, called Mr Knicks-off below stairs, bribed page-boys to visit his flat, which was a few minutes' walk from the Piccadilly.

'Did you go?'

'No, sir! My mother wouldn't have liked it.'

Unmarried staff slept on the upper floors of the club premises. Brownie in his leisure hours went to films and music halls, and strolled round Shepherd Market. He made friends with an old fishmonger there, who taught him how to open oysters and skin and fillet fish, and with various prostitutes on an uncommercial basis. A prostitute named Ruby would take him to a pub in the area and buy him a supper of a baby's head – a delicious kind of circular steak and kidney pudding.

He was paid the merest pittance to start with, perhaps £1 per week. But he had no expenses and was well fed, even if he managed to give Ruby the impression he was starving.

'We ate the leftovers from the members' dining-room. We fed like fighting cocks.'

Almost always throughout his adult life he so arranged matters that he was fed like a fighting cock.

And then he received tips. The Piccadilly along with other clubs banned tipping; but no rules or regulations were going to stop a gentleman who could afford to be generous from showing his appreciation of first-class service. Nothing was ever too much trouble for Brownie – fetching, carrying, walking a member's dog, standing in a deluge of rain to hail a taxi. He was blessed with the sunniest of tempers and the still rarer gift of being able to cheer people up. Inevitably banknotes were pressed into his hand and, in the dining-room, found by him beneath the side-plates of the members he had waited on. At some stage he was honoured to become a so-called 'trusted servant': he worked either as or with the club cashier and was allotted the mysterious task of overseeing the financial transactions in the Card Room. He was therefore handling large sums of money – and he benefited by often getting a cut of a gambler's winnings.

Moreover in due course he was permitted to open a Staff Beer Bar in a disused cellar, which must have been profitable.

Later on he swore that no alcoholic beverage had passed his lips until after the war. But is it likely he could run a bar for beer without touching a drop? And where did he acquire his taste for port if not at the Piccadilly, at which it was amongst his daily duties to decant the stuff?

Anyway, he said that in the latter stages of his employment he could count on average take-home pay of £27 per week, which would be the equivalent of £200 in today's debased currency: a fortune considering it was tax-free and pure pocket-money.

But money did not interest him, except from an intellectual point of view. He was completely unmercenary, although he loved to spin dubious yarns of how far a pound had stretched in his salad days – purchasing two seats at a music hall, programmes, chocolates during the show, ice-creams in the intervals, a four-course dinner and a bus-ride to the home of the piece of fluff who was ready for anything by that time. Where money was concerned, he acted as if he believed the Lord of lords would provide; and the strange thing was that the Lord did so, in spite of all Brownie's blaspheming.

The destination of most of his companions after a night out was the Piccadilly itself, which employed staff of both sexes. Maids cleaned the place and worked in the kitchens and, if they were single, also lived in. They were strictly supervised by an older housekeeper, and their rooms on the upper floors were sealed off from those of the lusty pages and waiters. Romance flourished nonetheless. Propinquity and sufficient opportunity performed their customary function. Brownie recalled not only formal evenings in theatres with girls who at any rate began by being on their best behaviour, but more earthy episodes on a dark stairway and behind an accessible chimneystack.

Round about the age of twenty-two he took a particular fancy to a pair of sisters with jobs at the club, Mary and Jenny.

Jenny was his favourite.

He married Mary.

Brownie's marital home was a flat he rented in Fulham.

Now he was a married man he was allowed occasional weekends off. On the Saturday morning of such a weekend he and his wife would go to see the sights at the Caledonian or Portobello markets. At length they would buy a whole branch of bananas – a hand of bananas, he called it. They returned to their flat and went to bed and stayed there until the Monday, just reaching out for a banana whenever they felt hungry.

The scene of the two of them in bed for nearly forty-eight hours, eating bananas and the rest of it, suggests happiness.

The fact remains that the monotony of marriage cannot have suited

Brownie's temperament. Variety was much more than the spice of his life: variety was its very bread and butter. Without change, excitement, challenges, and crisis and drama, which most people hope to get away from by marrying, he fell into a bored torpid state.

He was extraordinarily attractive to women of every sort, condition, age and class, notwithstanding his appearance, which struck other men as being on the unprepossessing side. Hereward once annoyed a vain Don Juan of his acquaintance by declaring that the greatest success with women he had ever known was Brownie.

And Hereward was simply telling the truth, not teasing.

Brownie was expert at charming, pleasing, surprising, interesting, engaging the sympathies of women and, above all, making them laugh. He seduced them physically or morally by means of the eternal infallible technique: tickling them.

Yet his attitude was ambivalent. Like rough boys, he scorned their frailties. He subscribed to jeering music hall opinions of pretty little dolly-birds, wives and mothers-in-law. He seemed to feel he was a battle-scarred veteran of the sex-war as well as the class-war, who must never yield or retreat.

The worst of it was that he came up against an extreme form of a common male difficulty. He could love but not live with women, generally speaking. Or, rather, he could and did win their love and attachment – and dull attachment was the last thing in the world he wanted. He aroused expectations which he had neither the intention nor the ability to fulfil.

Again and again he put himself in false positions that turned out to be untenable. He spoilt his women. He was such fun to be with, he pulled their legs, he gave them presents, he promised the moon, he was their slave. When he disappointed the hopes he had raised, he could not abide their shrill demands and reproaches – his nerves were not good enough.

Women were the chief representatives of that authority he was always opposed to. Drinking might have been an expression of the mutinous sentiments they inspired. It was easier to drink and forget than to tell a furious female he could not and would not and did not and was at the end of his amorous tether. Probably in pubs he recovered his sense of identity as a sex-war soldier together with other soldiers, refreshing themselves before slogging back into action against their fair and foul enemy.

That he should have married the wrong sister was typical. Setting aside his future causes of complaint, the women he was involved with were invariably wrong in one way or another – and subject to his critical ridicule and unflattering comparisons with men. He liked his liberty too much to be bothered with attempts at rectification. And it is perfectly possible that he let Mary lead him to the altar merely to oblige, when he wished to wed Jenny or not at all.

His conduct in 1939 tends to corroborate the notion that he had at least had his fill of nuptial bliss – by then he had been married for a year or two. He enlisted in the army before hostilities commenced. He was patriotic, he said – and why wait until he was called up? He persuaded the military doctors to pass him fit despite his hundred and fifty tumours.

Far be it from me to cast aspersions on his convictions and his courage.

At the same time his biographer is entitled to try to get to the bottom of his ambiguity.

He need not have been in such a hurry to enlist. He could have persuaded the doctors he was not a hundred per cent fit – he did in different circumstances. As it was he pauperised his wife unnecessarily soon, for a private in the army was then paid only a few shillings a week. The evidence is capable of the interpretation that what he could not wait for was escape from matrimony. He volunteered for service in a Scottish regiment. 'I told them I was half a Scot through my mother.' No doubt he omitted to add that his father had been Austrian.

TWO

BROWNIE'S recollections of his years in the army were a trenchant comment on the confusion and absurdity of war.

Whether or not he ever told the whole true story is debatable. I suppose that as usual he himself, not really the war, was responsible for most of the confusion.

His ambition to get into a Scottish regiment was realised. After spending a few weeks with the Highland Light Infantry, he transferred into the Black Watch. He was prouder of having served in the Black Watch than of any of his other achievements. He felt it was a social distinction. The regimental tradition of toughness was right up his street.

He was stationed at barracks in Edinburgh and Glasgow: Auld Reekie and Glasgie, he called them in his travesty of a Scottish brogue. He would emphasise the nordic cold of the parade grounds on which he learnt to drill the Black Watch way: 'It was so cold a man's hands froze to the barrel of his rifle.' But some of his drilling must have been done in or near cities in Southern England with their kinder climate, Bath in Somerset and Lewes in Sussex, for instance, which he knew well.

He wore a kilt and sporran and nothing underneath.

He readily expatiated on – and must have exaggerated – the Black Watch attitude to nether garments.

'Wearing pants under a kilt was forbidden . . . Before leaving barracks, we had to prove we were properly dressed or undressed to the NCO on duty in the guard-room – showing a leg wasn't in it . . . We weren't allowed to travel on the upper deck of a bus, because of climbing the stairs . . . We could only get permission to wear pants if we were going in for Scottish dancing in mixed company . . . One sergeant-major of ours had a mirror fixed to the end of his yard-stick, so he could peep under our kilts to check that none of us had pants on . . . Another sergeant would give the command: 'Battalion, sit down!' – when snow was thick on the ground. Any man who was able to sit in the snow without moaning and groaning was placed in close arrest.'

Brownie at once complained of cold weather such as he experienced in the army and elsewhere, referring back to its dire effects on a Scottish soldier's unprotected parts, and boasted of the circulation of his blood.

'I'm centrally heated – my blood's always on the boil – I have to sleep on top of my blankets with the windows wide in mid-winter – and on summer nights you could fry an egg on me!'

He was pleased to remember that he had become as tough as his comrades in arms – and in years to come to think he remained so. He described forty-mile route-marches across the Cairngorms, carrying a full load of equipment, and other tests of strength and endurance he had passed. Being a Sassenach amongst Scotsmen – although he might have argued that point – and Cockney and an ex-waiter with von Recklinghausen's Disease, obviously put him on his mettle. In his free time he joined in brawls and pitched battles with Canadian troops: 'We threw Canadians through shop windows.' He kept on winning a corporal's stripe and losing it for having taken part in some act of hooliganism, more than likely committed under the influence of alcohol – notwithstanding his far-fetched assertion that he was teetotal until after the war.

'We were savages – the local people were far more frightened of us than they were of the Germans,' he would say complacently.

He affected to despise the rest of the British army, not to mention the armies of our gallant allies.

With his future boss, who had been in the Royal Horse Guards, he indulged in competitive badinage.

'All the Brigade of Guards could do was spit and polish . . . Do you know our name for the Household Cavalry? We called them Piccadilly Cowboys . . . They did most of their parading behind the trees in Hyde Park after dark – with men in mackintoshes giving the orders . . . We were a fighting regiment!'

But then he let Hereward in on a secret cause of Black Watch embarrassment. A platoon was posted to guard a remote island in the Orkneys, where, it was later discovered, the men interfered with the sheep. They had wound their puttees round the beasts' legs to stop them running away, Brownie explained.

Thereafter his jibes at Hereward's expense could be countered by the single syllable: 'Baa!'

And Hereward would inquire: 'Who were the Black Watch fighting in the Orkneys? Have you heard the rumour that the sheep up there are giving birth to tartan lambs with built-in sporrans?'

Brownie had to laugh. The story amused more than it ever embarrassed him personally – and he was not averse to its publication. For it lent support to his mythology in respect of the licensed gang of roistering ruffians to which he once belonged, indiscriminately randy, lawless, afraid of nothing, belligerent and jealous of their reputation.

'We never retreated . . . We never shone our boots like your lot, we dubbined them, ready for active service . . . When the Guards saw the whites of the enemy's eyes, they sent for the Black Watch . . . The Germans meant it when they said we were devils-in-skirts!'

He played down the fact that owing to his qualifications he was soon in action in the Officers' Mess.

Meanwhile his daughter Peggy had been born.

His wife was all right for money, she had a well-paid job in a factory, and generously subsidised him when he was home on leave.

He waited on the Black Watch officers, picking up tips and compliments and contrarily preferring the authoritarians, just as he had at the Piccadilly Club, until his regiment was shipped over to France with the British Expeditionary Force.

Before long he was involved in the retreat to Dunkirk.

He made much of his war-wound. 'I shed my blood for king and country . . .' He was inclined to limp and confide in strangers that he did so because of the injuries he had sustained in battle.

Eventually, in response to Hereward's curious questioning, he provided a reasonably convincing answer.

'We were on the run,' he related.

Would he have admitted the Black Watch had retreated if he was not telling the truth? But you never knew with Brownie. He might have borrowed the whole scenario from a film.

'We were on the run,' he said. 'We were separated from our regiment – about a dozen of us with rifles and not even a Bren-gun. We were sheltering in the ruin of a cottage in the country, completely isolated – no other buildings nearby. An officer in a staff car roared up and ordered us to gather round. He pointed to the landscape in front, a few flat fields in the shape of a wedge with woods on either side. He told us: "You see the gap between the trees? Any minute a Panzer Division with tanks is going to start rolling through it. You're to stop that Division – do you understand? You're staying here to fight to the last man and give the regiment a chance to retire to a more strategic position. And good luck to you!" Well – the officer buzzed off. We were left standing in full view of the blasted gap. We scuttled back into our cottage pretty damn quick. Of course we were scared – a dozen riflemen against a Tank Division. My mates kept on pushing me forwards into the doorway to keep a look-out. I heard the report of a rifle and felt as if I'd been stung by a wasp or a bee. When something warm started trickling down my legs I thought I must have disgraced myself – that was how scared we all were. But suddenly I noticed my boots were full of blood. The next thing I knew was that I'd been taken prisoner.'

'Had you been stung by a bee or had you been shot?'

'Shot, sir.'

'Whereabouts?'

'In the leg, sir.'

'If you were shot in one leg, why did blood trickle down both of them and into both your boots?'

'I was shot in the thigh, sir, and high up the thigh at that.'

'You mean you were shot in the posterior?'

'More in the hip, please, sir. The bullet just missed my vitals.'

'How lucky for you!'

'You can say that again – if it's luck to be seriously wounded and a prisoner of war for a hell of a long time.'

'I'm sorry, Brownie – don't think me unsympathetic – I was concentrating on your vitals, which you were lucky to hang on to. But I want to try to get the picture straight. What happened between your being shot and being captured?'

'I passed out, sir.'

'Fainted, you mean?'

'No, sir. I lost consciousness because my life-blood was draining into my boots.'

'Did you come to in hospital?'

'The Germans treated me in one of their hospitals. But I had to do a tremendous march before I was anywhere near a hospital.'

'So you were able to march although you were seriously wounded?'

'There was no alternative, sir.'

'Were you still bleeding as you marched?'

'Not all the way, sir. I clenched the wound together with my hand.'

'Really? What sort of a wound was it?'

'A sort of deep graze.'

'Only a graze?'

'A sort of very deep painful graze.'

'I see. What became of that Panzer Division? Did it get through?'

'We couldn't stop it, sir. I was knocked out. My mates were captured along with me. Most of the Black Watch Battalion was caught in the bag.'

'And you tottered into Germany with your hand on your hip?'

'Beg pardon, sir – I wasn't ever in the Household Cavalry.'

On numerous occasions Hereward and Brownie resumed their droll duelling over the latter's experiences as a casualty and prisoner of war.

'Who shot you?'

'It was the Germans, sir.'

'You sound a trifle doubtful.'

'No, sir. Why should I be?'

'Well – you said the Germans were in front of your ruined cottage. The Panzer Division was on the point of advancing through a gap between two woods in front. And you were shot in the rear.'

'It was a ricochet, sir.'

'Are you quite sure you weren't shot by a friend or a foe of yours in the Black Watch? You said you were pushed forward into the doorway by the other fellows. Maybe somebody wanted a bit of space to take aim and plug you.'

'Never, sir! A trigger could have been pulled accidentally, because everyone was so dithery. But that's a different matter.'

'I agree. And don't get me wrong. But haven't you often told me old scores were settled and unpopular officers and men were polished off by their own side in the heat of battle?'

'I might have done.'

'How unpopular were you?'

'I was the original forces' favourite.'

On another tack Hereward inquired: 'Listen, Brownie – honestly – how was it you came to be shot in that particular part of your anatomy? You say you were facing the Germans in your doorway. Isn't the exact reverse closer to the truth?'

'The Black Watch never turns its back on the enemy, sir.'

'But you've confessed you were on the run.'

'We were running for cover to fight from.'

'Did you know that in some regiments a wound such as yours is considered to be conclusive proof of cowardice and grounds for a court-martial?'

'I know that if I'd been in the American army I would have got the Purple Heart.'

'Do you think you deserved a medal?'

'Definitely I should have got the Purple Something-or-other for what I suffered and where I suffered it.'

His sufferings included starving in a POW camp.

'I used to dream of babies' heads and two veg.' – babies' heads were the steak and kidney puddings obtainable in that pub behind the Piccadilly Club.

'Was it awful, Brownie?'

'It was until I was taken to hospital.'

'To have your wound dressed?'

'Yes, sir.'

'Weren't you taken to hospital immediately?'

'Not soon enough. The German doctors were more interested in my tumours than my wound. I'm a medical freak, you see.'

'Are you telling me you got to hospital because of your tumours – and your bleeding bottom never needed attention?'

'In a manner of speaking.'

'But I understood your wound was so serious?'

'That's right, sir – or it would have been if I wasn't a rapid healer. I heal as quick as an animal, probably on account of the gipsy in me.'

'Well – anyway – were the doctors kind to you?'

'Oh yes, sir. The Germans are a marvellous race. I never had any quarrel with the Germans. One of their doctors asked me to be his batman.'

'What did you say?'

'Yes, sir.'

'What?'

'It was better being his batman than mooching round the camp with nowt to eat.'

'But he was an enemy – you were betraying your country by co-operating with the enemy.'

'He was more of a gentleman than many I've worked for over here. And I'm half-Austrian, remember.'

'For heaven's sake, Brownie – did you join the German army in the middle of the war? Which side were you on? I'm getting in more and more of a muddle.'

'What's muddling? I did what I could to keep body and soul together. And I was only working for my doctor for a shortish spell. He issued me with a certificate of invalidity and then I was repatriated.'

'Sent home?'

'Yes, sir.'

'Because of your tumours again?'

'Exactly.'

'How long did you spend in the POW camp?'

'Six or seven months.'

'Six months! That's not a hell of a long time. My impression was that you were there for the duration. I've been feeling sorry for you for having been imprisoned for years!'

'It seemed like years, sir.'

Brownie added: 'Besides, I was recaptured and locked up in another POW camp before the war ended.'

The indubitable fact that he once more persuaded the British doctors to pass him fit to fight, when the Germans had come to the conclusion he was so unfit as to constitute no further danger or threat to themselves, was extra evidence of his courage – and the reason why Hereward felt free in a humorous context to call it in question.

He was re-trained by the Black Watch. He returned to France soon after D-day.

'I was part of the Allied Forces' spearhead.'

'Brownie – we know you were shot and wounded – did you ever shoot anybody?'

'Yes, sir.'

'How many of the enemy did you knock out?'

'One, sir.'

'No more than one?'

'And he was a mile off. But I got him in my rifle-sights and let the poor basket have it.'

'What makes you think you hit him?'

'He jumped in the air and rolled over like a rabbit.'

Brownie's second Stalag was worse than the first: 'We had to work on the land – the Germans were short of food and we were so hungry we ate raw turnips in the fields.'

But he adapted to circumstances as usual.

The polite version of how he did so ran as follows: 'I was detailed to work on a smallholding that belonged to an old Prussian farmer and his wife. I helped to look after everything on the smallholding, especially the pigs. They're beautiful creatures, pigs, and much cleaner than human beings. If I have to come back to earth in the shape of an animal when I die, I'd like to be a pig. The farmer and his wife were all over me, they were grateful, and gave me food, an egg or two and now and then a slice of bacon, which I smuggled into camp in my glengarry and shared with the lads.' His glengarry was the Scottish cap worn by the Black Watch. 'I kept quite a few of the lads going with the victuals I slipped them.'

The impolite version was less altruistic and more likely.

'The farmer was past it – he was about seventy. His wife Olga was thirty and a great blonde buxom thing. It was harvest-time when I started working for them – we were busy until late at night and again at the crack of dawn. They asked for permission to let me sleep in their house, which was really more of a shack – just a kitchen and a room above; and I promised not to try to escape and was granted parole. I thought I'd be sleeping in the kitchen. But on the first evening the farmer took my hand and led me upstairs and pointed to the double bed in the bedroom. We climbed into it together. Again I thought he wanted to check on my movements and stop me escaping. But he stayed on his side of the bed and began to snore – and Olga was in the middle. Of course it was ding-dong the whole night through. And afterwards Olga couldn't have enough. She even got at me in the pigsty. The most peculiar part was that the farmer was more grateful to me than ever for making his young wife happy. He used to say: "Brown do Olga good" – which was a funny way of putting it, considering. "Ja, ja, mein Herr, Brown done Olga good a couple of times today," I shouted back at him. And he laughed and patted my cheek – and she gave me another plateful of meat dumplings and sauerkraut. That Olga, she fed me like a fighting cock – none of your naughty comments, please, sir. She and her hubby were dead-keen on keeping my strength up. The fellows in camp couldn't understand why I got fatter and fatter while they were skin and bones.'

'Didn't you explain why?'

'No, sir – still tongue, wise head, as the saying goes.' He would tap his square forehead and declare: 'Five hundred thousand brain-cells in here and none of them filled with beeswax.' He often had recourse to a similar canny dictum: 'There are no flies on me – only the marks where they have been.'

'But didn't you smuggle any titbits from the smallholding into camp?'

'I couldn't smuggle meat dumplings and gravy in my glengarry, sir.'

'Didn't you smuggle anything? I've heard you telling people you provided your friends with victuals. Was that a lie?'

'No, sir. I'm no *proverber* of the truth.' He meant perverter. 'I'd smuggle an egg or a scrap of bacon when I remembered to. But I needed all the nourishment I could get, working day and night as I was.'

'And mostly flat out.'

'Thank you, sir. My friends wouldn't have smuggled and run risks and denied themselves to share their buckshee rations with me – they weren't stupid. And my religion was against it.'

'What religion?'

'The first and last commandment of my religion wouldn't have let me act any different.'

'What's that, Brownie?'

'Take care of number one.'

It was his biggest lie that he took care of number one.

He repeated and even seemed to believe that he was motivated by exclusive self-interest. In reality and on the contrary, his life was spent in taking care of others. In the midst of war, in prison camps, he found someone to take care of, for instance his German doctor, and again in a sense Olga and her complaisant husband and their pigs. His chief ambition was to please and indeed increase the sum of happiness in the world; and in order to fulfil it he was always prepared to renounce his ego.

At the same time it has to be admitted that he generally did what he wanted to do, what made him happy, and that he was infinitely crafty at turning every situation to his own advantage and far from blind to the main chance. He pleased – which pleased him – and as a rule he was rewarded for pleasing sooner or later. He was at once as patient as Job, and the person in the Chinese adage to whom all things come because they have been waited for.

He was either sensible and down to earth and practical, or cynical, depending on the angle from which he was observed. He would not shed a tear for his fellow-prisoners while he demolished Olga's dinners; how was he to appease their communal hunger? Why should he as well as they go hungry?

Moreover he lived for the moment. The gratification of Olga was his immediate concern and best bet. His inclinations, natural, physical and politic, obliged him to do justice to her cooking. Pointless qualms of conscience would have spoilt his appetite.

Hereward agreed that Brownie might be destined for heaven – but with reservations.

'He won't sneak past the pearly gates until he's explained to St Peter how it was that he fell on his feet over and over again, when his friends were falling on their heads.'

Hereward could have mentioned Brownie's use or abuse of religion for the sake of a joke – which was unlikely to endear him to St Peter.

'My God is punctuality,' he reiterated.

And he countered incredulity and scepticism by invoking and challenging the deity: 'Let the Lord God Almighty strike me dead as I stand here if I tell a lie!' – an oath not only foolhardy, but eventually counter-productive, since in the human ears of the initiated it was proof positive that the truth was being *proverbed*.

Anyway the war ended. His romantic story was that he was liberated by a female Russian soldier on a motorbike, who leant a plank against the wire perimeter fence of the camp and rode in over the top.

He also claimed there was a concentration-camp in the area, where Jews had been incinerated: 'We sniffed them like Bisto Kids provided the wind was in the right direction.' Again the Russians liberated the surviving inmates. Brownie, notwithstanding his shocking pleasantries, was distressed by the dreadful sights he said he saw. Yet he continued to proclaim his admiration for the Germans – objectively, genuinely, provocatively, and partly for racialist reasons.

His attitude to other races betrayed his social origins. His conscious considered opinion was that he had risen above the working class and its prejudices. Even if he sometimes called himself a peasant or a serf, he would speak in terms as patronising as they were scathing of the idleness, greed, irresponsibility and folly of the British post-war worker. Whether or not a beneficial phenomenon of our class system is that nobody can believe he is the common man, Brownie was justifiably convinced that he was uncommon – 'when they made me they threw away the mould' – or had become so owing to his contacts with the gentry. And his socially superior persona had a special liking for individual Jews and Negroes – he sympathised with their minority plight, told them he was a gipsy, teased them outrageously, and often established relations of mutual trust and affection. But in the event of trouble, in Jewish shops for instance, or when he caught sight of blacks queueing to draw the dole from a Social Security office, he cursed the races they belonged to. Instinctively and ineradicably he reverted to subscribing to the worst fear of poor people everywhere: namely of strangers muscling in on their scant preserves.

After peace broke out, and before he was demobilised, he transferred into the Military Police. The various roles he played between 1939 and 1946 – Highland Light Infantryman, Black Watchman, fighting man, Officers' Mess orderly, prisoner, German doctor's servant, invalid, pig-fancier, and finally, as he impressed simpletons by abbreviating it, M.P. – were more like transformations in a pantomime than official transfers or anything else. He remained in Germany, his principal task being to trace contraband which had been stolen from army stores for sale on the black market.

He must have excelled at it. He had a native genius for concealment – and developed it when he began to drink too much – so was in the position of poacher turned gamekeeper. In the same way that he loved to hide things and secretively cover his tracks, he loved to seek.

I can imagine him on the job: padding round the premises of suspected black marketeers, quieter than usual, his slightly bulbous eyes missing nothing, terrifyingly perspicacious. Once, he related, he and a colleague ransacked a flat in vain. They had examined every room in the place thoroughly and unsuccessfully. As they were leaving Brownie hurried back to the bathroom: the wife of the proprietor had been having a deep bath there. He pulled out the bath-plug. She was lying naked on dozens of tins of Spam.

Discoveries of another sort were in store for him in Civvy Street. His marriage was on the rocks, although he – or she – still hoped to salvage it. The problems of the Browns were typical of the times: they had been married for seven or eight years and only together for one or two.

What might have been more tragic for Brownie was the rejection of his application to resume work at the Piccadilly Club. Apparently he was told by a secretary that the club was now staffed by immigrant Italians, his former enemies.

THREE

His repudiation by the Piccadilly was cruel – and cinematic. It seems too neatly ironical, his job being filched by members of a race he had fought against, and that he should thus be penalised for his patriotism. It is improbable on several counts: the club authorities would have been crazy not to jump at the chance of re-employing him. For that matter would he have wanted to work anti-social hours in London, when he was living with his wife and daughter in Kent and doing his utmost to preserve his marriage?

The Piccadilly no longer exists. Brownie has covered his tracks.

He signed on at a Royal Doulton factory.

'Were you making lavatories?'

'No, sir – bone china!'

He then switched into the construction industry. He was engaged in building the West Kent Power Station. He worked as a labourer on one of the tall chimneys, some hundreds of feet above the ground. He was well paid and received extra danger-money. But he was always short of cash, because of the gambling on site.

'The men played cards and gambled all the time, even on the scaffold, and expected me to join in. They were a rough crew – you had to be rough to put up with the conditions in winter.'

West Kent Power Station is in the vicinity of the Thames Estuary. Almost throughout the year icy winds from the sea swayed the scaffolding alarmingly; and mud and wet cement on boots rendered the rungs of ladders and the catwalks of planking slippery; and hands were so chilled that they could not grip the poles. One day a fellow missed his footing and fell to his death.

'How did you react?'

'Badly, sir.'

'Well – no wonder.'

'I thanked God it wasn't Brownie – and stayed where I was, clinging on at the top, until they'd cleared the mess away.'

A contributory cause of his shortage of cash may have been his expenditure on liquid refreshment. No doubt the post-war hour had struck at which – he would admit – he had started drinking or drinking in earnest. He said that at the Power Station it was difficult not to.

'The best men on the scaffold swigged a quart of beer first thing in the morning. They just poured it down their throats – they wouldn't venture near a ladder without it. The beer relaxed their muscles. Otherwise they would have been too tense and jittery.'

'Did you follow their example?'

'Yes, sir. That's why I'm here today. The teetotallers were turned into strawberry jam.'

Additional pressures were driving him to or towards drink. In spite of his adaptability he had had by no means a cushy war. He came home to find his marriage in pieces and, possibly, that he was superfluous to requirements at the Piccadilly. In factories and on scaffolding he was wasting his talents – he was something like a creative artist denying his art and growing destructive or self-destructive in consequence. And he was not half as rough and tough as he pretended to be.

He was unhappy. He was drowning his sorrows. But he was never at a loss for such excuses. Life never failed to provide him with first-class excuses to overdo it as he pleased.

The pub became – or already was – the oasis in the desert of his existence. He knew by heart the name of every public house he had ever frequented: the way he rolled those names round his tongue evoked scenes of Dickensian brightness, warmth, jollity and good cheer. Pubs were his clubs, where he felt protected from the outside world of demanding women and authority; where with the help of a little of what he fancied – or a lot – he could shed his cares; where he chewed the rag and shot a line, and formed the sort of temporary friendships he preferred, which posed no threat to his privacy. For pubs were also the stages on which he performed semi-professionally, entertaining, imitating his bosses, clowning – he was not keen on members of his audience prying behind the scenes.

His troubles multiplied, perhaps not only as troubles are inclined to, but as they invariably did when he was in the grip of the demon.

Against his will he had been forced to join a Trade Union. He disapproved of Union methods, the intimidation and the blackmail, and eventually tore up his Membership Card at a public meeting. Then he had a fall from the scaffolding. He was lucky enough to land on a horizontal pole ten feet below and save himself; but he lost his nerve and his head for heights. The result was that he either resigned his job or was kicked out of it by Union officialdom.

Meanwhile Mrs Brown was dividing her time between her husband and the man she had lived with during the war: again I am quoting Brownie. Increasingly violent quarrels ensued – and crimes were committed that gave ample scope for unpleasantness in the future.

He had to scrounge the wherewithal to keep at any rate two bodies and souls together, his own and his daughter Peggy's. He had an allotment where he grew vegetables, a bicycle and a mongrel called Lassie. He was very fond of Lassie: she used to run along the street and leap into his arms when he rode home on his bicycle. One fine day Mrs Brown had the dog put down.

'For no reason?'

'No proper reason, sir.'

'Was nothing wrong with her?'

'She was three years old and in the pink, although my wife wouldn't have it.'

'You mean your wife said that Lassie was ill?'

'She said so. And she procured a certificate from the vet. But I know she did it to spite me.'

'I suppose you had your revenge?'

'Oh yes, sir. Nobody gets away with twisting my tail.'

A suspect feature of the story of Lassie was the mournful relish with which Brownie repeated it, in order to enlist sympathy, whenever the collapse of his marriage was mentioned. He added embellishments to wring the hearts of his listeners: no dog had ever been so obedient and faithful as his Lass.

But whether or not Mrs Brown really carried her spite to lethal extremes, she must have been provoked by her spouse's customary response to stress. He was poor and unhappy, therefore he squandered money in pubs and made himself miserable: that was his paradoxical theory – or habitual practice. He was under the common illusion of drinking people: he imagined a few drinks did him a power of good, sharpened his wits, enabled him to cope, whereas in fact they simply stupefied him.

And their after-effects in his case were psychologically as well as physically damaging. He suffered from guilt. Guilt and shame between them induced a passive masochistic state, which tempted the opposite sex in particular to vent its spleen on him. His boldness with women when he was sober emboldened them when he was or had been drunk: often they seemed to visit on his unprotesting person the accumulated bitterness of all their defeats in the war with men. To keep them quiet, and as penance, he renewed the solemn extravagant promises he could not and would not honour. He was again reproached, he had a few more drinks, he sank back into his infuriating lethargy, he asked for another dose of punishment, and the vicious circle was complete.

The upshot of this murky period of Brownie's life – unemployed, at odds with and more or less separated from his wife who was not kind to him, penniless, dogless, and probably half seas over – was that he decided to look for the type of work he was best at in London.

In 1950 he may indeed have applied in vain for his old job at the Piccadilly: by that time the club was in financial straits and its exclusive policy could have been to employ cheap Italian labour.

He managed to trace the club's pre-war hall-porter, who was now a commissionaire at a luxury hotel. He explained his predicament to Mr Triggs and said he was ready to go into private service. Should Mr Triggs hear of any decent situation, would he let Brownie know?

Soon afterwards Hereward Watkins began to play his part in Brownie's destiny, and vice versa.

Hereward was then aged twenty-three, while Brownie was in his mid-thirties.

Hereward had served his term in the Household Cavalry and been demobilised, wanted to write and was eager to apprentice himself to literature. But he was hard up, notwithstanding his well-to-do family and Watkins Hall in the Brecon Beacons. A married sister vacated her flat in the West End of London and suggested that he should take it and move in. Although he agreed he would work better there than in the spare rooms of hospitable friends, he said it was way beyond his means.

The flat was a maisonette on the two top floors of a large house in Windle Road, just north of Oxford Street. The place was owned and the rest of it occupied by a learned society, the Antipodean Archaeological Trust, which was disposed to lease its residential accommodation for a minimal rent to a recommended tenant.

Hereward had second thoughts. The maisonette was a bargain and thanks to his sister he was in a position to obtain the lease. Granted, minimal as the rent was, he could not afford it. On the other hand he might be able to sub-let the three rooms and bathroom on the lower floor.

By chance he met a Frenchman, Jacques Beausson, who was in a hurry to find somewhere to live. Jacques was a prosperous banker, thirty or so, and working in the English branch of his bank. He needed a good accessible address, since he had to wine and dine business contacts in the evenings, and room for a servant who would cook for and generally look after him.

He approved of the maisonette on being shown round it. His servant could have one of the rooms on the upper floor, leaving Hereward with two, which would do him nicely. The financial details were sorted out to their mutual satisfaction. Hereward felt it was worth investing most of his capital in the necessary furnishings.

Temporarily Jacques happened to be staying in the hotel where Mr Triggs was the commissionaire.

On the appointed day he therefore arrived at Windle Road with Brownie in tow.

At first Hereward did not take to him. And he was none too sure that he liked the idea of having to share his new home with a foreign acquaintance and a total stranger. But in time he changed his mind.

Jacques was not a typical Frenchman: he was taciturn and reserved. He worked hard, left for his office early and returned late, stayed with English friends at weekends and travelled abroad on business a good deal. He was careful not to impose upon or bother Hereward, and kept strictly to his own floor of the maisonette. His discretion was appreciated, while his contribution to expenses relieved Hereward of money worries. In addition Jacques was literary, respected Hereward's endeavours in that line, and his initial trials and errors, and encouraged him to persevere with the novels that eventually made his name.

Brownie – or Brown as he was called to begin with – struck Hereward as too obsequious.

My memory tells me I was present at their meeting. It was long ago – but I seem to remember climbing the stairs to Hereward's quarters and being greeted by a short smiling man with flat sandy-coloured hair brushed back and parted in the middle: he had emerged from the kitchen on to the top landing. Jacques, who was not present, must have admitted him to the maisonette and left him to his own devices – and perhaps I had been having lunch somewhere with Hereward preparatory to lending a hand with his unpacking.

'How do you do, sir – Brown, sir!'

He was standing to attention. He barked his name and the sirs. But he shook hands and smiled with a certain charm. He was thin in those days – thin, active, quick, lively, like a terrier. I noticed his broad face and square forehead and popping blue eyes. He wore a black bow-tie and white waiter's jacket.

'Is everything all right, Brown?'

'Yes, sir, thank you, sir. Would you like to inspect my room, sir?'

He led us into it. His shaving tackle was laid out with extraordinary precision on the shelf above the washbasin. A framed snapshot of his daughter was exactly in the centre of the bedside table. His blankets had been folded and piled with scrupulous neatness at the foot of the bed.

'You must have been in the army.'

'Six years and four months in the Black Watch, sir!'

'Really? Are you Scottish?'

'Half-Scottish, sir – my mother was a Macgregor.'

'Obviously you haven't forgotten your army training.'

'I was always regimental, sir.' By regimental he meant tidy. 'Is there anything I can do for you, sir?'

'Oh – no. No, thanks. Well, I'll see you later, Brown.'

Hereward expressed his doubts as soon as he and I were alone.

'I don't fancy that three-bags-full approach. I've never in my life been called sir so often in such a short space of time. He's too good to be true – he's smarmy. Anyway he's Jacques' servant, not mine. I know he's got glowing references, but I couldn't bear to have him dancing attendance on me.'

At four or five o'clock on the same afternoon, as I recollect it, there was a knock on the door of Hereward's sitting-room.

'Yes? Who is it? Come in!'

'Beg pardon, sir – I wondered if I could bring you a nice tray of tea?'

'How thoughtful of you, Brown. As a rule I don't stop for tea. I may fetch a cup in a little while. But don't you trouble yourself.'

'It's no trouble, sir. I've already laid the tray for two. Indian or China, sir?'

'Have you got both sorts?'

'Yes, sir – I've just been to the shops.'

'Well, in that case, China, please.'

'And some hot buttered toast with strawberry jam, sir?'

'What about Monsieur Beausson? Where's Monsieur Beausson? Won't he be wanting tea?'

'He said he'd only dash in to change his clothes this evening, sir.'

'Well – if you're sure it isn't too much trouble, maybe we will have toast and jam.'

'Thank you, sir.'

'No – thank you, Brown.'

Brownie was on his very best behaviour. He was out to prove he was not too good to be true. He was practising the seductive art of his dance of attendance. And his gratitude was sincere inasmuch as he was pleased to be given the opportunity to please.

But he was also acting a part – and with such expertise that neither Hereward nor I, although we had both been in the army, realised quite how much of his obsequious manner would have been called bullshit in a barrack-room.

Again, Londoners as we were, even if Hereward hailed from Wales, we failed to recognise in him that traditionally Cockney phenomenon of a person for whom every single aspect of existence is a potential joke.

We were slow in the uptake. It was some years before we got the point.

Jacques never got it. French people may be wittier than the English; they cannot be as relentlessly, broadly, inclusively humorous as Brownie, who was after all unique. Temperamental or national misunderstandings between employer and employee at Windle Road were to blame for future discord.

I must not anticipate.

The fanciful sequel to our first encounter that I visualise with hindsight is Brownie in some pub, holding forth over a frothing tankard and making mock of Hereward's efforts not to exploit him: 'I hadn't been in the house two minutes before my boss starts pressing the bell. That's what they think their fingers are for – pressing bells for flunkeys. Bring me tea and a stack of hot toast spread thick with best butter, he says. And he wouldn't touch the tea you and I drink, matey – not he. His tea's flown in fresh from China every day – I had to walk two miles to Fortnum and Mason and back again to buy it. The habits of the upper crust are peculiar, believe me! Mr Hereward Watkins, the Earl of Grimlingham, Graf von Twisch, Lord Tatters Tatham – I've known the lot. I could tell you stories about them that would make your hair stand on end.'

I often spent Sundays with Hereward. We would meet for lunch after each of us had done five or six hours' writing, then go for a long walk and probably to a movie, and have an evening meal and part at the nearest bus-stop. Occasionally other friends joined us. They were hard up, too, and impatient to hear what it was like to have a manservant at your beck and call.

Hereward satisfied our curiosity. He was equally intrigued by Brownie, whom he was beginning to appreciate. He in his turn was grateful for the opportunity to get on with his work without having to waste time on practicalities.

Officially Brownie was free to visit his family at weekends. But he was inclined to stay put in London – to save himself the expense of travelling to Kent, or because of his strained relations with his wife, or because he was afraid of yielding to alcoholic temptation on his home ground. In the early days at Windle Road he was either not drinking much, or his drinking had not attracted anyone's attention: a new job and new faces were exciting enough to keep him happy – and pretty sober.

On Sundays when he was in residence he would beg Hereward to let him do the catering. A card-table was erected in the little sitting-room on the top floor, and Hereward and I and any extra guests were duly fed and waited on. They had a special piquancy, those feasts served in princely style to our group of needy and even hungry aspirants for fame and fortune.

It was on Brownie's Sundays in London that I began to talk and listen to him, and mainly eavesdrop on the amusing serial of his dialogue with Hereward.

In passing, in defence of Hereward, I should explain that Brownie's offers of supererogatory service were only accepted in Jacques' absence. Hereward was always loath to seem to be taking the slightest advantage of his tenant's servant. And he was considerate, whatever the imaginative slander that may have been spread around in the local hostelries.

Apparently Jacques was aware of how difficult it was to stop Brownie acting out his role and had no objection to his being kept occupied. He was the opposite of a dog in the manger – he was delighted to think of Hereward enjoying the manger's contents when he could not. A side-effect of his generous attitude and his absenteeism was that up to a point Brownie came to regard Hereward as his boss, while Hereward was drawn into assuming more and more of a boss's responsibilities and obligations – which were later on to form his payment in full for all benefits received.

But again I must not anticipate.

Jacques' prime concern was that Brownie should learn to cook. He was satisfied with his dispositions at Windle Road except in that respect. He appealed for advice to the hotel – and its commissionaire Mr Triggs – where he had stayed on arriving in England. Consequently Brownie spent a few weeks studying in the hotel's kitchens.

He proved an apt pupil. Cooking expressed the artistic part of his nature. Cooking could be said to be the art he had always sought. He loved the challenge of it, and the drama, the thrills and spills, and the implicit snobbery, and the competitive and boastful avenues it opened. He was greedy, he was neat-fingered, precise, inventive, intuitive, and presented food beautifully – presentation and the look of things counted for more with him than reality: he had most of the attributes of the best cooks. He never felt he was a hundred per cent alive unless he was frantically busy, sweating and cursing, for instance over a hot stove.

The chefs at the hotel were French. He acquired their lingo along with the tricks of their trade. And he could have been imitating Jacques, when he travestied the glottal stop. He now started to speak of por-h-ridge, o-h-ranges and so on.

'What would you like for lunch today, sir?'

'Oh – bangers and mash.'

'*Les sausages* and *pommes pur-h-ée*. And a green *salade*, sir?'

'Okay, Brownie.'

He was an out-an-out culinary name-dropper.

'Brownie, I can't think of anything to eat – my mind's a blank. Make a suggestion, will you?'

'Well, sir, you could have Chicken *Napoléon* with *petits pois* and *pommes fantastiques,* followed by *chocolat soufflé* or a cold *o-h-range mousse.*'

'What's Chicken Napoleon?'

'It was dreamt up by the chef of *Napoléon,* sir, during the retreat from Moscow. All he had in his travelling larder was bread and butter and some *vin rouge.* The troops foraging in the countryside brought him a scrawny old fowl and a capful of *tomates.* He cooked his ingredients together in a pot over a camp fire and produced a very tasty dish. You should try it, sir.'

'How long does it take to prepare?'

'Five hours.'

'Five hours! But I only want a snack. What are *pommes fantastiques* anyway?'

'Balls, sir.'

'What did you say?'

'I said they're potato balls, sir. I scoop the balls from potatoes with my handy tool and roast them golden brown in the oven. They're like miniature crunchy *pommes rôtis.'*

'I see. But you misunderstood me, Brownie. I'm alone for supper and couldn't face a complicated meal – and I hate the idea of your slaving for hours on end to feed me.'

'Would you like a fresh *poisson,* sir, with *pommes allumettes?'*

'Do you mean fish and chips?'

'Yes, sir.'

'No. But I'll tell you what I would like: have you got a tin of sardines? Give me sardines and an apple, Brownie.'

'Very good, sir.'

The recipe for his Chicken *Napoléon* required dissection of the bird. He would illustrate the method of dissecting it on his own body.

'First you cut off its wings.' With his hand with fingers outstretched, simulating the blade of a knife, he would as it were carve from the side of his neck, down his chest and round and under his arm. 'Then you force its legs apart and cut them loose.' He would bend his knees and open his legs and carve from his groin up to his waist. 'And next you dig out its oysters.' He would turn and gesture graphically in the vicinity of the small of his back. 'If you need to separate the drum-sticks from the thighs you'll have to cut through here' – his hand sawed across his kneejoint.

He was liable to get his French wrong. He was taught to cook a savoury of ham and cheese fried between slices of bread, which is called *Croque Monsieur* in France. He called it *Coq Monsieur.* But maybe he meant to be rude. He had a lot of intentional fun with his description of *pommes fantastiques.*

His mistakes in English were also laughable, whether by accident or on purpose. He could not speak the word people except in the plural: 'I don't like a crowd of peoples.' He said Volga when he meant vulgar.

'No, Brownie – the Volga is the river where the boatmen sing.'

'Is it, sir? I thought I was Volga, and those boatmen were singing a vulgar song.'

Instead of 'a lick and a promise' he said 'a cat's lick and a promise': 'I've only given your room a cat's lick and a promise this morning.' Because of his fondness for pigs, or from more ambiguous motives, he adapted the phrase cat's whiskers: 'You look like the pig's whiskers, sir!'

He said poonah for puma – 'as fierce as the poonahs in the zoo'; adolt for adult – 'he ought to know better at his age – after all he's an adolt'; charmed for chimed – 'the clock charmed six'; dappy for dapper – 'he was dappy in his brand new suit'; dole for doll – 'she's as pretty as a little dole'; hammer and tonk for hammer and tongs; Japanese scrawl for Japanese scroll; loveable for lovely – 'we had a loveable duck for dinner'; maulers for molars – 'I can eat the toughest meat with my maulers'; pendulum for pendant – 'Madame was wearing a great pendulum of diamonds'; and pus for pith – 'when you're making my sauce of *o-h-ranges,* you must be sure to use the pus – it's pus that adds the special flavour to my *o-h-range* sauce'.

His cooking improved out of recognition after his course at the hotel. Then Jacques invited a friend to stay in his spare room, Madame Drey, who gave Brownie extra lessons. Madame Drey was about sixty. She was a bad advertisement for her skills with food, being skeletally thin. She had a cigarette in her mouth and a glass in her hand for most of every day. But she and Brownie shut themselves into the kitchen at Windle Road. And she put the finishing touches to his education.

Jacques began to entertain his business contacts, as planned.

Brownie shopped for and prepared and carried downstairs and served and carried up the remains of mammoth meals, infinitely more complicated than the one he had suggested to Hereward.

'What was on the menu last night?'

'*Consommé* and *croûtons* to start with, and *sole vé-h-ronique* done in a white sauce with peeled grapes, and a sweet *gigot,* still pink inside just as Monsieur Beausson likes it, and *haricots* and oodles of my *pommes fantastiques,* and a *soufflé* of *chocolat,* and a board of *fromages* and a bowl of *fruit.*'

'Did they actually eat all that?'

'Not Monsieur Beausson – he's a very small eater. But the others did. I had to go round the table twice with my *gigot.* And they got through three French loaves as long as your arm and a pint of cream with the *soufflé* and their coffee.'

'They must have been hungry.'

'A gentleman told me he'd been starving himself all day so as to make room for my dinner.'

'What did they drink?'

'Chilled white wine with the fish, and *vin rouge* at room temperature with the meat, and brandy with the coffee. And they had gin and vodka before they sat down.'

'Did you serve the wine or was it passed round?'

'I served it, sir.'

'Isn't such a big dinner party a bit much for you?'

'Oh no, sir! I love it! I was like a wet flannel by the end of the evening – the sweat was pouring off me.'

'Over the guests?'

'They were past noticing by that time, sir.'

'Well – please tell me if you ever find the work too much – I'd try to explain to Monsieur Beausson.'

'I will, sir, thank you, sir. But I feel fit today – I could easily do it again.'

His duties, onerous as they were on festive occasions, did not seem so to him because they were still a novelty. He was buoyed up by being good at his job, and getting better, by compliments, and by his mystique of inexhaustible toughness. And he himself in his enthusiasm doubled those duties. He would plead with Jacques for permission to cook a chicken with tarragon, although tarragon was out of season and he knew he would really have to walk to Fortnum and Mason to buy it. He walked unnecessary miles and scoured Soho for recondite herbs and spices which he rather than Jacques insisted on using.

He had great respect for his employer, and affection and loyalty, at least on the surface. He was flattered to ascribe the highest standards to his Monsieur Beausson, and the most delicate palate. He was responsive to the trust reposed in him and sensed the gentleness and kindness underlying Jacques' somewhat impenetrable manner. He was impressed by the princes of industry and commerce who came to gorge themselves at Windle Road, and the foreign visitors who stayed in the spare room, Madame Drey, Colonel de Chiffre and the rest.

But the Cockney mentality with Celtic trimmings of feyness and fantasy, and the logical Latin one, are poles apart. When Jacques asked Brownie how many guests he could manage and received the boastful reply: 'The more the merrier, sir!' – he took Brownie literally. When Colonel de Chiffre asked for the name of a reputable laundry in the neighbourhood and was told not to worry – Brownie would be delighted to wash Monsieur le Colonel's shirts – the same thing happened. There was so much of the Celt in Brownie that his native tongue should have been Gaelic, which does not include any equivalent of the word no. As a result he assumed an ever increasing work-load.

And Jacques was too preoccupied to take note of the problem.

The fact was – as he saw it – that Brownie had more than enough spare time in which to recuperate from dinner parties, despite his determined attendance on Hereward. He could go away for weekends if he chose to, and enjoyed completely free holiday spells while Jacques was travelling abroad and Hereward was down at Watkins Hall. He kept on saying the job suited him. He seemed to be settled and content.

His seeming contentment was always a danger signal. It could mean he was bored.

After he had been at Windle Road for about five years, his wife instituted proceedings for divorce and he had cause to console himself.

Or perhaps he started drinking again and thus gave his wife cause to sue for divorce.

He did not mention the extenuating circumstance of his emotional and legal tribulations until the deteriorating quality of his service was complained of.

Hereward, who was more often at home and lived at closer quarters to Brownie than Jacques, was the first to realise something was amiss. Brownie's breath began to smell of beer or alcohol – occasionally the whole upper floor of the maisonette smelt like a brewery. The white jackets he wore got grubbier, he took less trouble with his clothes, and another odour of stale sweat and dirty socks emanated from his bedroom, the door of which he now kept locked. He was apt to become unnaturally talkative and sentimental: 'Lord Tatters Tatham was the best of the bunch at the Piccadilly Club. I'd have gone through hell and fire-water for Lord Tatters!' He had a TV set in the kitchen: he would drop off to sleep in front of it and disturb Hereward in the adjoining room with his thunderous snores. After dinner parties downstairs, the process of washing up, and crashing and banging of cutlery and crockery, would continue into the small hours.

His cooking was no longer what it had been. At those dinner

parties, the meat was cold and the ice-cream was hot, there were extended intervals between courses, and he took it on himself to converse in a loud voice with the guests as he served them: 'Breast or thigh, Madame? You'll find a dear tender piece of breast by your right hand, Madame. And you must have lashings of my speciality *sauce de tomates* with *cognac* . . . It's thigh for you, isn't it, my lord? You gobble up your thigh, my lord, and I'll slip you a second helping . . .'

At length Jacques issued a mild rebuke in general terms. He too had his suspicions, he had been surprised by the amount of drink consumed on the premises, but did not like to broach such an awkward subject. Brownie confessed his sins. That is to say he described his marital catastrophe and apologised for having let it interfere with his work. He thanked Jacques for drawing attention to his absent-mindedness and promised faithfully that he would never have reason to do so in the future.

He was more or less believed, and steps were immediately taken to assist him through the temporary crisis.

Jacques acted on Hereward's theory that Brownie might be overworked. He engaged a daily lady to clean the rooms on his floor of the maisonette. She was Polish, called Mrs Kowscko, sixty-ish, squat and rotund. Brownie flirted with her, said she was more like a calf than a cow, relieved her of any job she considered doing, and soon demoralised her.

Mrs Kowscko began to arrive at eleven o'clock instead of nine, carrying several empty shopping bags and just in time for coffee and cakes in the kitchen. She dawdled over her coffee until twelve, laughing at and with Brownie. Then they adjourned to Jacques' flat, where they played games with their feather dusters. At one she returned to the kitchen for a square meal and at two she departed with her shopping bags bulging.

The household bills soared. Brownie did not hesitate to point the finger at Mrs Kowscko, who in her turn accused him of every crime under the sun. The next daily lady employed by Jacques was Mrs Whitworth, a severe middle-aged Scot.

Brownie's flirting took a different form. He told Mrs Whitworth that his mother had been a Macgregor, pronouncing the name with a marked Scottish accent, and he was ex-Black Watch. He softened her up by appealing to her nationalistic sentiments – Windle Road rang with his 'Och ayes!' and 'Och noes!' And he so brainwashed her, probably by exaggerating the demands made upon him – 'I'm butler, valet, cook, housemaid, telephone operator and errand-boy rolled into one: I'm on duty sixteen hours a day!' – that she could not speak civilly to Jacques or Hereward, whom she must have regarded as ruthless slave-drivers.

Luckily she had to leave for some reason. Brownie's unexpected attitude was – good riddance. For Mrs Whitworth was a secret dipsomaniac, he declared. His answer to the question of Monsieur Beausson's disappearing drink was that it had been poured down her throat.

Jacques' experiments in easing his manservant's lot by physical means were obvious failures. Brownie never could work with other people: he was too much of a perfectionist, in a sense too pernicketty, and he spoilt them, and was demoralised by as well as demoralising them. And he was unable to resist an opportunity to whitewash his own character by blackening theirs. It was almost inconceivable the dour brisk Mrs Whitworth was a dipsomaniac, or that Mrs Kowscko pinched a ton of food without his connivance. But his calumnies were nonetheless advantageous from his point of view. For they divided, if not removed, Jacques' suspicions in respect of the bottles on the drink-tray. And his boss ran no more risks with meddlesome daily ladies, who might or might not be bad influences.

No – clearly – assistance would have to be moral, psychological, verbal – and specific and straightforward, too.

Brownie's crisis was not so temporary as had been hoped. A year of it had already passed, his divorce was dragging on, and he was behaving more oddly than ever. Gone were the dinner party days when he was ready half an hour before the guests arrived – everything under control in the kitchen, the table laid with gleaming silver and glass, the wine decanted, and himself freshly shaved in a pristine jacket, his face pink and shiny, exuding health and happiness, and none of his five hundred thousand brain-cells filled with beeswax. Instead, frenetic and flustered, interrupting his last minute arrangements to plunge downstairs in response to the doorbell, breathless, his eyes popping and rolling, he under-cooked and over-cooked his party pieces and handed them round on wobbly platters, startling strangers with his muttered expletives – 'Mamma mia! Jesus!' etcetera; and was liable to fall asleep with his head on the kitchen table after serving the coffee weak and lukewarm.

Jacques protested.

Excessive drinkers put their real friends in an intolerable position. While drunkards wreak havoc in the lives of their nearest and dearest, the borderline cases create dilemmas. How addicted are they? Should somebody butt in before it is too late? Will disagreeable advice be understood, accepted, forgiven – or any use? Does one have the nerve to advise? Does one have the right? Yet rectitude cannot be equated with standing by and even negatively co-operating as a valuable person one is fond of goes to the dogs.

Jacques had been loath to stray into such an ethical minefield. He worked extremely hard in order to earn money partly to pay a manservant who would save him trouble – not make it. He had no energy to spare to fight on the home-front for Brownie's sobriety, and was disinclined to break the rule of his reserve.

But nature stepped in. Nature alone rescues us from the horns of horrid dilemmas. A combination of disappointment and irritation inspired him to speak out.

On a typical morning after the night before, he summoned Brownie and charged him with drunkenness.

'Oh no, sir – not that – I'm sorry you should think that, sir – it's not true, I promise – I've signed the pledge, sir – I swear it on the grave of my dear mother!'

Brownie was deeply shocked by the imputation. He rebutted it with tears in his eyes. Not a single drop of strong liquor had crossed his lips since he had been in Monsieur Beausson's employ. Moreover, if he had been drinking, he would never have touched the drink that belonged to Monsieur Beausson. He was not a thief! But he laughed at the whole idea – and invoked the members of his family in the Salvation Army, who had persuaded him to sign that teetotal pledge long ago. Not only his mother, but God Almighty Himself, were his witnesses!

Jacques was taken aback.

Brownie hurried on: 'I've been receiving nasty letters from my wife, sir. I know I promised not to let her get me down. But she's vicious, sir. You wouldn't believe the wicked lies she writes about me – they choke me, they do, and I can't settle to my duties as I should. Your good self and Mr Watkins have shown me nothing but kindness. May I ask you to be kind and patient for a little longer – just until my divorce is through and I'm less upset?'

Jacques began to apologise.

'Please, sir – it's all right, sir – I quite appreciate how you came to be mistaken,' Brownie said with magnanimity. 'And I'll try hard to keep my spirits up and give satisfaction. Will there be anything else, sir?'

Jacques managed not to capitulate completely. He had been bitten once before and was twice shy.

He wanted all his drink locked in the cupboard under the stairs.

'I'll do it now, sir. I was going to suggest it myself.'

Brownie carried the bottles in question into the cupboard, stacked them regimentally on the wine-racks, locked the door with an ostentatious flourish and presented the key to his boss.

Later the same day he relapsed into his woolly woozy state.

Brownie won his divorce and lost his excuse. But his daughter married, he said he had to fork out more money than he could afford for the wedding, and his debts became the scapegoat for his erratic conduct. When his debts were paid with the help of Jacques, he produced a new alibi in the person of a favourite brother who was dying by slow degrees: 'Mick's in pain, sir – I can't concentrate for thinking of his pain.' In between times, he claimed he was seriously ill with 'flu, toothache, conjunctivitis, lumbago and housemaid's knee. And he still had a trump card up his sleeve.

Hereward took over from where Jacques had left off.

He had recently published his first novel, which was successful, and was invited to attend a public reading from it. Brownie agreed to iron his suit for the occasion, at which he needed to look smart. He dressed in a hurry on the night, and arrived and mingled with the readers and the audience. He noticed a bad smell, and that the people who were introduced to him recoiled with expressions of embarrassment and disgust on their faces. He realised his suit was responsible for the stink – and tackled Brownie with the spontaneity of anger on the following day.

'What did you do to my best suit? No – don't tell me a lot of fibs! I'll tell you: you used a filthy washing-up towel as a damp cloth when you ironed it – you impregnated it with grease and detergent – you ruined it – and you made a proper fool of me at my function – I might as well have stepped straight out of a sewer. I suppose you'd been drinking again?'

As usual Brownie denied everything.

He had not been drinking; the towel he had used as a damp cloth was cleaner than any whistle; the suit had been as smelly as hell before he touched it – he had had to hold his nose while doing the job; but had simply obeyed Mr Watkins' orders, weighed down with work for Monsieur Beausson though he was – and so on.

Another incident provoked Hereward to speak his mind. If he was spending the weekend alone at Windle Road, Brownie would leave him snacks of cold food in the kitchen. The snacks were laid out appetisingly under sheets of greaseproof paper and the kitchen always appeared to be spotless. But one weekend Hereward, instead of removing the paper and consuming the food according to custom, decided to cook himself some hot sphaghetti. He reached for the middle-sized saucepan of the set on a saucepan-stand and lifted the lid: it contained the mildewed remains of stewed cabbage. None of the saucepans on the stand, which were burnished on the outside, had been emptied or cleaned. He opened the drawer reserved for kitchen implements – they had been thrown in dirty. He explored further and found stacks of unwashed plates, teapots full of stale tea, blackened frying-pans with fat in them, broken dishes galore, and squalid souvenirs of dinner parties, greenish *pommes fantastiques* in a lipsticked wine glass, a half-eaten *Croque Monsieur* swimming in a bowl of cherries with kirsch.

He duly vented his wrath on Brownie.

'Your kitchen's a disgrace. Look at this, look at that! Do you want to poison us? It's revolting – and I know why, even if you pretend you don't! You're going all to pieces because of drink!'

Brownie professed amazement at the sights he was made to see – 'I'd no idea it was that bad, sir.' However, he reminded Hereward that the previous week had been particularly busy and that he had stayed at his post, cooking dinners, on duty for sixteen hours a day, although fearful his brother would expire before he was at liberty to dash to the hospital. What with being worked so hard, and Mick at death's door, and his rotten tooth and his gammy knee, he had not felt up to tidying the kitchen properly. Of course he would give it a thorough blitz at once. It would be ready for inspection in a couple of hours. As for drink, he repeated that he did not partake.

Hereward was unconvinced. On the other hand he had to admit that his evidence was circumstantial, not to say flimsy. He had never caught Brownie in the act of partaking. He was impressed in spite of himself by the consistency of Brownie's denials.

In a word, he was gullible. In retrospect he was staggered by his gullibility. He had been slow in the uptake, as he was to see Brownie's jokes.

'The trouble is,' he used to say, 'Brownie's cleverer than me. He's always been a jump ahead, and for all I know he is still.'

And Hereward meant it, although most of his friends scoffed at such false modesty.

Certainly his aristocratic compassion for a dependant at the opposite end of the social scale, and hereditary feudal concern for a servant on whom he depended, were played upon by that essential craft of the lower classes which Brownie carried to the point of virtuosity. He was induced to feel guilty by hints of Brownie having to work too hard, of the consequent deterioration of Brownie's health, of Brownie having been divorced because of his devotion to duty, and his being denied access to the deathbed of his brother. Guilt tied Hereward's hands as intended, inhibiting his scepticism – and Jacques': for instance, since they as bosses could be the bone of contention between Brownie and his wife, neither of them liked to demand to see her vicious letters which he said were his undoing. Over the episodes of the stinking suit and the discovery of disaster areas in the kitchen, Hereward was at even more of a disadvantage, considering he had asked Brownie to iron his suit – a favour, and extra work, not specifically paid for – and he happened to be snooping in the kitchen because of Brownie's snacks, which came into the same gratuitous category. He had enjoyed those snacks, the preparation of which was part of Brownie's particularly busy week that might have prevented him from bidding his beloved brother farewell – and was therefore obliged to restrain an indignation deriving from his enjoyment, ungrateful and stony-hearted.

Again, notwithstanding his blue blood and anachronistic attitudes, Hereward was sufficiently imbued or infected with the spirit of the age not to want to seem to be grinding the face of the poor.

Yet again, as a normally truthful person, he could not conceive of Brownie's total disregard for the truth.

The resultant paradox was that he was exploited by Brownie, at least in a moral sense, rather than the other way round.

The only weak spot in Brownie's subtly aggressive defences, behind which he lived his private life and kept his secrets, was his charm. His chief strength, his amusing engaging infinitely plausible personality, was also his weakness: it was like a parable.

For Hereward had grown fond of him. He would miss a great deal more than menial services if Jacques decided to get rid of Brownie. He could not bear to stand by and take a detached spectator's view of the possession of his friend and in many respects his benefactor by evil forces.

He joined in the battle for Brownie's soul – or at any rate for his physical salvation and his job.

One morning he was too worked up over the situation at Windle Road to be able to write. He interrupted his rigid routine and went for a walk. And he ran into Brownie, who emerged from a pub in a back alley.

'What were you doing there?'

'Trying to buy half a bottle of cheap red wine for cooking, sir.'

'Why didn't you buy it from the grocer?'

'I forgot, sir.'

'Sorry – I don't believe that. I believe you were drinking.'

'No, sir – never.'

'Shall I check with the landlord?'

'I might have had a Guinness, sir. My doctor advised me to.'

'What about your pledge? What about all your swearing to me and Monsieur Beausson that you don't drink?'

'I only do it sometimes – under doctor's orders.'

'How often is sometimes? Every day?'

'If possible, sir, so as to keep fit.'

'You drink Guinness on most days – is that your story now?'

'Yes, sir – just a glass, sir.'

'You fool, Brownie! You're not yourself, you're making yourself sick, because you guzzle Guinness – don't you understand? Your doctor ought to be struck off the register if he really gave you that advice. Well, at last we know roughly where we are. I've caught you at it, because you thought I was writing and you were safe – and you'll have to stop. Obviously drink's been the problem all along. I'll help you. Instead of lying and lying, you should have let me help you before. As it is you're halfway down the drain.'

'Yes, sir.'

'Do you agree?'

'I'm sure I can pull back, sir.'

'Are you willing to have a shot?'

'Oh yes, sir! I agree it's not been good for me, in spite of the advertisements.'

'Seriously, Brownie?'

'Yes, sir.'

'In that case I won't say anything to Monsieur Beausson. We'll see what we can do together.'

'Thank you, sir.'

Brownie's thanks, and misleading passivity and malleability, his yielding to pressure in accordance with the theory of ju-jitsu, and then his reformations which were short-lived, lured Hereward deeper into the fray. He was an expert flatterer – and nothing flatters a person more than the idea that he or she can save the soul of another.

Hereward was pleased to think he had established a little bridgehead of truth: namely that Brownie drank Guinness in pubs and was willing to co-operate with a team-effort to curtail his alcoholic activity.

And perhaps Brownie was in earnest when – or whenever – he volunteered co-operation. Addicts are supposed to long to be free of their addiction. But he had been issued with the sort of challenge he could not resist. The more Hereward supervised and investigated his movements, where he was, what he was up to, whether or not he had had time to sink a Guinness, the more elusive and evasive he became. He began to drink not only because he needed to – also to put one over on his authoritarian mentor.

Hereward raged unrestrainedly now, as at a partner who had let him down. He threatened to divulge the secret they shared to Jacques, painted grim pictures of Brownie's future if he got the sack, tried conciliatory tactics, appealed to better feelings, gave innumerable pep talks and extracted as many solemn promises.

He was frustrated, exasperated, and in his exasperation inclined to go too far – thus making the very mistake he sought to correct, if verbally as opposed to alcoholically.

Again he caught Brownie emerging from a pub, inebriated beyond the shadow of a doubt.

'How could you?' he demanded.

'Oh, sir – I couldn't help it, sir – I heard today that my brother had to have his leg off.'

'You've always got some feeble excuse,' Hereward retorted.

He apologised afterwards. He had to apologise almost as often as Brownie did. His nerves were stretched near to breaking-point as the battle wore on.

In several of their skirmishes his defeats were mysterious. Since so many promises had been broken, he broke his and confided in Jacques. Between them they concocted a generally beneficial plot. In the course of a weekend, in Brownie's absence, Hereward thoroughly and in vain searched the kitchen for drink. On the Monday morning Jacques asked for and received every possible assurance that Brownie had no drink hidden in his locked bedroom. Jacques then accompanied Brownie to the shops to buy things for his dinner party in the evening. For the rest of the day, during which Brownie was forbidden to leave the premises, Hereward kept a sharp eye on him. Jacques, home from work, retrieved the bottles from the cupboard under the stairs and decanted the wine, and later he himself charged the glasses of his guests.

Brownie passed out nonetheless between the meat and the pudding.

Where, when and how had he obtained the means?

It might have been in connection with that episode, as inexplicable as it was inexcusable, that he played his trump card – or suggested he had such a trump literally up his sleeve. Under interrogation he referred to his tumours. He rolled the sleeve of his shirt to the elbow and displayed the lumps in his forearm.

He would recall that his mother had died in screaming agony of a tumour behind her eye and say he had been having headaches which frightened him out of his wits. He implied that his behaviour could in no way be accounted for, except by a tumour forming in his brain – and if so he was the innocent victim of a terrible error on the part of his bosses, who should pity instead of persecuting him.

More than likely he was crying wolf as before, although louder. Yet the mysteriousness of his addiction or disease or whatever it was tended to reinforce his latest threat – or defensive response to threats. He would pop round to the tobacconist's for a packet of Woodbines and return drunk in a matter of five minutes. He would trip lightly down the stairs to lay the table for a party and soon hardly be able to stumble up. And his health was unquestionably going to pot, Hereward's remedial efforts notwithstanding. He was at once thin and puffy round the jowls, and heavy-eyed, with none of his former zeal and zip. His clothes were slovenly and his kitchen past praying for.

Early one morning there was a commotion in the kitchen, shouts, curses, sounds of furniture being manhandled and breaking glass.

'What's happening, Brownie?'

'I've got a rat in here.'

'You've got a what?'

'A blasted rat, sir! It's as big as a dachshund!'

'What are you doing to it?'

'I'm shying milk bottles at it.'

Esoteric swear-words were heard, followed by a bang and the tinkle of more breaking glass.

Hereward and Jacques hurried to join Brownie, who was sweating profusely and trembling.

'Where is this rat?'

'It just went behind the fridge.'

'Right – I'll pull the fridge away from the wall and you two get ready to wallop it with brooms – okay?'

But the rat had vanished.

'I saw it, sir – large as life – it had a nasty sneering sort of expression – honestly, sir!'

'Where did it come from?'

'It stepped in through the window – it marched along the parapet outside and jumped in – it looked me straight in the eye – I'm not exaggerating, sir!'

'Well, it seems to have made itself scarce. I wouldn't worry any more, Brownie. You'd better clear up all the mess.'

The rat could have been real or a sad hallucination due to a brain tumour. But Brownie's bosses veered towards the opinion that it was a figment of his befuddled imagination – in other words he had had an attack of *delirium tremens.*

The climax occurred in the ninth year of the triangular arrangement at Windle Road.

Jacques gave a dinner party for Colonel de Chiffre, who was staying in his spare room. Hereward, having spent the evening out with friends, returned at ten o'clock and was climbing the maisonette stairs to the top floor. Brownie lurched from the kitchen bearing the main course on a platter – a loveable duck dissected, *pommes fantastiques* and vegetables. He was intoxicated. On the landing he subsided quite slowly onto one knee, while the platter tipped and pieces of duck slid off it and gravy dripped on the carpet and the miniature roast potato balls bounced down the staircase.

And gazing at Hereward horror-struck he mumbled: 'Oh sir – what will Monsieur le Colonel say?'

In the morning there was the worst row ever. But Brownie was about to go on his annual holiday. He managed to persuade everyone that after a fortnight's rest he would be a different person.

He departed, leaving his kitchen looking like a bomb-site and his bedroom locked. Hereward worked for two days at cleaning the kitchen, and then on an angry impulse swung himself through the window onto the parapet where the rat had marched, and edged along and peered into Brownie's room. Fifty or a hundred empty bottles of wine and spirits lay all over the floor. The bed was unmade – the sheets were greenish-brown. Putrid socks, shirts, trousers and shoes were scattered amongst the bottles. The washbasin was encrusted with grime.

Brownie's holiday did him no good. He had only the vaguest recollection of the places he had visited. Somewhere he had gone in for horseback riding: he said his legs were stiff and chafed and walked with them bowed like a cowboy.

But Jacques and Hereward were not in the mood for jokes. Jacques reminded Brownie of the fiasco of that last party, and complained of the shambles of his bedroom and his tipsy homecoming. He ran through the history of their association and what he had put up with. He declared that now Brownie must agree to see his – Jacques' – doctor and submit to treatment, or else they would have to part.

Brownie demurred once more. He dreaded the medical profession, which, he asserted, went berserk with excitement on catching a glimpse of the rarity of his tumours. He related that in the past he had consulted a doctor about a stye in his eye, was ordered to undress completely and ushered stark naked on to the stage in a theatre crammed with students. At Windle Road he had always recoiled from professional investigation of the various maladies he said he suffered from.

But he was hoisted on the petard of his recent inflation of those maladies. He could not warn his employer he was dangerously ill and refuse a request to prove it. He had to choose between accepting a condition he himself had caused to be imposed on his continued service, and dismissal from his job for drunkenness.

He saw Jacques' doctor, who sent him to hospital for tests. Apparently his liver, kidneys, blood, digestion and nerves were in a shocking state. Almost the only thing that was not wrong with him was his brain. He was advised, and received permission and encouragement from Jacques and Hereward, to do the necessary cure.

It seemed to be successful. Two months later, back at work, he did seem to have become a different person – pink-cheeked, clear-eyed, slim, no longer puffy, calm, clean, stronger and more active. He was full of the doctors, nurses and other patients in the hospital, who had thought the world of him.

He kept it up for about a fortnight.

As soon as he relapsed, Jacques announced that he had had enough.

Then Jacques was recalled to work in the head-office of his bank in France.

And at the same time the landlords of Windle Road realised they were charging too little for the maisonette and doubled the rent.

Brownie would be unemployed. Hereward was losing his tenant, and had neither the financial resources nor the temerity to assume sole responsibility for a new expensive lease of his home. Jacques packed his belongings.

After ten years together they all prepared to go their separate ways.

FOUR

JACQUES said goodbye, and arranged for his pieces of furniture to be removed from his flat, including the bookcase that had stood in the entrance hall.

The removal of the bookcase uncovered a two-foot-square hinged grille into the cupboard under the stairs in which Jacques had carefully locked his wine and spirits.

'Well, fancy that, Brownie!' Hereward commented. 'One mystery's solved at any rate. Now I know how and where you got hold of your drink without leaving the house. You just shifted the bookcase and reached in for it. And I used to think you were cleaning when I heard you banging about down here. You're too crafty by half – helping Monsieur Beausson to put his bottles out of harm's way and making such a palaver with the key – and having your own secret door into the cupboard all the time!'

Brownie pretended to be surprised by the revelation of the grille.

'But didn't you ever move the bookcase in order to dust behind it?' Hereward persisted. 'Either you were aware of the existence of a second door, and therefore in a position to open it and get at the booze, or you weren't doing the dusting part of your job properly.'

'I must have slipped up on the dusting, sir,' Brownie decided with a shifty giggle.

There had been no recurrence of his one relapse too many following his cure. He was still reeling from the implementation of the repetitive threat in which he had ceased to believe – irreversible now that Jacques was in France. He could not count on a blameless reference from his ex-boss. His future in his mid-forties was to say the least uncertain. He was probably trying hard not to compromise it further.

Hereward was paying his wages in the meanwhile, but explained that he could only afford to do so on a temporary basis.

He was a stricter employer than Jacques: he had more opportunities to be strict since he worked at home; maybe he was more dogged, more determined to win the battle for Brownie's well-being, or more competitive, more reluctant to admit he was beaten; and naturally he wanted to receive full value for the greater proportion of his income – and indeed capital – he was investing in Brownie's services.

The combination of his own abstemiousness and his shortage of cash to spend on alcoholic beverages for guests meant that Brownie was not exposed to temptation as he had been. He did not give parties. He did not have people to stay. He did not like to eat food flavoured with strange herbs unobtainable except in Soho. He attempted to lead a quiet regular life. Moreover he was English and had been in the army, he had a native understanding and some experience of the type of man he was dealing with, just as he was understood for the same reasons. He was also accessible and easy to talk to.

All this was good for Brownie, who began to demonstrate his trust in Hereward – whether or not his motives were as ambiguous as usual.

He described his time in hospital in more detail.

'They had genuine alcoholics there. They shut the worst ones in padded cells. We used to hear them howling and doing their best to bash their brains out.'

'That can't have been very nice.'

'We howled right back at them. We told them to put a sock in it. They were stupid. They smuggled in drink if they could. They bribed the nurses and porters to bring them drink. They couldn't think of nothing else. A terrible lot of drinking went on in the place.'

'Did you partake?'

'No, sir.'

Sometimes he spoke sympathetically of his fellow-patients.

'We got every sort in hospital, company directors, top executives – you'd be amazed. We had a vicar with letters after his name. He was the most pleasant gentleman you could meet in a day's march. His wife and his children had left him, and he'd lost his money and his house and his job – he was sacked for being paralytic in the pulpit. He said he drank anything – communion wine, meths, cider laced with the white spirit painters wash their brushes in, women's perfume. He'd drunk his whole life away.'

'I hope he taught you a lesson, Brownie.'

'Yes, sir. But I couldn't help feeling sorry for him. He was teetotal until he was forty. Then an old lady in his parish gave him a recipe for making wine from cowslips. He tried it, he got interested in making wine, and five years later he found himself in a padded cell.'

As a rule Brownie's reminiscences were less morbid.

'I did a spot of PT in the mornings, fed like a fighting cock, lazed around in the afternoons with the telly blasting, and in the evenings I played snooker with my Dr Martin. He was a beautiful doctor, sir. He thought I was the pig's whiskers.'

'You really enjoyed your cure, didn't you?'

'I did, sir – really.'

The latter statement was tinged with doubt.

'Was your treatment nasty?'

'No, not too bad, except for the electric shocks.'

'Did they give you electric shocks?'

'Oh yes, sir – I must have had half a dozen.'

'But what on earth for?'

'For my condition. I wasn't on the alcoholic side, sir. It was a hospital for nervous diseases with the alcoholics on one side and the rest of us in a separate building on the other. Dr Martin diagnosed my condition the minute he set eyes on me. He said I was nowhere near an alcoholic.'

'What did he say you were?'

'Schizophrenic, sir.'

'But, Brownie, you're no more schizophrenic than I am! That's ridiculous!'

'That's what he said, sir.'

'Did he talk to you? Did he go into your case thoroughly? I mean – did you talk to him?'

'Oh yes, sir, we had some long talks.'

'Well, you obviously tied him in knots if he was persuaded that your problem was schizophrenia. What else did he do to you apart from the electric shocks?'

'I had insulin, sir. I was in a coma for a couple of weeks. They pumped insulin into me and just woke me up to eat. I had to eat two meals at a time to counteract the insulin – two breakfasts of grapefruit, porridge, egg, bacon, sausage, a rack of six rounds of toast with lashings of butter and marmalade, washed down by a pint of white coffee – and the same again with lunch and tea and dinner.'

'How could you swallow so much food?'

'It was the dope, sir. I could have swallowed a horse. My appetite was awful.'

'Brownie – I still can't quite believe in the electric shocks. What were they like?'

'I was taken along to a kind of operating theatre. They fixed wires to my head and plugged me in. Afterwards I couldn't walk straight. I felt as if I'd had a few jars.'

'When did you begin to mend?'

'When they cut me off the insulin, sir. A nurse took me for walks in the hospital grounds with a packet of biscuits in her pocket. She handed me a biscuit if I got drowsy. Without the biscuit I would have slipped back into a coma. Dr Martin was very pleased with my progress.'

'I bet he was, considering he was treating you for a disease you didn't have.'

Hereward reverted to the topic.

'Listen – I'm bewildered by your account of what happened to you in hospital. You arrived there with alcohol coming out of your ears – and say you had to undergo a completely unnecessary cure for schizophrenia. My guess is that you talked yourself into the wrong stream on purpose. Didn't you even mention your drinking to Dr Martin? Did he have nothing to say about that?'

'He said it was a symptom of the schizophrenia, sir.'

'But schizophrenia means a split personality. Schizophrenics who require electric shocks are more or less up the pole. You must have played a pretty funny game with your Dr Martin. Did you put any other bright ideas into his head?'

'No, sir.'

'He passed you fit when you'd recovered from his treatment?'

'Yes, sir. I was over my malnutrition by then.'

'Malnutrition? What next, Brownie? I should think you had got over it with your double breakfasts and so on! But for heaven's sake – this house was knee-deep in stuff to eat when Monsieur Beausson threw parties. You can't convince me you were starved here.'

'I didn't bother to feed myself if I was on the sherbet, sir.'

'When you were on the sherbet – not if you were on it.'

'Yes, sir.'

'Well – now you're sober, and not under-nourished, and have been treated for schizophrenia, can you tell me why you let drink get the upper hand of you and ruin your prospects?'

'I mixed in bad company.'

'In pubs, you mean?'

'Not only in pubs. Those chefs in the hotel where I was sent for cooking lessons, they drank like a shoal of fishes. And you remember Madame Drey? She drank enough to sink a battleship – although she was so thin you could have sliced bacon with her. She killed a bottle of whisky stone dead during each of our sessions in the kitchen. And then the cleaning lady Mrs Whitworth – she was a wild beast for drink.'

'Are you suggesting nothing was your fault?'

'No, sir – but they got me going. Afterwards, when I was worried or needed cheering up, I was inclined to have one.'

'Or two or three.'

'Yes, sir.'

'What puzzles me is that you seem to be far more cheerful without drink than you ever were with it.'

'I know. I've been the biggest fool. But I've registered the message at last. And as they say, sir – better late than never.'

'Well – yes – I agree – and I don't want to bully you or rake over the past. But the most important question for both of us is whether the hospital produced any permanent late solutions, and if you're likely to feel in need of cheering up in the future.'

'I won't, sir – that I can promise you. I've seen the light, I swear.'

'Please don't swear, Brownie, whatever else you do. If you begin to swear, I'll be sure you're lying.'

Ambiguity must be contagious. Hereward had caught a dose of it. For while he sternly lectured and pedantically corrected and preached the virtues of sobriety in such conversations, he was half-hoping Brownie would get drunk again. In that case he could point to the failure of every experiment, and, following Jacques' example as an employer, call it a day. With justification he could lay down the moral and financial burden of Brownie – and concentrate on the more vital business of supporting himself.

His hope was disappointed. Butter would not have melted in Brownie's mouth in this interim period. He was subdued and acquiescent, alert, willing, and never caused embarrassment by inquiring into his boss's plans in the longer term. He conveyed the impression that he relied absolutely on Hereward, who was thus the more embroiled in his destiny.

Occasionally the past was raked over, in spite of Hereward's stated wish – or rather the past had its effect on the present. Why had it taken Brownie two hours to buy an evening paper – had he been up to his old tricks – how was he ever to be trusted – and how could he expect anyone to pay wages for the pleasure of being kept on tenterhooks? Brownie would establish his innocence without reproaching Hereward for injuring it. He was sad not be be given the benefit of the doubt he now deserved – he might shed a few crocodile tears – but quick to accept an apology and forgive and forget. His policy resembled the military strategy of coaxing an invader so deep into your territory that he cannot retreat.

Hereward had an uneasy feeling he was being subjected to Brownie's patent process, which converted masters into servants. To sack him as it were in cold blood was becoming increasingly difficult. To advance the base argument of money – or the lack of it – as the reason to terminate their close sort of friendship went against the grain. The passage of each impeccable week reinforced the extravagant notion of their having to sink or swim together.

Moreover Hereward was obliged to admit that Brownie was his chief material asset, if not his only one. He had been cosseted for ten years, and enabled to write his books without too many interruptions, by Brownie. Supposing he provided a roof over their heads, it was just conceivable that he could market the talents and some of the time of his manservant, while they continued to enjoy the apparently mutual benefits of co-habitation.

There were two large stumbling-blocks in the way of the scheme.

The prices and rents of suitable accommodation were prohibitive.

And no outsider was going to pay Brownie a penny for being drunk and disorderly.

Hereward's predicament was frightening. A roof over his own head, let alone Brownie's, seemed to be beyond his means. In the unlikely event of his finding a dirt-cheap flat with the right number of rooms, he could not guarantee that Brownie would not turn into his chief liability. As it was, day by day, he was squandering his resources on a maisonette in the West End that was far too big for him, and on a butler-cum-valet-cum-cook who was equally above his financial station. He saw himself on the breadline round the next corner, dragging Brownie after him like a ball and chain.

Then the same kind sister who had encouraged him to lease Windle Road came to the rescue. She was keen for him to buy a house for sale in a cul-de-sac in Hampstead. It was again a bargain, dilapidated yet potentially desirable, quiet and yet close to shops and bus-routes, and had a basement he could let. She offered to contribute to the purchase price.

He was touched by her generosity, grateful and hesitant. The house was of a size which frightened him almost as much as the prospect of homelessness. He would not be able to live there, and carry on writing, without practical daily help: which raised the question of Brownie in a more vexatious pressing form.

The fortunes of the Watkins family were mobilised in support of the project. Hereward's mother promised to chip in with money, and another sister with furniture. But he still hesitated.

He sought guidance everywhere. Should he commit himself to the swings and roundabouts of a haven in Hampstead plus Brownie? Or should he get rid of Brownie, repudiate extraneous responsibilities, travel light, and look for a lonely garret in the suburbs?

He discussed his quandary with an acquaintance, Dr White, a qualified psychiatrist, who told him categorically to steer clear of lame ducks at all costs.

The consensus of hard-headed opinion was that sooner or later Brownie was bound to be reclaimed by his alcoholic habits.

Eventually Hereward reached his independent decision.

He showed Brownie the house and asked if he would like to work there. He explained his finances fully – what revenue he could depend on, what rent from a basement tenant he hoped for, what annual salary he might rustle up. He proposed that if Brownie settled for Hampstead he should take time off as required to do dinners and odd jobs for other people in order to supplement his income. He said he refused to believe that history always repeats itself – he was therefore ready to gamble on Brownie sticking to the straight and narrow. The single string attached to the job was total abstinence.

Brownie was relieved and excited. He brushed aside Hereward's reminder that he could probably obtain more remunerative employment elsewhere. No other boss would be so good and kind, he declared.

On the strength of his reaction the deal was clinched with estate agents and lawyers.

That evening Brownie celebrated.

★ ★ ★

The following morning Hereward broke his word.

At least he suspended the condition of abstinence he had insisted on, and Brownie had accepted, the previous day. He was afraid his decision had been wrong, that Dr White and company had already been proved right, and he was now compounding his wilful foolish behaviour with his weakness. But his heart was not hard enough to be impervious to exceptionally contrite and credible appeals for one more chance. And he was reluctant to cancel all his elaborate plans twenty-four hours after he had put them into operation.

For better or worse Brownie looked at the matter from a different point of view. As he seemed to see it, Hereward was honouring his word under stress and re-affirming his trust and faith in the penitent sinner he was raising to the status of an indispensable colleague. Brownie was not only grateful and gratified, he was also confronted by the challenge of his new master's attitude: he too could act like a proper gentleman.

He said: 'I'll pay you back, sir – you'll never regret it!' which hackneyed assurances were remarkable in that they were nearly true.

The above sequence of events – Hereward's creation of a future for Brownie notwithstanding his awareness of the risks he ran: Brownie's instant destructiveness which Hereward chose not to penalise although entitled to – was a watershed in their story.

From then on water figured in it more than ever before. Brownie actually began to drink water when he was thirsty, or tea or coffee to cheer himself up. He grew more confidential the more he was certain he could have confidence in someone who had confidence in him. He substantiated the claim that Hereward had saved his life.

'I was drinking more than I let on, sir. I was horrible. I couldn't get out of bed in the morning without a snifter.'

'What of?'

'Whisky or vodka.'

'What do you call a snifter?'

'Well, a snifter's a snort, and a snort's a miniature.'

'I'm sorry – I don't understand – what's a miniature?'

'A miniature bottle, sir.'

'Don't those miniature bottles come in various sizes?'

'Yes, sir. I drank the sort that's half the size of a whole bottle.'

'You drank half a bottle of whisky or vodka before breakfast?'

'It was my breakfast, sir. I shouldn't think I ate a decent meal in three years. I couldn't fancy food. I didn't seem to need it – alcohol's nourishing, they say. But not eating played Old Harry with my insides and my nerves and the rest of me. Dr Martin said I was rotten right through at my first examination. He would have given me six months if I hadn't been treated in hospital. And if you'd given me the push the other day, sir, I definitely would have started again and drunk myself under ground.'

'What happened to you after drinking half a bottle of spirits for breakfast?'

'I kept topped up.'

'How?'

'In pubs, when I was meant to be shopping. I bought drink in off-licences, too.'

'And brought it home?'

'Yes, sir.'

'I knew you did. I knew you had it somewhere – and used to search for it at weekends and at other times when you weren't around. I found lots of empties, for instance in your bedroom during your last holiday, but never what I was looking for.'

'I hid it, sir. You remember the milk bottles I washed and lined alongside my sink? You probably thought there was water in them. In fact it was vodka or gin.'

He referred to that holiday which led to his final collapse and hospitalisation: 'It was crazy. One day I was supping cider in Somerset and the next I was riding horseback in the Isle of Wight. I couldn't have told you where I was or how I got there. I slept on beaches or in public parks. And every night I believed I'd wake up dead in the morning.'

He reminisced about his former involvement with the charity called The Blind Scribe.

'We collected money for it in a Working Men's Club I belonged to down Plumstead way. We organised weekly raffles, and on a Saturday every year we hired a coach and took a load of blind guests to a beauty spot, Canterbury Cathedral, or the tulip fields in Lincolnshire.'

'But the blind people couldn't see the tulips.'

'None of us could, sir. We were all intoxicated by the time we reached our destination. The coach pulled in at roadside pubs. After half a dozen pubs our guests were paralysed as well. We had an awful job, hauling them back to their seats.'

'Talk of the blind leading the blind!'

Brownie giggled ruefully and added: 'They loved the outing, sir. They laughed and sang, although once we got an awkward so-and-so who tried to batter somebody's head in with his white stick. It was just a bit of fun.'

'Tell me – what was your tipple in these innumerable pubs you patronised?'

'Ales and stout, sir – Guinness – and chasers. Often the chasers came in ahead of the ales and stout.'

'Is a chaser neat spirits?'

'Yes, sir.'

'What did you use for money?'

'I was in terrible debt. I owed money everywhere. When I was too skint for chasers I concentrated on beer. Now I can't stand a man on the beer near me – the stench makes me want to vomit. I wonder you didn't complain, sir.'

'I did, Brownie.'

'Sorry, sir.'

In the course of the move from Windle Road he showed Hereward an ornamental tankard he was about to pack.

He said it was a prize.

'What for?'

'Drinking.'

'How much did you drink to win it?'

'Twenty-one pints.'

'You're joking!'

'No, sir! I drank twenty-one pints in four hours. Here's a photograph of me doing it.'

He unearthed a luridly coloured snapshot of himself standing at a bar, crimson in the face, sweating and grinning with the tankard raised.

'I was ill for a fortnight afterwards,' he admitted.

On the day of the move, when the fridge was dragged clear of the kitchen wall, the dehydrated corpse of a rat was found to be lodged behind the motor.

Brownie was triumphant.

'What did I say? Look at it, sir! You and Monsieur Beausson thought I was seeing things. You thought I had DTs. But I was seeing straight – I was right all along! There's the rat to prove I was telling you the truth!'

It was characteristic of him to confess he had drunk twenty-one pints of beer at a sitting, and then assert that none of his senses had ever been affected by his abuse of alcohol. Naturally he was pleased to be vindicated. But he also wanted to retreat a step or two into his favourite shadows of ambiguity, from which he had allowed himself to be enticed. And as usual he could not let slip an opportunity to boast of his toughness.

Hereward's bank-balance was in a bad way while he waited to get into his house, in spite of subsidies from his family.

One morning he received a legalistic letter from his landlords at Windle Road, invoking the clause of his lease that enjoined re-decoration of the maisonette throughout before he left it.

He was stunned. He had not bargained for extra costs of maybe a thousand pounds to have the job done professionally. He threw the letter at Brownie, whose response was the more stoical the more frantic his boss became.

'We'll have to set to ourselves, sir.'

Whereupon he stripped off his white jacket and painted from dawn to dusk for a fortnight, tireless and always cheery, assisted by Hereward and an old-age pensioner by the name of Steve, probably a companion of his drinking days, whom he persuaded to help in return for free meals.

The work was finished, dead-lines were met, and Hereward's bill amounted to some thirty pounds for materials.

'You were marvellous, Brownie. I don't know how to repay you. I saved your life, you say. Well, you've saved my bacon. And you managed it on nothing stronger than cups of tea.'

They removed into 32 Trafalgar Terrace, N.W.3.

The basement had been converted into a self-contained flat, which was quickly furnished and let. On the ground floor were the entrance passage leading to the stairs, a bed-sitting-room for a lodger, Brownie's bedroom at the back, and a bathroom tacked on in the two-storey addition: Brownie and the lodger were to share the bathroom. His kitchen, where he had his TV and easy chair, adjoined Hereward's combined sitting and dining-room on the first floor. On the second and top floor were Hereward's bedroom-study and his bathroom.

They had more space than they were accustomed to. The rooms were larger with generous windows and higher ceilings. The front ones looked across the wide road at the flowers and trees in the gardens opposite, and from the rear ones the hillock of Highgate crowned with a church spire was visible. The house faced south-east and north-west, so that the sun shone in morning and evening. And the light seemed to be brighter, and the air fresher and purer, than at Windle Road. The season was spring: birds sang with rustic rapture in the dusty littered greenery of Hampstead Heath.

'What do you think of it, Brownie?'

'Champion, sir!'

The cul-de-sac was about a hundred and fifty yards in length. On one side of number 32 it was residential, on the other were the shops as in a village. All the houses, including those turned into shops, and the pub on the corner, were of roughly the same Victorian-Edwardian date. A central alley connected Trafalgar Terrace with the mews that ran along behind Brownie's kitchen.

A lodger materialised. The rents now flowing into Hereward's coffers allayed his dread of penury – and of no longer being able to follow his calling. He settled down and resumed his routine: breakfast at seven, writing until one, lunch and the afternoon off, a walk, tea, more writing, seeing friends if possible, and an early bed. Every three or four weeks he spent a few days with his family at Watkins Hall. As a rule he did not bother about an annual holiday.

Such disciplined regularity seemed to be the sort of straitjacket that Brownie needed. He rose at six forty-five, served breakfast and as it was being consumed gave Hereward's room a cat's lick and a promise, went shopping, cleaned the other rooms, cooked lunch, did more shopping in the afternoon and polished the brasses on the front door and gossiped with passers-by, switched on the telly at six, prepared and served supper, and then smoked and dozed in his easy chair until bed-time. At intervals he visited his daughter and son-in-law and grandchildren, usually when Hereward was away for weekends. Every year, in the second fortnight of August, he repaired to a Butlin's Holiday Camp.

He was too busy to get bored: soon he was not only doing the contractual minimum of cleaning for the male lodger, but valeting his clothes and running errands. To the pretty young female tenant of the basement flat he lent kitchen equipment, and he cooked titbits and washed up for her. Half the householders in the terrace entrusted him with keys of their properties: he was always having to hurry somewhere to let in a gas-man or walk a dog or accept a delivery or draw curtains to bamboozle burglars.

Hereward warned him not to repeat his mistake of making an impossible amount of work for himself.

'But I love it, sir. And I feel so fit! And I never could say no to peoples.'

While his life on the whole was sufficiently humdrum and monotonous not to fray his nerves, it did not lack the essential ingredient of variety. At Hereward's suggestion party-givers of his acquaintance tried Brownie out, and were predictably delighted. The telephone began to ring for Brownie almost as often as it did for his master, his diary was full of engagements, and once or twice a week he would leave the house at three or four o'clock and return at midnight, having produced more or less of a banquet. Thus he was kept on his toes as he described it – his culinary talents were exercised, his gastronomic snobbery was indulged, also his social snobbery, since he met all the nobs at his parties, and he reaped an abundant harvest of praise.

Incidentally, for Hereward, a special satisfaction was that Mrs White, the wife of the psychiatrist who had advised him to have no dealings with lame ducks, was amongst Brownie's more demanding clients.

In short the gamble was paying – literally. Brownie's low weekly wage was just adequate during bad patches without extra-mural dinners. But in a good patch he earned a small fortune in fees and tips over and above it – and his entire income was pocket-money considering he was boarded and fed. He was able to buy expensive presents for his family, invest in new suits and still put a bit aside.

His liquid assets were not draining away. Part of the secret of the success of Hereward's scheme was that Brownie was not boozing – apparently he was at last adhering to his resolutions. He retained certain habits he had formed in bars: for instance he swallowed his tea lukewarm and in a single draught from an enormous cup that held a pint, and measured his daily intake of tea in pints. He resorted to the substitute of fizzy lemonade, dozens of bottles of which he martialled regimentally within reach of his kitchen chair. And he could not altogether change his spots, that is to say his addictive personality: he started to eat too much, and similarly to smoke his pipe – in twenty-four hours he got through two ounces of the strongest tobacco on the market. But, suspect as his friendship with the landlord of the village pub might be, there was no evidence to suggest that Brownie was one of his better customers.

The other part of the secret was his happiness. He was personally succeeding where many had failed, he was winning general approval instead of disapproval, and working for an English or at any rate a Welsh gentleman in a gentleman's residence, and mixing with the gentry to his heart's content.

He whistled loudly and out of tune as he attended to his duties. He was so spontaneously happy that he omitted to affect an inability to whistle. Or he sang a snatch of the vulgar Black Watch version of *The Ball of Kirriemuir:* 'Five and twenty maidenheads / Lined up against a wall . . .' If he and Hereward were in London on a Sunday afternoon he pinned a Do-Not-Disturb notice on the door of his kitchen.

'May I come in?'

'Entrez, Monsieur.'

He would be sitting somnolent in his chair, replete after a gargantuan meal, enveloped in tobacco smoke, surrounded by lemonade bottles, watching a Western on his telly.

'Where are you, Brownie? I can scarcely see you for smoke. It's like a Turkish brothel in here.'

'Not much of a brothel, sir, without any goods for sale. All the same it's nice.'

Happiness is fattening. He became a jolly fat man with double chins and a belly that burst the relevant buttons on his shirts. He began to utter his complaint that modern clothes in the shops were made for queers, meaning persons thinner than he was. He would draw in his midriff and inflate his chest and flex his biceps and say his figure was too fine for the skimpy products of the rag trade.

At other times, if anyone criticised his girth, he would hold his breath until his eyes protruded alarmingly and his face turned purple, blow out his cheeks and thrust out his stomach, so that he looked like a gross apoplectic toad.

It was a joke, intended to show how little he cared.

But he was worried when he discovered he weighed nearly sixteen stone.

'You'll have to eat less, Brownie.'

'I've stopped drinking, sir. I can't stop eating. You'll want me to stop breathing next.'

He claimed he had heavy bones and was growing more muscular: 'I'm built on the lines of a bison.' He nonetheless went on a permanent diet, at least in theory. He would starve himself for a few days, or cut down to one daily meal instead of four, or resist bread and potatoes, or ration his pints of tea – and boast of his iron will.

But he was inclined to forget he was meant to be slimming. And the customs of his class were against him: he visited members of his family who expressed their affectionate feelings by stuffing him with great greasy cooked breakfasts, lunches on outsize plates, salmon salads and meat sandwiches at six o'clock, and a milky drink and a half-pound packet of Custard Cream biscuits before retiring. For that matter the nature of his work was no help: he had to taste, and no doubt he was tantalised beyond bearing by, the food he was employed to cook.

However, forgetfulness and extenuating circumstances apart, he again invested Hereward with an authority which he then seemed to be determined to flout. The thing he could never stop doing was to practise his deceptions.

'Brownie, what's become of the roast chicken we had for dinner the other evening?'

'You ate most of it, sir. And I had a morsel. And it was really a *poussin,* sir. I gave the carcase to a hungry old-age pensioner I know to make a bowl of broth with ...'

'Brownie, why are you cooking so much stew?'

'I thought you might have guests, sir. And I'll be needing a saucer-full. You can't run a car without petrol. Well – I can't run myself ragged for you for about a hundred hours a week without any nourishment. Besides, whatever's left of the stew won't be wasted. It'll keep me going for four or five days ...'

He exaggerated. His stews did not last so long. After twenty-four hours, when he had finished them, he would tell Hereward they had turned nasty. The saucer referred to belonged to his pint cup and was as big as a soup-plate.

Hereward, who liked his bread brown, would enquire: 'Why did I find a loaf of white bread hidden behind the glasses in the glass cupboard?'

'Is that where I put it? I was hunting for it all over. I'm so absent-minded! Thank you for finding it, sir. I bought it for your breadcrumbs. I wanted it to get stale enough to grate into breadcrumbs.'

'But it's only a bit of a loaf.'

'I cut the crusts off, sir, so it would get stale quicker.'

'But each of the crusts must have been a quarter of the loaf.'

'Oh no, sir. The baker told me it was a new shape. The crusts I cut were no thicker than shavings.'

'What did you do with them?'

'I chucked them out for a sparrow. I didn't eat them, if that's what you're thinking, sir. I'm on my diet, remember – which wouldn't permit me.'

Sometimes he played the game in a different way.

On being asked what he had done with crusts of forbidden bread he replied defiantly: 'I scoffed them with oodles of dripping!'

Hereward would laugh and comment: 'Well, it's your own lookout. I'd far rather you were fat than drunk. But I understood you were dead-set on losing weight. All I can say is you won't on bread and dripping.'

Brownie's defence of his lapses in this context included the taunt that he consoled himself with food because he was not allowed to consort with women.

'But you are, Brownie! I wish you did more consorting. You'd be less lonely and less likely to be tempted back into pubs. Why not marry again?'

'No, thanks, sir – I've been bitten!'

'You could consort without marrying. You've got your room downstairs. What goes on in it is your business.'

'Let a female foot in the door? Never, sir! There'd be hell to pay.'

'Consort elsewhere in that case. Take a woman to a cinema or a theatre. You can have as much free time as you like.'

'What about my work, sir? You've no idea how hard I have to work to keep you straight.'

'Nonsense, Brownie! You spend hours smoking in your kitchen chair. You might just as well be enjoying yourself with a member of the opposite sex. In my opinion it'd do you good.'

Hereward meant it. He was vaguely concerned by Brownie's reluctance to project the normalisation of his existence into normal social, not to mention sexual, intercourse. He guessed that a subsidiary bad habit of Brownie's was not to mix with people except in the street, in shops and particularly in pubs. He hoped that Brownie was now afraid of being pressed to have a quick one by hospitable friends and acquaintances. A sensible middle-aged maternal type would keep him safely and soberly under her wing and be company for him.

But Brownie was adamant. He refused invitations even to have a cup of coffee in another house. And he never returned to see his cronies in the Windle Road area – maybe because he had left unpaid debts behind him.

As for the question of women, Hereward was discomforted later on by his naive attempts to answer it.

Brownie's alcoholic preoccupations had been exclusive – and blurred every issue for ten years. Divorced, uninspired by drink, older and fatter, he seemed to lack libidinous initiative and self-confidence. He over-ate, he said his kitchen on a Sunday afternoon was not much of a brothel, and put the blame on his boss.

Hereward might have saved himself the trouble of encouraging Brownie, whose sex-appeal was at once magnetic and perennial. He could seduce any woman of any age and description in one way or another. He was therefore in a position to pick and choose – and if and when he felt like doing so, he chose not a middle-aged maternal type but the most nubile piece of grummet available.

At the same time he knew the score. He had had the lesson dinned into him not merely by his wife. By temperament he was too flirtatious and provocative, too fickle, and too vulnerable for the war of the sexes. He was cynical about women – he derided them, he dreaded their inevitable reproaches, as only a male chauvinist who has often been loved and hated can.

In principle – and in the meanwhile – he preferred his plaintive celibacy and to stay at home.

But there was always a gap between his principles and his practice. He could not help meeting women in the terrace. He showered terms of endearment on them indiscriminately: each was his sweetheart, his princess, his passion-flower, his luscious lump of Turkish delight, and more rudely his Polo Mint.

He would shout out to an old crock shuffling past in her bedroom slippers: 'How's your love-life, darling?'

His naughty jokes were rejuvenating. He could make even the sourest puss laugh. Almost every morning Hereward's writing was disturbed by shrieks of laughter from the street below. Brownie would be ringed round by a group of stout aggressive housewives, throwing back their heads and guffawing. He was so chatty, comical, quick at repartee and scandalously vulgar: married as no doubt they were to average dull prim husbands, it was not surprising that they fell for him. He offered to do their washing along with his own in the village launderette: 'My pants and your knickers could have a mad whirl together in the soapsuds.' He told them about a *budgeregard* – a budgerigar – and how it utilised the red-topped match it was given to play with. He went far too far, debunked, teased, and swapped recipes and insults.

'Never, Mr Brown! . . . Get away with you . . . None of your cheek now . . . You foul devil you!'

He fought their verbal battles with shopkeepers, who were terrified of his uninhibited tongue and talent for ridicule. He carried their shopping-bags and listened to their troubles and sympathised and cheered them up. He lent them money.

A pretty antique-dealer opened a shop in the terrace. Brownie developed a sudden interest in antiques. She resisted his light-hearted overtures. He had his revenge by spreading the story that she was a lesbian. Then she refused to speak to him. But one morning she called at number 32 and handed over ten pounds to Hereward.

She explained: 'I arrived at work the other day without my purse. I was desperate, in a rush, and didn't know where to turn. So I asked Brownie for a tenner. He's a dirty old man and a frightful liar. All the same I'm fond of him. And there's nobody else I would have liked to borrow from.'

He was generous – and receptive and unshockable – and the repository of secrets.

A girl in a flat across the terrace was deserted by her husband. She confessed to Brownie that she was being driven demented by the loss of her conjugal rights. She began to pester him with propositions.

Hereward suggested: 'Well, why not?'

'I can't fancy it.'

'The proverb says: don't look a gift-horse in the mouth.'

'She lives too close, sir. And another proverb says: don't mess in your own nest.'

A prerequisite of what he fancied was a sturdy pair of legs.

'I only go for girls with legs strong enough to crack a man like a nut.'

In spite of his ban on girls who lived too close, he did some consorting with a temporary neighbour named Maureen. The fact that Maureen was at least an amateur prostitute minimised his fear of involvement. After her departure he showed Hereward a photograph taken in her bed-sitting-room by a third party. In it he was fully dressed in his gentleman's gentleman's togs, dignified dark suit and overcoat and Homburg hat to match, and carried his rolled umbrella. But the umbrella in his right hand was raised as if to challenge the photographer to a duel, on his face was an expression of demonic glee, and his left hand was up Maureen's skirt.

There were a couple of real pros in the terrace, a mother and daughter, who apparently paid for everything with their favours, groceries, minicab rides. Brownie thought they were the accomplices of burglars and gave them the widest possible berth.

Once the harridan of a mother started to ask him leading questions. 'Why do you wear a white jacket? What do you and that tall fellow do for a living? What's your line of business?'

'We're abortionists,' he replied.

He got away with saying unforgivable things. He was always skirmishing with the Jewish family that ran the shop where he bought his tobacco. The wife of the proprietor attempted habitually, if in vain, to short-change him, he said. He concluded one of their public slanging-matches with the rhetorical exclamation: 'Why did Hitler let the ovens out?' Hereward was horrified when he was told about it. But Mrs Rosenberg reacted more in a Christian than a Jewish spirit. Turning the other cheek, she and her husband continued to sell Brownie his tobacco and laugh at his callous racialist sallies.

He did not reserve his offensive remarks which never seemed to offend for the weaker sex. He was friendly with a huge coal-black painter and decorator, Johnny Mgubba, who frequented the pub in the terrace. Johnny was apt to get drunk and to swagger up and down the street, beating his breast and bellowing: 'I am the Chief of all the Mgubbas!'

Brownie would greet him: 'Hullo, Johnny-boy! How's your health today? You're looking as white as a sheet.'

Before a General Election Brownie obliged Hereward by sticking a Conservative Party poster in a window.

Johnny Mgubba, who was passing, noticed and called: 'Hey! What are you doing? You're not Conservative.'

'That's right,' Brownie agreed non-committally.

'What's your politics then?'

'I support Enoch Powell.'

He was no respecter of persons, female, male, white, black, little, large, humble, grand – although superficially he could adapt like a chameleon to the class and susceptibilities of his companions. He was vulgar with the vulgar, common with commoners, refined with the refined, posh with the upper crust, and so on. But sooner or later he prevailed upon most people to rise or stoop to his basic level.

He laid siege to the daily cleaner from next door. She was in her fifties, married, respectable, even forbidding. He showed her snapshots of his grandchildren. They got on to Christian name terms. He began to escort her to her bus-stop in the afternoons.

One afternoon, as he assisted her into a crowded bus, he blew her a kiss and asked: 'Which night is it your husband's working, dear?' – so that everyone could hear.

On another afternoon he shouted after her: 'I never will believe it's my baby!'

The local chemist, a pal of his, employed an attractive bashful sixteen-year-old girl to serve his customers.

Brownie entered the shop and approached the counter.

'Oh – miss – I wonder – could I have a word with Mr Carter, please?' he enquired in a nervous tone of voice.

But Mr Carter had been briefed beforehand: mixing medicines behind a screen, he said he was occupied.

'Well, miss – it's like this, miss – I'm sure I don't know how to put it – I've never had much to do with ladies, miss – but my girlfriend's parents are on holiday and she's invited me to her place this evening and I don't want to get her in trouble – not the very first time, miss. Can you help me? Do you think – well – I ought to have something – take something with me – I mean just in case? Perhaps one of those things to wear – what are they called? And what size, miss?'

The wretched girl, having almost died of embarrassment, was revived by Brownie's involuntary laughter at his last question, in which Mr Carter, and she herself eventually, joined.

He had more fun and games in the houses where he cooked dinners, mainly with the maids, nannies, baby-sitters and au-pair girls who gave him a hand.

That could actually happen.

'Were you working on your own at the Lockett's?'

'No, sir. Their au-pair was with me in the kitchen.'

'What's she like?'

'Saucy, sir – we held hands in the washing-up water.'

He talked a lot about the capabilities and competence of a nanny in a certain house. Hereward's impression was that she must be the usual kindly old retainer. But then Brownie mentioned kisses.

'What sort of evening did you have?'

'Not bad – I got a kiss or two out of it.'

'Who kissed you?'

'Nanny, sir.'

'Really? And you and she kissed more than once?'

'Oh yes, sir.'

'I don't think I quite understand. Were these kisses pecks on the cheek?'

'No, sir – not pecks – proper knee-tremblers.'

He called proper or improper kisses either knee-tremblers or kilt-lifters.

'But, Brownie, what age is Nanny, for heaven's sake?'

'Eighteen, sir. She's a beautiful blonde with a figure like Marilyn Monroe.'

Hereward often warned Brownie not to practise his wiles on the youth and innocence of the girls he met in strange kitchens.

'The baby-sitter last night was a tasty bit of crackling.'

'I hope you didn't have a nibble.'

'Sir! She's younger than my daughter, sir! She's just a child.'

'That's what worries me. I don't trust you with female children.'

'They've all got to learn, haven't they?'

'Maybe – but not all of them necessarily from you.'

Sometimes one or other of the girls he had flirted with rang him up to propose that they should carry on in their spare time. He was disconcerted, and would protest coldly that none of his time was spare.

Once a client telephoned about her Fijian maid, who was sinking into a deep depression for unrequited love of Brownie.

'What did you do to her?'

'Nothing, sir.'

'I bet you led her up the garden path.'

But he was unrepentant.

He assumed that hackneyed hypocritical masculine attitude which is the strongest argument against permissiveness: 'Well – she didn't ought to have let herself be led.'

As a rule he succeeded in locking love out: his lust was so ruthlessly irresponsible. A former lodger in the room on the ground floor invited Brownie to his wedding. For a change he accepted, went along, kissed the bride, drank a glass of champagne to toast the happy pair, and ended by spending the night with a fellow-guest.

'She was full of the joys of spring. Women are pushovers after weddings.'

'Will you see her again?'

'I doubt it, sir.'

'Why not?'

'I'm not that keen.'

'Won't she want to see you?'

'I gave her the wrong telephone number.'

On holiday at a Butlin's Camp a girl he nicknamed Peanut became his partner for dancing etcetera. Evidently he was an expert dancer, rhythmical and light-footed, notwithstanding his bulk. He disengaged from Peanut by promising to meet her at the same time in the same place the following year – and promptly booked in at a different camp.

With the mistresses of the houses where he cooked he again had fun, if not the games he played with their staff. The titled ones he addressed as 'My lady' instead of 'Milady', and all those without titles as 'Madame' instead of 'Madam'. To the husband of a titled wife he would refer to her as 'Our lady', probably meaning to crack a sacrilegious joke although he kept a straight face. His eccentricities and absurdities were a part of the entertainment he was paid to provide.

'Can I press you to a Brussels sprout, Madame? . . . You must get outside another dollop of my mousse, dear sir!'

Meanwhile he gathered material for the book he planned to write about the bad manners and peculiar habits of his so-called superiors. Some of his clients tried to diddle him: for instance he would quote a price for a dinner for four and find he was expected to prepare cocktail snacks for twenty without any extra fee. Some were stingy: they would economise on food for him to eat, or want to know what he had done with the watery dregs of Dry Martini in the cocktail shaker, or haggle over his bus-fares. A woman who should have known better required him to quarrel telephonically with her grocer for refusing to deliver an order of a packet of salt at six o'clock in the evening. Another, more scatterbrained, would ask him to follow an abstruse recipe, hoover her sitting-room, fool around with her children and zip up the back of her dress simultaneously.

The hosts at these parties were liable to tempt him with drinks. The story he told Hereward was that he explained frankly and fully why he did not dare so much as sniff alcohol. He was resentful of a malicious gentleman who nonetheless forced him to taste every bottle of wine before serving it.

And he had his enemies amongst party-goers: a literary lion who sat sideways at dinner tables, impeding Brownie's laborious progress with platters, and a thoughtless professor who helped himself to more than his share of meals and made it look as if Brownie had got his quantities wrong.

In one house he had an enemy in the shape of a ferocious

bull-terrier. Moreover its owner and his clients were hardworking people – they gave him a key with which to gain admittance before they returned from their offices. When he first tried to do so he was bitten by their dog, waiting for him on the other side of the front door. His strategy on that and future occasions was ingenious as ever. He retreated, bought a supply of Mars Bars, pushed them through the letterbox, and while they were being masticated slipped in.

But on the whole he not only loved or at any rate was stimulated by his excursions into a world of fashion, and the representatives, the paraphernalia, the opulence and glamour of the social establishment – he was loved, even in the end by savage greedy dogs, and valued and treated well.

His particular favourite was Mrs Pemberton-Wicklow, a merry widow, a relentless hostess, and physically a heavyweight. She reciprocated his feelings: once on an unconventional impulse she embraced him.

'Was it enjoyable?'

'Yes and no, sir. She half-squeezed the life out of me. She's like a boa-constrictor.'

'Did you do any constricting?'

'I always do my bit, sir. No – seriously – I'll tell you what it was like. You know the advertisement on TV with a boy and a girl running towards each other in slow motion through a misty cornfield? I ran into Mrs Pemberton-Wicklow's arms and she ran into mine like that.'

After Hereward's father's death, his mother continued to live in a few of the rooms of the ancestral home, attended by her equally ageing Welsh housekeeper Mrs Williams. When Mrs Williams went on holiday, Brownie replaced her. And he began to accompany his boss to Watkins Hall to help with the work at weekends and at Christmas.

He soon won Mrs Williams over, in spite of her bucolic hostility to a smart operator from the metropolis. He said he was partly Scottish – Celtic as she was; and he brought her peace offerings, false jewellery and a pair of yellow satin knickers with a butterfly embroidered on the front. Screams of unwonted laughter issued from the kitchen.

One day Mrs Williams remarked to Hereward: 'Now you'll be ready for a quiet time down here, considering you're so busy in London.'

'I haven't been especially busy since I finished my last book,' he replied.

'I mean with the people you have in to lunch and dinner.'

'But I seldom have people in. Where did you get hold of that idea?'

'Your Brownie told me he was cooking for ten or twelve for every meal.'

'I'm afraid you can't believe a word he says.'

'Oh I don't,' Mrs Williams agreed hurriedly, mortified at having fallen into the trap of alien urban deceitfulness after all.

Back in Trafalgar Terrace, Hereward was chatting to a neighbour.

It was in the spring; and he volunteered the information that he had recently visited his mother; whereupon he was asked: 'Did you have good sport? Shoot any grouse?'

'Grouse? No! I shouldn't think there's a grouse within hundreds of miles of the Brecon Beacons. And I stopped shooting ages ago – and anyway it's the wrong time of year for shooting grouse.'

'Oh – I'm sorry – I understood you had a grouse moor in the grounds of the castle.'

'What castle?'

'Where your mother lives – Watkins Castle.'

'Actually it's called Watkins Hall – and it's a medium-sized manor house with a ruined Victorian wing. I suppose you've been listening to Brownie's fairy tales?'

'Well, yes – he said it had turrets and a flagpole for the family standard and a drawbridge.'

'Did he indeed?'

'And he likes being there because of the flighty red-headed French lady's maid.'

'What did he have to say about the grounds?'

'I got the impression you owned most of South Wales.'

Hereward confronted Brownie with his lies. But he realised that reform in this area was out of the question: in the first place Brownie could scarcely open his mouth without *proverbing* the truth, or at least exaggerating – and in the second an inherent class difference between them would never be erased. For Brownie's shamefully poor origins urged the widest possible publication of his present relative affluence and the other advantages he had wrested from the tight fist of fortune; whereas Hereward's wealthy aristocratic ones urged him in the opposite direction – towards playing down the privileges of his birth and understatement of his subsequent success or good luck.

'You've been at it again, Brownie – making out my mother queens it in a castle and I shoot grouse in her garden. I don't mind you boasting about yourself. But I won't have you misrepresenting me as a bloated plutocrat. Now I know why everything I buy in the terrace is so pricey. The shopkeepers must think I'm a millionaire – and a mean millionaire at that. You'll spread Communism.'

'I am a Communist, sir,' he retorted with his shifty giggle.

'Don't be silly! Since you were a boy of fourteen you've been dependent on Capitalism, financially, psychologically. If you don't vote Conservative you're just a humbug.'

'Yes, sir – that's what we Communists are, sir.'

He was teasing. But he was also resisting pressure to change his ways. He was too fond of basking in the imaginary glory he bestowed on his boss.

'You'll get me strung up to the nearest lamp-post when the revolution comes.'

'Have no fear, sir – Brownie's here!'

In fact, politically, he was on the extreme right. He loathed Bolshies and believed they were to blame for all our national ills. He advocated the control of mob violence with flamethrowers.

And his rhyming catch-phrase – 'Have no fear, Brownie's here!' – had an element of truth in it. He at once slandered Hereward – 'I have to empty his ashtray after every cigarette he smokes . . . I have to get on my knees to pull his muddy boots off . . . He can't do nothing for himself . . . One day he boiled an egg for an hour and wondered why the shell didn't go soft' – and protected him. He slept with a length of lead pipe under his pillow and gave instruction in the art of dealing with an intruder.

'Suppose a villain rings the doorbell in the middle of the night, or more likely in the middle of the afternoon, what do you do?'

'I tell you to answer it.'

'Thank you, sir. All right – provided I'm at home I tickle him with my blunt instrument. But suppose I'm not at home, what's your procedure?'

'I look out of the window to see who's there – and don't let him in.'

'But you won't know he's a villain however hard you look at him. He won't be wearing a black mask and carrying a sack over his shoulder. He'll be in a natty suit – and he'll say he's from the Council, or he's collecting money for nuns. Suppose he talks you downstairs, how do you open the front door?'

'Like this?'

'No, sir. You should step backwards when you open the door, so you've got room to kick him in the crutch when he rushes you. And where are you going to hit him?'

'But I've already kicked him, I've probably crippled him – must I hit him as well?'

'Definitely! Aim for his throat, chop him across the throat and block his windpipe, or blind him by sticking your thumb in his eye. And kick him again when you've got him on the floor.'

'Do I send for the police after I've finished with him, or an ambulance?'

'You should be able to send for the undertaker, sir.'

Brownie was specially protective of Hereward's bank-balance. He was a virtuoso of a shopper, carrying in his head and comparing the prices of almost every article in a number of shops, and thinking nothing of walking half a mile to save a few pence. He shamed profiteering shopkeepers, and got things cheap either because he intimidated them with his wit, or because his custom and goodwill were worth cultivation, or because he had spun some heart-breaking yarn.

He would tell a butcher he wanted to treat a starving arthritic pensioner to a square meal and bring back a bargain mixed grill for supper. He had no scruples about begging a bite to eat for his invalid father.

'I'll have a nice leg of lamb for my boss – and do me a favour and throw in a handful of scrag-end for my father.'

At length the local butcher inquired suspiciously: 'Just how old and sick is this father of yours?'

Brownie's answer, whatever it was, must have implicated Hereward, who was shaken when another shopkeeper said to him with a sly smile a day or two later: 'I'm glad you're feeling better, sir.'

Hereward liked none of the public roles in which he seemed to have been cast – millionaire, miser, tyrant, spoilt brat, and ailing father of a sort of confidence trickster who was his senior by thirteen years.

He felt he was being stared at by strangers as he walked down the street. He found it a particular strain to be abroad in his manservant's company. He was uneasily aware that together they bore a comic resemblance to Don Quixote and Sancho Panza. And Brownie was irrepressible and adept at causing embarrassment for a joke: witness the incident with the girl in the chemist's shop.

Once Hereward was commiserating with an octogenarian lady in a wheelchair when Brownie hailed her: 'How are the bowels, passion-flower?'

Again, they stopped to pass the time of day with some scaffolders who were working on the house next door. But after a few minutes Hereward had to hurry away. Brownie's quips on the theme of scaffold-poles and nuts and bolts were too crude to listen to.

Punctuality was his God. He would rebuke artisans who failed to arrive on time in the mornings: 'I know, I know – you lay too long in bed with your hand on your brains...' A corpulent official of the Gas Board, who was near retiring age, clocked in the regular couple of hours late for an appointment. Brownie said: 'Where have you been hiding, matey? Why can't you leave your missis alone – and do your work instead? I'll give you a piece of free advice: put it on the window-sill and bang the window on it...'

Hereward bought a car which he parked in his front garden. Other drivers were apt to block his exit with their vehicles. On one occasion Brownie caught a person at it.

In front of Hereward he shouted: 'Clear off! We're a team of brain surgeons, waiting for an emergency call. If you park there and stop us driving out, the patient could die. And we'd have you up for manslaughter.'

He also warned would-be parkers in the wrong place: 'Want me to run a six-inch nail along your paintwork? Want me to light a bonfire under your petrol tank?'

He was fearless, at any rate in speech, although he usually modified his aggressive remarks to members of his own sex by adding the word sir, even in conversation with the most oafish youth.

He was motoring somewhere with Hereward. They pulled in at a transport cafe, entered the shack of a building which was full of lorry drivers, sat on high stools at the messy counter and studied the gravy-stained menu. A lumbering negro came to take their order.

Brownie gave it: 'Fried egg and fried bread, bacon, sausage and tomato twice, if you'd be so kind.'

He continued in his fancy voice: 'And this gentleman here likes his fried bread golden brown, and his eggs hard on the bottom and soft on top, with a nice crisp frilly edge – sir!'

The negro rolled his eyes and Hereward blushed.

On another day in a supermarket they were standing in a queue at the pay-desk behind a shopper in a fur coat.

'Beg pardon, Madame,' Brownie addressed her: 'but I wonder if you've heard what they say about ladies in beautiful coats like yours?'

Luckily she laughed and lifted the hem of the coat to show she had clothes on underneath.

Brownie's affectations were a measure of how far he was prepared to go in search of amusement – his own, if no one else's.

He started to limp round Hereward's dining-table one evening.

A sympathetic guest asked him what was wrong.

'It's my foot, sir.'

'What have you done to your foot?'

'It happened in the war, sir. A German tank ran over my instep.'

'Oh dear – I'm sorry. But what a miracle you've got any foot left!'

'The terrain was muddy. I sort of sank into it. But my toes have never been the same.'

'I should think not!'

'I can't touch the ground with them. They will stick up in the air. Look, sir.'

And he exhibited his foot with the toecap of his shoe pointing upwards.

'That must be terribly uncomfortable.'

'It is, sir. But the doctors can't help me. I just have to make the best of it.'

Hereward intervened to say: 'Funny that I've never noticed anything the matter with your foot.'

'I'm a bit shy about it, sir. I've always tried to conceal it.'

'Let's see you walk, Brownie.'

He hobbled a few paces.

'But you don't walk like that normally.'

'I'm afraid the trouble's getting worse, sir.'

Later, alone with Brownie, Hereward expressed his scepticism more forcibly.

'May you be forgiven!'

'I shall be, sir. I'm telling the sober truth.'

To prove his point he hobbled everywhere within the house and in its immediate vicinity for several weeks, toecap vertical.

He was ready to suffer for his affectations. He pretended he could not – or rather refused to – regulate his intake of medicines, wishing to suggest he was too tough to be either healed or hurt by them. As a result he repeatedly poisoned himself.

'You haven't been drinking, Brownie?'

'Never, sir! But yesterday I went to consult my doctor about my wonky shoulder. And now I keep on seeing stars – it's as bad as being on the booze.'

'What did your doctor do for you?'

'He wrote out a prescription for tablets.'

'Have you started taking them?'

'Started and stopped, sir.'

'You don't mean you've taken all the tablets?'

'Yes, sir.'

'Where's the bottle? But it says here – one at night. How many tablets did you take?'

'I lost count. I swilled them down with a pint of tea – they were such tiny tots. And I never can be bothered with one at a time.'

'Well – you're a lunatic.'

'Maybe, sir. But I've given my wonky shoulder a fright. It hasn't dared to pain me since.'

He was stubbornly affected. He was affected even in adversity.

He was advised by his dentist, who had pulled out half a dozen of his teeth under a general anaesthetic, to rinse his mouth.

He was scarcely conscious, and his mouth was probably awash with blood.

But he replied: 'Sorry, sir – I don't think I will – because I'd have to swallow what I rinsed with – you see, sir, I can't spit.'

Towards the end of his long happy period at Trafalgar Terrace two incidents occurred which he described to Hereward – and Hereward then dined out on.

Brownie in his boss's absence received an unusual visitor at number 32.

'He was a plain-clothes police officer, sir – a charming gentleman. He said there might be a housebreaker holed up in the mews, and wanted to have a peep from our back windows. I told him a housebreaker would never be able to afford the rent of any house round here. But anyway I let him in – he showed me his identity card. I hope I did right.'

A week later Hereward returned home at about midnight.

Brownie in an excited state was waiting for him.

'They've caught Cat's-eyes, sir!'

'Who's Cat's-eyes?'

'Cat's-eyes Callaghan, the bank robber! The police arrested him. And I saw the whole thing!'

'What happened?'

'I was cooking my supper. I was cooking my pound of chipolatas when the doorbell rang. The officer who called the other day asked if he could position two of his men in the yard behind our basement flat. I gave permission – and hurried back to my kitchen and put my chipolatas on a plate and the plate and the mustard-pot on the draining-board by the window and switched off the light. The terrace was crammed with police-cars and constables – but everything seemed to be quiet round about the mews. A voice boomed through one of those loud-hailers. The next minute I thought I heard a door slam – actually it was a skylight being thrown wide open – and some glass broke. And somebody was running across the flat roof of the mews house opposite – he was just like a shadow although he was only ten yards from where I was watching. He got to the middle of the roof and the policemen in our basement yard shone their torches on him. He stopped. He was dressed all in black with a black beard. You could see he knew he was done for. But he ran on and jumped down from the roof of the last house in the mews. He jumped right into the arms of a posse of police.'

'What a thrill, Brownie!'

'It was, sir. I was leaning on the draining-board and dipping my chipolatas in the mustard-pot – I burnt my gullet to a crisp with mustard. But it was better than the telly.'

'Did you talk to the officer in charge afterwards?'

'Yes, sir. I said I couldn't help feeling sorry for Cat's-eyes when he stopped in the beams of the torches. He told me not to waste my pity on a nasty piece of work. And he laughed at my idea that the criminal he was chasing couldn't afford much of a rent. Cat's-eyes had twenty thousand pounds on him in a money-belt.'

'How long had he lived in the mews?'

'Six months, I believe.'

'Didn't you come across him?'

'No, sir. He was hiding and never set foot in the terrace by day. But he spoke to shopkeepers on the telephone. Every week he ordered a dozen bottles of vodka from the off-licence and a case of avocado pears from the greengrocer.'

'Nothing else?'

'No, sir.'

'Not a very healthy diet.'

'No.'

'Twelve bottles of vodka a week can't have done him much good.'

'I agree, sir,' Brownie replied smugly.

The other incident also involved the police.

Again Hereward was absent on the afternoon in question. Brownie was wiping over the floor of the hall when he heard a key turning in the lock of the front door. He opened the door – he imagined his boss was trying to get in. An insignificant weaselly tramp was standing outside.

The following exchange took place.

'Who are you? What do you think you're doing?'

'I was using this here key you give me.'

'What? What key?'

'This here key you give me in Wormwood Scrubs.'

'I didn't give you any key in Wormwood Scrubs! I've never been in Wormwood Scrubs! You were going to burgle my house, weren't you?'

'Yuss!'

'Get out of it!'

And Brownie administered a push that sent the fellow reeling backwards: he did not need to kick him in the crutch or chop him across the throat or blind him.

He pushed and pursued, banging the door shut, and asked a passing neighbour to ring the police without delay. The ineffective intruder was now slumped on the kerb of the pavement, speechless and with his head in his hands. Brownie stood over him, guarding him unnecessarily, and fuming on account of the allegation that he was a party to the planned theft.

Sirens wailed, and a police-car with flashing blue lamp, two policemen on motorcycles, a van containing four Alsatians and their handlers, and a Black Maria rolled up: 'An army arrived to arrest a shrimp!'

The shrimp was bundled into the Black Maria. Brownie was driven in the police-car to and from the police station, where he made and signed his statement.

On returning to the terrace he realised he had locked himself out of number 32. The door was shut and he did not have his own legitimate key in his pocket. As usual he seized his opportunity. He warned off other burglars by broadcasting the fact that he could not possibly force an entry.

'That place of ours is like a fortress!'

Eventually Hereward appeared on the scene, admitted him and was regaled with the story.

Brownie was duly summoned to speak his piece at a magistrate's court. In the witness-box he managed to create a mild sensation.

'Mr Brown, were you in Wormwood Scrubs Prison with the accused?'

'No, sir.'

'Were you ever in Wormwood Scrubs Prison?'

'No, sir.'

'Were you ever in prison anywhere?'

'Yes, sir.'

'What was that?'

'I said yes, sir – sir!'

'Please think carefully before you answer my next question, Mr Brown. Would you inform this court where exactly, when, and for what offence or offences you were imprisoned?'

'Germany – between 1940 and 1941 and again between 1944 and 1945 – for fighting for my king and country – SAH!'

FIVE

HEREWARD WATKINS was a generous friend. He often invited me round to meals at Trafalgar Terrace. With the royalties from his books, his rents and private income, he was richer than me. But that is not saying much – he was still worried about money. And wealth, whether relative or absolute, is by no means a synonym for hospitality.

Hereward was generous and Brownie always warmly welcoming.

'What a treat to see you again, dear sir.'

'No, it's my treat, Brownie. How are you?'

'Fit as a flea, thank you, sir. And yourself?'

'Oh, not too bad.'

'That's the ticket!'

The mere sight of his round rosy cheeks and comfortable corporation under his white jacket put an instant edge on my appetite. His confidence and optimism banished dull dyspeptic care. His relaxed conviviality was conducive to over-eating. His own greed, far from disgusting, was infectious.

Even a slab of Cheddar cheese served by Brownie seemed to taste better than cheese anywhere else. It was presented so temptingly: 'This is a crumbly mature strong Cheddar, sir – it'll blow your head off – it's more-ish!'

At Trafalgar Terrace he confined himself to cooking the sort of food most men prefer: grills with chips and roasts with roast potatoes, stews, eggs and paper-thin streaky bacon, crinkly and crisp, savouries of sardines or soft roes on toast. He was mad on fish: he said he would have cut his mother's throat for a wing of skate: which must have been why his breadcrumbed fillets of plaice were unparalleled.

He would carry a couple of tray-tables into the sitting-room, so that

Hereward and I could eat in the armchairs by the fire and watch the telly. But he was more amusing than the majority of programmes.

'What's the gossip, Brownie?'

He might hark back to the Piccadilly Club or his wartime experiences. He might dance for us – just a step or two – suddenly loose-limbed and extraordinarily expressive – also graceful, if a trifle grotesque. He might mention somebody in the terrace and imitate the way that he or she walked – 'You know him, sir, he walks like this!' He had a unique gift for imitating walks – and was as merciless as the best comedians: he could do cripples to perfection. Or he might expatiate on the subject of lodgers.

For instance that Mr Carstairs, who lodged in the ground floor front room for some months, had a weekend wife in the country and a mistress in town. For the sake of appearances he would sneak into number 32 at half-past seven in the morning, undress, put on pyjamas, get into bed, and yawn and stretch and pretend he had just woken up when Brownie called him at eight.

Another lodger was a refugee from Bulgaria. He had anglicised his name to Smith and was a door-to-door salesman of encyclopaedias. Brownie discovered that Mr Smith had been born a prince and never failed to refer to him as His Royal Highness.

'His Royal Highness gave me no end of trouble – he was a messy young pup.'

A married couple moved into the room. The husband was a martinet, the wife a martyr in Brownie's eyes. One day their car broke down. He sat in the driving seat and expected her to provide the motive power to get it started. And he encouraged her by yelling through the window: 'Push, you cow!'

'What else, Brownie?'

'The worst was Mr Boyd in the basement flat. He was a sex maniac. He came home with a different woman every evening. He used to chase them something wicked, singing *Jerusalem* at the top of his voice.'

'Did he catch them?'

'He must have, sir. Once he asked me to change his sheets. I needed a hammer.'

If Hereward had invited other people to a meal, we ate at the dining-table in a corner of the room. The ladies present invariably asked Brownie for his recipes. He would describe the speed or intensity at which he boiled liquids by reproducing the sound of the process.

'You bring the mixture to boiling-point, Madame – bllop, bllop! Then you boil it a bit faster – bllop-bllop, bllop-bllop! And before you pour it you step on the gas – bllop bllop bllop bllop bllop!'

He made lemon barley-water in the summer. It was wonderfully cool and refreshing, and sweet and sharp and bland. Even guests unaccustomed to non-alcoholic drinks consumed gallons of it. He wrote out that recipe repeatedly.

'Oh, Brownie, how good of you! Now I'll be able to have delicious barley-water for all my parties. Thank you so much!'

Of course he had omitted an essential ingredient.

Disappointed hostesses would interrogate him about their failures, his ready explanations of which confounded confusion: 'Are you sure you blanched your lemons, Madame? Are you sure you used the pus of the fruit? It wouldn't taste nice without the full flavour of pus.'

But sooner or later most of his victims saw the joke.

'You brute, Brownie! I've spent hours – days! – toiling over your fake recipe for barley-water. You fooled me completely! How could you? I kept on giving it to my husband, who thought I was trying to poison him.'

Hereward as host would remark ruefully that he was in the wrong place: he ought to be in the kitchen, and Brownie presiding at the head of the table.

'People enjoy talking to him more than talking to me. I don't blame them. I'd rather talk to him, too.'

In my view and in my memory they were complementary – Hereward aristocratic, pale and thin and attenuated, dignified, highbrow, accurate, preoccupied and on the melancholic side, and Brownie foreshortened, tubby, unbuttoned, bursting out all over, as common as muck in his own estimation, although in another sense exceptional, lowest-browed, whimsical, on the spot and always potentially manic. In music hall terms they were like a double act – the feed and the funster.

They both followed departing guests downstairs to the front door.

'Goodbye, Hereward – and thanks. Goodbye, Brownie.'

'Goodbye, sir.'

'Your dinner was pure poetry.'

'What did you think of my *Oeufs Trafalgar?*'

'Scrumptious! I meant to ask you: how are they done?'

'They're my invention, sir. They're simplicity itself. You soft-boil your *oeuf* and shell it under cold running water, and pop it in an individual *pot* and cover it with a loo-warm aspic mixture' – loo-warm equalled lukewarm in his phraseology. 'And then you drop slices of radish and chopped chives into the aspic before it sets, and serve out of the fridge.'

Hereward interposed: 'Is that the whole truth and nothing but the truth, Brownie?'

'Cross my heart, sir!'

'Your heart must be tired of getting crossed,' Hereward remarked.

'My heart's as sound as a dinner-bell – or it was until I started to work for you.'

The backchat and the laughter continued on the doorstep.

'Well – I really should be off.'

'Come again, sir.'

'I will if your boss invites me.'

'I'll see he does, sir.'

Walking or driving into the night, turning to wave by the alley into the mews, I used to feel I was leaving behind me an island of peace, order, compatibility and cosiness, amidst the turbulent seas of normal existence.

But an adage survives from the past in which the so-called leisured classes could find domestic staff to be served by – and to make a study of and draw conclusions from.

The ominous generalisation runs: 'Seven years a servant, seven years a friend, seven years a master.'

Brownie, not counting the period at Windle Road when he was employed by Jacques Beausson, had now been with Hereward for fifteen years.

The sun – and the stars – still shone on the island in Trafalgar Terrace.

Hereward's brave or reckless gamble on Brownie's sobriety had turned out to be his best investment. Apart from the obvious dividends paid, it had already enabled him to produce the seven or eight books which were likely to be the main body of his life's work. He would never have dared to become a householder, and thus receive his rents, without Brownie. He would never have managed to write as much, and thus realise some of his ambitions, without Brownie. He followed his vocation, or prosecuted his trade, resolutely. No doubt in different circumstances, say in that garret in the suburbs, in between grubbing round for a living wage, he would have tried to scribble. But he was not cut out for competition against the odds in an exhausting distracting worldly obstacle race. To write well and do a nine-to-five job is to refute history. He was too modest to aspire to be one of the gallant exceptions that prove that rule. For, with apologies to idealists, literature and art and culture are flowers that grow from the root of all evil: and money is hardly ever earned by artists and writers – or writers who are artists – when they need it. As it was, and had been for fifteen years, he could afford to buy not only his daily bread, but the sustenance equally vital to his spirit – time. He could wallow in the immaterial luxury of redundant energy which is the stuff of inspiration. Moreover his privacy was guarded and his routine doubly regulated, his loneliness alleviated, his blacker moods lightened, his necessary obsessiveness laughed into proportion and his very health maintained – by Brownie.

'They say that no man is a hero to his valet,' he observed. 'But my valet's a hero to me.'

There was a touch of Pygmalion in Hereward's attitude. His gratitude and admiration were tinged with pride. Brownie who had conquered an addiction supposed to be almost unconquerable, who seemed to have emerged unscathed and unscarred from the struggle, who was the embodiment of a success story – and had helped him to succeed – was in a sense his creation as well as his creature.

He claimed that he learned more from Brownie than he had ever taught.

Once he referred to a bereaved widower of his acquaintance, who had been happily married for half a century.

'He talked about his wife. He was in tears. He's turned against the house where they lived together. His children are kind, but busy. I felt so sorry for him.'

'Well, I don't,' Brownie declared. 'He was happy with his old woman for fifty years? And he's got kind children and a house? He's got the lot. He's had his lot. He ought to quit belly-aching.'

No doubt Hereward's exposure to the gritty realism of the representatives of a class lower than his own widened his horizons.

'You Watkinses think you're on the bread-line when we Browns would think we were on the pig's back ... The members of your family kiss each other on the cheek. If we kiss anybody we kiss on the kisser, as if we meant it ... Your ladies wear black clothes – ours never wear black – they wouldn't want to make things any gloomier than they are

... You cry over what we laugh at – if we started crying, where would we stop?'

Brownie was pleased to browbeat his boss with the stick of class-consciousness. But he also personified a summing-up of the pathetic fallacy of egalitarianism and the cause of workers' solidarity. Unlike those at the top of the social pile, who will always unite to defend their advantageous stations in life, he had no reason to defend his native station, he had no feelings of loyalty for his former equals – he despised and was quite ready to betray them in order to overcome his disadvantages.

He considered that he was fundamentally the superior of any man on earth. A certain self-reliant arrogance in him may have been typical of his class. He was chauvinistically vain: he would insist that the British or rather the Scots had won the war, not the Russians and Americans. At the same time he completely dissociated himself from the British postwar worker, for whom he had nothing but scorn.

'He's a lazy skiver on the fiddle – and he lets Commies push him around.'

He was without sympathy for the unemployed.

'They ask for it. They're too greedy for money. They open their mouths too wide – they're not worth the wages they want – of course they lose their jobs. They're *idiotick!*' He pronounced the last syllable of the word with a funny click. 'They hang out their paws for the dole and moan that they can't find employment. But they're stuck-up. Most of them wouldn't work on the buses or sweep the streets, like the blacks. They wouldn't work all hours in a corner-shop and be polite to everybody, like Indians and Pakistanis. Why don't they clean windows? Why don't they join the army or the police or emigrate? Why don't they go into private service?'

He would say less controversially: 'I've been in service on and off for forty years. I couldn't have asked for anything better. I've lived on the fat of the land and never had to pay a penny for it. I've got to know the nobs – it's been interesting.'

And again: 'It's our anniversary, sir. Sixteen years ago today we moved into number 32. Doesn't seem so long, does it? You've been good to me, I will admit that. I don't believe we've had a single quarrel.'

They would refer with renewed thanks to the ways in which each had rescued the other.

They were indeed the best of friends.

But Brownie had slipped into the habit of addressing Hereward as Master. Perhaps it was meant to be a mark of his respect. It was a joke, too, with a hint of satire. Hereward did not voice any protest, although it worried him slightly. Brownie's five hundred thousand brain-cells were full of paradoxes, if not beeswax. He might have decided to soft-soap his friendly boss or bossy friend by calling him Master, because he had reached the stage of presuming that he was actually in charge.

From another point of view the sixteen fruitful years of their association, or twenty-six including the ten at Windle Road, also alarmed Hereward. They were growing older. Brownie might die, which would be bad enough, or retire, which would be worse, or fall ill, which would be worse still – selfishly speaking. He merited a pension if and when he retired: how was it to be paid? Trafalgar Terrace would have to be sold and a proportion of the proceeds converted into some sort of annuity. At a stroke Hereward would therefore lose his servant and friend, his home, his income from lodgers and with it his financial independence and freedom to write.

'I hope you're putting money aside against a rainy day.'

'I've got my nest-egg in the Building Society, Master.'

'You'll need it. I'm afraid I've been very remiss; I've made no provision for your pension. I haven't had the cash – but that's a rotten excuse. Naturally I'll see you're as all right as possible by hook or by crook. But you must save now for your retirement.'

'I'm not retiring.'

'You may one day.'

'I'd go mad if I retired. Work's my everything. I'd be a dead duck without it – or a mad duck.'

'You may change your mind.'

'I won't. I'll die in harness. I'd rather – believe me. That's definite.'

Hereward approached the subject from a different angle.

'Listen, Brownie – I pay you too little. You know why: I'd pay you more if I could: and I know you do pretty well when you cook for other people. But if you're not booked by your clients, you don't receive the weekly wage you deserve.'

'I'm content, Master.'

'Well, I'm not. It doesn't seem fair. And I've been thinking. You should have at least ten active years ahead of you. Why don't you leave me and work for a real millionaire, or pop across to America and be an

English butler there, and make a fortune to carry you through your old age?'

'Not likely! In the first place, I've told you, I'll never be that old – I'll die young from knocking my navel out in your service. In the second I can't abide money – I wouldn't cross the road to pick up a five pound note. No, sir! It's kind of you to be concerned about my future. But religion says – or mine does: eat, drink and be merry.'

'Eat and be merry, Brownie.'

'Pardon me – eat and drink lemonade and be merry. No honestly – I'd work for you for nothing – or just a dry bed to curl up in and a corn of bread.' A corn of bread was his unappetising description of a crust. 'I would, sir! I'm staying put.'

The obstinate implications of Brownie's final declaration worried Hereward yet again.

'What if I went bankrupt and had to sell this house?'

'You won't. And we'd always get by somehow. Besides, Trafalgar Terrace suits me. I wouldn't want to be anywhere else.'

'But what would you do if I sold it?'

'I'd get a room in the caves.' The caves of the terrace were some slummy boarding-houses along at the far end. 'The shop-keepers are mates of mine: they're always after me to work for them. Or I might look for a job in a wet-fish shop. Nobody likes to work with fish, but I'd love it. And there's a bomb of money in fish.'

'What if I married, Brownie?'

'I'd divorce you, Master. I couldn't stand a woman over me, if you catch my meaning. I'd do my disappearing act – and pronto!'

Hereward was neither bankrupt, nor had he any matrimonial plans, for the time being.

He was touched by Brownie's offer to remain at his post for no pay whatsoever.

But his anxieties were far from removed. He could never let Brownie stay put and work for nothing – apart from the objective rights and wrongs of such a course, it would aggravate the sense of obligation he was already labouring under. And supposing Brownie were to take refuge in the caves for one reason or another, Hereward's inescapable duty would nonetheless be to prove his gratitude in financial terms and at exorbitant cost.

It occurred to him that he had tied their destinies in a knot which, if ever loosed, would unravel the whole fabric of his life.

Sometimes Brownie picked at the sore point in his boss's conscience. He would produce advertisements for qualified menservants culled from newspapers.

'Look at this one, Master: self-contained flat, car, five-day week, eight-hour working day, colour TV, foreign travel, and wages that are plain ridiculous.'

Maybe he was merely drawing attention to his disinterested loyalty.

But he made Hereward wince.

'Why don't you apply for the job?'

'No, thanks! It smells to me. In return for all that cash, whatever would a gentleman be wanting a servant to do for him?'

'Take a chance – you're not exactly innocent – pocket the wages even if they are the wages of sin – follow the advice I've been giving you!'

'Sir! My birthsign's Virgo, sir! I'm the only virgin in Trafalgar Terrace. I'd rather be poor and keep my virtue in one piece.'

Before the prospect of Brownie falling ill and becoming an invalid and a millstone, Hereward simply quailed: and illness was Brownie's main defence against his mortal enemy – boredom.

To amuse himself, or torment his boss in his intuitive teasing way, or both, he would invent lists of terrifying symptoms: difficulty with his speech, paralysis of an extremity, shooting internal pains, partial blindness, unbearably severe headaches. He was such an extraordinary actor that he could assume at will a facial expression of suffering bravely borne, or contort his hands into rheumatoid shapes. He enjoyed every minute of the rigmarole of playing the sick hero: yielding unwillingly to persuasion to seek help from the medical profession; bidding everybody farewell as he sallied forth to surgery or casualty department; comforting his fellow-patients with his devil-may-care jokes; swapping scabrous witticisms with buxom nurses; deceiving doctors; waltzing home with his bouquet of compliments – 'I never thought I'd have a good laugh in the waiting-room, Mr Brown! You're a tough egg and no mistake, Mr Brown!' – and then snapping his fingers at science and at fate by swallowing his supply of pills in a single gulp.

As a rule his own GP, a German refugee named Mannrich, pronounced *Mannrick* with a click by Brownie, called his bluff.

A poisoned whitlow under a fingernail was at last submitted to Dr Mannrich's examination.

'I can get rid of that for you.'

'Thank you, Doctor.'

'I can get rid of it quickly or slowly – which would you prefer, Mr Brown?'

'Quickly, Doctor, please – you don't know my boss – he's pitiless – he won't let me off work for half a day.'

'So – I can get rid of it quickly – but can you stand pain?'

'Doctor, I was in the Black Watch!'

Whereupon the whitlow was gouged out with a scalpel.

'Could you stand it, Brownie?'

'No, Master – I hollered!'

Dr Mannrich summarily dismissed the majority of Brownie's ailments. And Hereward did likewise. But once Hereward mistook what must have been a bout of pneumonia for a bad cold; he was full of rallying exhortations and references to Sir Laurence Olivier when he should have sympathised and served tea etcetera in his turn; and he was not allowed to forget it. He had to be more careful thereafter.

Moreover he and no doubt Dr Mannrich were cognisant of the threat of the card up Brownie's sleeve: their memories were jogged.

'What is it this time?'

'Nothing, sir – just my knee.'

'Do you mean your housemaid's knee? Or should I say your war-wound?'

'Have a heart, sir. I couldn't sleep with it last night. And my head's pounding like Big Ben, although I've munched a packet of Aspirin.'

'Oh well, what can you expect? Your cures are much worse for you than your diseases.'

'I had the headache first, sir. That's why I munched the Aspirin. I was never one to complain – '

'What are you doing now?'

'Explaining, not complaining, sir. I don't mind being ill. But headaches are something else. They put me in mind of my mother.'

'Whereabouts in your head is this headache of yours?'

'Behind my right eye.'

'But it couldn't be a tumour, Brownie. You haven't developed any new tumours for years.'

'Oh yes, sir, I have. The other day a couple came up on my big toe. Would you like to see?'

'No, thanks! How long have you had your headache?'

'A fortnight.'

'You never mentioned it.'

'I didn't want you to fret, sir.'

'Tell me another!'

'I'm telling you the truth, Master. May I go blind and bonkers and die in agony if I'm not!'

'In that case you'd better hurry along to your doctor.'

The word doctor was apt to promote a magical improvement in Brownie's condition. Yet he carried his pantomimes so far that he could not always wriggle out of their consequences. He was compelled to totter to the surgery of Dr Mannrich, who, again, had no alternative except to send the probably hypochondriacal but possibly moribund patient to a hospital for still more tests.

Brownie would return to Trafalgar Terrace beaming.

'How did you get on?'

'I had loads of fun, Master. The nurse who looked after me was a little blood-orange.'

'What about your headache?'

'They passed me A1.'

'Well – thank God.'

At such moments Hereward's relief was greater than his annoyance with Brownie for crying wolf. The homily he had prepared on the subject of blackmail boiled down to a glad speechless smile. For if Brownie had been as ill as he pretended, and had not died but had become more or less incapacitated, he would have been the complete financial and even the physical responsibility of his master and friend. Hereward's recurrent nightmare was that he would never be able to free himself from the debt owing to his stricken invalid of a servant, who might refuse to leave his house, who might have to be served and tended for ever. He could hardly scold Brownie for providing evidence that his nightmare was only a dream. He felt more than relieved. He was reprieved – temporarily.

In fact Brownie's constitution was strong but delicate. It was like his physique. He was indeed built on the lines of a bison, or a heavyweight wrestler: his powerful muscles were concealed by layers of protective flesh. At the same time he was the opposite of clumsy and could mend watches with his short thick fingers. His reserves of energy were almost inexhaustible and he seldom spent a day in bed. On the other hand he usually and genuinely had something the matter with him, a graveyard cough, a digestive disorder, a sprain or rheumatics or toothache.

Equally his nervous system, given a chance, was strong. He would not have tempted providence with his dire hints of tumours if he had been – say – as highly-strung as Hereward, and apprehensive and superstitious. He would neither have deliberately got into nor been able coolly to get out of his various scrapes. An element of his nature was imperturbability: he could not have cooked so well without it. Yet he was sensitive, easily upset by lack of appreciation and hostile criticism, excitable to a fault, and, while never moody, prone to panic and despair, for instance at the time of his divorce.

Of course he was drinking then. Drink had reduced him to a nervous wreck. There had been no signs of his being sucked back into or towards the vortex of addiction during his decade and a half at Trafalgar Terrace. Once or twice in the early days he smelt of beer, and he talked too much and his speech seemed to be slurred. But, as he put it, his boss had jumped on him. The intervals between these unpleasant episodes lengthened. Sobriety became the rule of the house rather than the exception.

Hereward's confidence in Brownie and Brownie's confidence in himself advanced in unison. They often discussed drink, congratulating each other on their emergence from the crisis it had caused.

'I do admire you for kicking the habit, Brownie – I don't know how you pulled it off.'

'I couldn't if you hadn't stood by me, Master. You've been a brick' – and so on.

They dwelt sanguinely on their precautions against a repeat performance of the dramas of Windle Road: the bareness of Hereward's drink cupboard, and his determination to check the slightest excess on the part of his version of Galatea; and Brownie's claim that he was allergic to alcohol since his treatment in hospital for schizophrenia or whatever, and his resistance to social life and its temptations, and his healthy dread of pubs. He no longer spent his annual holidays at Butlin's Camps with their bars – he went to his daughter who could be relied upon to keep him out of them. And he stayed with his brother Arthur, surely a model citizen, a skilled engineer by trade, now retired.

If Hereward was going to Watkins Hall for the weekend, he would urge Brownie to visit Arthur. For all his confidence he did not quite like to leave Brownie alone at Trafalgar Terrace.

But the passage of every temperate year helped to dispel his doubts. He was able to return home without a pessimistic sinking of his heart, even if Brownie had been on his own for a whole week or more.

Slowly and after many tests and much reinforcement, trust was built up.

Unnecessary, unacceptable as the thought might be, that trust could only be demolished in the same way.

Sometimes Brownie saw his sister Ada and brother-in-law Jack, who was a thriving builder in the north of England: Ada was one of the two sisters whose bed he had shared when he was a boy.

She wrote him exclamatory letters in a sort of transatlantic jargon to arrange meetings during Jack's business trips to London: 'Hi, lover-boy! How's tricks? We're rolling down the great white highway next Tuesday forenoon! Let's hit the town together! Mosey along to our usual dive at opening time! Bye, toots! Ever your kissable . . .'

After an evening with Ada and Jack, Brownie would enumerate the drinks he had had in a defiant tone of voice: two lagers with lime, a third of a bottle of hock, and a nightcap of another lager.

'But I don't mind you drinking so long as you're in control of the drink and not controlled by it.'

'I've got it under my thumb.'

'Well, that's okay. Did you enjoy yourself?'

'Yes, thank you, Master. It was a riot. I sent for the head waiter in the restaurant and pulled his ears about the temperature of the wine. Ada wet herself. And we were dancing in Piccadilly Circus at two o'clock in the morning.'

The even tenor of life at Trafalgar Terrace was resumed. Brownie did not appear to be unsettled by the odd celebration, while Hereward reflected that a change was probably good for him. The contradiction between his allergy to alcohol and enjoyment of lager and hock was somehow glossed over.

He continued to affect an absolute horror of all things alcoholic. If he was asked to sniff the dregs of a bottle of sherry which might have turned sour, he would warn that he was liable to vomit and beg to be excused. If he washed up empty beer glasses – and Hereward was present in the kitchen – he would hold them at arm's-length, averting his head and wrinkling his nose. Should wine be required for an unexpected guest at the last minute, he would protest at having to enter the adjacent pub in order to buy it.

On summer afternoons idle men with newspapers under their arms hung around outside the betting-shop or sat on the walls of front gardens in the terrace.

'Who are those men? What are they doing?'

'They're waiting for the pub to open. They're alcoholics, sir.'

Brownie was disapproving.

'Haven't they got jobs?'

'Some have. That one in the cloth cap – he runs a painting and decorating business from the saloon bar. But most of them are fit for nothing – or they're villains. The fellow with the briefcase deals in jewellery. He drinks neat gin. He's a terrible alkie.'

On another occasion Brownie remarked darkly: 'Burglars use our pub. I'm telling you, sir! That's why we don't get burgled.'

Again the contradiction between his showy reluctance to cross the pub's threshold for wine for his boss, and his intimate knowledge of who drank there and what they drank, was not explained. Brownie, if pressed, probably would have said that he had been gossiping with his friend the landlord. But how had they become friendly? When and where did he gossip with the landlord, who was hard at work every day? And what was his link with the thirsty burglars for whom number 32 was out of bounds?

Alcohol in the abstract, as a conversational topic, had clearly never lost its fascination for him. He would describe in exhaustive detail the merits and demerits of different beers and spirits. He derived a competitive satisfaction from being able to teach Hereward a trick or two.

'We ought to go on a pub-crawl together, Master. It'd make a break – just once! We'd start with a couple of pints apiece of best bitter from the wood at the old *Flying Cow* in Shepherd Market. Then we'd quick-march over the road to the *Shillelagh* in Half Moon Street to lubricate our tonsils with draught Guinness. Then we'd whip in to the *Tartan Banner* in Dover Street for a few drams of the water of life – a backyard brew from the Highlands that curls your hair. Then we'd snatch a fish supper and some noggins of light ale at the *Winkle and Shell* in Soho. And we'd finish with hot toddies at the *Dirk and Sporran* in Shaftesbury Avenue. And I'd carry you home.'

'You'd have to carry me home long before we got to the *Dirk and Sporran*. I can only drink half a pint of beer at a time.'

'Not with me you wouldn't! I wouldn't be seen dead with a half-pint man. Queers drink half-pints.'

Considering Brownie had avoided pubs like the plague for at least sixteen years – or so he said – his memory for their names was remarkable.

For that matter, considering he rarely went anywhere except to the residences of his clients, and of his daughter and brother, and exclusively patronised local shops, how was it that he had such a wide circle of acquaintance?

As well as embarrassing his boss, he could be embarrassed, for instance on expeditions to distant parts of the metropolis. A red-nosed codger with bleary eyes or a peroxided gaptoothed baggage with a ginny voice would fall on his neck at an underground station or a bus-stop.

'Brownie! Billy! Kitch! Terry! My old cock-sparrow! Where have you been shunted? What have you been at? Now don't you run away!'

But he did run, blushing. He was unresponsive and offhand.

'Who was he? Who was she, Brownie?'

'Oh – mates from years back.'

'How many years back? They recognised you without any difficulty.'

'I must be well preserved.'

'And why did they call you Terry? Terry sounds like an alias to me.'

'I've been called worse than that. The other day you were surprised I could remember the names of pubs. In some places they call me Jumbo, because I never forget.'

'Well – you seem to know a hell of a lot of people.'

'I know the whole world, Master.'

There still appeared to be no need to elicit straight answers to these questions. Brownie was – or was seen by Hereward to be – sober. It was inconceivable that the mutual trust they had built up brick by brick, behind and beneath which they had as it were sheltered from so many storms, could collapse like a house of cards.

Hereward shrank from contemplation of such a disappointment and catastrophe.

But the answer to one question was brought home to him by an external agency. He had wondered why Brownie had been dropped by several of his clients, including Mrs Pemberton-Wicklow. Hereward met her at a social gathering and was told a tale nastily reminiscent of Windle Road: ten guests for dinner – interminable delays – uneatable food – no washing-up done – Brownie snoring with his head on the kitchen table – and eventually having to be woken and turfed out.

Then another client telephoned Hereward: she was sorry, but could no longer employ a cook who swigged from a bottle of vodka in front of her children.

He girded his loins for battle.

'I understand from Mrs Pemberton-Wicklow that your last dinner for her was a drunken orgy.'

'Not drunken, sir. I was ill on that day. And I'd swallowed every pill I could lay hands on. She got me wrong.'

'And I hear you take vodka with you when you do dinner parties.'

'Vodka? Who have you been talking to?'

'A little bird. I hear you swig vodka in front of children.'

'Oh – that! That wasn't vodka – it was lemonade! I made believe it was vodka to those sneaky children for a giggle.'

'Well, your giggle and your pills are going to cost you money.'

'I don't want money.'

'But I do, Brownie – I want you to have it. I couldn't employ you for the wages I pay if you weren't earning extra money from other people. Don't you see? I wouldn't have the face! Anyway, if you start drinking again you'll be done for – and so will I!'

'I haven't started drinking. Instead of listening to old wives' tales, you should have faith in me.'

'I have! Or I had. I mean – personally I've no complaints. But now I'm worried about what happens when my back's turned.'

'Nothing, Master. My dinners out are exhausting – you wouldn't be able to guess at how much work I get through, shopping and cooking and laying the table and serving a tip-top meal and clearing and cleaning, not to mention travelling. But nothing else happens. I've never once given myself a booster. You tell me not to start tippling again. I can tell you I will start, if you don't stop racking me unfairly.'

Brownie was more formidable than he had been – he had the force of his sixteen reformed years behind him. In a manner of speaking he had broken his bonds and grown accustomed to freedom, which he was evidently determined to defend. Besides, he may have felt it was not any more the exclusive prerogative of his boss to be masterful.

Some of Hereward's counsellors supported Brownie, who ought to be allowed to do as he pleased at his age, have an occasional drink, live his own life for better or worse.

Too soon the drinks would not be occasional, Hereward retorted – and then Brownie would not live, he would die, and cause more widespread destruction in the process.

He was nonetheless influenced or attracted by such advice. He was unused to wasting his time and energy in altercation – and unwilling to. He was caught in a cleft stick after all: his puritanism might be counter-productive. He therefore refrained from delving deeper into the matter. He resolved not to base any future case on mere hearsay and suspicion. He settled for blissful ignorance in the meanwhile.

Peace broke out once more.

Yet now Hereward was alerted willy-nilly to changes that had taken place over a long period and without his noticing. Brownie's standards of cleanliness had slipped. His everyday clothes were less presentable. And piles of his dirty buttonless shirts and socks with holes in them accumulated in his bedroom, from which a pungent odour spread through the house.

'Go to the launderette for God's sake, Brownie – you're stinking us out!'

'I am going, Master. I've been trying to go for a fortnight. But you wouldn't let me – you put too much on my plate.'

After an overdue visit to the launderette he would omit to iron the damp washing in plastic bags behind his kitchen chair.

'What's the smell in here?'

'It must be the stew you had for lunch.'

'No – I wouldn't eat anything that smelt so bad – it comes from where you're sitting.'

'Thank you, Master.'

'What's in those bags?'

'My laundry.'

'Haven't you ironed it yet?'

'I haven't had a chance. You're a twenty-four hour job, you are! Anyhow, I've got to wet it and run it through the spin-dryer again.'

'Well, please do. I won't have our kitchen smelling like a rabbit hutch.'

Brownie's aversion to bathing became more marked. Hereward had always had to suggest he should jump into a bath. The main effect was grammatical.

'When did you last have a jump-in?'

Thus a verb became a noun with a new meaning.

'I can't remember.'

'You need one.'

'I don't want my body-oils disappearing down the drain. They're precious, you know – they're pure essence of Brown! And the body-oils of we Romanys keep us sweet.'

'That's where you're wrong.'

He would laugh, and promise to jump in later on, and predictably forget, and still give off his pervasive odour.

'How long have you been wearing your socks?'

Brownie glanced at his wrist-watch.

'Two hours and twenty-three minutes, sir!'

'My nose tells me you were wearing them yesterday and the day before.'

'If you'll forgive my saying so, you're too nosey – that's your trouble, Master. My socks are changed twice daily. My socks aren't to blame – it's my feet. I suffer from an uncommon affliction in the foot department.'

'I bet.'

'Truly, Master. It's the waiter's disease, called Carpet Feet – it comes from walking on carpets and it makes your feet all spongy and sweaty. Everybody on the staff of the Piccadilly Club had it.'

'I pity the members.'

'You would be on the side of the members, sir. What about us?'

He was humorous and good-humoured, but less malleable than formerly. He developed an effective contrary method of dealing with Hereward's corrections. His revenge for remarks critical of the smelliness of his bedroom and kitchen was to open the windows and doors wide even in winter.

'The house is freezing.'

'I'm airing my room, Master. I'd hate to have a frowsty room like yours. I keep my room fresh.'

'Well, I'm damn cold.'

'Are you, sir? You must be sickening for 'flu. I think it's healthy.'

Following weekend visits to his daughter or brother, when Hereward pointed to the unwashed crockery regimentally stacked in a kitchen cupboard, he would say: 'I'll see to it, sir. But what do you expect? You shouldn't have ordered me to cook your lunch on Saturday morning, and get your shopping, and press your suits, and have my jump-in and thoroughly scrub my feet, as well as cleaning the whole house. My mother wasn't frightened by an octopus – I've only the one pair of hands.'

Hereward was penalised for his slightest requests for service over and above Brownie's idea of duty. For instance, if he asked for the replenishment of a salt-cellar, it would be filled so full of salt that some was bound to be spilled.

'Look at this mess, sir!'

'Sorry, Brownie – but you filled the thing too full.'

'Of course it's my fault. Who wanted me to fill it? Well – it's your table.'

'All right – I'll sweep the salt off the table.'

'You wouldn't know how! Leave it to Brownie! Why keep a dog and bark yourself?'

He was more long-suffering, more the martyr, and his retaliatory teasing had a sharper edge.

If Hereward mentioned a dripping tap, Brownie would screw it so tight that nobody else could unscrew it. If Hereward said his bacon was over-cooked, Brownie would serve nearly raw bacon the next time round.

And the slanderous stories he spread grew taller.

A simple-minded neighbour enquired of Hereward: 'It's not true, is it, that you put on a special black top-hat before you sit down to dinner?'

Another neighbour remarked: 'You're a wonder, Mr Watkins – eating so much and keeping so thin! I'm sure that if I ate four meat meals a day I'd burst.'

Once a strait-laced spinster of advanced years buttonholed Hereward in the street: 'Can I speak to you for a moment, Mr Watkins? I received a postcard this morning. It was from the sea-side – one of those sea-side postcards – it really shocked me. I've heard that your Mr Brown is on holiday. And I can't be certain, because nothing was written on the postcard except my name and address, but I think he must have sent it. Will you please tell him I was not amused? I've had palpitations ever since I set eyes on the disgusting object!'

The excessive side of Brownie's nature was definitely gaining ground. A lady-client of his rang Hereward to say she could never again employ such a talkative butler: the previous evening neither she nor her guests had been able to get a word in. And Hereward had to agree that he saw her point. Now and then he was asked by his friends to parties at which Brownie officiated. The food and the way it was served might be miraculous. On the other hand, if Brownie was elated or flustered, the proceedings were in danger of deteriorating into farce. He dominated every conversation; his *soufflés* subsided, or his *pommes fantastiques* were so crisp that they broke somebody's tooth; he would electrify respectable members of the fair sex with his flirtatious compliments and endearments – 'It's your low-cut dress that's making my platter wobble, dearest Madame!'; or he would puff and blow and sweat and curse and speak disrespectfully to dignified gentlemen – 'Mind your back, dear sir! And don't you dare drop the serving spoon into my o-h-range sauce!'

One evening Hereward arrived at a cocktail party at which Brownie, instead of dispensing refreshments, was swaying on his feet and holding forth, announcing to all and sundry that he had been the *chef de cuisine* of General de Gaulle.

Hereward deduced he was drunk and said as much. Brownie denied the charge and stalked off angrily. Ten minutes later he reappeared stone cold sober.

How was it possible? What had happened?

Smart social occasions were apt to go to his head. A snobbish manic mood must have created a false impression of drunkenness. But underlying Hereward's immediate relief was his unease, which was becoming chronic. The mysteries he was afraid to plumb were multiplying, almost as they had in the old days.

In the kitchen at Trafalgar Terrace a photograph was added to the display on Brownie's shelves. It was of a young girl in silhouette on the seashore, posing prettily and provocatively in clinging jeans and jersey.

'Where did you get the pin-up?'

'Ask no questions and you'll be told no lies.'

'Come on, Brownie – if you didn't want me to ask about it you wouldn't have put it there – who is she?'

'She's a nymphomaniac and dipsomaniac and drug-addict.'

'Do you know her well?'

'I know her a bit.'

'I suppose you know the nymphomaniac bit of her?'

'Please, sir – she's just a child – she could be my daughter.'

'Female children are in trouble when you're on their trail. What's she called?'

'Brett.'

'That's an odd name.'

'It suits her.'

'Where does she live?'

'In a flat across the road.'

'Is she married?'

'No, sir.'

'Who pays for the flat? What does she do for a living?'

'She's sitting on a fortune – and not always sitting on it either.'

'Do you mean she's a prostitute?'

'She needs the money to buy her drink and drugs.'

'What sort of drugs?'

'All sorts.'

'She sounds a caution.'

'She is, sir – but lovely with it.'

Hereward did not take much notice. Brownie had been keen on innumerable stray girls before. But he seemed to be particularly intrigued by the cautionary aspect of Brett.

'She'll go with any buck nigger with half a barrel of beer inside him and a fiver in his pocket. I've told her she'll get her throat slit one of these days or nights. But she only laughs at me . . . She's over the top most of the time – she's no idea where she is – on her head or her heels or her back . . . She was a photographic model. She's got a little figure on her fit to make your mouth water. But she couldn't do a job of work any more. It's stupid really . . .'

He sympathised with Brett's stupidity for personal reasons.

'She's got everything – everything's in the right place – and there couldn't be no one nicer when she's talking sense – you'd agree with me, Master! But she's hitting it too hard. She'll be pushing up the daisies before she's thirty.'

'You're sorry for her, aren't you?'

'I can't help it. She reminds me of how I used to be. Do you remember, Master?'

'Do I not!'

'I keep on telling her about the patients in my hospital. I'd like to stop her zonking herself out of her mind with those blasted drugs at any rate.'

'What age is she?'

'Twenty-two – and life is so sweet.'

Hereward was more impressed. He grasped the fact that Brownie's feelings for Brett differed from other passing fancies. Apparently she had tapped the rich seam of his capacity for looking after people. In that case, if he was attempting to cure her of her addiction, he was the less likely to set a bad example by capitulating to his own.

Perhaps Hereward's wishful thinking was partly due to his being on the point of publishing his engagement to be married.

SIX

BROWNIE was the first person to whom he broke the news.

He had dreaded having to do it. He appreciated that his marriage was going to be a body-blow to his so-called servant – the sweetness of whose life for getting on for thirty years was attributable to the bachelorhood of his so-called master. He foresaw stormy weather, trials and tribulations for both of them, and indeed for Alice.

Brownie's spontaneous response was altruistically joyful. It revealed anew the excellence of his character and the largeness of his heart.

Hereward was at once reassured and almost sad to be happy at his expense. But he had never and could not have taken a vow of permanent celibacy for the sake of Brownie's peace of mind. From the beginning the mutual risk of matrimony had been an integral term of the contract they had entered into.

By accident or by design Hereward had recently arrived at his more optimistic estimate of Brownie's chances of survival. He would have married his Alice whatever the physical and moral state of any outsider. At the same time he was or chose to be encouraged by Brownie's attitude to Brett: which seemed to suggest his dependant and responsibility was at last so independent and responsible that he could look after another person in peril as well as himself.

Nevertheless Hereward wound up their conversation by saying: 'You won't worry, will you, Brownie? I don't know exactly what's in store – it's early days yet. You asked me once to have faith in you. Please have faith in me. But I can promise you here and now that I'll make sure your future's better than your past, provided you don't rush me.'

'I'll be all right, Master. It's you that mustn't worry.'

The two essential questions, whether or not Hereward and Alice would require his services, and whether or not Brownie would do his disappearing act as planned, were left hanging in the air.

In the circumstances they had to be. Hereward was preoccupied for – and by – the present. He was in his late forties: he was not in a position to procrastinate. He had met Alice in the autumn, their wedding was in January, and they set off for their honeymoon, having taken more than enough important decisions.

As for Brownie, he was over sixty. Where would or could he disappear to? He was too old to slink into the caves of Trafalgar Terrace and work in a wet-fish shop. He was too young and active to retire. Naturally he wanted to wait and see.

The period of general uncertainty was not necessarily more of a strain for Brownie than for Hereward, who had already reached private conclusions as daunting as they were inevitable.

Alice was exceptionally kind and good. But she had married one man, not two. Because she did not know Brownie well, she still regarded him as a shabby appendage with a lah-di-dah manner and an inflated reputation for wit: she felt like the singular child in the fable who realised the Emperor had no clothes on. And she was alarmed at the prospect of having to start life with her husband, and cook and care for him, under the eye of a professional who was probably jealous and possessive.

Equally Hereward could not start life with his wife on such an unsteady triangular footing, let alone expose her to the threats he had quailed before: Brownie falling ill and becoming a burden. For he had no doubt she would grow fonder of Brownie – and, if so, that she would be quite incapable of self-protective ruthlessness, in spite of having to bear the brunt of feeding and cherishing the dear invalid.

Hereward quailed worse than ever when he thought of Alice's involvement in that eventuality. And supposing Brownie was driven back to drink by subordination to a woman, what then?

On a less horrific level, Hereward recognised that Brownie's ingrained eccentricities – his bragging and bullshit, his blaring telly, his trailing clouds of tobacco smoke, his unwillingness to jump in, his odoriferous socks, his contrary reactions to correction and presumptions that he was or had been in charge – would never fit into the clean quiet fragrant home of Alice's fancy.

He recalled the apposite proverb and had to agree with it: new wine could not be put in old bottles.

Moreover, while on his honeymoon, he settled with Alice where that home would be: her flat in Pimlico rather than his house in Hampstead. It was more central and convenient, it had rooms of a better size and shape, it was not expensive; and she was attached to it, and for him it was only fraught with pleasant associations. It lacked accommodation for Brownie.

Hereward administered the bitter pill as soon as he dared, coating it liberally with sugar.

'Brownie – I expect you've been wondering what our plans are.'

'Yes, Master.'

'Well – it's no good thinking the three of us will be able to live together happily ever after.'

'No, Master.'

'You're a marvel, but you might get on Alice's nerves if you shared a kitchen. And she's a marvel, yet I know from experience that she'd get on yours.'

'Oh no, she wouldn't.'

'But you always warned me you'd hate to work for any female.'

'Beg pardon, sir – Madame isn't any female.'

'No – of course not – but what I'm trying to say is – we've decided to live in her place. Hang on! Wait a tick! We'll be there – but we're hoping you'll stay on in Trafalgar Terrace. You could come and do for us in the mornings and leave after lunch and attend to the house and the lodgers. What about it?'

'Thank you, sir.'

'Don't thank me. Do you like the idea?'

'I'd like to stay in my bedroom and my kitchen, if possible, sir.'

'I'm telling you that you can. But I'm afraid you won't be so fully occupied as you have been.'

Brownie was provoked to forget that he was being martyrised and ought to act accordingly. He expostulated. He ran through his usual repertoire of proof of his intolerable load of work.

'I'll be more occupied, not less. I'll have another dwelling on my hands, I'll be travelling two or three hours a day – and you'll want extra lodgers in your rooms to help pay expenses. I won't have time to light my pipe!'

'Well – is it going to be too much for you?'

'No! We Browns are not like you Watkinses. We never give in.'

'And I don't have to mention the condition, do I?'

'What condition? I might have guessed there'd be a catch in it somewhere.'

'Alcohol's not allowed.'

'Sir, if you asked me open a can of beer, I wouldn't remember how.'

'One more thing, Brownie: do you think you'll be lonely in the evenings without me?'

'I'll be glad to have a bit of rest and relaxation for a change.'

It was easier than Hereward had anticipated. Brownie had been fairly receptive and adaptable in principle. Anyway he had ended by laughing at the dislocation of his existence.

Hereward and Alice spent some months at the house in Trafalgar Terrace, while the flat in Suffolk Crescent was converted and decorated for their joint use.

And Brownie dropped his defences against Alice. He talked Cockney in her company, he was comical, coarse, and gentle and tactful. As a result she withdrew her reservations. She was charmed by his talents and sunny willing temper. She was spellbound by his stories of the Piccadilly Club and his military misadventures – and amused when she heard him spouting German to the milkman, who had also been in a prisoner of war camp. She asked him for recipes, which he wrote out wrong in his flowery script. She let him try to blind her with the science of his cookery. She commiserated when he said he had done his stretch of thirty years hard labour for Hereward. She was tolerant of his other peccadillos.

Her more friendly feelings were reciprocated.

Brownie conceded to his boss: 'She's tops – you don't deserve her.'

Then Hereward and Alice returned a day earlier than expected from a visit to relations to discover Brownie inebriated.

His explanation was that he had been to a friend's funeral and later drunk a single toast to the deceased – and the wine must have been either corked or spiked.

In private Alice interceded on his behalf.

'He only had one glass of wine.'

'Don't you believe it!'

'And he had been to a funeral.'

'Funeral my eye!'

'And the wine might have disagreed with him.'

'If he really was at a funeral, the wine wouldn't have been spiked. Nobody spikes the wine at funerals.'

'But you can't stop him doing what he wants to do in his spare time. It's not possible. It's not your business.'

'He wouldn't be here today if I hadn't made it my business.'

'Well, please, for my sake, give him another chance.'

'Give him a quarter of an inch and he'll take a mile.'

'I suppose you know best.'

'I should – I've reason to!'

All the same Alice soothed the savage breast of her spouse, who accepted Brownie's apologies and confined himself to a mild regretful rebuke.

The following morning he found a note slipped under the door of the conjugal bedroom.

It ran: 'Dearest Madame and Master – PG Tips from now on – Your Devoted and obedient servant, Brownie.'

Alice's argument in favour of forbearance seemed to be supported by events. Brownie recovered his equilibrium. His behaviour was faultless. Hereward had to admit he was pleased that his dictatorial impulse had been curbed.

Then – again – a week or so before the Watkinses moved into Suffolk Crescent they were invited to a buffet supper which Brownie was to cook for his client and their hostess. They arrived, were admitted by a hirsute Portuguese maid, were greeted and introduced to guests, and saw Brownie staggering round in the supper room, grinning foolishly and with his black bow-tie awry.

Hereward sought him out and hissed at him: 'You're drunk!'

'Oh sir! Hullo, sir! No, sir, not drunk, sir!'

'Yes, you are! How could you? I'm ashamed of you!'

Brownie, instead of meekly bowing his head according to custom, laughed in a recalcitrant jeering way and summoned the maid from the kitchen: 'Angelina! Come and get an earful of how my master speaks to me!'

Hereward commanded: 'Shut up, Brownie! Pull yourself together!'

But Brownie continued to address Angelina: 'Listen to him! That's how he always speaks to me! I told you, didn't I? He's worse than Hitler! He thinks he owns me!'

Hereward was forced to beat a retreat. The evening was ruined for him, even if the disasters he was expecting did not quite materialise – and although in Alice's opinion Brownie got through it amazingly well. The next day the traditional accusations and warnings and excuses and apologies were exchanged.

Yet an alien element had stolen into the routine. Hereward had not only criticised, he had been subjected to offensive criticism for the first time. The episode in the supper room was a sort of joke: in retrospect he saw its funny side. It was also a raising of the standard of revolt, however shakily.

The disturbing implication was that Brownie was tearing up the treaty on which he seemed to consider his master had already defaulted by marrying. He was declaring his intention not to abide by the provisions of it unilaterally, after the other signatory had repudiated them. He had revealed his reproachfulness and resentment, his sense of being the loser in his competition with his boss, his sense of being morally and metaphysically betrayed and abandoned.

His actions hinted at the new-fangled notion that drink was and would be not his downfall, but the remedy for his wounds – and his secret weapon in the next stage of the war he had to fight in self-defence.

Things returned almost to normal. The surface of the relationships at number 32 was once more unruffled. The armistice was brief. Hereward was dismayed by snippets of terrace gossip that reached him. Evidently Brownie was making references to redundancy payments. He was telling people he would take his boss to the cleaners if there was ever any question of unlawful dismissal.

To add to Hereward's anxieties as an employer, Alice's work would necessitate a trip abroad immediately after their removal into Suffolk Crescent – and it was fixed that he should accompany her.

'How long will you be out of the country, Master?'

'Two or three months – I don't know.'

'It'll be a nice holiday.'

'It won't be exactly a holiday. Alice has got her job to see to, and I'll be writing.'

'What am I meant to do?'

'You'll have the house and the lodgers, and our flat to keep an eye on. And I was hoping it'd be a break for you, too.'

'I'll be lucky!'

'But, Brownie, you must agree you'll be less busy than if you had the house and lodgers and us to clean and cook for into the bargain! Do you think you'll be able to manage?'

'Oh – I can manage!'

'You won't do anything silly? You'll be here on your own, remember.'

'On my own? I'll have the lodgers badgering me twenty-four hours a day.'

'Well – it's an experiment. Give it a whirl, Brownie! You say they're my lodgers. But they're your bread and butter. If you decide you don't like these new arrangements, we'll put our heads together and devise something different. I promised you, didn't I?'

'Yes, Master.'

'Listen – surely I've proved that you needn't feel insecure? I'm determined to get you suited, if it kills me.'

'I'm not complaining.'

'Not much.'

'Why – what have I said? I never complain. I may moan, but I don't complain. No! I'll be fine – I'll be having a high old time – that's fair, isn't it? You've got Madame – you worry about her! And you ought to follow my advice: just live for each other and let the world take care of itself.'

Hereward did so for three months.

But back in England, installed with Alice in Suffolk Crescent, he was informed by Brownie that their world had not taken care of itself after all.

Everything was wrong.

The lodgers had been playing up, not paying rent, subletting their rooms, harbouring undesirable personages, causing disturbances, and disobeying and abusing Brownie.

'You're too kind to them.'

'I knew it'd be my fault.'

'But you are too kind.'

'I was too kind to say I'd be responsible for that lot of pigs' blurts!'

One lodger had done a moonlit flit, owing both Brownie and Hereward a packet of money, and in due course compelling his landlord to sue for the forfeiture of his lease.

'Did you lend him money, Brownie?'

'No – but I kept an account for him.'

'In other words you did lend him money. I suppose you did his shopping?'

'Well – he was always asking me out to dinner.'

'Did you go?'

'Once or twice.'

'Where?'

'To the Wine and Cheese Bar.'

'What did you drink with your cheese?'

'Have a guess! I'd fool around with a glass of wine. But he was half an alcoholic. He'd bottle it and then he'd call me a lackey.'

'Have you any idea where he's flitted to?'

'If I had, he'd be singing soprano!'

Alice asked after Brownie's health.

He was not fit. He had never got over his accident: which accident was perhaps too unlikely to be untrue. He had been travelling from Trafalgar Terrace to Suffolk Crescent – he emphasised the point that he was about his boss's business. He was on the escalator in the Underground, when a boy ten yards ahead of him dropped a bundle of cricket stumps. The stumps hit him, tangled with his legs, tripped him, and he twisted and sprained his knee.

'I was black and blue and purple and yellow, Madame, like one of those baboons – except in another place. And my knee's still puffy – and it had to be my dicky knee, didn't it?'

No, far from being fit, he was lame, and his nerves were shot to pieces by the lodgers, and he had this bad arthritis in his hands which made them tremble, and his eyesight was not what it had been.

'Master says the flat's dirty and dusty. But I can't polish for the pain in my hands, Madame. And I can't see a speck of dust.'

He was at loggerheads with members of his family. His brother Arthur had married a year before Hereward, and even later in life. Needless to say Arthur's wife Edith had fallen in love with Brownie.

'She won't leave me be. She's on top of me the moment Arthur turns his head the other way. It's embarrassing, sir!'

Edith must have had a dominant personality. She dressed her conventional old husband in flowered shirts and persuaded him to wear a piece of false hair. At a family function a relative failed to recognise him.

'Who's that over there?'

'That's Arthur,' Brownie replied.

'Arthur? Never! What's he got on his head?'

'He's got a dead cat on his head!'

Marriage had been too much for Arthur, who had recently suffered a stroke and was laid up in hospital. Edith seized her opportunity or tried to: she pestered her brother-in-law to come and visit the sick man. When Brownie rejected these hypocritical appeals, her long telephone calls and letters grew spiteful.

Unfortunately Brownie answered her letters. Although so peaceable in his speech, he was a fire-eater of a correspondent. Edith was infuriated by the scornful home truths in his missives. She dipped her pen in poison in response, and began to ring in the middle of the night in order to wake him and whisper not-so-sweet nothings in his ear.

Apart from his persecution by Edith, which rendered it impossible for him to risk seeing Arthur, he had somehow quarrelled with Ada, with whom he was engaged in another acrimonious correspondence.

Hereward prayed that history was not repeating itself. For nearly two decades he had seemed to be right to deny that portentous dictum. Yet the history in question had been made in a preceding period, when Brownie was similarly troubled by aspects of his occupation, his plethora of ailments, by having the opposite sex at his throat and a stricken brother in the background, and by tremulous hands.

However, Suffolk Crescent received its cleansing blitz in the fullness of time. He arrived there on the dot of eight o'clock every weekday morning. He produced and helped to consume a delicious lunch, as he would and could not have done if he had been drinking deeply – and departed at two or three in the afternoon.

Sometimes in the evenings, should Hereward telephone through to Trafalgar Terrace, he sounded stupefied. But his reasonable excuse was that he had been asleep: because his nights were often disturbed by Edith's irate mating-calls, he was more than ever inclined to drowse in front of the telly.

'And you know me, Master – you could chop off my leg without my noticing when I'm drowsy – forty winks for me are like a general anaesthetic – and it takes me half an hour to come round.'

Occasionally Hereward felt impelled to voice the hackneyed query: 'Were you – are you – will you be really okay?'

Brownie's invariable answer: 'Yes, Master,' proved nothing.

Theoretically he ought to have been okay. He was working in Suffolk Cresecent, not particularly hard, for about thirty hours each week. His services for his lodgers at Trafalgar Terrace were meant to be minimal. His weekends were his own, he was no longer badly paid, he had no obligatory expenses, and could coin money at his clients' parties if he chose to. His conscientious boss was running a whole large house in Hampstead mainly for his benefit.

In practice he still moaned. His journeys to and from Pimlico by public transport were adding four hours daily to the six during which he sweated blood for Hereward. At Trafalgar Terrace he had to put in at least four more hours a day, making a total of ninety in a week. He was too knackered to do dinners for his clients. At weekends he could not enjoy his freedom, he had to rest his weary limbs – and so on.

'Well – cut your hours of work – arrive at the flat at ten in the mornings – it's entirely up to you!'

Brownie squashed such suggestions. He had set his mind on martyrdom. He preferred to blame Hereward – and punish him by being the bearer of bad news.

'I felt giddy on my crowded bus this morning – I thought I was going to flake out . . . A fellow stepped on my big toe with the tumours in the Underground – he must have weighed sixteen stone – it's been merry hell ever since . . . Sorry to interrupt your writing, Master, but I thought you'd like to know the rain's pouring through the ceiling of your old bedroom in Hampstead . . . There are definitely rats in your basement area, Master – I've seen their visiting cards . . .'

Hereward and Alice took to driving him home whenever possible. One afternoon in Trafalgar Terrace they had emerged from the car and were standing by it, when a girl carrying flagons of wine tripped towards them, calling as if to a pet: 'Kitchy – Kitchy – Kitchy – Kitchy – Kitchy – Kitchener!'

She was young and attractive and jolly.

'Don't forget, you're coming to my party tonight, my little Kitchy-Kitchener!' she cried.

Brownie, who had blushed crimson, addressed her in a warning tone: 'These are my bosses.'

'Oh!' She stared at Hereward boldly and curiously. 'So you're the boss!' She obviously knew more about him than he knew of her. 'Well, well!' She laughed and twiddled her fingers at Brownie – 'See you!' – and passed by with the flagons of wine for her party under her arms.

Alice enquired: 'Is that Brett?'

'Yes, Madame.'

'Isn't she sweet?'

'Oh yes, she's sweet enough. She's naughty but she's nice.'

Brownie was regaining his composure.

'Is she as naughty as you say? She looks so innocent.'

'That's it, Madame. But innocent's the one thing she never has been. And she's naughty company for me.'

* * *

The experiment had failed.

After about a year Hereward admitted it. The complicated design for living, which was costing him so dear in time, trouble, money and expense of spirit, had turned into the chief bone of contention between himself and its intended beneficiary. Brownie could cope neither with his novel range of duties nor his extra leisure, he refused to restrict one or the other or both, and was increasingly dissatisfied. He had too much to do, according to the familiar refrain – yet was at a dangerously loose end during his slack evenings and weekends off. If he was not already drowning his sorrows he soon would. Trafalgar Terrace, containing Brett, would then be the reverse of his salvation.

'It hasn't worked out, has it?'

Brownie agreed.

They began to think of alternatives.

The prospects or lack of them depressed Hereward. Whatever scheme he devised Brownie was likely to undermine – later on agreeing with complacence it had not worked out. Even sober and healthy – or fairly – he was threatening to become a millstone. Far from disappearing, he still spoke of dropping dead in harness. He could not be dismissed ungratefully, unlawfully and with an exorbitant golden handshake; he could not be insinuated into the employment of a stranger, who might actually exploit him and would certainly be encouraged to do so; he could not be condemned to solitary confinement in a new house – say a flatlet in the neighbourhood of Suffolk Crescent; and he could not be paid a full wage for part-time service by a boss he had deprived of lodgers and thus of revenue.

His receipt of the old-age pension would be a help.

'How long before you get it, Brownie? How old are you? Let's see – you must be sixty-four.'

Hereward based his calculations on the age of a friend of his, Adam Barlow, of whom Brownie had always made a special fuss, saying they were twins.

'Sixty-four? Don't be funny, Master! I'm coming up to sixty-two.'

'But Mr Barlow's sixty-four – and I thought you were his exact contemporary – you used to say you were and that virgins ought to stick together – have you forgotten?'

'Mr Barlow's birthday and mine fall on the same day – we're both Virgos – but he's my elder by two and a half years if he isn't my better.'

'Believe it or not.'

'I'll fetch you my birth certificate, Master!'

The birth certificate was duly produced. The entry under date of birth corroborated Brownie's claim. But it rather looked to Hereward as if the numerals had been tampered with.

Although the suspicion seemed preposterous, Hereward entertained it sadly. For no doubt Brownie was frightened of being asked to retire – and a spot of forgery would postpone that evil hour. In his present vengeful mood, in order not to mitigate his boss's predicament, he might be prepared to forgo a couple of years of pension.

Yet at last he relented to the extent of contributing an idea of his own to the debate. His client Mrs Hilda Stacey was a well-to-do widow with a house near Suffolk Crescent and accommodation going begging. She had offered him a home and a job at the time of Hereward's marriage.

Could he not live and partly work there?

Hereward wrote to Mrs Stacey, who replied enthusiastically. She was a strong-minded impulsive person, acquainted with and undeterred by Brownie's record. She admired him for having vanquished his vice, she appreciated his virtues, and would like nothing better than to have him in her house. His presence would be protective, and he could occasionally cook for her and her guests in return for a luxurious room and bathroom adjoining her kitchen.

The decision was left to Brownie.

It was explained to him that if he remained at Trafalgar Terrace, unsatisfactory as he found it, he would be safe, whether or not he was ill or got into trouble – at any rate until he reached pensionable age; whereas if Trafalgar Terrace were sold, and Mrs Stacey were to change her mind and evict him for some reason, he would have no roof over his head.

He was warned that Mrs Stacey was not the type to stand for nonsense or nurse him through an illness – and there would be nowhere else for him to go. He himself acknowledged that he was bound to come to grief in a secluded flat. Anyway he and his boss between them could not afford a flat in central London. If their second experiment failed, they would have to part. And even with a subsidy from Hereward in recognition of his services, he – un-pensioned by the state – would be poor. Trafalgar Terrace was still his for the asking – and the dependable and indeed rewarding devil he knew must be preferable.

He settled for Mrs Stacey.

'You're not just being contrary, are you, Brownie? You're not saying yes because I'm half-inclined to think you ought to say no? Are you convinced you couldn't carry on in Hampstead?'

Hereward also enquired: 'Is it that you want to escape from Brett?'

'Brett and others, Master. I need to be shook up. And Mrs Stacey's lovely. And I'll have made it to South West One, where the nobs live. And I'll only have to cross the road to be with you and Madame in Suffolk Crescent.'

Trafalgar Terrace was put on the market. Brownie showed possible purchasers over it. One man who was keen to buy the place mysteriously withdrew his bid. He informed the estate agent he was nervous of another flood.

'What on earth did you tell him, Brownie?'

'Nothing.'

'Did you mention flooding?'

'Well – we were flooded during that freak storm a few years ago.'

'But it was no more than a trickle of water under the basement french window! I suppose you said you could hardly keep your nose above it and were baling out all night?'

He giggled.

But in spite of his salesmanship the house was eventually disposed of.

Meanwhile Hereward had negotiated further with Mrs Stacey and drafted a document, a sort of charter, the prime intention of which was to safeguard Brownie from himself. He was to work for the Watkinses until after lunch for five days a week, and cook for Mrs Stacey and a strictly limited number of her guests on three evenings in lieu of rent. His weekday afternoons, his Tuesday and Thursday evenings, and his Saturdays and Sundays were to be free. The plan would cease to have contractual force in the event of any party to it being unhappy in any way. And Hereward guaranteed to extricate Brownie from Mrs Stacey's ground floor room at short notice, if requested.

Everyone signed on the dotted lines.

SEVEN

TRAFALGAR TERRACE was vacated; Brownie moved in with Mrs Stacey; each was pleased and then delighted with the other; they could not get over their good luck; and Hereward wondered if his problem was finally solved.

Life in this context seemed sweet to all, or sweeter. But the sweetest life cannot be lived without fear of the end of it, at least.

In the next twelve months Hereward's every fear appertaining to Brownie was realised.

Mrs Stacey began to find fault with him. She was sorry to – she was tentative – she was unused to dealing with menservants – she was appealing to Hereward for advice and assistance. Brownie was a splendid fellow; but why did he stack her plates dirty in the kitchen cupboards? Why could he not buy a shirt that buttoned across his tummy? How often did he have a bath? Had he always smoked quite so much of that positively fumigating tobacco? He was too kind to her, he was spoiling her – for instance he made her sit down to an elaborate tea although she had never before bothered with a mid-afternoon meal. Yet the other evening he had omitted to clear the dining-room table and had not even extinguished the candles after a party – he had simply gone to ground; and the lights had blazed in the kitchen and in his room until dawn, when she heard him washing dishes. It was worrying – candles left burning could cause a fire. Why had he vanished like that?

Soon she herself was able to answer the last of her awkward questions. Right in the middle of a party, between the meat and pudding courses, she had found him either asleep or unconscious in the chair in the kitchen, which reeked of alcohol and looked as if it had been hit by a bomb. She could not rouse him. She had to rescue the remains of the dinner, while he lay there spreadeagled and snoring like a grampus. Later, when she went to bed, he was still in his drunken stupor. It was worse than worrying – it was not nice. A decent woman of her age ought not to have to put up with it. Admittedly she was in receipt of an apologetic note. But how was she to be sure it would not happen again?

Hereward assured her. Brownie did likewise, having been accused, reproached, racked, implored and reasoned with by his boss. Mrs Stacey was mollified – she now had experience of what a lot she had to lose.

But in private Hereward was as pessimistic about the future as he had ever been optimistic. For Brownie had consigned his copy of the charter to the waste paper basket, practically speaking – and seduced Mrs Stacey into following his example. He not only served her tea when by rights he should have been resting, he fetched her morning paper from the newsagent's in all weathers, he spent his free afternoons shopping for her, and on his evenings off and at weekends he insisted on cooking her three-course snacks. He would not let her into her own kitchen: she reported that she had to choose between being fed by him and starving.

Hereward could imagine it: 'Why keep a dog and bark yourself, Madame? . . . Allow me, Madame – I've nothing else to do . . . When I'm not hard at it I feel dead, Madame . . . Who's coming to dinner today?'

Of course Mrs Stacey had never met anyone half as ambiguous. She had not yet learned that when Brownie said one thing he usually meant another. If she expressed a wish to nibble a biscuit and cheese for dinner alone, he seemed so cast down, so sorry for her in her solitude and disappointed for himself, that she rushed to the telephone and mustered an instant party, which he then held against her. She complained of being worn to a frazzle by having to entertain every Tom, Dick and Harry of her acquaintance for the amusement of Brownie, whose complaint was identical. She acceded to his demands for interesting new recipes: he reported that he had to sweat over them for six hours. And her grateful compliments egged him on.

Consequently overwork and exploitation were no longer the theme of his time-honoured radical teasing, but almost a matter of fact. He blamed Mrs Stacey to Hereward, and probably vice versa – while Hereward wrung his hands over the real incorrigible culprit. Under pressure Brownie admitted he had been *idiotick:* but having spoilt Mrs Stacey, how was he suddenly to stop?

He could not mend his characteristic ways. Without exaggeration he was exhausted. And his cure for exhaustion had always been drink.

The only hope was that Hereward and Alice were again going abroad in connection with her job for three months. Certainly Brownie could, and perhaps he would, take it easier during their absence. On the other hand he might cave in completely without his boss to prop him up.

Soon Mrs Stacey was writing the Watkinses desperate letters.

Hereward did not need to read her detailed accounts of the calamities he had dreaded.

On his return he raged at Brownie and sent him straight to the doctor – his hands were palsied and the whites of his eyes bright yellow. And he did his best to convince Mrs Stacey he had not inveigled a total alcoholic into her house by false pretences.

Dr Mannrich tested Brownie's liver and warned that if he went on drinking he would kill himself within a few weeks. As a result there was much talk of PG Tips and lemonade henceforth. His health improved. He was given a last chance. His excuses for his collapse in the summer counted for more with Mrs Stacey than with Hereward, who had heard them before: his brother Arthur had one foot in the grave and his virago of a sister-in-law had again got him down, having discovered where he was living. He swore solemn oaths on the heads of his daughter and grandchildren, and so on.

It was too late. Guilt because he had been drinking, or still was, reduced him to being everybody's abject contrite slave. He was the more prodigal of his involuntary and compulsive services for Mrs Stacey. In the mornings, after fetching her newspaper and before he arrived at Suffolk Crescent, he was cooking breakfast for her daily lady, called Noreen. He was doing most of Noreen's household work. He was even shopping for Noreen.

The autumn jolted by.

Christmas came with its festive spirit or spirits.

He was intoxicated for three weeks. Apparently he never went to bed: he slept in Mrs Stacey's kitchen chair at night, snoring and groaning horribly. He slept and groaned in the Watkinses' kitchen by day. He slept if he sat down, and woke drunk if he could be woken. He was incapacitated – and beyond Hereward's authority.

Mrs Stacey invoked the clause of the charter that guaranteed his removal from the wreckage of her ground floor.

Hereward told him.

He added: 'You know it's the end of the road for us.'

Brownie was so shocked and startled that he played the trump card he had kept up his sleeve for many years.

He was iller than his master knew. The pain in his head was like a pneumatic drill, he was permanently giddy and dizzy, he had not been able to see properly for ages, and his sleepiness was abnormal. Drink was by no means the whole story.

Hereward packed him off to Dr Mannrich, who fixed an appointment in hospital for the following day.

'He wants them to scan my noddle.'

'But you've had tests in hospital on other occasions.'

'No, Master. It's different this time. Doctor's opinion is that I've started a tumour on the brain.'

'Did he say so?'

'He's afraid so.'

'Truly?'

'Why should I lie to you now?'

Once more Brownie was turning the tables on Hereward.

'When is your appointment?'

'Ten o'clock.'

'Well – please go and rest. And I'll ring you at nine tomorrow.'

'But at eight I'll be trotting round to get breakfast for yourself and Madame.'

'Don't think of it, Brownie! I couldn't bear you to get our breakfast when you're bound to be feeling ropey.'

'I'd rather it was business as usual, Master. I'd rather keep busy while I can.'

'Are you busy this evening? Shall I speak to Mrs Stacey?'

'No, I will.'

'You ought to have an early night.'

'Leave it to me.'

'What? Yes – just as you like. And I'm sorry.'

'Thank you, Master.'

Hereward might have been more sceptical and less sorry, but for Mrs Stacey and Alice.

Mrs Stacey was spoken to – and appalled by her misinterpretation of the issue. Instead of sympathising with and organising prompt medical attention for Brownie, who had heroically striven to do her bidding as he approached the terminal stage of his disease, she had given him two weeks' notice. She had acted heartlessly in her ignorance – thanks to Hereward, she implied. She should have been fully informed about Brownie's tumours, one of which on the brain could account for all his extraordinary behaviour. His drinking was understandable and pardonable – and he was not necessarily fibbing when he said he had never drunk much. Although her unkindness was not her fault, she deeply regretted it.

Alice's regrets were even deeper. Brownie had no home to call his own – and she felt responsible. If she had not spirited Hereward from Trafalgar Terrace, if she had included Brownie in her residential arrangements, he would not have been unsettled, insecure, drunken, harassed, and perhaps in consequence sick to death. She had grown to love him – and might as well have stuck a knife in his back.

She was aghast at the injustice recently meted out to him. His boss and her husband had been certain he knew better, obviously wrong, and cruel. For he had brushed aside patent symptoms of illness, dismissed pleas of innocence, hounded his faithful retainer to the edge of the abyss, and made a perfect misery of his probable ultimate days.

Hereward's defences crumbled. If the tumour was not a trump card but the lethal reality it was beginning to seem to be, he would never forgive himself. He had judged the present in the light of the evidence from the past – Brownie's alcoholic tendencies, his previous crises, his play-acting, and inventive genius for extenuating circumstances. Yet the past had been survived: and history was not always repetitive. Error stared him in the face – it would be typical of Brownie to have the last laugh at his expense by dying: in which case his praiseworthy attempt to save Brownie's soul and body, his high-minded hectoring, and rows and recriminations, would look like sheer inexcusable tyranny. His maltreatment of his afflicted benefactor and best friend had already antogonised his wife. He was regarded as a monster by Mrs Stacey – and could be short of time in which to repair the damage he had done.

He dared not argue sceptically. He was sorry for lots of reasons.

He passed a wretched night.

Brownie appeared in the morning. He was punctual and sober. He ate a hearty second breakfast with Hereward and Alice.

'Did you manage to sleep?' Alice asked tearfully.

'Like a top, Madame!'

'You weren't too worried?'

'Worried? No, Madame! I often shook hands with death in the war.'

'Oh, please, Brownie, don't talk like that!'

Hereward broke in: 'You shouldn't have bothered to come round to be with us. I told you not to. I hoped you'd lie in. Still, it's lovely to catch a glimpse of you.'

'I couldn't have stayed with Mrs Stacey, Master. She saw me off – she got up specially. She was choked!'

'Poor Mrs Stacey!'

'And Noreen was blubbering all over the place.'

'Well, you're everybody's favourite.'

'I know, Master – it's awful!'

Alice asked: 'More tea, Brownie?'

'I wouldn't say no, Madame. Tea's my tipple. I'm like the main drain where tea's concerned.'

He was so brave and cheery, even so challenging with his claim that tea was his tipple, that Hereward felt he could inquire: 'What exactly happened when you went to Dr Mannrich yesterday afternoon?'

'He rang through for today's appointment.'

'At once? Didn't he examine you?'

'He took one look at me and said it.'

'Said what?'

'As I walked into the consulting-room he said: "I can guess why you're here, Mr Brown – it's a tumour on your brain, isn't it?"'

'What an odd thing for a doctor to say!'

'Wasn't it just? It brought me up in goose-pimples. It reminded me of my mother. She died in agony from a brain-tumour, Madame.'

'Yes, I've heard, Brownie.'

'Brownie – would you mind repeating Dr Mannrich's diagnosis? It strikes me as incredibly unprofessional.'

'He looked me straight between the eyes and said: "You've got a tumour on the brain, you have."'

Alice giggled apologetically.

'I wish you wouldn't make it sound funny, Brownie.'

Hereward also laughed a little at the black humour of the situation, and Brownie himself joined in.

'Well – I should be going.'

'Let me drive you to the hospital.'

'Oh no, Master. You get on with your writing – don't let me interrupt it. And I'd prefer to find my own way there.'

'I could keep you company while you were waiting to be X-rayed.'

'For pity's sake, Master – you'd kill me on the spot with embarrassment.' He blushed uncomfortably at the very idea. 'No – I'll telephone as soon as I've any news.'

They said goodbye.

The Watkinses waved at him from a window with their fingers crossed.

He telephoned at mid-day: 'All clear, Master!'

The general relief had its rueful sides.

Hereward was mortified that he at least had not known better than to jump through Brownie's hoops before he needed to. He should have protested that no doctor in his right mind would greet a patient with the words: 'You've got a tumour on the brain, you have.' As likely as not Dr Mannrich's examination had disproved the tumour theory – and the appointment for a brain-scan was another figment of Brownie's dramatic imagination and an unavoidable part of his confidence trick: which would explain his reluctance to be accompanied to the hospital. Naturally, if so, it was easy for him to seem to be brave and to sleep like a top, while the courage of Hereward's sceptical convictions evaporated and he was kept awake by remorse.

The relief was also short-lived.

Doubtless Brownie had made himself feel mortally ill. Conceivably he had hoped that death would spare him dishonour. Whatever occurred or did not occur in that hospital where he might or might not have had an appointment, he must have realised he had run out of excuses and the game was up. He surrendered – to his grief at having got the sack, his humiliation, his horror of retirement, his addiction.

Two or three days later Mrs Stacey, whose anguish had turned into anger, requested Hereward to rid her of the oblivious hulk in her kitchen within twenty-four hours.

But the story of William Kitchener Brown was more of a comedy than a tragedy.

Hereward persuaded him that, in accordance with the charter they had signed, he would have to move out of Mrs Stacey's house and into a small hotel nearby, while they worked out the details of his gloomy future.

'At such short notice, Master?'

'Yes, Brownie.'

Again the shock of these rapid developments was sobering. The beeswax cleared from his five hundred thousand braincells. He was dignified in defeat, amenable and uncomplaining at last. His valour or lack of it had been a disputatious old joke between himself and Hereward. The argument was settled by his attitude to his latter days stretching ahead, minus his boss, fraught with memories of failure, apparently impoverished, solitary, bleak, and the graveyard of his rare gifts and talents.

Hereward was surprised not only by his stoicism.

When he was helping to pack Brownie's clothes and few belongings – the treasured copies of his own books; the brown-paper-covered cookery books with greasy thumb-marks; the framed photographs and rack of pipes; the collection of ornamental tankards, including that prize for drinking twenty-one pints of beer in an evening – he observed: 'I'd forgotten how many tankards you accumulated over the years.'

'Yes, Master.'

'You bought them in antique shops and curio shops, didn't you?'

'Yes, Master,' he smirked.

'Brownie, were they prizes, too?'

'Yes, Master.'

Hereward ventured further into the maze of his ex-manservant's secrets.

'When did you start drinking again?'

'Not when you married. You pass the word to Madame. She's been an angel to me – I wouldn't want her to think she drove me back to drink. No! I was at it long before. I was sure I could stop the minute I needed to. That was my mistake.'

'Was Brett a bad influence?'

'Yes and no.'

'Who was a bad influence if she wasn't?'

'Arthur.'

'Your brother Arthur – who died a month ago? But I thought he was teetotal! I was always encouraging you to spend your weekends with Arthur! You led me to believe you'd be safe!'

'I know,' Brownie giggled.

He either confessed or seized on the pretext of his late brother, who was in no position to disagree: 'He was worse than me. All my brothers were drunkards. We Browns were born with beer instead of blood in our veins. Edith says I killed Arthur by boozing with him. She's been on and on at me about doing him in. But really it was the other way round.'

Hereward enquired: 'Why didn't you tell me? Why didn't you allow me to help?'

'I was too proud – and craft's my middle name.'

On an unquestionably truthful impulse, when Hereward asked if he would ever cut out alcohol – if he could – if he wished to – he admitted: 'It's my life, Master.'

His fate had been sealed by Mrs Stacey's ultimatum. But his revelations imposed limits on plans for his retirement. It was established that he would live the rest of his life somewhere near his daughter Peggy at Margate in Kent. The Watkinses' initial idea was to settle him in a boarding-house, where he would have the company of his fellow-lodgers and his landlady would fall in love with him. On second thoughts they appreciated that even the most loving landlady might take exception to his anti-social habits, which he had said were unbreakable – especially in the summer season when rooms at a holiday resort were at a premium. He would be better off in a self--contained flat, provided he could afford the rent, was not too lonely, did not let it get too dirty, or annoy his neighbours by singing *Sweet Adeline* and passing out on the staircase. Even a flat purchased for him rather than rented would be subject to the same disadvantages.

For thirty years he had been saying that if he won the football pools he would buy a cottage in the country. Admittedly in a detached cottage of his own he could be as sober or as drunk as he pleased.

Hereward applied to an estate agent in Margate. One day he received particulars of a house in the street where Peggy lived. It seemed ideal, and to be going cheap, although Brownie was unselfishly opposed to the investment of such a large sum of money on his account.

Six months ago the price would have been unthinkable. But in the meanwhile the Watkinses had sold 32 Trafalgar Terrace; and since they were already installed in Alice's flat in Suffolk Crescent, they did not need the cash for alternative accommodation. Thus Hereward had the chance at once to discharge his financial debt to Brownie, who had worked for him for a pittance through poorer years, and to shed the burden of those practical responsibilities which weighed on him more heavily than ever.

The little house in Margate, across the road from Peggy's, as it were sheltered by a family umbrella, would solve every problem – combined with some sort of pension.

Arguably, Brownie himself had supplied that solution by foiling Hereward's previous schemes for his welfare, just as he had created the problem in the first place. In his crafty fashion he had turned up his nose at a mansion in Hampstead and a high-class flatlet in South West One, and brought about the present concatenation of events from which he was likely to derive the maximum profit. From a cynical point of view he seemed to be on the verge of achieving his heart's desire by having behaved badly. His opposition to his boss's projected expenditure might have sprung from an ethical inkling that virtue, not vice, should be rewarded.

But Hereward was prepared to be pushed around as well as to push in the cause of a sort of emancipation. He had been constrained by his anxieties for too long. He had been punished enough for his happiness with Alice. He acknowledged that his marriage had wounded Brownie's competitive susceptibilities, perhaps chronically, whatever might be said to the contrary. He recalled that at the beginning of the last act of the drama he had pleaded for a postponement – a few weeks of peace in which to finish his current book. He now suspected that his pleading had been Brownie's chief incentive to wage total alcoholic war, even at the cost of his health and his job, in order to distract or attract his boss's attention.

They had traversed the charted areas of service, friendship, and assumptions of mastery on Brownie's side – and in a sense were locked in combat in a dark and barren no-man's-land. Hereward was willing to pay any ransom to get out of it.

Moreover he still wanted to keep his promise. In principle and on paper, each of his post-nuptial experiments had been better for Brownie than the one before. The little house would be the best. It could not be improved upon.

And after all the grudging part of Brownie's ambivalence was beneath the surface. It existed, it had expressed itself in action, and was perhaps not to be wondered at, and justifiable. But it was subterranean and possibly subconscious. He had scarcely uttered a single resentful word, and never scoffed or sneered at his boss's invidious marital state. And Hereward was aware that in an emergency, or if he were to suffer a setback, he – and his wife – could again count on Brownie's absolute and infinite devotion. He had enjoyed the unique privilege of being the object of that devotion for nearly a third of a century. He could not forget that Brownie had saved his bacon by painting the maisonette at Windle Road in a fortnight. He remembered how good Brownie had been to him when he was ill at Trafalgar Terrace, and the myriad jokes cracked by Brownie that had kept his melancholy at bay, and the mountains of Brownie's food he had eaten with relish, and the blessings Brownie had showered on his literary career, and the perennial fun they had had together.

The little house and the wherewithal to live in it was the very least he could do in return.

Brownie, informed of the decision of Hereward and Alice, was overcome by gratitude, scolded them for their kindness, said goodbye and departed for Margate.

He was always a lucky devil.

But then his luck was merited by his moral qualities – setting aside his weakness for a bottle. In fact his courtship of fortune was usually successful more because he was careless of the outcome, was ready to do without fortune's favours, than because he was machiavellian. He got the things he wanted by not wanting them unduly – and never asking for them.

Thus it was with the little house, where the Watkinses hoped he would be happy, too.

He had to hang around for three months before he could obtain possession of it.

His first letters in his curlicued writing were extravagantly positive. 'Darling Madame and dearest Master – you are a pair of solid gold bricks . . .' He was staying with Peggy, feeding like a fighting cock, walking for miles along the sea-front in the early mornings, playing with his grandchildren whose sweets and treats were breaking the bank, and having the time of his life.

But soon he wrote from a different address. He was no longer staying with Peggy, who did not really have room for him. He was in temporary lodgings, not seeing much of his family, having difficulty in finding employment, and feeling the pinch: he was unaccustomed to having to pay his way, since his weekly wage for thirty years had been pocket money. The only job he had been offered was looking after the deck-chairs on the beach – he added exclamation marks to this sentence and underlined it ironically. Gentlemen's gentlemen of his age, and top chefs, were not required in Margate.

He was trying to draw the dole. In the past he had waxed violent on the subject of Social Security scroungers. Yet almost in the same breath he would say: 'When I'm on my uppers, I'll bleed that Social Security white! I'm entitled, Master – I fought and rotted in prison for my country – I'm not a lazy layabout . . .'

He had set about bleeding it. His references to what he was up to were contradictory. He had extracted a couple of pounds from the welfare people, he was getting a tenner a week, he had got fifteen pounds, he had been invited to dinner by the nice lady in charge of such handouts, who thought he was a most deserving case – and evidently had no idea that he was receiving an adequate pension from Hereward. Nevertheless he was not making ends meet, he wrote. He was having to economise all round – his weekly subsidy from the state was a mingy seven pounds and fifty pence. He was often hungry, and bored, and hated having nothing to do, and pined for his master and mistress.

He in his turn had not forgotten how to play upon his ex-boss's anxious affections. He had twisted his ankle on one of his walks – his leg had swollen to the size of a bolster. He was afraid he was growing old: he took to signing his letters, 'Your obedient old servant'. He rang Hereward constantly to inquire: 'Any worries or troubles, Master?' – a question designed to cause dismay, considering it meant that he was worried and troubled, and he only asked it when tipsy.

At last he was able to move into his house.

The proprietorship of property on a small scale is invariably good for the soul. The plaintive correspondence and nagging telephone calls ceased. After three or four weeks Brownie wrote: 'My dear Madame and Master – Sorry I haven't been in touch – I've been on the go from dawn until late at night – My new house is a miracle . . .'

At about the same time, Hereward met a friend of his, Nancy Creston, who was eager for news of Brownie. Formerly Lady Creston had been a favoured client – Brownie used to say he could gobble her up – and she reciprocated his special feelings for her, if less carnivorously. Now, when she heard he was out of a job, she wanted to offer him one.

'Do you think he might come to my rescue, even for a day or two a week?'

She was a gentle sensitive person, abstemious yet tolerant, aware of his proclivities, under no illusions, convinced she could control him, or anyway that the effort of attempting to was worthwhile.

She contacted Brownie, whose response was eagerly affirmative.

Again that summer the Watkinses went abroad for three months.

'Dear Madame and Master,' ran the letter that awaited them on their return. 'Trusting you are both fit, as I am. I've settled into my house, which is the best in the street. I keep it regimental, not a spot of dust, wood floors polished so you can see your face in them – and I'm painting it bit by bit. Last week I bought a clock that charms for my lounge – half price – fell off the back of a lorry, I suppose. And I got my three-piece suite, settee and two comfy chairs – can't wait for you to try them. I've been travelling up to town to help Lady Creston Tuesdays and Thursdays. Her Ladyship takes a lot of beating – she is A1. My room there is gorgeous and I sleep between sheets with a coronet on them!! We have great jokes together, and she asks her family in for meals, and they all think I'm the pig's whiskers. The extra money is handy. And I still touch my other lady from the Social Security – not what you're thinking, sir!! So I'm quite flush for the present. At weekends I blitz my house, do the shopping, see my grandchildren, and lean on the garden gate, smoking my pipe and chewing the cud with neighbours. Dear Madame and Master, you have done me proud. I know I was wicked and should have been shot. Instead you've given me everything I ever dreamt of. I don't know how to say thank you . . .'

Hereward spoke to Brownie on the telephone.

'You seem to be well?'

'I was never better, sir.'

'And the house is a success?'

'It's a smash-hit – and keeps me out of mischief.'

'And your arrangements with Lady Creston suit you?'

'Down to the ground.'

'I'm so glad.'

'Any chance of seeing you, sir?'

'Come round when you're next in London.'

'What about Tuesday? I could cook lunch for yourself and Madame. Her Ladyship isn't expecting me till the afternoon.'

'That'd be a pleasure for us.'

'No, no, sir – my pleasure. I'll look forward to it.'

'Same here, Brownie.'

On Tuesday he did not arrive at the appointed hour. The engagement could have slipped his mind, or maybe there had been a muddle about which week he was coming round. Hereward clung to such sanguine explanations until the evening, when Nancy Creston rang to tell him Brownie was missing. They drew the disappointing conclusion that he had relapsed alcoholically: they could not communicate with anyone and make sure, since neither he nor Peggy had telephones in their respective homes.

The next day they sent him a telegram, to which they received no reply. They had been reluctant to sneak on him to his daughter; but now they disregarded their scruples to the extent of sending a telegram to Peggy, who reported back that her father's house seemed empty. Four days passed. They were unwilling to inform the police for fear of the scandal that would finish Brownie if he was found to be merely drunk in some ditch or gutter. No doubt the members of his family were restrained for similar reasons – and because they believed he must be misbehaving in London. Then Hereward sent a third telegram to Peggy. Brownie was discovered dead on the floor of his kitchen.

He had died of a heart attack, instantaneously, and probably on the preceding Tuesday morning, for he was clasping his railway return ticket to London in his hand.

Innumerable doctors had fussed over his tumours and his liver. Not one had noticed that his heart was in a perilous condition.

He had fooled the medical profession for the last time – and Hereward for that matter. To put it another way, Hereward had failed to see through his final deception. But who was to say whether Brownie marched through the pearly gates drunk or sober, or as a direct consequence of his having had his last one too many? His death was as ambiguous and secretive as his life.

It was all very sudden and sad. He was too young to die at sixty-three or sixty-four or however old he was – mentally youthful and vital at any rate.

The compensating factor was that his luck had held good.

When he died he was not a boozy casualty of the class struggle, used and discarded, sacked and in disgrace, with nothing to show for his fifty years of kind service except Carpet Feet and the shakes, unable to adapt to retirement and the ageing processes, a burden to his friends and relations, a victim of his own stupidity – but a householder, a man of means and substance, still on the best of terms with his boss who had cared for him enough to make his dreams come true, forgiven as he forgave, perhaps enjoying himself more than ever before, looking forward to his future, and at work, in harness, just as he had wished.

So in a sense the comedy had its happy ending.